Praise for Lesley

Her Mother's Daughter
Crewe's talent lies in rendering characters that readers can actually care about. They have been hurt and they have hurt others, but their essential goodness shines through.
—Atlantic Books Today

Hit & Mrs.
If you're in the mood for a cute chick-lit mystery with some nice gals in Montreal, Hit & Mrs. is just the ticket.
—Globe and Mail

Crewe's writing has the breathless tenor of a kitchen-table yarn...a cinematic pace and crackling dialogue keep readers hooked.
—Quill & Quire

Ava Comes Home
She expertly manages a page-turning blend of down-home comedy and heart-breaking romance.
—Cape Breton Post

Shoot Me
Possesses an intelligence and emotional depth that reverberates long after you've stopped laughing.
—Halifax Chronicle Herald

Relative Happiness
Her graceful prose...and her ability to turn a familiar story into something with such raw dramatic power, are skills that many veteran novelists have yet to develop.
—Halifax Chronicle Herald

LESLEY CREWE

CHLOE SPARROW

Vagrant
PRESS

For Tata

Vagrant Press is an imprint of
Nimbus Publishing Limited
PO Box 9166
Halifax, NS   B3K 5M8
(902) 455-4286

Printed and bound in Canada
NB1692
Cover design: Heather Bryan
Author photo: Nicola Davison

This novel is a work of fiction. Names, characters, places, and incidents are either the product of the author's imagination or are used fictitiously. Any resemblance to actual persons, living or dead, events or locales is entirely coincidental.

Library and Archives Canada Cataloguing in Publication

Title: Chloe Sparrow / Lesley Crewe.
Names: Crewe, Lesley, 1955- author.
Description: Series statement: Lesley Crewe classics | Previously published: Halifax, NS: Vagrant Press, 2014.
Identifiers: Canadiana 20220455260 | ISBN 9781774711903 (softcover)
Classification: LCC PS8605.R48 C45 2023 | DDC C813/.6—dc23

Nimbus Publishing acknowledges the financial support for its publishing activities from the Government of Canada, the Canada Council for the Arts, and from the Province of Nova Scotia. We are pleased to work in partnership with the Province of Nova Scotia to develop and promote our creative industries for the benefit of all Nova Scotians

CHAPTER ONE

THE ONLY THING YOU NEED TO KNOW ABOUT ME IS THAT ALL MY wishes come true.

It can be a curse.

The wishes have random outcomes; sometimes they don't happen the way I imagined them, which can be extremely upsetting. It started when I was fifteen and told my parents I wished they'd shut up.

They did. They died in the middle of an argument later that day in front of our Victorian row house in Cabbagetown. Dad was up on a metal ladder while Mom kept it steady, yelling he didn't know his ass from his elbow and to get down from the utility pole with the hedge clipper before he hit a wire.

After their funeral, mom's older sister, Aunt Ollie, and my Gramps let me stay in my parents' house, since they lived right next to me and we shared a front porch and a backyard. They didn't want me to lose everything, they said. I think they were just alarmed at the thought of me underfoot. Whatever, the arrangement's worked for ten years. The only downside is listening to the two of them argue through the plastered walls. It's the same thing every morning: muffled shouts of frustration coming from the bathroom.

"Did you take my teeth again?"

"Why would I want your miserable teeth?"

"You're taking my money too! Don't think I haven't noticed. I'm telling Chloe."

After giving my cat, Norton, a tremendous farewell squeeze (the best part of my day), I'm on the bus heading to the CBC Building on Front Street West in downtown Toronto. I don't own a car because they destroy the environment and make us all slugs. Gramps ferries me around in his ancient station wagon with wood-panelled doors when buses or bikes aren't convenient; I guess I don't mind him destroying the environment when it suits me.

Every morning the same people surround me as I sway to the lumbering rhythm of this familiar bus beast. When an elderly lady gets on, I stand to give her my seat, and then scowl at the three able-bodied young guys who sit there and pretend they don't see her, using their iPod, iPad, and iPhone as decoys to fake oblivion and escape guilt.

It's wet and wild out on this early June morning, and the feeling of being rumpled and damp lingers even as I take the stairs to our office. It's my only exercise.

"Why do you wear that nasty sweater all the time?" is the first thing out of spray-tan Amanda's mouth when I get to my desk. I untie the belt of my comfy, hooded, cable-knit wool cardigan.

"It's cruel to wear leather."

"What about the flock of sheep running around buck naked?"

Amanda and I are assistant editors and producers for television productions here at the CBC. I'm sorry to say she was entirely miffed when I was hired because I'm ten years younger than she is, but when I told her my orphan story she gradually warmed up to me.

Every morning the first order of business is to get coffee. Our lunchroom has one of those fancy new coffeemakers.

When we stampede to line up at this temple of caffeine, the latest rumour is unleashed, usually untrue or at the very least embellished, but that never stops us.

"Word has it that we're about to launch another news program," Amanda says.

This makes my heart race. "You're kidding."

"Don't get excited. This one's mine."

"Who told you that?"

"Have you tried the hazelnut flavour?" Amanda has a terrible habit of changing the subject.

"Why do you think you'd head up this new project?"

"I believe I'm allergic to hazelnuts."

"What about me?"

"Sorry, Chloe, you look like you're still in high school."

"My appearance has no bearing on which assignments I get."

"Oh, you sweet, innocent child. How you look has a bearing on *everything* in this world."

Can I just say that I can't see Amanda heading a serious news program? As nice as she is, she's got an orange tinge to her skin and she can never make a decision.

"What about this Bold French Roast cup, or maybe English Breakfast tea?"

The entire day I dream about my new assignment, so I don't get a thing done. Since my work evaluations are always excellent and my boss tells me I'm going places, it's not impossible to think I might be picked for this project. Everyone knows my career is everything to me. It has to be. I don't have anything else in my life. But I don't dwell on it. Mother always said, "It's no good feeling sorry for yourself because most of the time we make our own misery." That was the advice she gave me when I didn't get invited to a party in grade one.

My cellphone bursts into song around four in the afternoon. It's Aunt Ollie's number, and since she never calls me at work, I'm sure Gramps is dead. Too frightened to answer the phone, I allow Beethoven's Fifth to continue unabated.

Amanda drops her neck backwards so she can peek at me from her workstation. "Are you going to answer that or do we have to hear the entire symphony?"

I press the answer button. "H...Hello?"

"Don't panic!"

This isn't a good thing to say to me over the phone. Not with my history.

"Your Gramps backed over Norton with the car!"

"Oh my God, is he dead?!"

"Who's dead?" Amanda jumps out of her chair and stands beside me, prepared to burst into tears if the situation requires it.

"No, but I think his front paw might be broken. We're taking him to the vet."

"Okay, I'll meet you there!" I throw the cell in my purse and scramble around gathering my things. "Gramps ran over Norton!"

"Your next-door neighbour? The one with garlic breath?"

"Not Norman, Norton—my cat! I have to get to the vet's office. Call me a taxi."

"Do you want me to drive you?"

I could kiss her. "Would you mind?"

"No problem. Let me get my stuff."

We hurry out of the office, our high heels clattering on the cement of the parking garage as we run to her car. The interior of Amanda's SUV is like nothing I've ever seen. If I didn't know better I'd say she lives in it with her husband and two toddlers.

"Don't mind the stink. The kids spilled milk yesterday and I forgot to mop it up."

The smell is putrid, but I pretend I don't notice, since she's doing me a huge favour. We race down three levels of parking garage and emerge onto the street, the late afternoon sun blinding us momentarily.

"Poor Norton. What if it's really serious? He's my best friend."

"I've been meaning to talk to you about that." Amanda thinks that because she's thirty-five and married with two children, she knows everything. "It's not a good sign when your best friend is a cat."

"Cats are nicer than people."

We swerve around cars and trucks. Amanda is rather exceptional behind the wheel, and I'm about to compliment her when she says, "Dogs are nicer than people, not cats. But you know what's even better? A man. Find one, for God's sake. You're twenty-five and you've never had a boyfriend."

"I have so."

"Not since I've met you. I know you're busy, so go online like the rest of the world."

"Ugh."

"I'm fixing you up."

"If you love me at all, you won't."

"I only like you." She screeches the tires in front of the vet's office. "Do you want me to wait?"

"No, that's okay. I'll call you later." I burst out of the car and into the vet's office, startling an enormous husky. He howls his displeasure, which sets off the felines and makes a small mutt pee on the floor.

"I'm sorry!" I sprint to the front desk. "Please, can you tell me if my cat is here? Norton Sparrow. He was hit by a car."

"Yes, the couple who brought him in are with the vet now."

"I have to see him, I'm his mother."

People who work in vet clinics have heard it all. "First door on the left."

Now I rush to the door and charge in, hitting Gramps on the back.

"Ow, watch it!"

He deserves it anyway. All I see is Norton lying on the table.

Aunt Ollie wrings her hands. "He's not dying. He'll be fixed up in no time."

Norton seems happy to see me. Pushing my way over, I reach down to rub his head, giving him kisses. "It's okay, I'm here."

"Norton will be fine," the vet says. "The right front leg has some torn ligaments but no broken bones."

I didn't realize the vet was in the room.

"I told ya I didn't run over him. I barely touched him."

Aunt Ollie points her finger at Gramps. "You back out of that driveway too damn fast. What if it was a child? I'm having your driver's license taken away."

"You do and I'll smother you in your sleep."

"Not if I poison your food, old man, so don't cross me."

While I'm used to this sort of conversation, I'm acutely aware that other people are not. I turn my back on the vet so I can glare at my relatives. "Why don't you two wait in the car? I'll handle it from here."

They shuffle out and the silence is a relief. Time to turn around and pretend I have a normal family. "Sorry about that. What should I do now?"

"Stop calling your cat Norton."

"Why?"

"Norton's pregnant."

"How did *that* happen?"

"The usual way, I imagine...wine, a nice dinner."

For the first time I look at the veterinarian and not at his white coat or stethoscope. He has a pleasant smile, but then he ruins it.

"I'm surprised a woman like yourself has to be told to fix their cat, especially in this day and age."

"I thought he was fixed! There was no evidence of....you know."

"That's because female cats don't have testicles. How did you not know the sex of your pet?"

"I don't get out much."

He turns his head to hide his grin. "I'll bandage the leg to give her support. I can't give her a sedative because of the pregnancy. She'll be stiff for a few days, but otherwise she's in perfect health."

I reach down, expecting to retrieve my expensive cat carrier, and see there's an old wicker picnic basket with a towel in it instead. "This is how they brought him in?"

"Her. Ingenious, don't you think?"

We carefully place Norton inside until she's comfy, and I close the cover.

"Thank you."

"You're welcome."

It's quiet on the trip home, since Gramps and Aunt Ollie aren't speaking to each other. I'll tell them about Norton later. For now our new mother needs a lot of peace and quiet, two things in very short supply when my family is around.

❀

THE NEXT DAY I'M RELUCTANT TO GO TO WORK, THINKING I SHOULD be with Norton, but Aunt Ollie assures me she'll take care of everything. It doesn't give me a lot of comfort. My only female relative has a screw loose.

It's only while I'm on the bus that I begin to wonder whether I should wish to be the producer of the new series. No, I'm above that sort of thing. I need to get it on my own merit...but what an opportunity to advance my career. How many wishes do I wish? Not very many. It's not like I'm greedy.

It's raining again, so of course the minute I get to my desk Amanda asks me why I wear my nasty sweater. She's starting to bug me.

I head into the washroom to make sure my hair still looks good. I put it up this morning, mindful of Amanda's comment about looking too young. I have a lot of wavy brown hair almost to my shoulder blades. There's a can of hairspray on the counter, something I've never used in my life. I spray some around my head, but it's revolting. The price for beauty is too high, if you ask me.

One last thing, and I make it as watertight as I can, since flubbed wishes make me break out in hives.

I wish to be the producer of the new series at the CBC. Here in Toronto. In this building. The one being announced this morning. The series Amanda talked about. At the coffee machine. Amen.

We assemble in the conference room to hear the big news, all of us with our lattes. There's excitement in the air. *Please let it be an informative and insightful documentary program, something that might make a difference in this crazy world we live in, a show that speaks the real truth.*

Amanda pokes me. "Why are your eyes watering?"

"Are they?" I hadn't noticed, but they are rather itchy.

Our boss arrives, a man named Herb Gardner, which couldn't have been easy growing up. I admire him greatly; he always seems so sure about everything. He looks down at all of us sitting around the conference table.

"We're jumping on the bandwagon. We're going to produce our first reality show."

I'm on it! Gritty reality, like investigating the housing concerns in First Nations communities, the heartbreak of Maritime families whose breadwinners have to work in camps and oil fields in Alberta to make a living, the impossibility of being a farmer in today's world. The list is endless. I can't wait. My God, what if it's about political espionage or drug cartels? I'll just die!

"You've heard of *The Lonely Bachelor*. The Canadian version will be called *The Single Guy*."

What?

I rub my eyes in disbelief. Everyone around me is shocked into silence. We are the CBC. *The Lonely Bachelor* has busty women disembarking from a stretch limousine, pledging undying love to a guy they've never met. How does that help society?

Mr. Gardner continues. "And we've decided that the producer we need for this particular project is our wonder girl, Chloe Sparrow. Everyone give her a big hand."

Oh. My. God.

"Come up here, Chloe."

As I get to my feet, Amanda pulls at my skirt. "What's wrong with your lips?"

My dismay is such that I fumble as I make my way towards my superior. My colleagues are looking at me but their faces are distorted. Catching sight of myself in the glass wall behind Mr. Gardner, I realize I've morphed into a Teletubby.

Fade to black.

AMANDA'S WITH ME AT THE HOSPITAL, GIVING ME HELL FOR using hairspray that wasn't mine. The epinephrine the paramedics pumped into me to counteract my allergic reaction has me jumpy and talking like an auctioneer.

"What is he *thinking*? I don't know anything about bachelors or bimbos. You'd be better at that."

"I'll forgive you because you have chipmunk cheeks."

"This isn't what I signed up for."

"Enough! This should've been my job. Do you hear me moaning about it?"

"You're moaning about it now."

"I have to go."

After Amanda leaves to go back to the office, I lie there and count the holes in the ceiling tiles. To my horror, the doctor suggests I stay overnight on a gurney in the hallway just to be safe. She tells me my reaction was severe, so I call Aunt Ollie. Gramps picks up the phone.

"What's shakin'?"

"It's Chloe. I have to stay overnight in the hospital, but it's not serious and I don't want you to worry."

"Likely excuse."

"Gramps, make sure you feed Norton."

"You got two boyfriends?"

"Is Aunt Ollie there?"

"She's always skulking around. Ollie! Pick up the gee-dee phone."

"Helloooo?"

"Make sure you feed Norton, because I won't be home tonight. There are cans and bags of dry food in the pantry."

"I already fed her."

"Stop snooping in my house when I'm not there."

"How dare you suggest such a thing? By the way, I'm mending the holes in your socks and soaking a few of your bras."

❁

AFTER A FITFUL NIGHT'S SLEEP ON AN UNCOMFORTABLE SLAB that's too high off the floor, I wake up with the world's worst hangover. The nurse assures me this is normal for people pumped full of adrenaline. She tells me to take it easy for the rest of the day, so I take a cab home. It's much easier than asking Gramps to come get me. I don't have the stamina for him right now.

The relief is overwhelming the minute I cross my own threshold. In my house everything is orderly and has its own place—a result of too many nights alone. Nothing's changed since the day my parents died. It's comforting to keep it this way. Although after ten years some items are wearing thin, like sheets and towels. Whenever I have a bad day I go to my parents' closets and hang out there for a while, or I go to the library and read their books. Both of them were University of Toronto professors. They expected great things from me, and I still live in fear of disappointing them.

In the weeks following their accident I was, of course, grief-stricken. I cried out one night that I wished my parents were still with me. And believe it or not, I've been living with two poltergeists ever since. Dad slams doors and Mom rattles the dishes. At times the thermostat goes crazy, too. I'm assuming it's my mom around when it becomes unbearably warm. All she did was complain about hot flashes.

Upstairs, Norton is on the canopied bed my mother wouldn't let me get rid of because she said it was a sin to waste money. It doesn't go with the black walls that I insisted I wanted when I turned fifteen. A decade later, I'd kind of like to paint the walls pale grey, or soft linen, but I still can't bring myself to do it.

Norton rolls over onto her back and waits for me to rub her belly. It's our ritual.

She showed up on my doorstep one night after I had a terrible argument with a friend. Stomping home through the snow, I wished for a new friend. Lo and behold, Norton was at my front door. At first I thought she was a fat racoon. The minute I put the key in the lock she walked in like she'd been doing it all her life. We understand each other perfectly. I'm also a stray.

At five o'clock, I'm still sleeping when the phone jars me awake.

"I've made beef stew. Dinner is in ten minutes." Click.

The thought of eating beef stew leaves me cold, but Aunt Ollie has guilt issues and insists on feeding me periodically. I trudge to the bathroom and for the first time look in the mirror. I'm a wax candle that's been left in the sun too long. Hopefully hot water will shrink my skin back in place. I'm not vain, but right now I look like my grandfather.

Naturally, the other two don't notice a thing wrong with me. They've been locked in battle for so long the outside world has ceased to exist. Their entire realm is this atrociously messy house, which will be lethal one day, because Gramps is very careless with his pipe. My aunt and I have tried for years to get him to stop smoking. He said he'd quit smoking the day Aunt Ollie lost her spare tire, so I wished for Aunt Ollie to lose some weight. She got sick and lost ten pounds while she was in the hospital. I realized I had to stop interfering or I'd knock off my whole family.

Aunt Ollie passes me a plateful of beef stew. She knows I'm a vegetarian, but she conveniently forgets.

"What's going on at work these days?"

She sits and scratches her head through a hairnet. Sometimes I want to yank out the two pink plastic rollers that are forever curling her bangs. I don't think I've seen her hair unadorned in a decade. At fifty-one, Aunt Ollie looks as old as Gramps, and he's seventy-three.

"I got a promotion. I'm the field producer of a new series for the network."

Gramps takes tobacco out of his pouch and fills his pipe. "That's one thing I'll say for you: you're smart, like me."

Aunt Ollie passes me a huge bowl of maple walnut ice cream before I've even taken a bite of the stew. "Will you get a raise?"

"I'm not sure." That's something I hadn't considered.

"What's it about?" Gramps asks.

"It's a reality show."

"Which means?"

"People go on television and pretend they're living normal lives while a camera crew follows them around."

Gramps's bushy eyebrows quiver. "The whole world has gone to the dogs. Who in their right mind would want to have a camera stuck up their arse all day and night? Where do they find these lunatics and why do I want to watch them?"

"I love *Say Yes to the Dress*," Aunt Ollie sighs. "You should've seen my wedding dress."

Gramps lights his pipe with a match. "Trust you to still be talking about it."

Aunt Ollie slams her spoon on the table. "Why shouldn't I?"

"It was over thirty years ago! Drop it already."

Before I can say anything, Aunt Ollie makes her martyr face and rushes out of the kitchen. I'm left to defend her.

"Why are you so mean? She's the only daughter you have left."

"She loves it. Olive's been a drama queen since she was born. I get her riled up so she can blow off steam. What else has she got to look forward to?"

He kind of has a point. Since I'm not hungry, my food goes in the garbage and I start to clean up. Gramps leans back in his chair. He's still a good-looking man, despite the grey facial hair sprouting out of his nose and ears. It's his awful glasses that have to go. They hang off the edge of his nose and are so full of fingerprints it's a wonder he can see.

"Yeah, the poor little bastard got run over by a backhoe. No wonder. He was about five foot nothin', only skin and bones. Just as well he met his maker before the wedding. Ollie would've smothered him on their wedding night."

"I hope you've never said that to Aunt Ollie!"

"Might have...once or twice."

"No wonder she hates you."

The dishes loaded, I start the dishwasher. Only the pot to scrub in the sink and I can escape.

"So what's your reality show called?"

"*The Single Guy*. It's about a bachelor."

"And what do you do with him?"

"He tries to find a woman who will marry him."

"You're going to follow this numbskull all over the city?"

"No, they're delivered to him on a platter."

He sucks on his pipe for a few moments. "I believe I was born in the wrong century."

I'm back in my Barbie bed by seven-thirty. I spend most of my time in my room, despite its gloominess. The rest of the house is always in darkness. It seems disrespectful to use superfluous electricity in the rooms my parents lived in, since that was the manner of their death. I confirmed my instincts one evening when I decided to turn on all the lights in the house as an experiment. Dad opened and slammed doors shut the entire night, and there was a broken coffee mug on the kitchen floor the next morning. It would have to be my favourite. Thanks Mom.

I am almost always alone, but it never feels lonely when Norton is on my bed. What would it be like to have a man here instead? Impossible, I guess. He'd want the lights on.

Norton has her good paw over her eyes, which means she doesn't want to be disturbed. Trouble is, she's lying on the remote. When I gently remove it, she tightens the grip on her face, stretching her back paws until they tremble, toes splayed in annoyance.

I decide a little television will put me to sleep. Wouldn't you know, *The Lonely Bachelor* soundtrack fills the room as the camera sweeps over the palatial estate where this nonsense is filmed. Ordinarily I'd switch it off, but now I have to do research, so I reach for the writing pad I use to jot down my dreams and hold a pencil aloft, ready to do battle. An hour later there's not a single word written down. A minute after that Amanda's on the phone.

"Did you watch it?"

"It's...terrible."

"The mud-wrestling segment was over the top. We shouldn't do that right off the bat."

"We shouldn't do it at *all*. What has mud-wrestling got to do with anything? Ever? This is going to be a disaster." My notepad slides off the bed and I sink into my frayed sheets.

"Hike up your big-girl panties. We have to start casting soon."

"I don't think I'm the right person for the job."

"You're not, but am I holding a grudge?"

"A little."

"Which is understandable, given the circumstances. I am your senior."

"Your life is perfect, Amanda."

"Perfect? At this moment, the love of my life is snoring on his recliner with a jumbo bag of chips on his chest."

"At least you have someone in the house with you."

Norton opens one eye and gives me a dirty look.

"Something occurred to me today as I was driving home," Amanda says. "We're going to be surrounded by gorgeous women for months. I think I'll have streaks put in my hair and maybe get a little Botox for these frown lines."

"Are you serious?"

"Sparrow, you have no idea what you're in for. These women are going to walk all over you. You look twelve! It might help if you cut your hair—gotta go, one of the kids is crying."

I haul myself into the bathroom and take a lengthy look in the mirror. This is when a mom or a sister would come in handy. The only thing Aunt Ollie has ever said is that my eyes are too far apart and my lips are pudgy. The longer I stand here, the more aware I am of the lingering scent of the hairspray that nearly took my life, and that reminds me of my ridiculous wish.

No more wishes. No more hair.

❊

MAKING A HAIR APPOINTMENT IS LIKE TRYING TO GET INTO A sorority. Amanda recommends a few salons downtown, but they're booked for months.

I'm at my desk eating yogurt and fruit for lunch when Amanda sits back down in her swivel chair, and I ask, "Why can't I go to your hairdresser?"

"No way."

"Why?"

"It's the quickest way to ruin a friendship. If you hate it, you'll blame me."

"I will?"

"Yes."

In the end, I go to the local hairdresser at my closest strip mall. They take me right away, which should have given me pause. An hour later, I'm bald. I tip the girl because she's so proud of herself.

When I go back to work, Amanda claps her hands together like a little kid. "A pixie cut, I love it! You finally look your age."

On the way home, I notice people on the bus looking at me, wondering if I'm the same girl who's been riding this bus for years. It's amazing how you know when someone's staring at you. Even the lazy bums who never stand for an elderly citizen sneak a peek. That must mean I look great.

Or not. When I show up at my grandfather's house, my Aunt Ollie covers her face as soon as she sees me and runs down the crowded hallway towards the kitchen.

Gramps limps out of the living room. "What the hell happened to you? Did someone attack you with gardening shears? I'll go kick his head in."

"By all means, go kick the girl working her butt off in our struggling local hair salon."

"You *paid* to have this done?"

There's no reason for me to stay out in the hall with my grandfather, so I leave him and go to the kitchen, where Aunt Ollie proceeds to sniff and shudder every time she glances at me.

"I got my hair cut. People do it several million times a day."

"You look like you have cancer."

"Thank you."

"Your beautiful hair!"

"Okay, this is astounding. You've never once in my life told me my hair was beautiful."

"I didn't want you to get a swelled head."

Gramps returns to sit in his rocking chair by the stove. "People are too conceited as it is."

"Did you ever once tell your daughters they were pretty?"

"They weren't."

"What a terrible thing to say!"

"He's right," says Aunt Ollie. "I'm surprised your mother found a man."

These two make me want to pull out the little hair I have left. "I can't stay. Could you keep Norton over here during the day? I don't like leaving her alone now that my hours are unpredictable."

"That fur bag?" Gramps says. "The place won't be fit to live in."

"This house is a garbage dump. A little fur isn't going to spoil the overall look."

"Of course we'll take her." Aunt Ollie wipes her eyes. "Norton's better company than old misery-guts."

"Hey, I resent that."

Back home I deliver the bad news to Norton. "I apologize in advance for the hell you'll go through living next door."

CHAPTER TWO

WE'RE SWAMPED WITH APPLICATIONS. ARE THERE THAT MANY desperate bachelors out there? Amanda and I spend an entire week going through the pile in the small, second-floor back room that we're using as an office. It's quiet and private and prevents our female co-workers from sneaking peeks over our shoulders.

Reading about the personal lives of strangers takes an enormous amount of energy and concentration, not to mention a nose for bullshit, something I haven't honed yet.

"What about this guy?" I read the application out loud. "He's a Rhodes scholar, a surgeon, has a black belt in karate, and runs his own charity for orphans when he's not doing heart transplants or competing in triathlons."

Amanda rolls her eyes at me. "Honestly, Chloe, does he sound real?"

"He could be."

"What's his name?"

"Biff."

She leans over and grabs the paper out of my hand, throwing it behind her. "Next."

The next application floors me. "Wait a minute, I know this guy."

Amanda looks up. "Who is he?"

"He's the vet who helped Norton." I look for his name. "Dr. Austin Hawke."

"Let me see."

When I pass it over, Amanda's eyes widen. "Dear God!"

"What?"

"He looks like Ryan Gosling!"

"Who's Ryan Gosling?"

Amanda slams her hand on the table. "Why are you in charge of this show? You barely watch television! Everyone knows who Ryan Gosling is. He's a gorgeous Canadian movie star. How is it possible you don't know this?"

"I do *so* watch television...documentaries, and the news..."

"Please tell me you watched TV when you were a kid."

"I was allowed to watch *Mr. Dressup* and *Sesame Street*."

"It's like you're from another planet," Amanda moans.

I find it very strange that a man like Dr. Hawke would want to be on a television show. He doesn't strike me as the type, but then again, what do I know about men?

After a long and gruelling process, we ask some of the women on our floor to help us during their lunch hour. Amanda lays out the pictures on the conference table and passes out pencils.

"These are the final thirty," I say. "We've weeded out the obvious lunatics, criminal types, and mama's boys. It goes without saying that they have huge egos."

"How do you know?" Debbie from acquisitions is always the first to question everything.

"They want to fondle strange women in front of a camera and have it broadcast on television. What does that say about them? Please put a checkmark beside the men you find attractive. We're going on looks alone at this point."

There's no sense ignoring the fact that women like men who are deemed attractive by other females. That's what I've read, anyway.

They circle the table. Debbie uselessly puts a checkmark on every one of them. Fortunately, the rest are choosier. We thank them for their time and gather up our papers, counting the marks for each man. Based on that scientific criterion, we whittle the bachelors down to ten, and Amanda contacts them with the good news.

❀

FOUR DAYS LATER, THE FINALISTS FROM ALL ACROSS CANADA are cooling their heels in a downtown hotel—except Austin, who declined a room because he lives in town.

I decide to let Amanda handle the interviews of these gentlemen. She's pleasantly surprised that I trust her with the job. It's more about me being a big chicken, but she doesn't need to know that.

We are now seated in chairs at a round table in one of the back rooms. Each candidate will be brought in one at a time from the annex room next door.

Amanda pokes me. "Stop frowning. If Mr. Gardner finds out you despise this sort of show, you'll be yanked outta here before lunch."

True. There's my new raise to consider, so I give a big grin.

"Okay, now you're overdoing it."

"Did you buy a blouse just for today?"

Amanda strokes the front of her new purchase. "Nice, isn't it."

It won't be by the time the spray-tan molecules bleed into the collar. Why she needs to look like she stepped off a plane from the Dominican every day of her life is a mystery to me. But then, so are most things.

It's a hideously long day, hours upon hours spent talking to Ken dolls, but Amanda has a blast and spends so much time grilling these alpha males that I'm ready to wring her neck.

"I can see the Situation going on here," she mumbles.

I whisper, "What situation?"

"Never mind, you don't watch *Jersey Shore*."

One fellow points out that not only is he incredibly handsome, he graduated from M.I.T. and is a millionaire on paper. I pass a note to Amanda that says *I'm a millionaire too.* Later that afternoon we have a guy who winks every time he says something. It borders on creepy.

"I've got a great job." Wink.

He probably lives at home with his mother.

"I'm a real gentleman." Wink.

Maybe he's a flasher.

I escape to the ladies' room for a minute, but what I desperately want is more caffeine, which I track down in the lunchroom. The copy girl is taking the last of the cream. "Are you having fun?" she asks. "Are the guys hot?"

"As hot as my coffee. Any more cream?"

"You're, like, so lucky." She takes her creamy java and leaves. There's only skim milk in the fridge. If there's anything I can't stand, it's skim milk in coffee.

I wish I had cream.

It's amazing how quickly my resolve about not wishing disappears when I want something. After counting to ten I look in the fridge again. There's the cream, in the back on the top shelf.

We're down to the last interview, but the minute Amanda sees my coffee she wants one, so she ducks out. The intern waltzes in the other door with Austin Hawke. He thanks the intern and fixes his jacket sleeve before advancing towards me. He's the only man to reach over the desk and shake my hand.

"Austin Hawke. Nice to meet you."

"Hello, Dr. Hawke. It's nice to see you again."

He looks puzzled. "We've met before?"

"I'm Chloe Sparrow, Norton's mother."

He still looks confused. Obviously I made an impression on him. "Sit down, please."

He settles in his chair and gives me a charming smile. Amanda comes in with her coffee mug and momentarily stops dead when she sees my veterinarian, but quickly gathers herself and sits beside me. Austin reaches over to shake her hand too.

"Austin Hawke. Lovely to meet you."

"Amanda Partridge, and the pleasure's all mine." She sounds like she's purring, which strikes me as funny, but it's been a long day so I cut to the chase.

"Why on earth do you want to be on this show, Dr. Hawke?"

Amanda jumps in. "What Miss Sparrow means, is why would you like to be a part of this fabulous new series?"

He hesitates. "I have to be honest. My sister dared me to apply. It was a joke, but then I found out the bachelor gets paid, and since I'll do just about anything to pay off my student loan, I thought I'd see it through."

He's forthright, if nothing else. "You think you can propose to someone you never met in twelve weeks' time?"

"I have no idea, but my mother says I'm a hopeless romantic. The girls at the office call me Dr. McFurry."

Amanda is melting into a pile of goo beside me. She grills him for an hour, asks him about everything, from what he likes for breakfast to his favourite hockey team. Finally, I thank him for coming and he shakes our hands again, and looks at me more closely.

"I remember you now. You've cut your hair since we last met. It looks very nice."

Now I'm blushing.

When the door finally closes behind him, Amanda hits me on the arm. "He's absolutely perfect! He's the one!"

"Just because he looks like an actor I've never heard of? Is that a good enough reason?"

Amanda's spray tan seems to be fading, always a sign of fatigue. "You know why you're the producer? The bigwigs upstairs think you're young and hip and have your pulse on what the eighteen-to-twenty-five-year-old demographic wants to watch. They don't know there's a middle-aged woman rattling around under that tight, luminous skin of yours."

"But is it a conflict of interest because he's my cat's vet?"

"Who's gonna know and who gives a shit? He's the best of the bunch."

"Fine, if you say so."

❀

AFTER WORK I HIT A VIDEO STORE AND ASK FOR A RYAN GOSLING movie. The girl hands me *The Notebook*. Sounds boring.

The bus ride home soothes me as I stare out the dirty window watching the world go by, but the best part of my day is walking from the bus stop to my house. My street has narrow Victorian row houses like mine, but also a few arts and crafts bungalows and gingerbread houses, a perfect backdrop for the charming urban gardens all the young families are planting around me. The idea of planting flowers is nice, but they'd only die on me so I've never bothered.

When I show up to take Norton back to my house, he's on Gramps's lap being rocked to sleep. The minute Gramps realizes I'm there, he starts gesturing. "Take this damn cat, will ya? She won't leave me alone."

Then he looks annoyed when I take the damn cat. Once Norton is fed and cuddled at home, I gulp down a grilled cheese sandwich while standing by the stove. Then I take a bath, get in my flannel pyjamas, make some popcorn, and put on the DVD. Press play. Two hours later I'm sobbing into my empty popcorn bowl because I'm in love with Ryan Gosling and I want his babies. I call Amanda.

"Hello? Who is this?"

I blow my nose into my buttery napkin. "It's me."

"Chloe? You sound like you have a head cold."

"I just watched *The Notebook*."

"*I know*. Didn't I tell you he was perfect?"

"Oh, he is. He is."

Norton looks a bit fed up with my blubbering. I can't blame her. She's supposed to be resting.

❀

I'VE WANTED TO WORK FOR THE CBC SINCE I WAS A YOUNG teenager. My parents had a love affair with their news anchor, Knowlton Nash, and I grew up listening to the sounds of mortar fire in the background of terse news clips, delivered by brave male and female reporters telling Canadians the score in the hot spots of the world. This is serious stuff. People need to know what's going on, and I was always determined to be part of it, which is why I studied journalism and television production at Ryerson and graduated at the top of my class. I know what you're thinking and yes, I admit it. I did wish that I'd graduate at the top of my class, which made me feel bad for a while, but then I thought what the heck. It's not something I'm going to brag about in a social situation, and I certainly would've passed anyway. So I don't feel guilty about it.

Not really.

The best thing about working for the CBC is coming into the building and walking through the atrium. The vast space floats over my head. A deep well of knowledge hangs in the air. Just knowing there are floors and floors of busy little beavers informing us about the world and our place in it gives me a chill. Although some days I also think how cool it would be to put up clotheslines and hang our laundry out.

I also love walking into the hustle and bustle of our newsroom and studio, everyone busy at their desks or rushing by with armfuls of paper. There is a constant murmur of people on their phones or conferring with each other about important news items. Featured guests and artists wait in what we jokingly call the green room, which is a couch and coffee table by the entrance door; however, we do have bottled water and a dish full of peppermints they can help themselves to.

When I need a break, I walk to the wall of windows that overlook the city and watch the traffic and people going about their business, everyone in a hurry to get somewhere. Toronto is a centre for business, culture, and sports, all pulsing together to create a vibrant and modern dynamic. It's beautiful and upscale, surrounded by older and unique neighbourhoods like my own Cabbagetown, Chinatown, and Kensington, with its famous market.

As I walk up the stairwell to work a week after my *Notebook* revelation (I've watched it five times now), I gird my loins, knowing the female interviews are coming up. It was hard enough picking one bachelor, never mind twenty women. I tell myself yet again that I've been given an opportunity that everyone (Amanda) seems to want, so I'm going to stop whining and do my best. This isn't the kind of show I'll produce forever, and the reality is that networks make money on reality shows, so I'd better get with the program. In 2011, money makes the world go round, and I'll hop on this carousel with enthusiasm and hold on tight.

Three days later, I feel faint and want to get off. Amanda and I are worn out and punchy, and if I see another pair of enhanced breasts I may have to kill myself. So far the most popular answers to the question *Why do you want to be on this show?* are as follows:

"I want to be married."

"I'm looking for love."

"I need a man."

"I want to be a star."

"I don't want to die alone."

The traffic of women is a blur, until a candidate shows up who's almost as flat-chested as I am. She reaches over the desk to shake our hands before sitting down. Austin's going to love her.

"Hello, I'm Jocelyn Dove."

A Hawke and a Dove? This is television gold. By the time we finish our interview, Amanda and I realize that Jocelyn's so perfect, *we* want to marry her.

We eventually have our list and go through it one last time.

"So their average age is twenty-five," Amanda says. "They all have jobs, but I'm not convinced that Sydney isn't a pole dancer. What does she do again?"

"She's supposedly an actress. Naturally, Jocelyn is a kindergarten teacher, and Lizette is a race-car driver, which is impossibly cool. Tracy is a graphic designer, and Mysti is a law student. Holly and Molly are flight attendants."

"Chloe, are you sure having twins is a good idea?"

"They aren't identical, and maybe it will be a disaster, but isn't drama what we want? What's going to be a nightmare is that we have two Jennifers, two Kates, two Sandys, and two Sarahs."

"Don't forget Rebecca, Becca, and Becky."

"Emily and Erin round it out. That's twenty girls, all of them better looking than me."

"Don't be so hard on yourself, Chloe."

"They're better looking than you, too, not to mention younger."

"Up yours."

We need a drink very badly, so we pack up and head to the nearest bar. As always, the minute we walk out of the building and around the corner, the wind hits us full blast and we're trudging forward like pack animals, but at least the wind is warm and the rain's cleared up. We race to get to the bar door first. Three drafts and a platter of nachos later, I'm happy with the world.

"Can you remember any of their names?"

"The Dove girl...Jocelyn."

"She is *so* winning this competition. Let's just plunk the two of them in a hot tub and watch them mate. What would you call the offspring of a dove and a hawk, anyway?"

"Hovedawk?"

"How about Warren Peace?"

The two of us crack up before I knock back my glass.

"You're always showing off, Sparrow."

"Do you know what else just occurred to me? We have a Hawke, a Dove, a Sparrow, and a Partridge."

"Don't forget Ryan Gosling. What do you think it means?"

"How the flock should I know?"

"Oh, snap!" She gives me a high five.

I put my elbows on the table. "What's it like to go home to somebody at night?"

"Not everything it's cracked up to be when you come home late. We should shove off." She raises her hand in the air.

"No, no, no. I'm definitely paying for this. My treat. My treat." I fumble around and try to locate my purse, but it seems to have disappeared. "Holy shit! My purse is gone."

"It's hanging on the back of your chair."

"Oh."

At that moment a guy walks over and stands beside me. "Excuse me, my name is Enrique. Would you mind if I sit down?"

Yes, I do. I don't know what to say to this guy, but Amanda and Enrique are looking at me. "Okay."

So he sits down. Amanda is amazingly helpful now that she's rolling her paper place mat and not looking at me.

"What is your name, little one?" Enrique asks.

"Are you talking to me?"

"Yes," he grins. "Your name?"

I'm pretty sure you shouldn't give your name to a strange man right off the bat, but I can't think of another one until I blurt, "Amanda."

Amanda stops rolling the paper and gives me a dirty look.

"And what do you do, pretty Amanda?" He downs his drink.

"I work."

"Where?"

"Here."

"In this bar?"

"In Toronto."

"Doing what?"

"This and that."

He laughs and traces his finger down my arm. "We should do this and that together."

Amanda grabs her purse, my purse, her coat, and my nasty sweater in a matter of seconds and then yanks me out my chair. "Oh, no you don't. Get lost, Enrique." She pays the bill and we're out the door in a matter of minutes.

I'm nodding off when she pulls the car up to my door. With the engine still running, she turns to me. "That guy at the bar was a player. If a man touches you without your permission five seconds after knowing you, that's a sign to stay away from him."

"I didn't want him to sit down. I did it for you."

"Promise me you won't go to a bar alone. Not for a very long time." Her phone dings and she reads her text. "Hubby's wondering where I am. Gotta go."

"Thanks for the ride."

There's no outside light on and the house is in darkness. Damn. It's so depressing. Things are closed up and dark at Gramps's, too. I wonder if they ever worry about me coming home late at night. There's a note on my door. *Brought Norton back at nine.* I'm feeling pretty sorry for myself by the time I get to my bedroom and fall across the bed. Norton asks me how my day went. I wish she wouldn't. I never have anything exciting to tell her.

CHAPTER THREE

IN THE MORNING I WAKE UP WITH A HANGOVER. THAT'S TWO IN the same month. This is not good, because I have a production meeting and my first face-to-face with Austin and then his harem. Contracts need to be signed and a meeting with the realtor has been arranged, and then I have to present a report to Mr. Gardner at the end of the day. All the while my head feels like a kaleidoscope.

A hot shower helps, and so do the painkillers, but my saving grace is the gigantic travel mug I found in a sales bin last year. I fill it with bubbly Coke to settle my stomach, after giving Norton her breakfast and a big sloppy kiss. "Aunt Ollie will be here at eight to take you next door. I love you. Please don't have my babies until I get back."

The last thing I do is look in the full-length mirror behind my bedroom door. This morning I have on a brand new suit. It's charcoal grey with a fine pinstripe. The pencil skirt hits me just above the knee, and the jacket has a smart tailored bow at the small of my back. The saleslady who helped me loved the feminine detail. That was nice of her. My dad had a charcoal pinstripe suit. I feel strong and powerful wearing it, or I would if my headache would only disappear. I'm ashamed to say my physical condition causes me to ignore the little old ladies on the bus today. My behind remains firmly in my seat. They're on their own.

"Love the suit!" Amanda says when I walk through the door at work. "You actually look like you know what you're doing."

"What would I do without you, Amanda?"

The production meeting lasts almost three hours, everyone reporting on the logistics of the show, recommendations for location shoots, and financial matters. Company lawyers go over legal mumbo-jumbo and break down what's expected from the bachelor and what's required of the ladies and also explain the confidentiality contracts. I almost pass out when I see the amount of money budgeted for alcohol.

"Is this necessary?"

Everyone swivels their heads to look at me. The host of our show, Trey Withers (who's smarmy, if you ask me, but comes highly recommended), launches into a detailed explanation as to why alcohol is essential for creating a more dynamic atmosphere on set.

"We want to keep the contestants buzzed from morning until night so they have no inhibitions, get into cat fights, say stupid things to Austin, and create uncomfortable situations 24-7."

"That's creepy."

Trey gives me a withering look. "Reality television is about people behaving badly. That's what today's audience wants to watch, Miss Sparrow. You better get used to it, since you're the producer of this show. Millions of dollars are now your responsibility."

He's right, of course, but I still feel sleazy and slightly sick when I think about it. When we adjourn I take more painkillers before I meet with Austin in the small office where we first interviewed him. I check my cellphone. He's ten minutes late, which annoys me. Does he want this job or not?

There's a knock at the door.

"Come in."

Austin walks into the room wearing an open-collar white shirt and black dress pants. He is clean-shaven and smells divine. He reaches for my hand and gives me a smile. "Miss Sparrow, I'm sorry I'm late. I had a dehydrated gerbil show up just as I was leaving."

"No worries, Dr. Hawke. Please sit down."

"Thank you. And please call me Austin."

I fidget with my pen. "You must be wondering why you're here."

"To deliver Norton's kittens?"

"Not yet. We want you to be our single guy. You are our first choice."

Austin adjusts himself in the chair, looking slightly overwhelmed. "To tell you the truth, I didn't expect to win. I thought only big dumb jerks are chosen for shows like this."

"They are."

He gives me a look.

"Sorry, that was my attempt at a joke."

"Good one."

"Austin, this assignment is quite a commitment. If you have any doubts about this, tell me now. I don't want you to be halfway into a shoot and decide you don't want the job."

"May I ask you why you picked me?"

"Trust me, you were the best of the bunch. You have many attractive qualities, one of which is that you look like Ryan Gosling."

"Who?"

"Thank you! I'm not the only one on the planet who didn't know who he was. Anyway, it's not important." I gather up the paperwork. "You have to sign this confidentiality agreement. Please read it over carefully. As well we'll need blood work and you'll meet with a psychiatrist."

"You're kidding."

"We can't have lunatics and sex fiends running around infecting women with STDs on national television." I get to my feet. "Please look over these papers and I'll be back to witness your signature."

My hand is on the doorknob when he says, "You look amazing in that outfit."

"Need I remind you that I'm not one of the contestants?"

"Good thing. I'd kick you off first."

"Just sign the papers, Ryan."

I'm halfway down the hall when he shouts, "The name's Austin!"

Now into the lion's den. Amanda has the frenzied female contestants cooped up in the boardroom down the hall. The minute I open the door and enter, Amanda collapses into the nearest chair with a sigh of relief.

"Good morning. I'm Chloe Sparrow, the producer of *The Single Guy*. We met briefly at your interviews, but right now I'd like to say congratulations for being chosen the best single gals in Canada!"

I wait for their hysteria to settle down before I resume speaking. "As wonderful as you think this experience is going to be, it's real life. This is a three-month commitment and your hearts are on the line. Honestly, if you think you are emotionally fragile or know that you won't be able to handle it, please, please say so now."

Complete silence. Gee, there's a surprise.

"Okay. I see that Amanda has handed out your contracts. I need you to read them and understand them, especially the section on the confidentiality agreement. In this day and age, when everyone and his dog knows what you're doing on

Facebook, you need to be vigilant about not posting anything until this show has finished the last episode. If you do not respect these terms you will immediately be sent home and could be fined, so I suggest you take this seriously."

In the space of a minute I've sucked the excitement out of this room. Now they look worried, and well they should be. "Amanda will witness your signatures and I'll be back."

Amanda stands up and whispers in my ear as I go by. "If you lose your job you can always be a prison warden."

After giving Austin a good twenty minutes to look things over, I re-enter the room. His contract is on the desk in front of him.

"Everything all right? Any questions?"

"Am I contractually obligated to sleep with these women?"

A flush of heat rises from my neck to my ears. I hate it when I have flaming ears. "Of course not."

"Just checking."

I hand him my pen and indicate where he should sign before I initial it. "Okay, follow me for blood work. I'm going to take you down the back way so your concubines don't see you."

In the emptiness of the stairwell, my heels sound ten times louder, so I start to ramble to cover up the noise. "Since you're here, is there anything I should do for Norton before the birth of the kittens?"

"You could always make a nest of sorts, a box with some towels, or some other comfortable space away from prying eyes."

"Excellent. Thank you."

"No problem."

Just before he leaves me, I blurt, "They won't die, will they?"

"The kittens? I shouldn't think so. The mother is a healthy specimen."

"Good to know, thank you. We'll be in touch." I click my way back up the stairs. Maybe I'm being paranoid, but I think I feel his eyes on me as I go. I can't look around to check because that would be mortifying. This hangover is addling my brain.

❦

THE MANSION THAT WILL BE OUR SET IS IN THE NEIGHBOUR-hood of Bridle Path, a wealthy enclave twenty minutes from downtown. Amanda and I are in a daze at the size of the place.

"Can you imagine cleaning this?" Amanda says.

"It feels lonely."

The realtor doesn't like me very much. He sniffs the air when I make a comment, so I wander off without him, but now I can't find my way back to the kitchen. After opening twenty doors and shouting hello into every one of them, I hear a voice.

"Down here!"

We gather around the kitchen island, which is the size of the swimming pool outside, and Amanda goes down the list. "So we have the luxurious grand entrance for the limo shots, the games room, the multiple terraces, the banquet hall, the great room, five fireplaces, six bedrooms, ten bathrooms, the gym, the hot tub and sauna, the library, this state-of-the-art kitchen, and the guest house next door is great for Austin and the crew. Is there anything I'm forgetting?"

"The elevator and the helicopter pad," the realtor says.

"Are you serious?"

Mr. Real Estate doesn't acknowledge me. I've had enough. "I'm sorry, I have a meeting. Thank you again, great choice."

❦

WHEN WE GET BACK TO THE OFFICE, LUCKY AMANDA SAYS GOOD night, but I still have to go upstairs and report to Mr. Gardner.

Waiting outside his office is nerve-racking. His secretary is a stern woman who never cracks a smile. I'm in a sweat just looking at her. Eventually she indicates that I can proceed into the inner sanctum. Mr. Gardner is at his desk.

"Come in and sit down, Chloe. How's everything going?"

"Very well, sir."

"What did you think of the location? I hear it's quite something."

"It's perfect for our needs, but personally I think it's shameful that only two people have been living in that house when there are so many other human beings on this planet with inadequate housing, people living in slums, tents, refugee camps, and in the streets. It's depressing."

"The world isn't fair, Miss Sparrow. Now fill me in."

When I eventually leave his office, I am bone weary. I'm grateful that he seems pleased with our progress, but at this moment I don't give a rat's ass, as Gramps always says. My bus ride home rocks me to sleep, so I miss my stop, but fortunately a kid screams at his mother and I wake up in time to get off at the next one, so I don't have too far to plod. It just seems like it.

I walk right into Aunt Ollie's because their door is never locked. Someday I'll find them dead on the floor, victims of a home invasion. I've asked them a hundred times to lock their door, but they never do. Aunt Ollie is at the kitchen table playing solitaire. Norton is snuggled in Gramps's lap, while he rocks. It's only then that I realize I haven't eaten all day, so the first thing I do is slump in a chair.

"You guys have any peanut butter?"

They both nod. This is the part where I'd love one of them to jump up and make me a sandwich, but they don't, and why should they? They're twenty-six and forty-five years older than I am.

While I'm at the counter, Gramps says, "You look like your mother."

"That's nice."

"She used to come home looking like crap, too."

While I eat my sandwich I tell them about my coming schedule. "So I'll be staying at the guest house when the day runs late, but I'll call and let you know because I don't want Norton to be alone."

"She's not alone, I've got the nursery ready," Aunt Ollie says. "It's in my bedroom closet. She can stay with us from now on."

"Besides, she likes it here better than your place," Gramps informs me.

I burst into tears.

"What on earth is the matter?" Aunt Ollie yells. "I thought you'd be pleased. It took me a long time to organize that closet. I even gave her two of my old wool blankets to snuggle up in and I put three pillows on the floor."

"I *am* pleased," I sniff. "It's been a long day."

Gramps gives me a searching look. "Are you sure you can handle this job?"

"Of course I can handle it. I'm just not sure I want to. It's too ridiculous. Do people actually think they'll find true love in front of a camera?"

"People can fall in love anywhere," Aunt Ollie says. "Take me and Howie..."

"Let's not," Gramps says.

My aunt ignores him. "We met when I ran him over with my bike."

"A precursor to the backhoe," Gramps mutters.

Aunt Ollie flicks her dishtowel at his head. "Shut up, you old fool."

My energy is waning. "I better go. Thanks for the sandwich."

"You took two bites out of it. Do you want some meatloaf?"

Should I tell my aunt yet again that I don't eat meat? I can't be bothered. I kiss the three of them on the head and secretly hope Norton follows me down the hall, but she doesn't.

I wish Norton would come home with me.

Norton jumps off Gramps's lap and chases after me down the hall.

"Hey! Where ya goin', you ungrateful cat?"

❀

THE LAST TWENTY-FOUR HOURS HAVE BEEN NIGHTMARISH, getting the ladies settled in the mansion with their luggage. The elevator is smoking by the end of it.

Finally I'm able to gather everyone into the great room to introduce the ladies to our production team: the cameramen, the lighting guys, drivers, the makeup and hair people, and most importantly, the host, Trey Withers. I try a few times to get everyone's attention, but they don't listen until Amanda puts her fingers in her mouth and gives a shrill whistle.

"Enough, people! Simmer down and listen to the boss."

All eyes are on me and I immediately regret not dressing more formally. I look like the assistants in the corner, with my jeans and sweater on. The ladies, on the other hand, have clearly tried to outdo each other. I wonder if they can keep this up.

Public speaking is not my thing. The fierce grip I have on my clipboard while I hold it against my chest leaves me breathless. *I wish to get through this speech without messing up.*

"Here we are, for what I hope will be a rewarding experience for all of you. Our team will do their best to help you with any concerns that arise, and I'm sure we will be fast friends by the end of this adventure. *The Single Guy* is the first show of its kind here in Canada, and we are committed to making it as professional as possible. The one thing we ask from you is to be authentic. Don't try to be someone you're not. We picked you because you are amazing women, so don't forget that in the coming days. This will be an emotional journey, and one you'll never forget."

The girls buzz with excitement.

"Now, if you'll be good enough to give your full attention to our fabulous host, Mr. Trey Withers, he will introduce you to the crew and fill you in on the coming days. We are extremely lucky to have Trey with us. Please give him a hand."

Applause breaks out, and Trey rushes over to kiss my cheek before extending his arms towards his groupies.

"Hello, my beauties! Are you ready for a good time? Let's do this thing!"

The place erupts. My part is over and I get out as fast as I can. Amanda follows me into the kitchen, where the kitchen staff has laid out some goodies. She grabs a doughnut and I grab cheese.

"You were great in there," she says with her mouth full. "Well done, you."

"They only listened because you told them to. Where did you learn to whistle like that?"

"I have five brothers."

I take another piece of Brie and a grape. "Wow. What was that like?"

"Smelly." Amanda picks up a glass of wine and hands it to me before taking one herself. "What shall we toast to?"

"To coming out alive on the other side."

"And staying friends."

"Amen, sister."

When Amanda heads home for the night, I wander through the garden path to the guest house on the property. This is where the crew will be staying if necessary, with Austin. I made sure I gave him the biggest room. My bedroom is down the hall at the back of the house and overlooks the garden. It will afford me some privacy, I hope. I've been a loner for too long to relish the idea of other people milling around in their bathrobes every morning.

A black-and-white Mini Coop zooms up the driveway and parks off to the side. Austin gets out just as I walk up to the back bumper.

"I love your car."

He pops open the trunk. "Thank you. I'm fond of it myself."

"Can I help with your bags?"

"Certainly not. You're the big cheese." He gathers up a duffle bag, and a couple of backpacks. Before he locks the car, I spy his suit hanging off a hook in the back seat. "I'll take this, shall I?"

"I suppose I'll need that. Thank you."

I lead him upstairs and open the door to his room. "I hope this is suitable."

Austin looks around. "It's bigger than my apartment."

"If you think this is big, don't go next door. It'll blow your mind."

He puts his belongings on the bed and I hang up his suit. "I'll let you get settled. If you need anything, I'm just down the hall."

"Thanks, Chloe."

"Sure thing."

"Chloe?"

I turn around. "Yes?"

"Are you sure I'm what you want?"

I don't have a clue.

"You're perfect, Austin."

CHAPTER FOUR

TODAY IS THE DAY WE FILM THE INTRODUCTIONS, AND I'VE never been so nervous in my life. This has to go very well. It will set the precedent for the rest of the shoot. I hand out the schedules and itinerary to my crew. I'm aware that the minute my back is turned they roll their eyes at my detailed strategies for every possible scenario, but at least they know it's coming.

Trey Withers doesn't. He marches over to me. "We're filming the introductions, the cameos, and the charm ceremony all in one go? That'll take twelve hours."

"I'm not going to tell everyone to go to bed and have them come back in the morning wearing the same fancy dresses, with the exact demeanour they had the night before. It's fake otherwise."

"Hello? This is television. It's not real."

"Maybe so, but that's the way it's going to be."

Trey gives me a dirty look. "I'm not used to being ordered around by a Girl Guide."

Everyone stops and looks at me.

"And I'm not used to being insulted. I'm the producer, Mr. Withers, and what I say goes. If you don't like it, I'll hire someone else."

That shuts him up.

At that very moment, Austin comes up from the garden path and walks to the front of the mansion. He's in a sharp navy blue suit, with a white shirt and black skinny tie. All the women on set stop what they're doing and gawk. Not me. I run over to him as quickly as I can.

"You look great, Austin. Like James Bond!"

"Thanks, boss. I didn't want to disappoint."

"Now, remember, you have to be bigger than you are."

"Bigger?"

"You're on television, so it has to be grander. Do you understand?"

"Right, grander."

I pat his shoulder like a dog. "Good, good."

What looks like an intimate moment between the Single Guy and his future wife on the TV screen is actually a three-ring circus. There are camera, sound, and lighting guys littering the front of the mansion. Trey, still smarting from our earlier encounter, smokes a cigarette down to the nub while he waits for his cue. He looks like a thug who ratted out his mother.

Amanda is down at the end of the driveway babysitting twenty women in a bus. The limousine driver knows to drive four contestants slowly up to the entrance and open the door for the emerging lady. Once the car is empty, he'll zoom around the back way and pick up the next four.

Amanda is out of breath as she runs up the driveway. "They're ready to go whenever you give the signal."

She disappears behind a big potted plant within the girls' position's sight line, so she can pretend to slit their throats if they ramble over their allotted time. Not that we haven't warned them in advance to keep it under a minute, but at this point they're so enraptured with the free wine that none of them will listen to a thing we say.

I'm wearing a headset that wraps around my ear with a small mike in front of my mouth. The limo driver can hear me.

"Okay, we're ready. Make sure you have the heat cranked in the car. The girls aren't dressed too warmly."

We start rolling. The limousine pulls up, and Sydney is the first one out. We had quite a discussion about who the first woman should be, and it was agreed that sex sells, so why not put our sex kitten up first.

It's a good thing we can edit film. The look on Austin's face when he sees Sydney is one of dismay. That's because her nipples are walking ahead of her.

"Stop! Stop, everyone."

Amanda and I run to Sydney. "You're going to have to do that again. Has anyone got masking tape or duct tape or something?" I turn to Amanda. "Tell the driver to bring Sydney up again and fix this situation for all the ladies."

One of the makeup girls produces a roll of tape and the three of them jump back in the limo before it speeds away. I can only imagine the scene that's unfolding at the end of the driveway. When I look behind me, the guys are smirking behind their hands.

"Oh, grow up. You've never seen nipples before?"

"Not quite like that," Austin says.

"You're pitiful. Pull yourselves together. We have to do this twenty-four times tonight, and I want this to be the best damn introduction ceremony on television."

Austin nods. "Yes, boss."

Amanda jogs up the driveway again. "Jesus, why am I doing all the running? I'm going to have a heart attack."

"Have you got it under control?"

"Forty nipples are being held hostage as we speak." She vanishes behind the rubber plant. We start again. When Sydney gets out of the limo and approaches Austin, we stare at her boobs. All is well.

The crew and I lay bets on which girl will light up Austin's face the most. As I predicted, Jocelyn is the favourite, but he likes Lizette the race-car driver too. Amanda thinks Kate P. has a chance. Mysti's all over him like a bad rash, and Tracy and Sydney do nothing but giggle. One of the twins—Holly, I think—says *ditto* a lot. Nerves, probably. Most of the others don't seem to get a huge reaction. Except for Rebecca, who says she has tattoos all over her body.

"Who says that to a man they just met?"

Amanda grunts. "I bet half of them would strip naked if they thought they'd get away with it."

By eleven that night, we've taped Trey talking to Austin, Austin talking to the girls, the girls talking to each other...no, the girls talking *about* each other. It's amazing how quickly it happens. Already alliances are brewing, and more than half of them seem upset with the other half.

Everyone's exhausted. I'm worried that I was wrong about the schedule but push on, despite Trey's dramatic sighs. The last thing to do is the charm ceremony. Each of the ladies receives a charm bracelet at the start of the shoot and if Austin wants to keep them, he'll present them with a charm. Then, when they go on group dates, he'll give one girl a charm before the ceremony so she's safe for another week. Honestly, who makes up this stuff?

I'm not surprised when Austin picks Jocelyn first. He dismisses a girl who hasn't opened her mouth (Jennifer H.) and one who wouldn't shut up (Sandy D.). My lead cameraman, Brian, and I crawl into the limousine to film each girl separately. It's only fair to give them the last word.

Jennifer H. wipes her eyes with a tissue I hand her. "I don't know why he didn't want me. I thought he was the one, you know? I quit my job to come here. I don't know what's wrong with me. I can't get a man."

Okay, this is way too painful. "There's not a thing wrong with you. This is just a television show. I'm sure there are lots of men out there who would love to date you. Isn't that right, Brian?"

Brian, the coward, refuses to show his face from behind the camera. "Sure."

She looks at him, or at least tries to. "Are you married?"

Sandy D. is pissed. "Who the hell does he think he is? He can't see awesome when it's staring him in the face? All those bitches hanging off him and I'm in the limo? He can go fuck himself."

Obviously we'll bleep that bit out.

Finally, thank God, it's a wrap, and we leave the mansion to the giddy ladies and the security guards. I sent Amanda home a long time ago. A group of us go back to the guest house, and some of the guys break out the beer to unwind before bed.

Austin takes off his tie and sits on a stool. "So, how do you think it went?"

"They're all in love with you, so keep it up."

When the guys laugh, I feel my ears get hot. Austin dismisses them with his hand. "Don't mind these idiots."

"I won't. Good night."

The weariness is bone deep as I drag my carcass up the stairs to my room. The only way I ever seem to go to bed is to fall from a great height like a skydiver and stay splayed like that for the entire night. My face goes unwashed, my teeth go un-brushed, and my body is clothed. Talk about pathetic.

There's a sound that keeps interfering with the wine-tasting session I'm having with Ryan Gosling. He says, "Are you going to answer that?"

When I drag my eyes open, my cell is lit up like a Christmas tree. Holy shit, it's three in the morning. Adrenalin courses through my body and levitates me off the bed, even as I answer the phone. "What's wrong?"

It's Aunt Ollie. "The kittens are coming! Should I boil water?"

"Don't worry, I'll be right there!"

There are advantages to being dressed in the middle of the night. I grab my purse, run down the hall, and knock on Austin's door. "Austin! Austin!" The stupid man keeps snoring, so I open the door, rush to the bed, and hold his nostrils with my fingers. Eventually, he springs up in bed, gasping.

"The kittens are coming!"

"What?!"

"The kittens! Can you drive me to my house?"

He looks around. "Did you just try to smother me?"

"No! Yes! Where are your car keys?"

"If the kittens are coming, then Norton obviously has everything under control."

"But they might die and I won't be there!"

"You are a lunatic. Get out while I get dressed."

I hyperventilate in the hallway until he shows up. I try to rush him along, but he looks grumpy. I get to his car first. Unfortunately, in my haste I keep pulling the door handle before he has a chance to unlock it.

"Get your fingers off that handle, and while you're at it, my face."

"I'm sorry. I truly am."

"I don't believe you."

Once we get the doors open and put on our seat belts, he starts the car.

"You have to hurry."

He turns around to face me. "Hurry where?"

"Cabbagetown. I'll show you."

We drive through the dark streets. I try to think of something to say. "There's not much traffic, so that's good."

"That's because most people are in bed."

"Thank you for this."

"Did I have a choice?"

"But this is life and death. It means everything to me."

"Life and death means everything to most of us."

"I can't breathe." I roll down the window and stick my head out like a dog.

"As a medical person, I can safely say you're not having contractions."

"I'm having sympathy pain."

"You're having a panic attack."

"God, is that bad?"

"No. I'm about to have one too."

We make it to Aunt Ollie's in twenty minutes. I don't wait for Austin to park before I'm out the door and running up the porch steps. "I'm here!"

"There are two of them," Gramps says from the threshold.

Aunt Ollie shouts from her bedroom, "She's struggling, what should I do?"

"Austin!" I scream before I realize he's behind me. I grab his sweater and drag him down to the hall. "I brought Norton's vet with me."

"You went to the poor bastard's house and hauled him out of bed?"

"She did, can you believe it?"

"Get in here!" Aunt Ollie hollers.

Austin goes in ahead of us. My aunt's hairnet is askew and her curlers are sticking up on end. She points at the closet. "I woke up out of a sound sleep and there were one and then two but she's having trouble with this one."

Austin kneels down in front of the lined box in the closet and I kneel by the side of the bed.

I wish for this kitten to live.

"Hold on, it's the cord."

I can't watch. The silence as the seconds tick by is unbearable. And then there's a mew.

"Here we go." Our hero places the kitten by the anxious mother, who starts licking her baby with purpose. Aunt Ollie and I tackle Austin while he's still on the floor.

"Thank you, thank you!" I give him a big kiss on his right cheek. Aunt Ollie takes care of his left. We gaze at the three little beings cuddled into their mother's belly.

"Will there be any more?"

Austin examines Norton again. "That's it. It's better for mom when there's not too many."

"This is the best gift ever." In no time I take twenty pictures of the new family on my phone.

"What are we going to do with three kittens?" Gramps asks.

"Keep them, of course."

"You're prepared to have four cats in your house?"

"Yes."

"Right now they're in my house," Gramps says.

Aunt Ollie waggles her finger. "And here they stay, because this is my house too."

"Your name isn't on the mortgage."

"Please don't argue. Norton needs to rest."

"So do I," Austin says. "It's four in the morning."

"I don't want to leave them. Please take good care of my babies, Aunt Ollie. I'll be back as soon as I can and I'll call you every day."

"Get her out of here," Aunt Ollie yawns. "I have to go to bed."

Austin takes me by the shoulders and marches me out the door. We get into his car and that's the last thing I remember.

❄

I'M IN A DARK ALLEY, HIDDEN BEHIND A GARBAGE CONTAINER with my hands tied behind my back. I try to scream but I have tape over my mouth. Austin kneels beside me.

"Don't move or you'll be sorry."

There's a horrible rumbling noise and without warning, a stampede of nipples rush by.

My eyes open.

I'm on my bed in the guest house, under a blanket, with yesterday's clothes still on my back. Oh my God, he couldn't wake me up. What if I snored or drooled? The clock says 8:30. I was supposed to be up by six. Fifteen minutes later, I'm showered and dressed in shorts and a t-shirt with a sweater wrapped around my waist. The last thing I grab is my backpack and run down the stairs. There are breakfast remnants on the table, but the only thing I can find is a banana and a container of yogurt, which I throw in my bag.

Running through the garden, I hear the waiting bus. Amanda is hanging out of it, waving me on. "Hurry up!"

The minute I jump on board the driver closes the door behind me. After I catch my breath I tell him, "You shouldn't leave the bus idling. It's not good for the environment."

He ignores me and pulls away from the mansion entrance at top speed. By the time I right myself and get to the top of the aisle, everyone is waiting to give me heck.

Trey taps his watch. "We were supposed to leave a half an hour ago."

"I'm sorry, everyone. It won't happen again, but last night I had three little kittens!"

"Did they lose their mittens?" Austin shouts from the back.

"I have pictures on my cell if anyone wants to see them."

No one does, which irritates the hell out of me. How many dog pictures have I looked at on people's phones?

"Okay then, we're off on our first adventure today. This is a group date consisting of ten of you."

"Where are we going?" Jocelyn asks.

"That's a secret. Relax and have a good time." I move to the back of the bus to sit near Amanda, Trey, Brian, and Austin.

"Why didn't you wake me up last night?"

"Are you serious? You were out cold before we got to the end of your street. Your cheek mark is still on my window."

"Chloe, now that you're a big mucky-muck producer, I wouldn't go mooning people in a car," Amanda says.

"Bite me." Which reminds me of my banana.

An hour and a half later we pull into Niagara Falls, an iconic Canadian spot if ever there was one. We'll showcase a lot of Canadian landscapes in the weeks ahead. We have a beautiful country, so why not show it off to the rest of the world? Everyone is excited, except for Becca.

"Niagara Falls? I came here on a school trip in grade five. It was a bore then and it's still a bore."

Amanda and I glance at each other. Charm is not Becca's forte.

The minute the girls get off the bus, we become a circus sideshow. The cameras attract people, who crane their necks to see if there's anyone famous in the group. All the contestants lean over the fence, looking at the water in their shortest short-shorts, which means no one is paying attention to the magnificent falls only a few hundred feet away. The power and sound of millions of gallons of blue-green water falling over the edge of the cliff is breathtaking. The roar and energy generated is almost deafening as it drops to the bottom and into the swirling rapids below.

"All right, everyone, we have to line up for the *Maid of the Mist* tour." This is a boat that takes tourists into the mist at the bottom of the falls, so it looks as if we're disappearing into the falls themselves. We have to wear rain gear or we'll get soaked.

"I'm not going down there," Trey says. "I'll ruin my hair. I can interview Austin up here with the falls behind him."

"Fine, whatever."

"I'm off to get a cappuccino."

Out of the corner of my eye I see a mutiny brewing, now that the girls are putting on their big yellow raincoats and sou'westers. They've turned into lobster fishermen. Amanda handles the situation, so I don't feel the need to get involved, but Becca comes looking for me.

"Are you kidding me? I look like a rubber condom. How am I supposed to get Austin to notice me?"

"If you're here yapping at me, he won't. The other girls don't seem to mind."

That's a bit of a stretch. The others look annoyed too, but good old Austin is doing his best, standing at the bow of the ship listening intently to something Emily is saying. I think he's mesmerized by the water dripping from her hat and her nose. When Sarah C. pulls Austin away, Emily stands there with her mouth open in shock. She better close it or she'll drown.

Amanda eventually stomps over. "Whose stupid idea was this?"

"Ours, don't you remember?"

"Shit, I hoped it was someone else."

Now Brian finds me. "We can't keep the water droplets off the camera lens."

"This is perfect."

Our attention gets dragged away by a commotion on the stern of the boat. Rebecca, Becca, and Becky have stripped off their rain gear and are now dancing in the middle of the crowd. "Come on, everyone, a wet t-shirt contest!"

My cameramen come from every direction to film this astonishing scene, no doubt for their private collections, because this isn't making it on air. It's a spring break video. The captain gets involved and passengers with children hurry them away. Austin makes his escape with the crowd.

When we eventually disembark, we march the ladies up to the bus and we're off. We can't do interviews when most of them look like drowned rats. As we lumber out of the parking lot, I hang on to the front seats so I won't pitch forward.

"What you ladies get up to in the hot tub at the mansion is none of my business, but it *is* my business when we are out in public. You need to behave with some decorum. The last thing I need is for any of you to be arrested for lewd behaviour and public indecency."

Becca points her finger right at me. "There's no need to get high and mighty with us, Miss Television Producer. You're in charge of a show that's about sex and trying to get into the bachelor's pants, and not only that, you want to broadcast it across Canada...from sea to sea to shining sea."

I'm mortified, but there's not a damn thing I can say. She's right. I quickly fall into the seat behind the bus driver, which in retrospect wasn't bright; if I'd been at the back I might have noticed Trey running after the bus, waving his hands in vain.

Amanda and I have a tête-à-tête later that afternoon, going over the planned day trips. We can't afford to screw up another one because I want to come in under budget. Amanda's distracted by the platter of sweets on the table. Her hand hovers over the selection.

"Maybe I'll take a muffin instead of a doughnut."

"Muffins have more calories."

"Do they really?"

"That gigantic one there has enough calories for the entire day."

When she hesitates, I grab it and stuff it in my mouth. "Mmm, this is good."

"I hope you get fat."

"I won't. I forget to eat."

"I hate your guts." She hovers once more, as if the goodies are giving off a signal she can hone in on. Austin happens by and grabs a Boston cream.

"That was mine," she grumbles.

"You snooze, you lose. Did you hear from Aunt Ollie?"

"Yes, the kittens are great."

"Good. So I think I'll kick off Becca. She's got a big mouth."

Amanda waggles her finger at him. "I don't agree. Keep her around for awhile; she makes great television."

"You can't tell him who he can kick off."

"I'm asking him to consider keeping her because she causes havoc and that's good for ratings."

"You two don't have to kiss her."

"You don't have to kiss anyone if you don't want to," I tell him.

"But the more he does, the better for us."

"So who do you like?" I ask him.

"It's a secret."

After he leaves, Amanda says, "I want you to come to supper on Sunday."

"Why?"

Amanda stands up and collects her papers. "The correct response is, *Thank you Amanda, I'd love to*, or *How sweet of you, I can't wait.*

"I *would* like to, as long as it's you and Jason and the boys."

"You're twenty-five and a cat lady already. I despair."

❀

AUSTIN KEEPS BECCA AND LETS EMILY GO. A FEW OF THE GIRLS are surprised by that. Becca is triumphant and gives me a big smirk.

Brian and I wait for Emily's meltdown in the limo. It happens in seconds, the tears, the look of agony and disappointment. I should have more compassion but I want to shake her.

"What did I do wrong? I can't understand what I did wrong. I didn't even get to go on a one-on-one date."

Brian and I are beginning to hate this ritual.

"You've only known Austin for two days. Don't be heart-broken."

She looks at me with puppy-dog eyes. "I was always the last one picked in school."

A circumstance I know well. A flood of empathy fills me, so I clasp her hand. "Everything's going to be fine."

"That bastard can eat shit and die."

I drop her hand like a hot potato and bolt, Brian and his camera right behind me. When she's safely out of sight, we look at each other. Brian shakes his head. "Nothing surprises me anymore. Sometimes I wonder if there are any ladies left in the world."

"As a female, I resent your sexist comment, but as a producer I'm also beginning to have my doubts."

❋

WE BEGIN TO EDIT OUR FOOTAGE, WHICH IS ALWAYS TRICKY. You can slant a story any way you want, but we don't have the right trajectory yet. More needs to happen with the personalities involved.

Speaking of personalities, Trey seeks me out in the rose garden, where I drink my coffee in peace. He must be desperate, since he usually avoids me at all costs.

"I need to speak with you." He sits on the other end of a garden bench. "And this must remain in the strictest confidence."

"Okay."

"The lighting engineer and I are...together."

"I wasn't aware. It's none of my business, but if it makes you feel better, I'm glad you got it off your chest."

He glowers at me. "I'm not coming out to you, Miss Sparrow. I don't need absolution. Jerry and I had a tiff and I've just seen yesterday's rushes. He's lighting me in such a way that I look like a cadaver on screen, and I'm not going to tolerate it."

"I'll have a word with him."

"If you would, I'd be grateful." He walks away.

Maybe it's not that bad. I seek out the film editor and go through the tape.

It's bad. I look for Jerry and eventually find him by the pool. When I stand in front of his chair and block the sun, he looks up. "Can I help you?"

I sit in the chaise next to him. "I've had a conversation with Trey."

He makes a face. "I can just imagine. Did he mention the sock? Or the fried egg?"

"I don't care about socks or fried eggs, but I do care if my host looks like he's dead, so whatever your disagreement with Trey, keep it between yourselves and don't ever light him like that again. Are we clear?"

"How old are you?"

I jump up from the chaise. "Why?"

"Have you ever been in love?"

I stand there.

"That answers my question." He gets off his chair and walks away.

"You haven't answered my question."

"We're clear," he shouts over his shoulder.

My excuse to Austin is a wonky camera and he'll have to tape his interview again. Trey gives me the briefest of nods when he sees the new rushes. I'm grateful I got that much.

❧

IT'S A DAY OFF FOR EVERYONE, AND BEFORE I GO OVER TO Amanda's for dinner, I take the bus to visit my family. I can't wait to see the kittens, and I miss Aunt Ollie and Gramps, too. Their loud voices are the background of my life. It means safety, that they're nearby if someone breaks in, like a burglar or a zombie.

The minute I get there I give them a big hug. "Did you miss me?"

"No, being a new mother is distracting."

"That's a fine thing to tell the child. I missed you."

"Thanks, Gramps."

"Rub my foot."

He takes off his slipper and holds out his leg, but I hurry down the hall to Aunt Ollie's room. There's my sweet Norton, looking happy and content with her little brood tucked in against her tummy. She looks up and gives me a sweet *purr-meow.*

"Oh, Norton, I've missed you so much. I love you, I love you, I love you."

She tolerates my kisses up to a point, but when I disturb the kittens, her look says *back off,* so I lie on my stomach and watch them. Aunt Ollie sits on the end of the bed.

"I'm missing my television programs because I spend all my time in here."

"I'm grateful, Aunt Ollie. I never could have done this stupid job if it wasn't for you."

"You still don't like it?"

Rolling over, I lie on my back and think about the question. "I like being the boss, and for the most part I do it well, but the show itself is so..."

"Stupid is what you said."

"How does a person fall in love when they're surrounded by thirty people watching their every move day and night? It's exhibitionism."

"But on the other hand, these young people want to fall in love, and they're hopeful, so it's not all bad."

"Why don't they do it on their own time?"

"Maybe they're busy, like you."

"Someone asked me the other day if I'd ever been in love and I didn't know what to say."

"Of course you were. Don't you remember Shawn?"

"Shawn?" I rack my brains. "No."

"He was your partner in kindergarten. You kissed him all the time. The teacher had to call your mother about it."

I put my arm over my eyes. "How humiliating."

"Your mother and I had a great laugh over it."

"She and Dad were in love, weren't they?"

Aunt Ollie shrugs. "They were always together, but they had their moments like everyone else."

"How did you know you were in love with Howie?"

"I got warm and fuzzy in my Mary-Ellen."

❀

NATURALLY I TELL AMANDA WHAT AUNT OLLIE SAID THE minute we're alone in her untidy kitchen. She nearly drops the pan of lasagne she's taking out of the oven. "Aunt Ollie? The one with the hairnet and compression stockings?"

"She wasn't always old—not that fifty-one is *old* old, she just looks old."

"For some reason I don't picture old people with sex organs."

"Okay, drop it. Elderly genitals aren't appetizing."

"You brought it up."

Amanda yells out the back door for Jason to bring the boys in for dinner. They have two high chairs they lock their kids into. Their boys are only nine and a half months apart, which always ticks Amanda off when you mention it. She seems to feel like she failed some mommy course and was caught screwing when she should have been comatose like all the other new mothers.

It's a relief to see only three placemats put out—she didn't invite anyone else.

Being with Amanda and her family is so much fun. Jason is a sweetheart and he's definitely a nerd. Ask him anything and he knows the answer. He works for some computer games company. J.J. and Callum are fair-skinned like their mom, with big blue eyes and perpetually runny noses. J. J. spends most of his time trying to hit his brother with his plastic utensils. Their dog, Ernie, stations himself between the high chairs and noshes away on the bits of food that are catapulted to the floor. But what I love the most is the way Amanda and Jason look at the boys and laugh about their antics. They are a unit, complete in this bubble of sweet contentment. I say as much to Amanda.

"Stay until bedtime, Chloe. It's amazing how the love fades into resentment when they refuse to stay in their cribs."

Halfway through the meal the doorbell rings. Amanda and Jason glance at each other before she jumps up and goes to the door. I'm immediately suspicious.

Jason takes a swig of his wine. "I wonder who that can be."

"I'm going to kill that woman."

Amanda comes back into the dining room. "Look who's here. Chloe, this is my youngest brother, Steve. Steve, this is my friend and colleague, Chloe Sparrow."

Steve smiles and shakes my hand. He's rather nice looking and that makes me instantly nervous. He's also tanned. It must run in the family.

"It's okay, Chloe. Amanda has a habit of embarrassing people with her hookups, but I like free food, so why not."

Everyone laughs. I join in.

Steve talks non-stop. So do Amanda and Jason. Even the boys babble endlessly. Without even asking, I find out that Steve manages an art gallery downtown, has never married, and likes the Toronto Maple Leafs. His favourite dessert is apple pie, and his mother tries to set him up with her friends' offspring because she wants more grandchildren.

That's nice. A mother who's interested in you.

"What do you do in your spare time, Chloe?" Steve asks me.

"I read."

He looks like he expects me to say something else. "And what do you read?"

"Everything."

Amanda glances at me like I've done something wrong. I do read everything—should I list the subjects for him? Steve continues to unburden his soul and now I'm worried that I'm pathetic. I lose track of what they're talking about. When Amanda gets up to serve coffee and dessert, I excuse myself and head to the bathroom. When I return, I overhear Steve and Amanda talking in the kitchen.

"She doesn't open her mouth."

"She's shy."

"I know shy. She looks bored out of her mind."

"Give her a chance."

"She's not my type, Amanda. Thanks, but no thanks."

I'm crushed. Who does he think he is? I'm not eating dessert with someone who doesn't like me. Maybe I'm acting like a big baby, but out the front door I go.

CHAPTER FIVE

I'M LATE FOR THE BUS AGAIN. THIS IS BECOMING A HABIT. ALL night I tossed and turned, brooding about that idiot Steve, hence the bags under my eyes. On top of that I forget breakfast. As soon as I'm on board I stay in the front seat, away from everyone else. This hockey segment had better go smoothly. I'm not in the mood for failure.

While we're stuck in morning traffic, Amanda comes up from the back and sits beside me. "Good morning."

"Hi."

"Why did you bolt?"

"He said he didn't like me, so I left."

"You didn't try very hard, did you?"

Count to ten.

"I didn't try very hard because why should I? He was your guest. You invited him, I didn't. You put me on the spot and I don't appreciate being seen as your charity case. I felt awkward and embarrassed. I'm perfectly happy on my own."

"I agree with everything you said except the last sentence."

"You don't think I'm happy?"

"No, I don't. I think you've been unhappy for a long, long time. It's the condition you're used to. You need to spread your wings and do something foolish. All these girls are your age. Think about that. They're having a blast down there and you're up here going over your schedule."

"That's because I'm managing a difficult job and the only thing they have to do is slobber over a guy. Go away, Amanda."

"I'm not trying to be mean. You feel like my little sister, and I worry about you."

"You do?"

"Of course I do."

"Well, that's nice, I guess. Thank you for dinner."

She kisses my forehead. "Have fun today."

When we arrive at the rink, the van with the hockey gear is nowhere to be seen. You can't skate without skates. My phone is glued to my ear while I try to find the van driver, and when he finally shows up I'm all over him before he's even out of the vehicle.

"Where were you?"

"Cool your jets. I'm here now."

People never apologize anymore, but there's no time to argue. By the time everyone is outfitted, two hours have gone by and we don't have a single frame of film. There are no skates to fit Brian, so he has to go out on the ice in his sneakers. I have visions of him cracking his head open. Our insurance premiums are sky high as it is.

Eventually we get the so-called hockey game going. There are two teams of girls chasing Austin around the rink, but he skates like the wind. Most of the girls stay on their feet and a few of them are good, but our twins Holly and Molly spend the entire time on their asses, or crawling up the boards—and each other—trying to keep upright.

"This is hard!"

"Ditto!"

Austin tries a few times to teach them how to stand straight, but it's like they're both made of rubber. Amanda claps her hands in glee; the more miserable the girls are, the funnier the show.

Amanda pokes me. "Go skate."

It looks like everyone's having a good time; even the cameramen are throwing snow at each other, so I put on a pair of skates and get out on the ice. My dad took me skating once. Of course, that was twenty years ago, when I was five. I stay by the edge of the boards so I can hold on if I need to. Before long I pick up a little speed, but I'm still looking at my feet.

Amanda shouts from the bench, "This is how to have fun, Sparrow!"

Then a puck comes out of nowhere and hits me in the face. I go down like I've been shot. There are coloured stars all around and then a big lump between my eyes, which I realize is my nose. Austin gets to me first.

"Am I bleeding?"

"Uh...yes. Stay down."

Fade to black.

❀

AMANDA, WHO I'LL KILL LATER, TELLS ME AUSTIN TOOK CHARGE and even yelled at the twins when they came over to see what was happening and almost sliced my fingers off with their skate blades.

At the hospital they tell me my nose is broken.

"Does it look bad?" I ask Amanda.

"Well, it doesn't look good."

"Let me see a mirror."

"I wouldn't do that if I were you."

"Get the mirror."

She looks through her purse and produces a compact, blowing on it to get the powder off first.

I've got two black eyes and a boxer's nose, as well as chip in my front tooth. I glare at her with my swollen eyes. "This is why I don't have fun."

When Amanda drives me home from the hospital and walks me through Aunt Ollie's door, for the first time in my life I see my aunt and grandfather visibly shaken about something that pertains to me. Gramps insists I sit in his rocking chair.

"Oh, your poor face," Aunt Ollie cries into her apron. "You were always such a beautiful girl and now you're deformed. Who'll marry you like this?"

Amanda looks gobsmacked. "What on earth are you saying? She's not deformed, and of course she'll get married. Just because she broke her nose and chipped her tooth..."

"You chipped your tooth!"

"You're right, Ollie," Gramps nods, "she'll be an old maid like you."

Now Amanda's spray tan turns a dark bronzy colour. "Chloe, would you like to come home with me? I'd be happy to put a mattress in the boy's room."

The thought of sleeping on the floor with two stinky-diapered toddlers is not my idea of a solution.

"Thanks anyway. I'll be fine."

"Are you sure? You shouldn't be alone tonight."

It's beginning to dawn on Aunt Ollie that Amanda is upset with her, so now she gets her back up. "Chloe is perfectly fine here, missy. She can sleep in my bed."

Oh joy, oh bliss.

"Call me if you need anything."

"Thanks, Amanda."

The first night is a bit of a disaster. Despite my happiness at seeing Norton and the kittens, I can't bend down because it makes my head throb, and I can't see them when I'm standing up. Aunt Ollie opens a can of beef and vegetable soup and butters a whole row of crackers for me. I try to eat around the little chunks of beef swimming in the bowl. After only two crackers I know that my head will explode if I chew anything else.

Aunt Ollie hovers as I crawl into her bed, then she passes me painkillers and a glass of water. "I'll be as quiet as a mouse when I come in later."

"Thanks, Aunt Ollie."

"I suggest you get rid of your snotty friend."

Painkillers that could put someone in a coma are no match for Aunt Ollie going to bed. She comes in to gather her toiletries but doesn't turn on the light. Since she can't see what she wants, she takes one bottle at a time over to the light of the street lamp coming through the window. "Oh, that's it."

Out she goes, only to come back a second, third, and fourth time to collect her nightie, her hairbrush, and her eye drops. She's not aware she's muttering. "Where are my slippers? Did you take my slipper, Norton? Oh, for heaven's sake, it's under the bureau. Silly me, I'd forget my head if it wasn't attached. Funny, my mother used to say that."

When she eventually gets in the bed, it's like being lifted on the crest of a wave. I hang on to the edge of the mattress so I won't roll down and smack into her broad bum. She fusses and fumes, lies on her side and kneads her pillow until it's just right, and then sticks another one between her knees. She grapples with the blanket, and then there's silence.

For two seconds.

"Dear God, please make Chloe's nose pretty again and don't let her get hurt anymore. Also, she needs to gain a few pounds. Watch over the old crank. Don't let him fall and break his hip because my life won't be worth living if that happens. Please keep Norton and her children safe and let me win the lottery this week. Amen."

I'm drifting off when Aunt Ollie begins to snore. It's like nothing I've heard before: a combination of a steam engine and vacuum hose. Fifteen minutes later I take an extra blanket and curl up in Gramps's rocker in the kitchen. Norton deserves a medal for staying in that room.

The next morning Aunt Ollie is annoyed with me. "You should've slept on the living room couch if you weren't comfortable."

She's right, but I would've had to take six gigantic stacks of newspapers and magazines off it first. I'm back in Aunt Ollie's bed for breakfast. Norton and the kittens are at the end of the mattress. They are so adorable; they make me forget the pain I'm in.

"What should we call them?"

"Bobby Orr, Wayne Gretzky, and Sid Crosby," Gramps yells from the bathroom.

"You sure can hear when you want to!" Aunt Ollie yells back. "I thought after spices. Cinnamon, Sage, and Rosemary."

Gramps shows up at the door. He's more invested in this conversation than he lets on.

"Why don't we all choose a name?" I say. "That's fair."

The doorbell rings. "That's odd. It's nine in the morning, who can that be?"

"I'll go." Aunt Ollie disappears and we hear her talking before she comes back down the hall. "I've got a surprise for you."

She comes in with a lovely bouquet of summer flowers.

"I bet they're from the CBC, trying to avoid a lawsuit," Gramps says.

"Gosh, they're pretty."

Austin sticks his head in the door. "They're from me, actually."

I'm in a stained nightie that belongs to Aunt Ollie, my face is smashed in, and I've got major bedhead and morning breath. Otherwise I look great.

"Thank you, Austin, they're very nice."

"I'm sorry for the early hour. I'm supposed to be back by ten."

"Isn't today Canada's Wonderland?"

"That's right. I'm taking Lizette. Since she drives race cars, I figured she'd go on the roller coasters with me."

"She'd do just about anything for you."

"I feel terrible about your accident."

"*You* didn't shoot the puck. Who did?"

"Becca."

"That's not surprising."

"She cried when they took you away."

"Did she blubber into your chest and hang off your neck?"

"How did you know?"

"Just a hunch." I point to the end of the bed. "What do you think of the kittens?"

"Growing like weeds."

Aunt Ollie says, "Can you tell us what sex they are? I don't have a clue."

"That seems to run in the family." He picks up each one and takes a peek. "It's pretty early to tell but if I had to guess, I'd say you have two females and a male."

"We're trying to think of names for them."

"I guess Becca's out."

The phone rings and both Gramps and Aunt Ollie race out to get it, leaving Austin and I alone. I wish he'd leave or stop looking at me like I'm the victim of a heinous crime.

"So when do you think you'll be back?"

"Tomorrow."

"As soon as that? Shouldn't you rest?"

"Resting is for sissies. Not that I don't trust Amanda and everyone, but my name is on this show, so it has to be perfect."

"I can't imagine you failing at anything, other than skating."

"I didn't break my nose skating. It was broken by a lunatic."

"True enough. I'd better go."

"Thank you for the flowers."

He gives me a cheeky grin and disappears.

The rest of my day is spent arguing about cat names. Nothing is ever simple in this house. I feel like King Solomon, with both Aunt Ollie and Gramps sitting on either side of my bed waiting for my opinion.

"Since I'm a man, I should get to name the male kitten."

"I want to name the one with the black patch around its eye."

"That's the male. You can't name the little guy Cinnamon."

"Why not? Norton is a female. Isn't that right, Chloe?"

"I thought she was a male when I named her. Does it really matter? Let Gramps name the boy cat. Otherwise you'll never hear the end of it."

Aunt Ollie crosses her arms. "I don't want a cat named Gretzky."

"And I don't want one named Oregano!"

My head is throbbing. *I wish this ridiculous argument were over.*

I point to the third kitten, the tiny runt Austin saved. "I'm naming her Peanut."

"Then I'm naming the other one Rosemary."

"And this little critter is Bobby Orr."

"Can I get some sleep now?"

They leave, but I don't sleep. I only wanted them out of the room. After an hour, I start to wish I could sleep, because I'm not used to lying in bed thinking. It brings up stuff I'd rather not deal with. If I'm being truthful, it shocked me when Amanda said she doesn't think I am happy. What is her idea of happy? What's *my* idea of happy, for that matter? I should be happy. I have an education, a great job for someone my age, and a house that is prime real estate. My parents invested well and left me a lot of money that's sitting in a bank collecting dust as well as interest. I have four cats and Amanda is my friend. I only have one friend?

I wish I were asleep.

❧

WHEN I SHOW UP FOR WORK THE NEXT DAY, AMANDA IS HORRI-fied.

"You can't come back yet!"

"Why not?"

"Look at your face! You need to heal."

"A broken nose is not the end of the world. I may look terrible, but the old brain still works."

Amanda turns around and whistles for someone. Turns out it's one of the makeup artists. When she runs up to us, I have to ask.

"Do you always respond to a whistle?"

"Not usually, but Amanda can't remember our names."

"That's because there are too many women running around. Do something with her poor face, will you?"

So I submit to some makeup to cover the worst of my bruising. Whatever her name is, she's very gentle, and when I look in the mirror I'm shocked.

"Wow, I look better than I usually do."

"You should use a little makeup on a daily basis. I can show you how to do it yourself."

"That will never happen, but thank you."

Everyone welcomes me back, saying how great I look. Maybe makeup is the way to go.

Today we are off to a dude ranch. Austin picks Sydney, Mysti, Molly, Holly, Becky, and Sarah C. to accompany him. They will ride horses along a very picturesque trail led by real cowboys. Since we're paying for the entire day, the ranchers will come back in the afternoon and accompany us out. That should give us the time we need for Brian to shoot lots of film of Austin riding by himself. These shots we'll use for his off-camera monologue later, about how he loves the outdoors and wide-open spaces. I suggested he wear a plaid shirt and cowboy hat to look like a rugged cattle driver. We want millions of Canadian women thinking he's a man's man, ready to brand and lasso steers.

Poor little cows. What did they ever do to anyone?

No one wants me to go riding. Austin tells me it's a terrible idea, but I'm not prepared to spend my day in a barn. Amanda says the only way she'll let me come is if I ride a donkey, because if I fall it won't inflict too much damage.

So here I am astride a donkey that is being led by a rope attached to the saddle of a horse ridden by the Lone Ranger. Donkeys are very sweet, and I'm in love with this little fellow by the time we get to the picnic area. Here, Austin and the girls will have a campfire lunch, once they supposedly gather the wood themselves. One of our assistants threw a bunch of kindling around the campfire, so it looks like they're finding random sticks themselves. Someone else will cook the hotdogs and beans and hand it to the group before the cameras start rolling, otherwise we'll be here all day, but the girls insist they want to make their own s'mores.

While Austin is being filmed trotting around on his horse, the girls keep themselves amused. Sydney, our sexpot, spends the entire time bent over, making sure the crew has a clear view of her cleavage. I'm mesmerized.

"Do men think those are real?" I ask Amanda.

"Men don't care what they're made of, as long as you've got a pair."

"Why are men so fascinated with breasts?"

"Why are women willing to mutilate their bodies to impress them, is more to the point."

Eventually Austin has had it with riding around aimlessly and Brian has enough footage, so they head over to the campfire. The girls practically push each other into the embers in an attempt to sit next to him. Austin doesn't seem to notice, or he's doing a good job ignoring these silly games. Once the shots are taken around the fire, the s'mores get passed around. Sarah C. makes one for me.

"I've never had one before."

Austin makes a face. "You've never had a cookout, or been to a bonfire?"

"No, I keep telling you. I don't get out much."

Now everyone watches as I take my first bite.

"Okay, I'm living on these things from now on."

Since the official part is over, the team gathers around the fire to eat up the leftovers and have a little downtime. Thirty minutes later, Sydney, Becky, and Sarah C. jump up and start retching in the grass, quickly joined by Brian, Amanda, and the cook himself.

I'm responsible for killing the cast and crew.

There is complete chaos for ten minutes, people trying to help other people, but it doesn't seem to be working.

Amanda brandishes a wiener wrapper in the cook's face while he's doubled over. "These are past their best-before dates, you moron!"

Which leads to more panic. Austin tries to assure everyone that while they may feel sick, they aren't dying and that the vomiting is a good thing, but no one believes him. The cowboys are not due for another hour. I have to make an executive decision, so I turn to Austin.

"There are some horses still here. Everyone who's sick can start riding back to the ranch now. I can send a couple of the healthy crew with them just in case. That way they'll be back in civilization with bathrooms. The rest of us can walk back. The cowboys will be coming soon anyway."

Between the two of us we get the afflicted on horses and send them on their way, despite Amanda's objections.

"This isn't right. You can't walk, Chloe. Your nose will fall off."

"We've still got the donkey," Austin says. "She can ride that."

"Make sure she does."

As all the sick people ride off into the sunset, Austin and I return to the campfire to face Mysti, Holly, and Molly. It occurs to them at the same moment that they are being left behind. By their faces you'd think I've left them on the moon while everyone else took off with the rocket. I've never heard such griping in my life.

"How far is it?" Mysti pouts.

"Three kilometres."

"What? That's insane!"

"This wasn't very well organized," Molly says.

"Ditto."

"Look, you can sit here and whine if you want to, but we have to start walking back before dark."

"The cowboys will get here before too long, so let's go," Austin says. "It'll be an adventure. Gather up your things."

While they grumble and gather their sweaters, Austin leads the donkey over to me.

"Let me help you on."

"Now, this is going to go over well. I get to ride and they have to walk."

"Do they have broken noses? You're looking pale, so no arguing."

Off we go, Austin leading the donkey like I'm the Virgin Mary and the other three bitching behind us.

"This sucks," says Molly.

"Ditto," says Holly.

"I have asthma," Mysti points out. "If I can't breathe, it's your fault."

"Why aren't we flying on helicopters like the American show?" Molly asks.

"That might happen yet. I have to look at the budget."

That seems to cheer them up for two minutes. After that they start again.

"I'm getting a blister."

"Ditto."

Mysti waves her arms around. "These bugs are ridiculous. It's the donkey that's attracting them. You should leave it behind."

I turn in my saddle. "Leave this delightful little creature by itself? Never."

"From where you're sitting I'm sure he is delightful, but we just walked in his poop."

I wish Austin would tell them to knock it off.

Austin shouts over his shoulder. "Why don't you guys stop talking and save your energy for walking?"

Now we have threatening storm clouds gathering overhead. The temperature drops dramatically. Apparently this is my fault as well.

"If there's thunder and lightning, I'm going to freak out," Molly says.

"Ditto!"

"Can't I get a turn on that donkey? I'm out of air."

"Austin, stop!"

He stops. I get down from the donkey. "By all means Mysti, please take the donkey." Now I have no choice but to face Holly. "You say *ditto* a hundred times a day. Who does that? Can't you say *I agree* or *you're right* or *I feel the same way* or *me too*? There are thousands of words out there. Use them."

"You should keep your mouth shut," Molly says.

"Ditto!" Holly yells in my face.

My mind goes blank after that. I walk as if the devil's after me. When the rain starts I don't even notice it. All I can think is that this is my life and Amanda's right. I am unhappy. I hate my job, I hate these insipid girls, I hate the CBC, and I even hate Austin, because he wants to be on this ridiculous show. I only love Gramps, Aunt Ollie, my cats, and that dear little donkey. I've broken my face and teeth for this job and for what? I'm going to resign the minute I get back to the barn. I'm not spending one more minute in this foolish situation.

That's when I trip over a root and fall face first into the mud. I'm worried about my nose, but my ankle throbs and I can't process two injuries at the same time. Once again, Austin is the first one I see. He's obviously bad luck, and I'm sick of sprawling on the ground in front of him.

"Leave me alone. I'm fine."

I try to get up, but that's not going to happen. Despite my objections, he picks me up in his arms and turns to put me back on the donkey—but Mysti is still comfortably seated, so he whips around and keeps walking. The insulted twins talk smack about me behind our backs.

"You should put me down. I'm fine."

He jostles me in his arms to get a better grip. "*I'm fine* doesn't apply in this situation. We're in the rain dragging three brats behind us and I'd like to get out of here."

"Me too, and I'm quitting the minute we get back."

"No, you're not."

"Yes, I am."

"You're going to quit over ditto girl?"

"If I feel like it. God, *I wish this day would end!*"

I instantly realize my blunder and feel sick. "I don't want it to *end*, end. Not an apocalypse-type ending, where the ground opens up and swallows you whole."

"By any chance, did you hit your head when you fell?"

When the cowboys appear over the horizon at that very instant, I'm extremely grateful.

"Thank you, that's exactly what I meant."

❦

THE DOCTOR ON CALL BANDAGES MY SPRAINED ANKLE AND tells me to keep off my feet for a few days. I'm more concerned with all the pukers, but they are on the mend and feeling much better, which is a huge weight off my shoulders.

The best part of the day is when Austin kicks the twins to the curb. Brian tells me they had a meltdown in the limo and started pulling each other's hair. That I can't wait to see.

CHAPTER SIX

Because I have to stay off my feet, I set up shop by the pool, as I need to be available to everyone at all times. This should have been my strategy all along, to let people come to me, instead of the other way around. I'm very popular, because people know I can't jump up and run away. July's heat makes this a pleasant experience. If this keeps up I'll be nearly as tanned as Amanda.

Trey pops by in his shorts and designer shades to rag on Jerry. "He's back to his old tricks."

"The lighting thing again?"

"No, he's doing everything he can to make me crack up on camera."

"Don't look at him."

"That's your sage advice?"

"What do you want me to do? Fire him?"

"It might come to that."

I'm starting to realize that Trey is high maintenance, like most television personalities.

"Trey, I want you to be happy on this shoot. Would letting Jerry go accomplish that? I doubt it. We'll be on the road for quite a while. It can get lonely."

I think he's considering what I've said, because it seems like he's looking at the sky, but I can't see his eyes behind his mirrored frames.

"He'll knock it off if you ignore him long enough."

His head turns in my direction. "You're probably right, as much as I hate to admit it."

"Good."

He gets up to leave. "How's your ankle?"

"I'll live."

"Good."

He might be warming up to me.

Sydney seeks me out one morning and lies on the chaise beside me. "Austin says he likes me, but I think he's stringing me along."

"He's stringing all of you along. That's what he signed up for. How does he find out who he wants to spend his life with if he doesn't have relationships with everybody?"

She sighs as she slathers herself with baby oil. "He's the nicest guy I've ever been with."

"You shouldn't do that. You might get skin cancer."

"Do you always listen to the experts?"

"Pretty much."

"No wonder you never laugh. Why don't you come and spend some time with us? What do you do at night in that guest house?"

"Read. Sometimes I go and visit my family."

"Do you have a boyfriend?"

"No."

"You should. You're pretty."

"Even with a crooked nose?"

"You don't really notice it after a while."

"I've got a chipped tooth."

"Keep your mouth shut."

"I'm flat-chested."

"That's unfortunate, but you can do something about it. My

enhancements were well worth it. Guys look at me wherever I go."

"Do you want them to?"

"Chloe, you're a strange girl."

When she eventually wanders away, I sit back and realize that I like Sydney, big tits and all.

Amanda dumps more and more office work on me, since she's picking up my slack, so I'm on the phone, making arrangements for trips to other parts of the country, when at some point I drift off. When I wake up, Austin and Lizette are in the pool and she has her bikini top off. I'm not sure where this pool business is going, but I'm out of here. I slide off the chaise lounge and attempt to cross the cement patio on my hands and knees, with my bum foot dragging behind me. I keep near the bushes and am almost at the corner of the house when I hear, "What on earth are you doing?"

"I'm looking for my contact."

"Do you need help?"

"No."

I keep crawling and run into Amanda. She wants to know why I'm on my hands and knees. When I tell her, she runs off.

"Brian! Get out to the pool quick. We're missing some good stuff!"

I hate this job.

The next day is more of the same, people hounding me while I work. I've decided to get crutches, and then I can at least walk away. When my cell rings, I hear it but don't see it and end up emptying my bag filled with folders on the pool deck to find it.

"Hello?"

"Hello! Is this Chloe Sparrow?"

"Yes."

"I'm sorry to bother you, dear, but I got your number from the CBC office. I'm Harriet Hawke, Austin's mother."

"Hello, Mrs. Hawke. It's nice to talk to you."

"And you dear. Austin has told me all about you."

"He has?"

"I was very surprised when he decided to do this. Apparently his sister Julia put him up to it, which is certainly typical of their relationship. Austin is sensitive, so I hope he doesn't get his heart broken. Don't tell him I said that, he'll get annoyed, but a mother can't help worrying. I'm sure your mother is the same way."

"Uh..."

"Austin's not answering his cellphone and I need to get in touch with him. His great-uncle died yesterday and we're having the memorial on Tuesday at noon. I hope he gets time off so he can be with us."

"Of course. I'm very sorry for your loss."

"Uncle Sam was a bit of a waster, but family is family."

"I understand."

"Thank you, dear. I hope we get to meet one day. Perhaps Austin can bring you for dinner one night."

"That sounds nice."

"From now on, call me Harriet. Goodbye!"

What a nice woman. Rebecca walks by with her colourful tattoos, so I wave her over. "Do you know where Austin is?"

"If I did, I'd be with him. He's ignoring me."

"You're still here, aren't you? I need to speak with him ASAP."

Ten minutes later Austin saunters over to me. "What's up, boss?"

"Sit down."

"Am I in trouble?" He sits on the chaise beside me.

"Your mom called."

"My mother? What's wrong?"

"Call her back. She said it's important."

"I know my mother. She told you."

I put my sunglasses on the top of my head. "It's not my place to say anything."

"Tell me."

"Your great-uncle Sam died. His funeral is Tuesday at noon."

Austin stares at the pool. "Poor old Sam. He always was a bit of a waster. Want to come with me?"

"Not really."

"We can go over to Mom's afterwards for lunch. I think we need a break and some homemade food."

"Okay."

That's how I end up in his mother's kitchen with a boat-load of relatives. Everyone's having a jolly time; clearly Uncle Sam won't be missed. I hear from ten more people that Sam was a bit of a waster but family is family.

Harriet looks like a mom, the kind of woman who wraps a scarf around you twice. It's Austin's younger sister, Julia, who surprises me, with her blonde dreadlocks and pierced tongue, carrying her guitar everywhere she goes. She played "Knocking on Heaven's Door" at the memorial, and she was awesome. I corner her at one point. "I have a colleague who's a music critic at the CBC. Would you mind if I told him about you? Maybe he could point you in the right direction."

Her face lights up. "Are you serious? You'd do that for me?"

"I'm not promising anything, but you never know."

"I'm singing at the Pregnant Toad downtown this weekend."

"I'll tell him. If he's free he might take a run over."

"Wow. That's the nicest thing anyone's ever done for me, and I don't even know you."

"Glad I could help."

When I meet Austin's Uncle Tony he thinks I'm one of the bachelorettes. "I hope he picks you. We could use some fresh blood in this family."

Austin keeps bringing his mom's food trays over so I can sample her wares, but I haven't eaten this much in a decade. I break out in a fine sheen of sweat. When he circles with his mother's chicken kabobs I hold out my hand. "Please, no more."

The surprising thing is that when I go to bed, I sleep like I've been drugged.

❀

TODAY IS EDGEWALK DAY AT THE CN TOWER, AN EXTREME adventure where people go out on a five-foot ledge and are attached to an overhead safety rail via a trolley and harness system. You can lean backwards or forwards off the edge, 1,168 feet, the equivalent of 116 storeys, above the ground. Austin selects Erin, Tracy, Lizette, Jocelyn, and Jennifer P. to go with him. After they come indoors, whoever Austin gives the charm to will stay and have a romantic dinner at 360, a restaurant that has a spectacular view of the city. The girls take a change of evening clothes with them. Participants have to be in perfect health. Now that I know I'm not going out there, I'm full of confidence for the others.

"You'll be fine. It's the safest ride in the world, they tell me."

The girls are quiet as we get in the van. Austin, on the other hand, can't wait. He rubs his hands together.

"Make sure someone takes a picture of me so I can text it to my mom. She'll freak."

Brian taps me on the shoulder. "I will drink poison if you make me go out there."

"Now you tell me." I roll down the window of the van and yell for Brian's apprentice, Jeremy. "We're going to need you on this venture."

Poor Jeremy gets instantly green around the gills. Not a great sign.

"Go get Gary, too."

"Who thought this one up?" Jocelyn asks.

Amanda holds up her hand sheepishly. "I was drunk at the time."

I'm ashamed to admit that I've never been to the CN Tower. The thought of taking Gramps and Aunt Ollie always left me weak, but I didn't want to go alone. So now here it is on this strange bucket list we've created for other people.

Amanda and I do our best to keep everyone in great spirits, but they're not fooled by our hilarity. This day will all come down to who can suppress their nerves long enough to make an impression on Austin, who's happy and excited by the adventure. They have to be happy and excited along with him, and right now the group is fifty-fifty.

When we stand outside the CN Tower, the enormity of it shocks me. We're going up there?

We're herded into the high-speed elevator before I realize that this baby has a glass front and two glass panels in the floor so you can enjoy the ride as you whisk up the side of the building at thirty kilometres an hour. I quickly find the nearest chest and press myself into it with my eyes closed. It happens to be Austin's. His after-shave is killer.

"Chloe, you've got to look at this," he says. "You can see the whole city."

He's wrong. I don't have to do a damn thing.

I'm the first one off the elevator, and I admit I accidentally speared a few toes with the rubber end of my crutch. Amanda collects the girls and clucks over them like a mother hen before handing them over to the people who run the EdgeWalk experience. She'll watch the proceedings from inside. I sit on a couch farther away from the window and put my leg up. Maybe it's my imagination, but I can feel this tower swaying. If it's coming down, I should call home.

"What's shakin'?" Gramps says.

"This building."

"When are you coming home? Ollie doesn't do a thing but play with the kittens."

"I miss them."

"They're little hellions, but Bobby's a big softie. Right, Bobby?"

"How are you feeling, Gramps? Everything all right?"

"Yes and no."

My heart jumps. "What do you mean?"

"I had a little chest pain the other day."

I stand up without my crutch and wince. "Did you go to the doctor?"

"Ollie wouldn't take me."

"Let me speak to her right now."

"Ollie? Ollie? Pick up the phone!"

"Helloooo?"

"Why didn't you take Gramps to the doctor? It could be serious."

"It could be, but it wasn't."

"Are you a doctor? I don't think we should take any chances. He's not getting any younger."

"I'm still on the phone. You're not getting any younger, either."

"He had chest pain because the old fool found my box of depilatory and tried to wax the hair off his chest."

"Gramps, you made me think you were having a heart attack."

"I don't believe I uttered those exact words."

"Now I know why I'm a basket case. Goodbye."

My legs are wobbly, so I collapse on the couch and take deep breaths. Maybe I can score some anti-anxiety medication on the street. As I sit and stew, I hear a commotion coming from the EdgeWalk ledge. No doubt all the harnesses have broken and everyone has fallen to the earth, *splat*. I'm not bothered by that notion.

Amanda brings in Erin, who apparently froze when she got out there. Tracy's in hysterics and Jennifer P. has gone mute. The only two left are Jocelyn and Lizette, and they're on either side of Austin, pretending to be superheroes flying off a building.

"Amanda?"

She plunks down beside me. "What?"

"Remember the good old days, when we used to sit behind a desk?"

"We had good times, didn't we?"

"I don't think I'm going to make it."

"If you don't, *I'll* get the helm."

I poke her with my crutch.

The participants eventually come inside. Austin is pumped. When he gives the charm to Jocelyn, Lizette is pissed off. I don't blame her. She was outside hanging off a building ledge for him, and not only that, she showed him her boobs in the pool.

I know Amanda wants to be home with her kids, so I stay with Brian while he films Austin and Jocelyn at dinner. The people at the restaurant have an extra table for us and say we can have dinner too, which is thoughtful. I'm nervous about sitting near a window, which is my bad luck since the entire outer wall is nothing but windows. While I'm reading the menu, something dawns on me.

"Brian, is this place moving?"

"Yeah, it's a revolving restaurant."

"It's unscrewing itself."

"Have something to eat. You'll feel better."

The motion is making me nauseous, so I don't eat, but it doesn't stop me from drinking vodka cocktails. I'm looped in no time. As Brian eats his way through a rack of some poor pig's ribs, I pick his brain.

"Do you have trouble getting women?"

"I've had my fair share."

"What's a fair share?"

He licks his fingers. "Chloe, you ask too many questions."

"You make that sound like it's a bad thing." As I focus on Brian, it occurs to me that he looks like a cross between a bear and a lumberjack. "Are you married?"

"What is this? Twenty questions? If you must know, I'm divorced."

"Why's that?"

"It's none of your business."

"Were you cheating on her? Why do men do that, anyway? Why are some guys so cruel?"

He picks up his napkin and wipes the barbeque sauce off his beard. "You don't have a very high opinion of men. Has someone hurt you in the past?"

I stir my drink with my red plastic sword. "I remember once I wished this guy would notice me and when he asked me to go for a drive I was so excited. He drove me to an out-of-the-way spot and tried to take off my clothes, so I wished that he'd leave me alone. He did. He pushed me out of the car and drove away. I had no money and my dad always told me not to hitchhike. It took me four hours to walk home."

"The guy was a dick. We're not all dicks."

"I'll have to take your word for it. I don't know that many men."

Brian glances behind me. "I better go get some romantic footage."

My glass is empty, so I nibble on a bread stick until Brian comes back to the table.

"Those two really like each other."

"Jocelyn's the one; I said that from the beginning. Can I go home now?"

Brian tells them we're leaving. We get on the elevator and I hide my face in Brian's shirt. The rest of the trip home is a big blur, except I think I reached up and tried to kiss Brian outside my bedroom. And I am pretty sure he patted the top of my head and pushed me in the door. I do remember hanging my head in the toilet bowl.

❦

I MAKE AN APPOINTMENT WITH MY DOCTOR. HE HASN'T SEEN any of my recent injuries and I want to bring him up to speed. Dr. McDermott is my pediatrician. He still lets me come to his office because he feels terrible about how I lost my parents. He helped me in the early days of my new reality.

It's awkward sitting in the waiting room surrounded by three-year-olds and mothers rocking their infants in sexy strollers.

One perfect mother leans over to me. "You seem to have forgotten your baby."

"I left her in the car with the engine running."

She recoils and then gets up and talks to the receptionist, pointing her finger at me. The receptionist waves.

"Hi, Chloe, you can go in now."

As I sit on the examining table, I reach for the paper and crayons Dr. McDermott always keeps on hand. My chart is filled with creations I've drawn over the years. He says a picture tells him more about what's going on in a child's life than anything else.

I'm almost finished my drawing when Dr. McDermott comes in. He's a gruff old goat. I'm not sure why kids aren't afraid of him—probably his gentle hands.

"My favourite patient. How are you, Chloe Sparrow?"

"I've been better."

"Let me see." He takes my picture from me. "So we have a girl standing under a big black cloud, being rained on."

I point to the sky. "There's also thunder and lightning and a tornado coming. That's a tsunami in the distance."

"Oh, dear."

"I broke my nose. I chipped my tooth. I tore the ligaments in my ankle and I haven't had a period in five months."

"Are you pregnant?"

"No."

"Are you sexually active?"

"I believe you have to have a boyfriend for that."

"Not necessarily. You don't have anyone in your life?"

I shake my head.

"That must get lonely."

Shrug.

"Hop on the scale."

It clunks when I step on the cold, shaky platform. Dr. McDermott shuffles the metal pointer around, but I can never read the weight fast enough before he whacks it back into position. "I see."

"What does that mean?"

"You weigh one hundred and two pounds. That's why you're not getting your period. You need to gain at least ten to fifteen pounds."

"I forget to eat."

"That's ridiculous."

My eyes well up momentarily. "Don't be mad at me."

He holds my head. "Let me look at your nose. Whoever set it did a good job. A slight bump is normal after a break. You can hardly notice it. Show me your tooth."

I give him a big smile.

"Piffle. You can't even see it, but you can get it fixed. You've got health benefits. Now let me see your foot."

"I have a cankle. It's lumpy."

His fingers gently press all around. "The swelling will go eventually, but not all of it. We are our wounds, my dear."

He listens to my heart and lungs, looks in my ears and down my throat, takes my blood pressure, and fills out a prescription pad. "I want you to have blood work done and a urine sample. I'm sending you for chest X-rays just to be careful, and I want you to come back in two weeks and we'll see how much weight you've gained. Then every two weeks after that. Are you still a vegetarian?"

"Yes."

"You can get all the protein you need on a vegetarian diet, but not if you don't work at it, and I know you. You don't sit still long enough to make yourself a meal. That has to stop. An occasional hamburger isn't going to kill you. I wish you'd eat some fish and chicken too."

"Fish and chickens have faces."

"I also want you to choke down two protein drinks a day. You can get them in a chocolate flavour."

My shoulders slump. "I hate my job."

"So do three-quarters of the people on earth, and last I heard you weren't smashing rocks in a quarry. Look, if I liked quick fixes I'd send you off with a bottle of pills, but that's not going to help you in the long run. You have to eat better. You should get some exercise—swim, and work with weights to build up your strength. Try yoga and meditating, anything that relaxes you and gets you out of your own brain. I have a feeling it's a scary place to be."

He waits for an answer.

"All right."

"Boundless enthusiasm! That's what I want to see. Now get out of my office." He squeezes my upper arm before I go. I can feel the warmth on the bus all the way to the hospital, where I sit in a room with sixty people who look like Aunt Ollie and Gramps. Maybe it's my fate to end up like Aunt Ollie. Gramps will die and I'll look after her, but who will look after me?

I'm in the bathroom at the hospital trying to catch my urine "mid-stream." Is this really necessary? It's pretty horrible to squat over the toilet with a tiny bottle between my legs, but it's nothing compared to having a guy open the door and flash me to the entire waiting room. He shuts it in a hurry, but the damage is done. With my pants around my ankles, I shuffle over to lock the door I thought I locked before. Now I have to stay in here until everyone has gone home.

This strategy lasts two minutes. I'm never going to see these people again. I exit with my head held high and don't look back. The nurse puts the pee bottle in a little rack. Then she rolls up my sleeve and drains away the last of my energy. I'm being bled as if I lived in Tudor England. In the X-ray department a crabby nurse shoves me into a cubicle and tells me to take off my blouse and bra and put on an enormous green Johnny shirt. The X-ray technician laughs when I ask her if my heart is broken.

On my way home in a taxi, I lean forward to speak to the driver. "Can you stop at McDonald's first?"

He looks at me quizzically in the rear-view mirror. Maybe he doesn't speak English. I mime stuffing my face.

"McDonald's? Big Mac?"

He gets it.

I've never been at a drive-thru, so I'm not sure what the protocol is. "May I have three Big Macs, three French fries, and three Cokes?"

"So you want three Big Mac combos?" the mechanical voice says.

"Okay."

"Anything else?"

"What do you have?"

There's a long pause. "Everything."

"I'll have a strawberry cheesecake, too."

"We don't have strawberry cheesecake."

"You said you had everything."

"You can have a McCafé Strawberry Shake or a Strawberry Sundae."

It occurs to me that strawberries are low in calories. "Do you have anything with caramel in it?"

"You can have a Hot Caramel Sundae."

"I'll have three of those, too."

"Anything else?"

The kid will ask me this question until I say no. "No, thank you."

When I walk in to Aunt Ollie's with my McDonald's bags, she and Gramps give me a look.

"Where did you get that?"

"Dr. McDermott says I have to gain fifteen pounds. This is medicine."

The three of us chow down. Why do cows have to be so darn tasty?

CHAPTER SEVEN

IT'S NOW BEEN TWO AND A HALF WEEKS SINCE WE STARTED filming, and the mansion still gives me the willies. I much prefer the guest house, where there is some semblance of coziness.

Today we interview the ladies who weren't picked for tonight's date, a particularly nice one for Rebecca, who is bubbly and wide-eyed. Austin is taking her to the Toronto Symphony and then dancing afterwards. Austin tells me he's afraid he'll fall asleep at the theatre. He arrives at the door to pick up his date wearing a tux. The harem collectively sighs at the sight of him. Rebecca preens a little before she blows them a kiss goodbye. The ladies wave their hands and shout that they hope they have a great time, but the minute the couple leaves, the bleating begins.

Trying to keep these women focussed enough to create a narrative we can weave into an actual segment is getting harder as the days go by. All of them either love or hate each other, and half the time I feel like I'm still in the cafeteria at middle school.

We break up into teams lead by Amanda, Trey, and me. We take them into different corners of the mansion and spend all day gathering the interviews this show is built on. We need lots of this type of footage, so we can pick and choose which bits will make it into the final product. We even have Jeremy as a rogue cameraman roaming around filming the girl's faces for reactions that we might need for any situation later on.

We store them up and use them in the editing room. That's how I know Sandy W. is never without gum in her mouth and Sarah F. yawns a lot. I've also noticed Becca's mouth is exceedingly big. Hardly surprising.

I've got Mysti, Jocelyn, Lizette, Sydney, and Tracy in my group. We're in a sunroom off the kitchen, and I made sure to have Brian with me. Sometimes the only way I can get through the day is to roll my eyes at him, which makes him giggle. A big guy who giggles makes me feel better.

I'm hoping for fireworks, since Jocelyn and Lizette are fierce rivals, but Jocelyn never puts a foot wrong so she may keep quiet. Mysti is plain crazy, Sydney is Marilyn Monroe, and Tracy is so sweet she makes my teeth ache.

The five of them are already chattering like squirrels. I try to get their attention, but it isn't working. Since I can't whistle like Amanda, I bang my pen against a water glass. The sound is pitiful, but Sydney realizes what's up and tells the others to hush.

"Firstly, I'd like to know if this experience is what you thought it would be. We'll start with you, Sydney."

"It's fun, but it's really hard to watch Austin go out with other women."

"But you knew that he would."

She bounces in her seat and claps her hands. "I know, but I thought he'd take one look at me and the game would be over!"

When the laughter dies down I point to Jocelyn.

"It's been amazing. Austin is wonderful and so are my new friends. I love this experience."

"It's all good, then?"

"Certainly. Every new experience teaches us about ourselves."

Jocelyn could be a Miss Canada contestant.

"What about you, Lizette?"

Lizette is by an open window so she can smoke. She inhales on her slender cigar and blows smoke at the ceiling. "I'm not here to make friends. This is about Austin and me. All the rest is nonsense that needs to be ignored. The woman who wins will be the strongest mentally, and fortunately I require extreme focus on the racetrack. It's the same with my men."

Instantly the other four women shrink a little, and Lizette gives them a lazy smile. This girl is formidable.

"What about you, Tracy?"

"How am I supposed to top that?"

Again, pretend laughter fills the air.

"Whether I'm the winner or not, I've had such a great time with these beautiful women. That in itself has been rewarding."

"So no one thinks this experience has been difficult?"

Mysti makes a face. "Please. They're all liars, trying to make themselves look good on camera, like butter wouldn't melt. It's a different story when we're not being filmed. I've never heard such bitching and backstabbing in my life."

"That's because you're the bitch doing most of it," Lizette says.

Tracy jumps in. "You can't talk to Mysti that way."

"Lizette thinks she's the favourite. That's not what Austin told me."

This is getting bad...or good, as the case may be. I don't know anymore.

Lizette stubs out her cigar. "It's women like Mysti who give the rest of us a bad name."

"Shut up, you witch!" Mysti jumps up and gets in Lizette's face. "Just because you drive a car around a track doesn't mean you're better than the rest of us."

"With you as the competition, I think it does." Lizette gets up and walks out of the sunroom.

Tracy wrings her hands. "Why can't we all just get along?"

❀

TODAY WE'RE OFF TO MUSKOKA, BEAUTIFUL COTTAGE COUNTRY only a few hours from Toronto. Kate P. and Kate M., Jennifer P., Sandy W., Mysti, Becky, and Erin are going with us for a day of swimming and sailing at a fancy resort surrounded by beautiful lakes. Austin will then pick one girl to have dinner with on a millionaire's yacht in the harbour. We've arranged for fireworks at the end of the evening.

I'm at the back of the bus trying to meditate, but it's not going well. My eyes are closed and that's about as far as I get. It's easier to look out the window at the emerald trees, pink granite, and sapphire lakes. My cellphone alarm goes off every hour so I remember to eat, which means I can't relax. I had some cheese earlier. Right now I'll have a box of Smarties, and next a banana.

Austin is at the front of the bus with the girls. Amanda has her earphones on and is singing along, too loud and completely out of tune. Brian is snoring with his mouth open, while Trey and Jerry are playing Parcheesi on their laps.

Austin appears when I'm halfway through my Smarties. "Do you mind if I sit down?"

"Not at all."

He sits and watches me put one Smartie at a time in my mouth. "Don't you want to pour the box in all at once?"

"No."

"I need to talk to you."

"Fire away."

Austin looks tired and a little dishevelled. He has a habit of running his fingers through his hair. It's like nervous tic. "This is a lot harder than I thought."

"No kidding."

"I don't like hurting people."

I hand him two red Smarties. "There. That will cheer you up."

He pops them in his mouth. "This started when my sister Julia accused me of being a perfect specimen of conformity. Someone who does everything right, gets an education, gets a job, pays taxes, and then retires and dies without ever being spontaneous."

"She's the rebel musician who's cool."

"So cool she lives off Mom."

I give him more Smarties.

"When I found out that I'd be paid for this gig, it seemed like a no-brainer. Trouble is, in my mind I glossed over what I'd have to do to get it."

"You're picking a nice girl to fall in love with."

"And making nineteen others miserable."

"I hate to burst your bubble, Austin, but these girls will recover. You're not Ryan Gosling, after all."

He pushes my shoulder with his own. "How do you manage it?"

"What?"

"You look like Ariel, but underneath you're Ursula, the Sea Witch."

"Who are they?"

"You're kidding me. No, never mind—you don't get out much."

The day is the best yet. Everyone has a relaxing time at the beach. It's perfect for what we need, all our gals in bikinis and rolling around in the water and the hot sand. Amanda and I are the lifeguards, while Brian and his gang follow the ladies. In the centre of the activity is Austin, doing his best to drown the girls with great scoops of water as they scream at the top of their lungs.

"I'm glad I have sons," Amanda says.

"Why's that? Want some sunscreen?" I pass her my bottle.

"This is SPF 60! No wonder you look like Snow White."

"I look like Ariel, if you don't mind. Why are you glad you have sons?"

"No matter what their age, females are screamers on the beach. It's like a drill going through your brain."

My alarm goes off. "I forgot my food."

Amanda sits up in her chair. "Again? You'll have to put me in charge. I always have food—except for right now, sorry."

I spy Brian about to open a bag of chips. "I'll give you five bucks for those chips."

"Get your own."

"My doctor says I have to gain fifteen pounds."

"My doctor says I have to lose fifteen pounds, but I'm still not giving them to you."

"You're a jerk."

"Yes. Yes, I am."

"Please?"

He tosses the bag over. "Take them. I hope you get fat."

"I hope so too." I rip the bag open and offer him some. He takes a huge handful and grins. "Where's my five bucks?"

Once the beach segment is over, we set up on the boat we'll be sailing in this afternoon. It's impressive, with a gorgeous deck of mahogany that will look great on camera, large enough to fit the girls, Austin, the captain, his crew, and two cameramen. I'm grateful I'm on the smaller sailboat that will accompany the bigger vessel, so we can get exciting shots from the water.

It's a glorious late July day in Ontario. The clouds in the pale blue sky look as if someone swept them along with a broom. There are speedboats, jet skis, and sailboats in the water, their canvasses puffed out by the wind, with cottages dotted in and around the edge of the lake, beautifully land-scaped among the fir and pine trees, some larger than a house in the city. This is where the rich have their hideaways.

I've never been in a sailboat and I'm leery of my weak ankle, but Amanda tells me I'll be fine, so I believe her.

After an hour I have concluded that this sailing business is heavenly. We race through the swells beside the large boat, shouting and waving back and forth. Gary gets some great distance shots of Austin at the wheel, steering the boat with confidence. He certainly looks like a natural, with his sweater draped around his neck and shirt collar up, wind ruffling his hair.

The wind starts to die down, which means we're going at a more leisurely speed. This is even nicer; you don't have to hold on so tightly.

Amanda's hair and my own look like rat's nests, and Gary insists on pointing the camera at us.

"Knock it off!"

"I can't. I'm taking it back to show the others what our esteemed leaders look like."

Stupidly, I stand up to go over and grab the camera from him. The skipper starts to come around and yells "Duck!"

I put my hand to my forehead to block out the sun so I can see the duck. "Where?"

The boom thumps me and I'm in the water before I've even registered flying through the air. The water hits me like a wall as I flail about, trying to get to the surface. All I can think of are the life jackets back on the boat. How incredibly idiotic that I didn't insist on wearing one. If I drown, someone else will see my black-walled bedroom with fraying sheets. How humiliating.

My head pops up, and I see the sailboats and people panicking, which makes me panic.

"Hel...p." I'm coughing on the water, but there's someone swimming through the waves towards me. *I wish you'd hurry up and get here!*

It's Austin. I've never been so glad to see him.

He grabs me around the waist and shouts in my ear, "You're going to be all right. Stop fighting. I've got you."

Now there are life rings around us, and people hanging over the side reaching out to get a hold of my arms. Austin pushes me up out of the water, and I'm hauled into the larger yacht like a tuna, courtesy of Brian. Amanda is yelling from the other boat. People wrap me up in a variety of things, everyone asking me if I'm all right.

Of course I'm all right. I'm alive, but covered in goosebumps, probably from fright.

Brian hauls Austin aboard too.

Mysti runs over and grabs him, crying. "I'm so glad you're safe! You could've drowned!"

He pushes her aside and comes over to me. "That was a stupid thing to do."

"You're going to yell at me?"

"You've got a weak ankle and you're standing on the edge of the boat that's moving. And not wearing a life jacket, I might add."

"You weren't wearing one."

"You have to be more careful."

"Thank you for saving my life. Now stop lecturing me!"

"How dare you yell at Austin? He rescued you."

"Keep out of this, Mysti," Austin shouts.

That's when the violent shivering starts. Fade to black.

When I open my eyes Amanda is sitting beside me as I lie on a gurney in a cubical surrounded by white sheets. "Please don't tell me I'm in a hospital."

"How are you feeling?"

"Like a fool."

"We're waiting for the doctor to release you. Then we can head home. It's been a long day for everyone."

I sit up and swing my legs over the side. "I'm sore."

"You could've been dead. Austin was in that water almost as fast as you were."

"He got mad at me. Yelled in front of everyone like I was a kid."

"He got a fright."

"Who did he pick for dinner?"

"Kate One. Then he gave Mysti the boot. She didn't go quietly."

The doctor arrives and lets me go after taking my pulse and blood pressure. "Keep warm and eat something."

❦

THE FIRST PHASE OF OUR PRODUCTION IS WINDING DOWN. Now we will head out on locations around the country. We chose

Vancouver, since it has such a beautiful backdrop, but now I'm wishing we weren't going so far. I've made arrangements to fly back to Toronto to see Dr. McDermott while we're on our jaunt. It's the only way to keep both him and Mr. Gardner happy; my boss wants me on site at all locations. Amanda and I had hoped to share the duties, so she wouldn't be away from home for long periods of time. She's no doubt bawling her head tonight before heading to the airport in the morning. I'm surprisingly teary myself. I've never been away from home.

Aunt Ollie helps me with my ironing.

"Don't talk to strangers."

"I won't."

"Don't go out late at night."

"I won't."

"Don't hang around street corners smoking a cigarette," Gramps says. "Someone might mistake you for a hooker."

"I won't."

"Keep your money in your bra," Aunt Ollie says.

"I don't carry money. I have plastic."

"You should always carry money. What if you were kidnapped and had to find a phone booth to call someone?"

There's no use explaining. "You're right; I'll carry money in my bra."

"Call us and check in from time to time," Gramps says.

"Okay."

We spend my last evening eating pepperoni pizza and playing with the pussycats. Bobby spends the entire time on Gramps's lap. Peanut is trying to climb a curtain, and Rosemary is fascinated by something under a bookcase. Norton is on the windowsill, looking at the neighbour's dog.

"Are you sure you guys are going to be okay without me?"

"We'll be fine!" Aunt Ollie sobs into her apron.

I've never seen her like this before. "Don't cry."

"I'm not crying."

Gramps wipes his eyeglasses. "Knock it off."

My amazement knows no bounds. I've never seen them like this. They never care what I'm doing or where I'm going, and now they're upset that I'm leaving. Guilt kicks in.

"Maybe I shouldn't go."

"That's up to you," Aunt Ollie sniffs.

"I'll be back to see the doctor. Make something fattening for me to eat."

"That she can do."

"Shut up, you."

"Make me."

In the morning, I go next door for a final goodbye when the taxi pulls up to the curb a bit early. One more round of kisses before I leave with my suitcase. While the driver puts my luggage in the trunk, Aunt Ollie and Gramps stand at the window with the kittens, waving their paws goodbye. I wave back until I can't see them anymore. Who would've guessed? They'll miss me.

Amanda looks miserable when she arrives at the airport. Her distress at leaving her family is evident—she forgot to spray tan before she left home. I hardly recognize her.

"Are you going to be okay?" We punch in our information at a ticket kiosk.

"The boys were crying and hanging off me. It was terrible. I've never left them for so long before."

"I've never left Norton and the kittens for this long, either."

"Are you honestly going to compare leaving a bunch of cats to me leaving my kids?"

"The kittens are my kids."

"I can't talk about this right now."

This is my first time flying, which is pretty pathetic. Brian sits by the window, Amanda in the middle, and me in the aisle seat. Austin is across from me and the girls are scattered around like chicken feed. They're excited about going and I'm happy for them.

I'm the only one who listens intently to what the flight attendant says. I open the brochure that tells us how to get out in case of emergency and study it. The flight attendant comes over and points to Brian.

"Sir, you're sitting in the exit seat. Is that something you're okay with?"

"Sure."

"In case we need to evacuate, you have to pull the handle up and in so the window is released, and then throw it outside."

"Okay. No problem."

She's about to leave. I hold up my finger. "Sorry, but that sounds terribly easy. What's the guarantee that the window won't accidentally open in mid-air?"

"Don't worry. Everything is secure." She's about to leave again.

"What's the protocol? Do women and children go first?"

"The best thing is to get out and free up the space for others to come behind you."

"Okay, thank you."

She leaves in a hurry. Amanda, Austin, and Brian grin at me.

"What? I don't know what the rules are. They tell you if you have any concerns, to ask them."

It seems like we wait forever for the plane to start taxiing to the runway. It's always mystified me how something that weighs tons and tons can get off the ground just by driving quickly down a runway. I look at the heads all around me. The plane is full. I wonder if that's bad.

I assume we're cleared for takeoff, because there is a surge of power and we're moving faster and faster. Surely we'll lift off soon...but we don't. We're going to run out of runway. My heart starts to pound. I get a slight dipping sensation and I know for a fact that the bottom of the plane is about to scrape off on the pavement.

But we're up, and the ground gets farther and farther away. I'm in a giant tin can hurtling through space, and I can't get out. My whole life depends on the person in the cockpit who I've never met. Maybe that person is having a bad day. Maybe they found out their kids are on drugs or their partner's cheating on them and they're not concentrating on anything else.

There's a horrible grinding noise.

"What's that?"

"The wheels."

"Are they falling off?"

Amanda pats my hand. "They're retracting. You'll hear that noise again when we land."

There are binging noises. Does that mean something's wrong? I don't want to ask the others, so I sit tight. But then the captain comes on.

"Ladies and gentlemen, we'll be encountering some turbulence over the Great Lakes. It shouldn't last long. Go back to your seat and make sure your seat belts are fastened."

My seat belt is digging into my ovaries.

When the bumping starts it's overwhelming. We're going to fall out of the sky. Why did I come on this stupid trip? Why did I take this stupid job? Who will look after Norton and the kids if I'm killed and something happens to Aunt Ollie and Gramps? My fingers dig into my armrests as we experience another scary jolt downwards. Austin leans across the aisle and touches my arm.

"It's okay. This is normal."

Another dip and I plant my face in Amanda's left boob. She holds my head like a baby.

"It's all right."

And then I remember. *I wish for this plane to stay in the air and take us safely to Vancouver.* I let Amanda have her boob back.

"Sorry, I'm okay now."

The rest of the trip is uneventful. Both Brian and Amanda are watching movies, but my speakers don't work, so I make lists of things I have to do when we get to our hotel.

"Chloe?"

I turn my head and look at Austin. "Yeah?"

He leans across the aisle. "I'm sorry I yelled at you on the boat."

"You're forgiven. No one else jumped in the water to save me. Now I know who my friends are."

"So we're good?"

"Of course. I'm used to people yelling at me."

He doesn't look convinced.

"I'm joking!"

"I'm never sure with you."

At one point I lean over Amanda and Brian to look out the window. The view of the Rockies is spectacular. The entire landscape is made up of giant mountains of craggy rock reaching for the sky, with snow at the top of the peaks. I take some pictures before Brian tells me to sit down. "Your knee is digging into my thigh."

"Sorry."

About a half an hour before we land, the captain comes on to tell us we'll be passing through a thunderstorm. It doesn't faze me in the least.

The plane goes up and down and almost sideways. A few people scream. Amanda now has her head in my lap, praying for God to forgive her for leaving her children. I calmly rock back and forth with the plane. The ominous black clouds that surround us make the inside of the plane dark and murky, as if we're underwater. Brian cracks.

"Jesus...get us outta here!"

And then we fly out of it. The captain comes on. "That was a wild one, folks, but everything's fine now. We'll be landing in ten minutes."

The passengers clap and smile at each other.

"I can't believe how calm you were," Amanda says.

"I rely on a higher power."

CHAPTER EIGHT

VANCOUVER IS BREATHTAKING, A CITY IN THE MIDDLE OF A rainforest. I've never seen such magnificent trees, bushes, and plants in my life. It's as if the entire area is sprinkled with fairy-dust fertilizer and the vegetation just continually grows. Houses look like mushrooms underneath the forest floor, with huge canopies of evergreen and cedar draped above. Downtown looks like it's made of glass, with shining tall towers between the blue water and the incredible mountains.

My mouth is open all the way to the hotel. The driver gives us a bit of a tour first, pointing out the Lions Gate Bridge and Stanley Park. All I want to do is get out and hug a gigantic tree, but it's raining heavily, so that will have to wait. The hotel is located on the famous Robson Street, the place to be if you want to shop and eat, and despite the rain the street is filled with people, all holding colourful umbrellas and wearing rain boots. The entire scene is enchanting. I wish I were here as a tourist and not someone who has to worry about keeping to our schedule.

Amanda and I share a room together. It's like having a sleepover, each of us with a double bed to ourselves.

"I have to call Jason. I can't believe I'm alive to talk to him."

"I'll give you some privacy."

So here I sit on the edge of a tub on the other side of the country, far from home. It feels like another world. I've been living with blinders on, content in my own corner. There are places to go and things to see. I need to shake off my dreariness and embrace new adventures. When I call home to tell them I've arrived, Aunt Ollie says there's nothing new and hangs up. I'm glad they're not missing me.

We gather in the hotel restaurant for supper. It's the first time I've eaten dinner with the girls. It reminds me of a sorority gathering. Most of them order salads, salmon, or grilled chicken.

The waiter looks at me.

"May I have the pasta Alfredo and chocolate cheesecake?"

It's very good, but I can't finish my meal and pass it off to Amanda.

With her mouth full of my dessert she says, "Stop it, you're such a pest."

It's now almost nine and my eyes are closing, but the girls are just getting revved up. They order drinks and it looks like a party. It's true what Amanda said. These girls are my age, and yet I feel a generation older. I must make more of an effort to join the fun...but not tonight.

Amanda says she'll be along eventually, so I ride the elevator alone up to my floor. When the doors open, Austin is there.

"You're not going to bed, are you?"

"I'm tired."

"You should come down for an Irish Coffee with lots of cream on top."

"It's bedtime. I know that's lame."

"It's been a long day."

"You're a nice guy, Austin. I hope those girls down there don't break your heart."

"Good night, Chloe."

❧

WE INTENDED TO GO TO THE CAPILANO SUSPENSION BRIDGE TO do our double date with Austin, but the desk clerk tells us to go to the Lynn Canyon Suspension Bridge instead. It's not such a tourist trap and it's free. Works for me.

Austin picks Becky and Tracy to go on this date. He can only choose one of them at the end of the evening, and the other girl has to leave and go back home. Becky has been in the background so far, but her confidence seems to be growing. Once the drama queens pause for breath, the quiet ones have an advantage. They haven't made as many enemies or stupid blunders.

When we get to the site, there's a wobbly suspension bridge crossing a deep ravine with waterfalls, bubbling rapids, and rock formations in the middle of an amazing stand of trees. The trails are on the other side, so you have to cross the bridge. The mist rises up to greet you as the water runs below, an echoing sound in this quiet place. You can imagine it as it was hundreds of years ago: ancient, damp, and earthy, the birds calling from high up among the treetops.

The team has to go over the bridge first, so we can capture Austin and the girls traipsing over it. As people make their way across, the bridge moves up and down. It gives me heart palpitations. Trey and Jerry stop in the middle to look down and marvel at the view. They're insane.

Amanda hollers across the canyon, "Hurry up, Chloe! It's not as bad as it looks!"

"You guys go first."

"Are you sure?" Austin asks.

"Positive."

So Austin, Becky, and Tracy start out over the bridge and cameras roll. Once again it sways from side to side. Becky is more hesitant, so Austin takes her hand and leads her across. I can tell from here that Tracy wishes she'd thought of that.

Amanda isn't pleased that I'm still standing on the other side of the divide. "Stop being such a chicken!"

There's no way around it. *I wish for this bridge to hold up.*

Just because I know the bridge won't collapse doesn't mean I enjoy the feeling of swaying on this rope. I can see a couple of hundred feet down through the rope mesh and wooden slats. As I inch my way forward I hear something, so I slowly turn my head. There are two beautifully sleek athletes in Lycra behind me.

"Do you want to pass?"

"If you wouldn't mind."

So now I edge closer to the rope, and suddenly realize I didn't wish not to fall off. But once you start a wish, you can't change it mid-stream.

"You should wear trainers on this," the guy says as they breeze by—running, mind you.

Amanda shouts encouragement, and Brian says he's getting it on tape because it's priceless.

"Turn that camera off."

"Come and make me."

He's fired. Don't look down and put one foot in front of the other.

"Chloe, the clock's ticking!"

"I can't," I whisper. If I speak too loudly, I'll fall off.

This is how it ends. My lifeless body crushed on the rocks below. They'll send my remains home by plane. I'll be buried next to my parents and soon forgotten, which means someone will buy my house and see how awful it is. Why am I living in a mausoleum? It's getting harder and harder to breathe.

Suddenly, I feel someone's hand slip into mine. Austin is beside me.

"Keep looking at me. I won't go fast."

He gets me off that death trap. I'm grateful and relieved. "Thank you. You're always coming to my rescue. Can I book you to assist me on the way back?"

"I'm not sure. Have you got any more red Smarties?"

❀

IN THE AFTERNOON, I'M IN A CABLE CAR GOING UP GROUSE Mountain, an incredibly foolish thing to do after you've been traumatized by a rope bridge. Yes, the scenery is breathtaking and it's amazing to see snow on the mountaintops in the middle of summer and the city glittering like a diamond in the azure blue sky. At least, that's what they tell me. I'm looking at the floor.

We've made arrangements for Austin and the girls to have a lunch outside, with the fabulous mountaintop as our backdrop. The people in charge are very excited to see us, because when this is broadcast across the country it will be free advertising for them. They've been kind enough to make boxed lunches for the rest of us. Things like this make all the difference on a shoot, because it can be a boring process day after day. People start to rub each other the wrong way. Trey got in a snit because Jerry took the last seat on the cable car and he had to stand.

To make my life easier, Amanda has taken over giving me something to eat every hour on the hour. She's my dealer, passing me a box of chocolate raisins on the sly, or a granola bar. The trouble is, she's gained five pounds and I've only gained two.

Our trio are well into their lunch and so far it's as boring as hell. There is absolutely no chemistry between any of them. What a colossal waste of time.

Trey comes over and whispers in my ear. "Watching paint dry is more exhilarating."

"Tell me about it. I *wish* something exciting would happen."

Oh no, I didn't mean that!

Just then, Tracy pops a grape into her mouth. She gives a strangled kind of cough and jumps up from the grass, her hands around her throat.

I start to run. "Oh my God, she's choking!" I'm killing someone else.

"Help her! Help her!" Becky shrieks.

Austin leaps to his feet and puts his arms around Tracy and gives her the Heimlich manoeuvre, once, twice, three times. She's a rag doll before the grape flies out of her mouth.

It lands at my feet.

All of us are in such shock that it's a moment or two before we notice something is wrong with Tracy. What with the jumping, squeezing, and manoeuvring, her blouse has come completely undone and her bra is around her armpits. I stare at her. She has no breasts. What she has been using for breasts are now on the ground. At first I think that maybe she's had a double mastectomy, but her chest is unscarred—flawless, even. The trouble is, it belongs on a man.

The entire crew gawks at her while Brian captures every painful moment. Austin looks stunned and Becky's jaw drops.

"You're a *guy*? Are you kidding me? We share a room!"

"Surprise!" Tracy shrugs. "Fooled you."

Amanda smacks her hands together. "This is genius. We have a hit on our hands."

Austin shakes his head at Tracy. "Did you think I wouldn't eventually find out?"

"It's the journey I wanted to go on, not the destination."

"What does that even mean?" I shout at him. "You lied to everyone."

"Sorry, but being a dame was on my 'fuck it' list. I'm ever so pleased with myself if that's any consolation."

Have you ever been on a cable car with people who aren't talking to each other?

❧

TRACY IS SENT HOME WITH HIS PENIS BETWEEN HIS LEGS.

"I can spot a drag queen a mile away," Trey tells me. "He was good."

Amanda and I are on her bed that night sharing a box of chocolates, but she's eating two to my one.

"I have to stop eating and exercise," she says.

"Do ten push-ups right now."

"You do them with me."

We lie on the carpet in front of our beds.

"Okay, go."

"One...two..."

"One..."

We collapse in a heap.

"This is ridiculous." Amanda crawls back up on her bed and faces the mirror. "Look at this gut." She jiggles her belly fat.

"You've had two babies."

"And a week's worth of your food in two days."

I manage to scramble back onto my mattress. "I'm firing you from the food job. It's my responsibility, not yours."

Amanda drops backwards onto the bed. "I miss my kids. I miss Jason."

"That must be a nice feeling."

"It's not. It's a horrible feeling, like your guts are missing, or your right arm is gone."

"Still, you know they're going to be there when you get home."

She turns over on her side to face me. "I know I'm a nag, but you should put as much effort into finding a mate as you do your career."

"Who gets married at twenty-five anymore? That's ludicrous."

"I don't want you to get married. Just find someone to spend time with. What if you choked on a grape at home? There would be no one to save you."

"Aunt Ollie and Gramps are next door."

"I'm sorry, Chloe, but your relatives are not dependable. Aunt Ollie would yell, *'Your face is turning blue and you'll never find a man looking like that!'*"

We start laughing and can't stop, each of us snorting in turn, which makes us howl even harder. Tears fall down my cheeks as Amanda kicks her feet in the air. The two of us roll around like banshees. I can't remember when I had this much fun.

We're completely spent by the time we regain our composure, each of us panting and sweaty.

Amanda fans her face. "That, my dear, was better than sex."

"I wouldn't know."

She stops fanning her face and gives me an astonished look. "What?"

"Don't judge me."

"How is this possible?" She jumps out of bed and hugs me. "You dear little thing."

"Hey! I'm your boss."

"Stop rubbing it in. How can someone be so worldly and yet so innocent?"

"Who was I going to talk to about sex? Aunt Ollie?"

"Yes! She's had warm and fuzzy feelings in her Mary-Ellen. Your mother died when you were fifteen. You never talked about sex before that?"

"She told me to go to the library. The books told me how to do it, not why."

Amanda shakes her head and holds me by the shoulders. "The fact that you're in charge of this show is hilarious. We have to hook you up."

She cackles to herself as she heads to the bathroom to brush her teeth. I'm left to wonder why I blurted it out. It's a secret I've been carrying for a long time.

❀

THE NEXT DAY AUSTIN, SYDNEY, JOCELYN, LIZETTE, ERIN, AND Rebecca are going zip-lining through some amazing scenery at Whistler. Sydney and Rebecca are not happy, but that's par for the course. There's not one activity we've done that hasn't had someone in tears, but the point is Austin wants a woman who likes adventure, because he's a big kid at heart.

Guys who live in front of their television sets playing video games don't apply to shows like this.

I'm still a bit stunned that I told Amanda my deepest secret, but it's freeing in a way. On the bus this morning she was very sympathetic.

"You've basically raised yourself, Chloe. You're an anomaly."

"Which is a nice way of saying I'm a freak."

As the ladies wait for their turn on the zip-line, Lizette and Jocelyn are once again the gals with the most enthusiasm and determination. Rebecca is biting her nails to the quick, Erin yelps before she's even in the harness, and Sydney is praying for salvation while she kisses the cross around her neck.

"It's not that bad!" I reassure her.

"Then *you* do it!"

"Would that make you feel better?"

"Yes."

"Okay. Are you coming, Amanda?"

"Not on your life."

The things I do for this show. The zip-line guys put me in the harness, and I stand on the platform surveying the tree-tops and deep valley I'll glide into. It's breathtaking. But I'm not stupid. *I wish to get to the other side.*

"Are you ready?"

When I nod, a staff member releases me and off I go, flying through empty space. The sound of the rope whizzing above my head reminds me of a giant angry bumblebee. I know I'm laughing but I can't hear myself. I'm about halfway across when I realize I'm racing across this landscape faster than everyone else. My screams alert Austin and a worker waiting on the finish line deck.

Austin yells, "Slow down!"

Did anyone tell me how to slow down? I can't remember. Frantically, I try to figure out what to do, but I draw a blank. Once again, my wish isn't specific enough. I'll get to the other side, but I may not be in one piece, so I keep hollering. It may be the last anyone hears from me.

The guys brace themselves to stop me before I smash into the equipment at the end. The only thing I remember is the look on Austin's face as I hurtle towards him. When I slam into his chest, I instinctively wrap my arms and legs around him and hang on for dear life. I need a moment to realize I'm not dead.

"Are you okay?"

"No." I hide my face in his shirt. "I'm humiliated. This didn't happen to anyone else."

"You go faster if you're a lightweight," the zip guy says.

"Your brochure didn't mention warp speed." I untangle myself from Austin's embrace and try to regain my dignity. We hear Sydney before we see her and when she comes into view, she's completely upside down. She's going to kill me and herself.

That evening Austin lets go of Erin. She confesses that she's relieved. "I'm missing home. I'm not a front-runner, so I'm leaving before it gets really painful."

That evening in the hotel room I'm on the phone with Aunt Ollie getting my daily fix of kitten news when Amanda panto-mimes hanging up.

"I have to go. I'll be home in a couple of days. Love you."

Aunt Ollie hangs up immediately, as always. It wouldn't kill her to say goodbye to me first.

"Get dressed and come with me," Amanda orders.

"I'm in my pyjamas."

"It's eight! Even my babies don't go to bed this early."

"Where are we going?"

"It's a surprise."

One of the town cars with the tinted windows waits at the hotel entrance. Amanda drags me by the arm and throws me inside. Jocelyn, Lizette, and Sydney are in the back.

"Surprise!"

Amanda slams the door shut behind me.

"What's this?"

"I told the girls you've never gone to a male strip show and they thought that was a shame, so off we go! The more, the merrier!" She pops open a bottle of champagne.

By the time we get to the venue I've had two full glasses of bubbly and I'm feeling fine. We join a whole room full of women we've never met, who are pumped and ready to let it rip.

I'm astonished at what goes on but pretend otherwise. One of the guys pulls me out of my seat and makes me sit in a chair on the stage. He gyrates and throws off articles of clothing about six inches from my face. Talk about baptism by fire.

Amanda and the others urge me on, laughing at my predicament, so I laugh too, because Amanda is a pal and she's arranged this so I'd loosen up, which is something I don't do often. I slip some money in the guy's G-string, which sets off another round of posturing by him and hoots from my friends.

My friends. That has a nice ring to it. By the time we head for home, I'm a weepy drunk who throws my arms around them and pledges undying love. We speed through the city singing at the top of our lungs while the driver makes exasperated faces in the rear-view mirror.

Amanda is as drunk as I am. "So who's gonna win this thing?"

The girls throw up their hands shouting, "Me!"

My hand goes up. "Am I allowed?"

"NO!"

"Why not?"

"You're a virgin!"

The laughter stops. Amanda throws both her hands over her mouth. The party's over.

The minute we get to the hotel, I get out of the car and don't look back. Amanda chases me through the lobby. The elevator doors close in her face. Once I'm in my room I deadbolt the door. When Amanda shows up and bangs on it, I completely ignore her.

"I'm sorry Chloe! You have to forgive me."

After five minutes of begging to be let in, she wanders off. I don't care where she sleeps, as long as it's not with me. This is what it means to have a friend. They always let you down.

❧

IN THE MORNING I LEAVE A NOTE FOR TREY SAYING I'M HEADING out a day earlier than planned and then take a taxi to the airport. Because it's short notice, I can only get on a flight that has a long layover in Edmonton, but thankfully I sleep through most of the flight. By the time the taxi pulls up to my house, it's late and Aunt Ollie's windows are dark, so I don't disturb them.

It's such a relief to be home I don't even mind my bedroom. "Hello, canopy bed...hello, black walls...did you miss me?"

The first thing I do is take a hot bubble bath to ease the tension that threatens to overwhelm me. Everything is quiet and peaceful as I close my eyes. Then the bathroom door slams open.

"Aaaah!!!"

Gramps is above me, holding a baseball bat, Aunt Ollie behind him with a rolling pin. She is furious.

"The water was running, we thought you were a burglar!"

"What are you doing here?" Gramps shouts.

"I came home a day early and didn't want to wake you up."

Gramps is breathing hard. "Next time call us."

"Normally you don't care what time I come home."

"That's when you're in the city, not across Canada."

My bubbles are fading fast. "I'm sorry! I won't do it again. Can I have some privacy? I'll be over in the morning."

"That's the thanks we get for thwarting a robbery," Gramps complains.

Aunt Ollie nods. "Next time we'll let them take everything." The two of them totter out.

"Could you shut the door, please?"

"Certainly, your highness." The door slams shut.

"I love you guys!"

Silence.

This calls for more bubbles and hot water. I'm up to my chin in scented froth when it occurs to me that I'm not speaking to my work family and now my real family's not speaking to me. So what does that add up to?

I need to change.

At midnight I raid the fridge, but there's nothing in it. Thank goodness for crackers and peanut butter. Since I'll be weighed in two days, I eat as many as I can. Sitting on the bed, I go through old photo albums. There are no pictures of my parents and I having fun together. We never went on vacations, and I always had to be quiet so I didn't disturb them in their studies, which is why I never invited classmates over. I'm almost certain they loved each other more than me. So it's okay that I don't know much about love. I can teach myself, like I do with everything. This is my new mission. I'm tired of feeling like an outsider.

In the morning I go next door and kiss my relatives several times, tell them I love them and I won't scare them like that again. They're appeased. We spend the entire day playing with Norton and the crew and then I order Chinese food, hoping the sodium will swell my body so I'll be bloated at the doctor's office.

The sodium doesn't do the job. Dr. McDermott is annoyed. "You've gained two pounds in two weeks. That's not enough. Your iron is low, you're practically anaemic. You're not bingeing and purging, are you?"

"Of course not! I'd never do that when so many people in this world are starving to death."

"Look at the black circles under your eyes. Your schedule is interfering with this process. I insist you take a couple of weeks off."

"I can't!"

"You most certainly can, it's doctor's orders. Look, Chloe, not having a period for months on end at your age is not a good thing. You're worrying your calories away. This television job is the worst thing you could be doing right now. It's taking a toll on your health. So if your boss has a problem with that, you get him to call me."

"This is a disaster."

"No, the disaster is you getting very ill. I mean it. Two weeks off, and then come see me."

I hop off the examining table. "Um...before I go, can you write me a prescription for birth control pills?"

He looks at me over his glasses. "Can we get your period back first?"

This kind of news has to be delivered first-hand, and I'm worried sick as I take the bus to the CBC. Waiting outside Mr. Gardner's office is very uncomfortable. His secretary is annoyed that I've upset the delicate balance of her appointments.

Mr. Gardner opens the door of his office. "Come in, Chloe."

"Thank you, sir."

He indicates for me to take a seat. I break out in a cold sweat that makes it very clear I'm going to stick to this leather chair.

"How is everything going?"

"Fine, sir. We're on budget, the crew is first rate. This Vancouver segment is going very well, absolutely breathtaking backgrounds that will impress the viewers."

"Did you make the right choice of bachelor? How's he doing?"

"Austin is wonderful. He always keeps his cool, which is sometimes difficult. The same can't be said for some of the ladies, but they're in a pressure-cooker situation and we have to make allowances."

"Like finding out one of your ladies was a lad."

"Even the psychiatrist missed that one."

"No matter, it'll make the show more interesting."

"Mr. Gardner, I'm here today because I had my doctor's appointment this morning."

"I trust it went well?"

I'm aware I'm wringing my hands. "As a matter of fact, it didn't. My doctor is worried about my health and has asked me to take two weeks off."

"Two weeks?"

"I told him I can't, because everyone is depending on me, but he insists. He said he is available to discuss this with you. I realize that means I'll miss the Calgary portion of the shoot, but as I say, our team works very well together and I know that between Amanda and Trey, things will run smoothly. I'm positive I'll be able to rejoin the crew in Quebec City."

He leans forward and clasps his hands together on his desk blotter. "Obviously we'll have to listen to your doctor. I'm assuming you'll be available via cell and internet to stay abreast of what's happening?"

"Oh, definitely. I'll be in touch with Amanda and Trey every day. Don't worry about that."

He gets to his feet. "I certainly hope you feel better soon, my dear."

I un-glue myself from the leather and shake his outstretched hand. "Thank you so much. I'm sorry to be such a bother."

"No need. There's an old saying...shit happens."

Once I'm home in my pyjamas I call Amanda. The minute she hears me, her voice catches.

"I'm so sorry. That was something you told me in private, and I had no right to share it with anyone. I got drunk and carried away. Please forgive me."

"Okay."

"That's it? You're not going to call me a couple of rotten names?"

"No, because I can't come back and you're going to be left with all the work."

"Seriously?"

"Dr. McDermott insists I take two weeks off. I tried to talk him out of it, but he wouldn't budge. I told Mr. Gardner this morning. I promised him I'd be in touch with you every day and I will."

"Rats, it won't be half as much fun without you here."

"You and Trey can handle this, right?"

"Excuse me? I don't think you'll find *me* in the hospital every second day."

"What's happened since I've been gone?"

"Becca and Kate M. are the latest casualties. We pack up and head to Calgary in the morning."

"I'm sorry I left you with this."

"Don't worry about it. I'm grateful that we're friends again."

"Just know that the next time you see me, I'll have sorted out my little problem."

"What? What are you talking about?"

"Nighty-night, Amanda."

"Don't do anything foolish! Do you hear me, Chloe—"

I shut off my phone.

CHAPTER NINE

DOING RESEARCH IS MY SPECIALITY. THERE ARE ABOUT A hundred thousand dating sites on the internet, and that's just in North America. All of them promise to find me a soulmate in a matter of weeks. Their confidence is unsettling. So if I can't find someone then it's my fault, not theirs. That's a lot of pressure.

On day one of my return to health, I enlist the help of my relatives.

"I have to rest for two weeks, but I'll be going out for walks and maybe even to the YMCA to swim. Gramps, I'll pay you to pick up my groceries and I'll pay you, Aunt Ollie, to make my meals. Take this cookbook and I'll mark off what I'd like to eat. Please note this is a vegetarian cookbook and the ingredients might not be exactly what you're used to preparing, but I'll make it worth your while. I need to gain weight so I can keep my job."

"I thought you said your job was stupid," Aunt Ollie says.

"It is, but it's mine."

"How often do I have to go to the grocery store?"

"As often as Aunt Ollie needs something."

She opens the book and thumbs through the pages. "What on earth is kale? Or lentils, for that matter?"

"The people at the grocery store will point it out to Gramps and you just follow the recipe. It might be a good idea if you tried this food regimen. It's very healthy."

"I'm not sure about this," she frets.

"Aunt Ollie, it's just a meal. If something goes wrong I'll order in, but please try for my sake. I don't ask for much."

She puts her hands on her hips. "Don't ask for much? Your grandfather and I have been looking after your cats since the day they were born! They wake us up at all hours, running back and forth down the hall."

"And you should see the state of the furniture," Gramps says.

"I'm surprised they found any furniture to scratch."

"Who cleans their litter box? Not you."

"I'm sorry, you're right. I do ask a lot of you. But this is only for two weeks and then I'll be out of your hair. There's still a month and a half to go before this production wraps up. After that things will return to normal."

They grudgingly agree. I'm not optimistic that this is going to work, but at least it gives them something to do. In case it's a disaster, I've got a few vegetarian restaurants on speed dial.

I lied about the swimming, but I will walk to the bus to meet men for coffee. That's if I can find any.

My strategy is to place my particulars on several online dating sites, since making appointments for individual dating agencies would sap what little strength I have. My laundry list of preferences is long. There doesn't seem to be enough space to type them all in. I'm free to browse through the picture galleries. This is sort of depressing. Everyone always uses their best photo, which means there's nowhere to go but down. I am now one of those desperate people who sent applications to our show. I wonder if I would've picked me. Somehow I doubt it.

While I'm waiting to be hit on via modern technology, Amanda calls me from Calgary.

"How's tricks?"

"I'm not turning any, if that's what you mean."

"That's exactly what I mean."

"I am capable of living my life without your guidance."

"I'm not so sure about that. Just promise me you won't do anything foolish."

"Can't, look at my track record. How's Calgary?"

"We had a flat tire on the way in from the airport. Then Trey and Jerry got lost when they went for lunch. Lizette and Sandy W. had a huge argument over misplaced makeup and Sydney's come down with the flu."

"How's Austin?"

"He's quiet."

"What does that mean?"

"I don't know, he's probably tired. Listen, do me a favour. Go visit Jason and the boys. I want to make sure they're doing all right."

"Sure. Keep me posted."

I get a few texts from the team. Trey tells me Jerry is being a jerk. Brian hopes I'm feeling better and then there's one from Austin. *Everyone misses you.*

Three days later I'm waiting at a coffee shop at noon to meet Ralph. He passed my rigorous standards and all my deal-breakers, which means he doesn't smoke, drink, do drugs, or belong to a cult. He has a job, an education, loves pets, and wants children.

He says he'll wear a blue shirt and red tie. I see him crossing the street as I sit on a stool by the window. As he gets closer I know he's everything I don't want, so I run and hide in the bathroom. I'm in there so long someone knocks on the door.

"Are you all right?"

"Yes. Has the man with the blue shirt and red tie left yet?"

"A blue shirt..."

"...and red tie. Could you take a peek for me?"

She walks away and comes back a few minutes later. "He's not out there."

I open the door and rush by her. "Thank you. You've been a big help."

Two days after that I arrange to meet Sebastian. We shake hands before I run out the back exit. Same thing with Derek, except he ran after me and I had to hop into a taxi to get rid of him.

When I get home I unsubscribe to all of my dating sites before I go next door for dinner. Aunt Ollie puts a plate of something in front of me. "What's on the menu tonight?"

"Damned if I know...quinoa, tofu, spinach, and portobello mushroom goulash. The only thing I recognized was the spinach."

My babies sit in the kitchen chair beside me and watch me take my first forkful.

"This is quite nice, Aunt Ollie. Thank you."

Gramps points at my tofu. "I took a bite of that white Styrofoam."

"It's called tofu."

"It should be called nofu. It's not food if it has no taste."

Norton jumps up and lies down in front of me. She sniffs at my dinner.

"Since when is she allowed to be up on the table?"

"Since you left her with us."

That's when I find the hotdogs Aunt Ollie hid in the goulash. Before I can say anything, she jumps up from the table.

"You can't get fat without eating something fattening. I've got a big tub of ice cream in the freezer. Eat that."

"Listen to your aunt. She's an expert on fat."

"Be quiet, old man."

"I'm stating the obvious."

This arrangement is not going to work.

❋

HOW DO YOU GO TO BED WITH SOMEONE ON SHORT NOTICE? I figured out why meeting men for coffee didn't work. I'm not looking for a relationship; I'm looking to get laid. Think like a guy, Chloe.

I call an escort service. "I'm looking for a man."

It's unbelievable that I'm having this conversation. My hands are clammy.

"Any type in particular?"

"What do you mean?"

"Blonde, tall, short, fat..."

"It doesn't matter, as long as he's not older than thirty."

"Okay, where and when?"

"First tell me how much."

"It depends on what you want."

"Oh, I didn't realize I had options."

"You name it, they'll do it, for a price."

"Really? That's fascinating. How does one decide which option is worth more than another option?"

"Are you a cop?"

"Am I the only person who's ever asked a question?"

"Kind of."

"Tell me this, then; are your escorts disease-free?"

"No, they all have genital warts. Of course they're disease-free."

"Do you have documentation?"

"Look, lady, do you want to do this or not? I don't have all day."

"Oh God, I guess so."

"I'm not twisting your arm. You called us."

"Right. I'll have the normal option."

"There's no such thing as normal."

"Regular then. To put it plainly, I don't want to be a virgin anymore."

"Why didn't you say so? You want the Cherry-Buster special, and that's four hundred bucks per hour."

"Good grief! It could take more than an hour?"

"I'm going to hang up."

"Is this person nice?"

"I'll give you Ramon. I've had no complaints about him."

My desperation is the only possible explanation for me giving the man my credit card number. Now the people who work in the billing department at Visa will know how low I've sunk. On the other hand, the paper trail will help the police find Ramon if he decides to murder me.

Naturally this rendezvous cannot take place at my house. I'll have to meet him at a hotel in the afternoon, which is so cheesy it's frightening. After an hour in the shower shaving every hair on my body, clipping my toenails and plucking my eyebrows, I stop. Why am I primping for this guy? I'm paying him to impress me, not the other way around.

My plan is to not think. I don't think at the liquor store, where I buy myself a bottle of wine to settle my nerves, and I don't think as I register under the name Jezebel Duckworth. By the time I hear the knock, I've been so busy not thinking, the wine is gone.

My mouth is so dry I can't swallow as I cross the room and

open the door. A very nice-looking guy with dark hair gives me a big smile.

"Hello, beautiful. My name is Ramon."

I stare at him.

"May I come in?"

"You're not Ramon. You're Steve. Amanda's jerky little brother who said thanks but no thanks."

He looks more closely at me. "Shit...Chloe?"

"Yes, Chloe, the girl who's not your type."

"Can we have this conversation inside and not out here in the hallway?" He pushes his way in and closes the door behind him. "What are you doing here?"

"I could ask you the same thing. Is this your job? Is this how art gallery owners snag clients?"

"Yes and no."

"I can't believe this." I turn my back on him and sit on the end of the bed, defeated.

"You can't tell Amanda."

"If you're ashamed of what you're doing, why are you doing it?"

"Look, I'm not exactly proud that it's come to this, but I lost my job six months ago and my family doesn't know. I have to pay the rent until I get another job, which isn't easy in today's economy."

"When that happens to normal people, they work at McDonald's."

"I can't make four hundred dollars an hour flipping burgers. Please don't say anything."

"Fine, I won't tell her. Just give me back my money."

"Can't. Company policy."

"That's complete bullshit." I flop back on the bed. "What do I do now?"

He sits beside me. "Why don't we go through with our plans? We never have to see each other again. No one has to know."

This suggestion makes me stand up. "I'll know, you idiot!" I pace around the room. "Why is this so hard?"

"Why is what so hard?"

"Having sex. According to the newspapers, magazines, all the internet sites, every movie ever made, and all the news shows ever aired, the entire world is doing it constantly except for me."

"Why is that? How did you make it out of high school and university without someone noticing you?"

"They did notice me, but I'm picky."

Now he points his finger at me. "That's what drives guys crazy. We work up the nerve to ask a girl out and she sticks her nose in the air because we don't chew our food properly. If you think you have it bad, ask a guy who's been rejected a few hundred times how it feels to stick his neck out and be laughed at by a girl and her posse in a bar."

"Everyone has a sob story." Now I plunk into the desk chair and twirl around, seeing as how I'm drunk.

"Technically, I'm yours for an hour. Is there something else you'd like me to do?"

"What's worth four hundred bucks? Maybe you could sand my wooden floors or clean out the gutters, but that would require work, something you obviously avoid."

"Are you hungry? I can take you to lunch."

"You want to have lunch with a girl who isn't your type?"

"I apologize for that remark. It was rude."

My twirling slows. He seems genuinely sorry and I'm starving. "Do you know where I can get fattening food?"

He stands up. "Now, *that's* refreshing."

That's how we end up at a heavenly German bakery with café tables for patrons to eat in. I'm drinking dark hot chocolate and Steve has coffee. Arrayed in front of us, with not an inch of tablecloth showing, are plates of *Apfel Maultaschen*, *Streuselkuchen*, *Buttergeback* and *Erdbeertorte*—which translates into apple turnovers, crumb streusel, German butter cookies, and German strawberry tart cake.

We don't even talk, just mutter, moan, and groan after every bite, pointing to the dishes we love best. Impossibly, we inhale everything. There's nothing left on our plates but cookie crumbs and flakes of golden pastry. Our bellies hang out like wasted old men drunk on mouthwash.

"Now, that was better than sex," he says.

"Your sister told me laughing was better than sex."

"They run neck and neck."

"Why can't you tell her about losing your job? It's not a sin."

He wipes his mouth on a napkin. "My family are overachievers. I've always been the disappointment, flitting from one career to another, not having my own family. My parents despair that I'll never grow up and become a responsible adult."

"They might have a point. You're a prostitute at the moment. Is this the only option to remedy your financial situation? I can think of a hundred others."

His brown eyes flash at me. "You are very direct."

"The truth is the truth."

"So tell me the truth. What's the real reason you've never been intimate with anyone?"

"I'm afraid."

"Of what?"

"People leaving me."

Steve shoves his hands in his pockets and leans back in his chair. "Dating is a minefield. Everyone's afraid of people leaving them, but they put themselves out there anyway."

"Then everyone is braver than me."

He smiles. "It's pretty brave to call an escort service. Not many people would do that."

"You have a problem, you find the solution."

"Didn't work though, did it?"

"That's because *you* showed up."

He checks his watch. "We still have three minutes left on the clock."

"Thanks, but no thanks."

Steve smiles again. "You're never going to forgive me for that, are you?"

He pays the bill and hails me a cab, handing the driver money before opening my door.

"Goodbye, Steve."

"Bye, Chloe. This has been the best hour I've ever spent."

"You don't get out much."

When I turn to look out the back window he's still laughing.

❀

AUNT OLLIE IS NOT HAPPY THAT I CAN'T EAT MY DINNER. "Do you know how hard I slaved making this Veggie and Orecchiette with Arugula-Walnut Pesto?"

"Looks like moldy cat food," Gramps says.

"It looks delicious. I'll eat it tomorrow and you can have a day off."

Aunt Ollie folds plastic wrap over the plate and puts it in the fridge. Then she sits at the table, looking done in. "Now I know why vegetarians are so thin. They wear themselves out chopping and peeling ugly vegetables."

Norton jumps up on my lap and rubs her head under my chin while I stroke her smooth fur.

"Anything new with you guys?"

"There's never anything new." Gramps puffs on his pipe. "We might as well be in prison."

"So go out! Take Aunt Ollie to the zoo or go to a Blue Jays game. There's nothing stopping either of you from enjoying yourselves."

"Yes, there is! I'm cooking you meals that require four hours of prep work, and he's running like a jackrabbit all over town trying to find these blasted ingredients."

They do look tired.

"You're right. This is not your responsibility. It's mine."

"So what do I do with the three packages of goat cheese your grandfather bought?"

"I'll take them with me, and the cookbook."

"Thank Christ." Aunt Ollie turns to Gramps. "Go get a bucket of chicken. At least I know what's in that."

Later that night in bed my cellphone rings. It's Austin, of all people.

"Hey, you, I'm glad you're still alive."

"So you heard about the bull incident."

I sit up. "What bull incident?"

"Amanda didn't tell you? I was nearly trampled by a bull at the rodeo."

"Good God, how did you get away?"

"A rodeo clown, but even he was rattled."

"So I leave Amanda in charge and she nearly kills my star. At least I only almost killed myself."

"How are you doing?"

"I had to fire Aunt Ollie from making my meals, turns out she hates vegetables."

"Why is everyone else in charge of your food? If it's not Amanda doling out chocolate bars, it's Aunt Ollie cooking your supper."

"I can't cook."

"So learn."

"Do you know how to cook?"

"No."

"How do you overcome this obstacle?"

"I go to my mom's for dinner."

"That's what I'll do. I'm calling her as soon as you hang up."

He laughs. "Do it. She'd love to have you over."

"I'm joking."

"Seriously, she thinks you're great. Give her a shout."

"Maybe I will."

There's a long pause on his end.

"Are you still there?"

"I let Becky and Rebecca go this week, but last night it was Sydney. She cried and cried. This whole thing sucks."

"Please don't quit on me."

"What difference would it make?"

"It's my show, Austin. It's the only thing I have, I need it to succeed."

He doesn't speak.

"Obviously, if you feel you can't continue, then there's nothing I can do about it, but I hope you'll reconsider."

"Sorry. It's been a long day."

"If you need to talk, I'm always right here. I'm your friend, Austin. I care about you."

"Do you?"

"Of course. Who else comes to my rescue once a week?"

"I better go. Take care of yourself."

"Ditto."

He chuckles before we lose the connection. I immediately call Amanda.

"You nearly killed Austin?"

"So he told you."

"Wasn't it *your* job to tell me?"

"What were you going to do about it in Toronto? He's fine."

"Is he? He sounded pretty down about letting Sydney go."

"We were all in tears. She's such a big softie and it was terrible, but that's the way reality shows work. People get hurt. Did you go see Jason?"

"I forgot."

"Chloe, I'm busting my ass here breathing in dust and the smell of cow dung. The least you can do is see if my husband and children are all right."

"You don't text them every ten minutes?"

"That's not the point!"

"Fine. I'll go tomorrow."

"Thank you."

"Thank you, too. I'm sure you're doing a great job."

"Better than you."

CHAPTER TEN

IT TAKES ME ALL MORNING TO MAKE BROWNIES FOR JASON AND the kids. I've used every bowl in the kitchen. I know my mother's interfering, because I put the wooden spoon on a trivet but when I go to get it, it's beside the mixer. Then the measuring cup falls to the floor and I am not anywhere near it.

I wish you'd stop! It's not like you ever baked me brownies.

Nothing happens after that.

Gramps does me a favour and drives me over to Jason's house so I don't have to get on the bus with a plateful of brownies. He demands two as payment and ruins my presentation. I shut the car door and lean through the open window.

"Thanks. Can you pick me up or shall I take the bus?"

"Get the bus. Ollie and I are heeding your advice and going out to eat and then catching the early show at the cinema."

My mouth drops open. "For real? That's great! What are you going to see?"

"Something called *Bridesmaids*."

My mouth closes. Do not dissuade him. "Have fun."

When I ring the doorbell, Jason shouts from inside, "It's not locked."

I open the door and take in the chaos at my feet. "Shouldn't you find out who's here before you invite them in?"

"You see that stuff on the floor? It's a trap for burglars. I'm in the kitchen."

When I creep through the debris and enter the kitchen, the entire scene is adorable. The place is a mess. The boys are in their highchairs. J. J. is nodding off with a plastic spoon in his fist while Callum stirs yogurt on his tray with his chubby hands. Jason is sitting down between them holding a jar of goop, with a dishcloth flung over his shoulder. He looks like he slept in his clothes.

"What have you got there? Please say it's adult food."

"I'm not sure if the boys are allowed brownies, but I took a chance."

"Never mind the boys. Hand them over."

I unfurl my creation and place the plate on the table in front of him. Jason grabs one and pops it in his mouth. He makes a face.

"What's wrong?"

"You forgot the sugar."

"Damn! Did I?"

"Yep, I'm eating them anyway. Pour me a glass of milk so I can choke these down."

I do as I'm told, but then grab my cell and take a picture of them. "I'm sending this to Amanda so she knows you're okay."

"Does this look okay to you? I can't see out of my glasses because I have snot smeared on them."

"Let me help." I gingerly take them off his head and carry them between my fingertips over to the sink and wash them with hot, soapy water, whereupon I gingerly place them back on his nose.

"Oh, hi, Chloe. I didn't realize it was you."

I sit back at the table. "Amanda misses you three terribly. I've heard her cry sometimes in the bathroom after she's talked to you. How are you managing?"

"We're okay. The boys aren't in daycare because they have colds. I work from home when that happens, not that much goes on until they're tucked in. Look, if you don't mind, I need a wicked piss." He passes me the jar and spoon. "Just put it in his mouth. He knows what to do after that."

Away he goes and I'm left with this child staring at me.

"Hello."

Callum bangs on the tray with both hands.

"Okay, sorry. Here you go."

I put some unknown substance on his spoon and slowly bring it closer to his face. He seems fascinated by this process. I'm afraid I'm going to hurt him so I inch forward and he does the same. We meet very carefully in the middle, and then he grabs the spoon with his teeth and won't let it go.

"Okay, Callum. I need the spoon."

He grins at me while keeping it locked in his teeth and then he shakes his head like a dog with its favourite rag. The only thing I can do is let go of the spoon and watch. He waits for a reaction, but I'm stumped. As long as he doesn't stick it down his throat I'll wait for his father to come back. He senses the game is over and spits out the spoon, so I grab it and offer him something from another jar. He turns his face away from me slowly, like that girl in *The Exorcist*.

When Jason reappears I point at the kid. "Why's he doing that?"

"You've obviously never given a toddler green beans."

"I must introduce him to my Aunt Ollie."

We hear the front door open and a guy shouts, "Jason!"

"In here, man."

Steve appears in the doorway. We both do a double take.

"You're busy," he says. "I can come back."

"No, we're not. You remember Chloe, Amanda's friend. This is my brother-in-law, Steve."

"Hi, Chloe. Nice to see you again."

"You too."

"Sit down, what brings you here? Got the day off?" Jason wipes Callum's face and hands with the dishcloth.

"Yeah."

"While you guys talk, I'll do some dishes," I say.

"You don't have to do that."

"It's no problem." Anything to keep myself busy.

Steve sits down. "I came to pick up the DVD."

"Which one?"

"*Game of Thrones.*"

"It's upstairs. Let me get it for you."

Jason leaves the room while I collect the dishes, and Steve talks to his youngest nephew, since J. J. is out cold.

"Hey there, buddy! High-five." Callum sticks out his hand and high-fives him.

"That is amazing! Did you teach him that?"

"No, his dad, but watch this." He takes out his cellphone. "Find Angry Birds."

The kid takes the phone and swipes the screen a few times, presses a button, and the game pops up. This floors me.

"Do you mean to tell me that babies know how to work these gadgets?"

"Hey, it's in their DNA. They'll never know anything else."

I fill the sink with hot water. "That's sort of scary. It makes me feel old."

"Before Jason gets back...do you want to go out for lunch? I know a greasy spoon that injects fat into their poutine."

This makes me laugh, which is dangerous. "It's probably not a good idea."

"For who?"

"Me, you, Amanda…"

"I'm not taking you to the Ritz-Carlton."

I hear Jason running down the stairs.

"All right."

J. J. wakes up and doesn't see his dad, so he shrieks, but then stops the instant Jason appears.

"Hey Steve, give me a hand with them. They need their diapers changed."

The two big guys and two little guys leave the kitchen and I have room to really go to town. I hate housework, but doing it in someone else's house is less painful. By the time they come back, I've even mopped the floor. I take a picture of it to show Amanda, but then delete it. Show-offs are pathetic.

Jason thanks me profusely. "This makes up for the godawful brownies."

"Good. I should shove off."

"Can I drop you off anywhere, Chloe? It's no problem," Steve says.

"Okay, thanks." I give Jason a kiss. "You're a great guy. Amanda is very lucky."

"Yes. Yes she is."

"See ya, bro."

"Yeah, thanks for the DVD."

Steve is driving a sports car, but don't ask me what kind. He opens the door and I get in. Once he's behind the wheel, he smiles at me.

"This is nice."

"I have the solution to your money problems. Sell the car."

He winces. "Damn. You break my balls every time."

"Just sayin'."

The poutine is to die for. We stuff our faces and talk about absolutely nothing. At one point he reaches over and caresses my hand.

"Don't do that."

"Why not?"

"I don't know where it's been."

"You are the most fascinating woman I've ever met. You say whatever comes into your head regardless of how I might take it."

"You're spending your days doing God-knows-what, to God-knows-who. It's a valid observation."

He slaps the table. "You see what I mean? You state the absolute truth and yet it doesn't feel like an insult."

"What I'm trying to understand is, why you do this. I understand the circumstances that make some people resort to desperate behaviour, but you're not desperate. You can come clean to your family, tell them you lost your job and are seeking another. You can sell your car to hold you over until you receive a salary again. It's not that difficult."

"Other people's problems are easy to solve. Take you, for instance. You want to know what it's like to have sex. I offered to help you—"

"It wasn't out of the goodness of your heart! You cost me four hundred bucks."

"You're right. Why didn't you let me earn it?"

"You're Amanda's brother. And I was hurt by what you said."

"I was completely out of line. Now that I know you, I think you're very special. Any guy with half a brain would snap you up in a minute."

"Take me home, please."

I walk out of the restaurant and stand by his car until he comes out and unlocks it for me. Before I get in he says, "I'll be back in a minute."

He goes off, but before I work up the nerve to jump out, he jumps back in. We don't say anything while he drives me home. When we arrive, Gramps's car is still gone.

"Look, I'm not proud of myself..."

"Shut up, Steve." I lunge over the gearshift, grab his face, and kiss him smack on the mouth. It takes him about half a second to respond in kind. I'm not sure how long we're at it before I realize that Norman, my next-door neighbour, is peering at us through his opera glasses.

"Let's go."

I jump out of the car and Steve follows. My fingers aren't working as I try to unlock my front door. He has to help me. The minute we close the door, my Mary-Ellen is crying for attention. We're waltzing down the hall trying to take each other's clothes off kissing the entire time. He pushes me into the living room.

"No! My dad's chair is in there."

"Okay, where?"

We continue to bounce back and forth off the walls until we reach the next room. "God, no! That's Mom's study."

We go a little farther. "How about in here?" He's kissing my ear when Dad's library door slams shut in front of us.

He looks incredulous. "Holy shit! Did you see that?"

I kiss him back to attention. "It's my father, the ghost. Kiss me."

He kisses me all right and then comes up for air. "Remind me to ask you about this later."

"Okay." Smooch.

"What about your room?"

"Never!"

He turns me around. "There can't be that many places left. "The kitchen?"

"Okay. I never eat in there."

We stumble past the bathroom and hall closet, tripping over our dripping clothes. We get to the kitchen and my mess is all over the kitchen table. "Sorry, I'll clear this up."

He takes his arm and sweeps everything on the floor. "There. Problem solved."

And that's how I lost my cherry: on top of a table covered in flour.

❃

WE'RE DRESSED AND DRINKING COKE AT THE NOW-INFAMOUS kitchen table. We even picked up the dishes and washed them.

"So, how was it? Did you get your money's worth?"

"How would I know? I've never done it before."

He shakes his head. "You have no feminine wiles at all."

"It's a terrible question. If you don't mind, I'd prefer it if you were gone before my grandfather gets home. He's old-fashioned."

"Right."

We both get up from the table.

"I want to give you something first." He reaches into his pocket. "Here's your money back."

"Keep it. You earned it."

He presses it into my hand. "Tonight I was on personal time."

I walk him to the door. He reaches out to touch my chin. "Will I see you again?"

"I honestly don't know."

"Good night, Chloe."

"Good night."

I close the door and wait for him to drive away before I go back out on the porch and sit in my rocking chair. It's a glorious summer evening. The sunset is purple and pink and casts a blush-coloured hue over the street, while the trees are outlined in black against the sky.

Now that I'm a member of the club, do I feel any different? I'm grateful that this is off my to-do list, but I'm not sure what the fuss is all about. Getting to the kitchen table was fun, but once I was on it, it was no great shakes.

Gramps's car drives slowly down the street and turns into the driveway. Once they get out and start up the stairs, I ask them how the movie was.

"It was a riot!" Aunt Ollie laughs.

"What did you think, Gramps?"

"Best snooze I've had in years. By the way, those brownies were crap."

❀

A FEW DAYS LATER IN THE EARLY AFTERNOON I'M BURNING RICE in my kitchen. The smoke alarm goes off and I flap the back door that leads out to my balcony. Aunt Ollie shouts out her kitchen window.

"Is your house on fire?"

"Sorry! The rice burned."

"Health food will kill you. We're having sausages tonight."

"No, thanks."

The phone rings. It's Austin's mother, Harriet.

"Would you like to come over for supper tonight? It's nothing special, but Austin thought you might like some company."

"That's so sweet." I glance at the bottom of my pot, which is black as coal. "I'd love to."

It's only about twenty minutes to get to Markham, where the Hawkes live. I leave a little early so I can pick up some flowers at the supermarket. When I arrive with a bouquet of Shasta daisies, she's thrilled.

"Look at that beautiful pink colour! Thank you, they're lovely. I'll put these in a vase."

We head towards the back of the house. It's an ordinary bungalow style, but the mature trees outside make it feel private on this busy street.

She tends to the flowers and puts them on the dining room table. "Please sit. I'm not sure if Julia is joining us or not. She's a free spirit—or a kook, according to her brother." She disappears and comes back with a large casserole dish. "I made macaroni and cheese. Austin tells me you're a vegetarian, so I thought this might be best."

"You're very kind. It looks delicious."

She fills my plate with cheesy wonder and offers warm tea biscuits and butter, and then sits down and serves herself. "Do you mind if I give thanks?"

"Certainly not." I bow my head.

"Thank you, oh Lord, for these thy gifts we are about to receive. Amen."

After taking my first mouthful, I'm in heaven. "Oh, Mrs. Hawke, this is divine."

"Call me Harriet, dear."

"I can make Kraft Dinner, but that's it."

"You live on your own, then? How old are you?"

"Twenty-five."

"You and Julia are the same age. Tell me, how did your mother get you out of the house? I'm looking for pointers."

"She died."

"Oh sweetheart, I'm sorry, and here I am joking."

"That's okay, you didn't know. My dad died on the same day. It was an accident."

She stops eating. "Oh, you blessed child. How old were you?"

"Fifteen."

Harriet's reaches over and covers my hand with her own. "That's dreadful. What a brave young woman you are. I hope I haven't upset you."

"Not at all."

"Let's talk about happier things."

That's how I find out that Austin cried on his first day of school and every day after that for a week. He'd bring home stray cats only to find that they belonged to the neighbours. He had a dog-walking business in junior high that was quite lucrative, and his dream is to go to Africa and see mountain gorillas.

The back screen door opens and Julia comes to the dining room looking like a street kid.

"What's for dinner? Oh, hi, Chloe! I was going to call you."

She spoons some dinner on a plate and sits with us. "Your music critic came to the club and he liked my stuff. He gave me the name of a few people he knows and I've picked up a couple of gigs through them."

"I'm so glad to hear it."

"Just having those names and numbers is like gold. It's the people you know who make a difference in whether you get discovered."

"I wish I could sing like you do. If you ever get a record deal, I will be first in line."

"I'll hold you to that. Sorry I have to eat and run, but I have to rehearse. See ya." She takes her plate of food and disappears downstairs.

"Austin and Julia are like chalk and cheese, as you may have noticed."

"Austin told me."

"Did he, now? He tends to keep things private."

"Austin is a great guy. I hope he picks the right girl."

She quickly looks down at her plate. "I hope he does, too."

CHAPTER ELEVEN

WHEN I STEP ON DR. MCDERMOTT'S SCALE AT THE END OF TWO weeks, I've gained seven pounds. He's pleased.

"You have colour in your cheeks, and you're sleeping better. Keep this up. Your period should kick in when you gain another five to seven pounds. If it doesn't, come to see me. Remember, good food, walk every day, and do some strength training to fill out those skinny arms. Being strong is being healthy."

I'm very proud of myself, despite the fact that I had to buy new pots and pans. At least I'm feeding myself.

The gang is back from Calgary, and I can't wait to see everyone, but I give them the weekend off so the locals can see their families and take some downtime. I visit the girls who are back at the mansion. Since Sarah F. was the latest casualty, there's only Jocelyn, Lizette, Kate P., Sarah C., Jennifer P., and Sandy W. left. All the troublemakers are gone. It's time to get serious. In my gut, I think Jocelyn and Lizette will be the finalists, and I believe that's sinking in with the other girls, even though they won't admit it.

I join them out on the patio as they have lunch. "Did you miss me?"

"No!" they laugh.

"You look really good," Jocelyn says.

Lizette passes me the chips and dip. "Eat up."

"Thank you." I shovel the chip through the dip. "How did Amanda do?"

"She was great," Jennifer says. "Always got to the bus on time, unlike *someone* I can mention."

Sandy nods while looking at her cellphone. "And we weren't held up waiting for you to come back from the emergency department of every town we went to."

"Gee, thanks."

My room at the guest house hasn't been touched since I went on sick leave. I'm tidying up my belongings when I hear a car pull up. It's Austin's Mini, so I stick my head out the window.

"What are you doing here? Go home and see your mother!"

"Hi, Chloe." He waves and disappears, and then I hear him thumping up the stairs, so I walk out of my room into the hallway.

"Good to see you," I smile.

He comes right over and gives me a hug. "Let me look at you. It's amazing! You look fresh as a daisy."

"It's miraculous what good food and rest will do."

We grin at each other. It occurs to me that he looks changed from the man who took care of Norton almost two months ago. "Are you all right?"

"I'm tired, but that comes with the job. Reality's a bitch."

"Why are you here? You're not due back until Monday."

"There are no groceries in my apartment, and it's hot and stuffy from being locked up for so long."

"So go to your mom's."

"Julia and I had an argument. It's easier to be here."

"Are you hungry? We could go out to eat and visit the kittens afterwards."

Now he gives me the smile I remember. "Sounds great."

We end up going down to the Harbourfront, where we buy bagged lunches and head to HTO Park to sit in the sandpit on

Muskoka chairs under enormous yellow metal umbrellas. We look out over the water enjoying the cool breeze, eating our egg salad sandwiches, and drinking lemonade.

"Have you and your sister always been at odds?"

"No. Julia's great when she's not taking advantage of mom, who works hard for her money. She should get a real job and contribute, instead of singing in bars sporadically."

"But you did what you wanted to do. Why shouldn't she?"

Austin takes a gulp from his bottle. "Point taken."

"I totally missed you when I came home."

"I missed you too."

"You guys feel like family now. It's a nice feeling." I smile.

He glances at me and then turns his head and looks out over the water, so I get a chance to watch him. He really is someone you could take home to your parents and they'd be happy about it.

"Now that you're halfway through this crazy journey, are you sorry you did it?"

"I'm not sorry that I met some great people and travelled the country, but if I had to do it over again, I wouldn't. I'd rather meet someone at work or be set up by a friend. That way Trey and Jerry wouldn't argue everywhere I go and Brian wouldn't film my every move. I'm not looking forward to watching myself kiss girls on television."

"Between you and me, are you in love? And who is she?"

"I am in love, but I'm not telling who with. You're as bad as Julia. She never stops yapping about who I should pick."

"I think it's Jocelyn, she's perfect."

"What if I don't want perfect?"

"You'd be a fool. Who doesn't want that?"

He doesn't answer, and I leave it be. "It's getting hot. Let's go see Norton's brood."

"Good idea," he says.

Aunt Ollie and Gramps hardly let Austin in the door before they're pumping him for free veterinarian advice. Austin doesn't seem to mind.

Peanut is in my arms. "This is the one you saved. Just imagine if you hadn't been here, this little life might never have had a chance. It's so admirable, your choice of profession. When I was a little girl I wanted to have a pet, but Mom said no."

"She was mean," Aunt Ollie tells Austin.

I'm taken aback. "Don't say that."

"It's the truth." Gramps nods.

"Don't talk about my mother like that. She's not here to defend herself. We have to go." I put Peanut down and leave their house and enter my own.

Austin is a few moments behind me. "Chloe!"

This anger is consuming me. "Maybe Mom was mean, but she didn't deserve to die a horrible death, and I still miss her. I don't care if she was bat-shit crazy; a lousy parent is still better than no parent at all."

Tears fall from my eyes and there's nothing I can do about it. Austin stays close but doesn't touch me. That's probably something he learned in vet school. Don't approach the anxious animal, just keep calm and it will feed on that energy. It works, because soon I want to hug him. He puts his arms around me protectively, but not tightly. That makes me cling to him. He doesn't tell me to *stop* or *shush*. He leaves me be.

"Come sit."

We go to the couch and I lean against his shoulder. "I always feel better when you're around."

"Thank you. I feel the same way."

"You feel better when you're around too?" I smile up at him. He leans forward and kisses me. Austin and I are kissing. What the heck is going on? He and I are on this couch and I've got my fingers in his hair and he's kissing my broken nose. I'm about to object but Mary-Ellen tells me to stay put. Mercifully, the constant tickertape of my inner voice grinds to a halt, and I'm in this moment that I've never experienced before, when the world gets smaller and smaller and the only people in it are Austin and me.

And Aunt Ollie.

"Chloe?" she shouts from the front door.

My extra seven pounds come in handy. I push Austin away from me with more force than I intended and jump up, smoothing down my clothes and hair. Then one more leap gets me into my father's recliner across the room. Austin stays on the couch looking slightly stunned.

Aunt Ollie shows up at the living room entrance. "Are you mad at me?"

"Not anymore."

"Okay then." Out she goes.

As soon as the front door closes, I run back to the couch and we pick up where we left off. So *this* is how good necking and fooling around and other dangerous things feel: so good I don't ever want them to stop. I'm beginning to understand this obsession with lovemaking.

Until I remember who I am and who he is.

I wiggle away and get to my feet. "I have no idea what just happened, but this has to stop instantly! I'm going to lose my job! Someone will find out and Mr. Gardner will string me up. There are millions of dollars riding on this. You have to propose to Jocelyn and live happily ever after. There's nothing else to be done!"

He puts up his hands. "Calm down."

"Sorry I pushed you, by the way, when Aunt Ollie showed up. I didn't mean it."

"Chloe, I've been dying to say this to you. Ever since we met—"

I literally run out of the room and run down the hall. "I'm not listening!"

Now he chases after me. "What are you doing, you crazy fool?"

I'm so freaked at this point I jump on a kitchen chair and then hop on another one when he comes closer. "I don't want you to talk—I don't want to hear—"

"You don't even know what I'm going to say."

"I do. And before you say it, I forgot to tell you I have a boyfriend."

He stops and so do I.

"He's an art gallery owner."

"You never mentioned him."

"I'm your boss."

"Is it serious?"

"It's ongoing, if that's what you mean."

"Do you love him?"

"That's implied."

He looks annoyed. "Why can't you ever answer a question outright?"

"Sorry, I'm a bit flustered. Please don't be upset with me because then I'll forget to eat."

He looks like he wants to shake me but he doesn't. "I'm not mad at you."

"You're a wonderful kisser, by the way."

"So are you."

My ears perk up. "I am?"

"No one ever tell you that before? Your boyfriend never mentioned it?"

"He's reserved."

He puts his hands through his hair, the gesture of frustration that I've come to know. "I'd better go. Thanks for the great day. I'll see you on Monday."

He turns and walks down the long hallway to the front door. I scramble after him.

"So what do we do now? How do we behave? This was a momentary slip, so we shouldn't let it affect our relationship because I do think you're wonderful…"

His hand is on the doorknob when he faces me. "You figure out what you want to do and let me know. Obviously my opinion doesn't matter to you. You have a very bad habit of not listening to anyone but yourself, so I hope you know what you're doing." He shuts the door.

Aunt Ollie's offer of a grilled cheese sandwich for supper is declined.

Amanda calls me later that night. "Jason tells me you were a godsend the day you came over and cleaned the kitchen for him."

"It was nothing."

"Believe me, when you're a parent, those kinds of gifts mean the most."

"Have you had a nice weekend?"

"The boys are adorable and the sex has been great. I don't want to go to Quebec."

"Too much information."

"Jason tells me Steve drove you home that day. So you're not holding a grudge after all?"

"Sorry Amanda, I have to go. Someone's at the door."

"See you at the airport!"

There's no one at the door, of course. The house feels very empty.

❋

LE CHATEAU FRONTENAC AND OLD QUEBEC CITY ARE ENCHANT-ing. It looks like we're back in eighteenth-century France, with narrow cobbled streets and courtyards flanked by stone row houses with leaded windows. You can take tours on horse-drawn carriages of the surrounding landscape and see sites like the Plains of Abraham, with the mighty St. Lawrence River meandering below. Standing high on a bluff, the hotel is an historic landmark. I've always thought it could have been used as Hogwarts in the Harry Potter movies.

We plan on being in Quebec City for four days. Brian and the guys take miles of film the first day because everywhere you look, there's something beautiful to look at. Austin and his dates will go to the Citadelle de Québec, a massive fortification that sits above the city and also to one of the oldest churches in Quebec, Notre-Dame Basilica-Cathedral. The *funiculaire*, a little cable car on rails poised on an inclined plane that connects the upper and lower part of the old city, is adjacent to Le Chateau Frontenac. Amanda and I go up and down a few times, but just wandering around Place Royale and Le Petit Champlain, a street of fabulous restaurants and shops, is enchanting.

Trey and I catch up over the magnificent breakfast buffet in the dining room, as he heaps his plate and waxes poetic about the food.

"Look at this apple butter, Trey. Have you tried it?"

His mouth is full. "No, I'm too busy sucking up this maple syrup. I can't believe we're staying here, I thought for sure the CBC wouldn't spring for it."

"We're doing the charm ceremonies on the balcony, so it's mutually beneficial."

My plate holds only fruit. Trey looks horrified. "We are at the Chateau Frontenac, one of the best dining experiences in the world. Please tell me you're going to eat more than that."

"I'm not hungry today."

"You're the second person to say that. Austin didn't want much either. If you ask me, he's running out of gas. He's definitely not the same fellow that started this, but he puts up a good front on camera."

Austin and I are wary of each other. We're polite, but we busy ourselves by talking to others, although he often glances at me and I confess I do the same.

Brian is filming Austin and Lizette in a horse-drawn carriage at noon. Amanda and I are in a carriage behind them.

Amanda asks the driver, "Can you get closer to the carriage ahead of us?"

"Not too close, mademoiselle. The horse, she kick."

"Can you go by them?"

The driver flicks his thin whip in the air, and the horse picks up speed. The other driver takes it as a good-natured challenge. We pull up next to them, horses clopping in sync. Amanda waves and Lizette shouts at their driver to go quicker. "*Plus rapide!*"

"I knew she'd do that!" Amanda laughs. "She is so competitive."

Their carriage takes off and we are left behind. Our driver is more sensible. We soon lose sight of them.

"What did you do that for?"

"I'm bored. I feel the need for speed."

"You are full of beans."

Amanda claps her hands. "I've got it! Remember, we needed another segment. Why don't we find a place with go-karts, and the girls can chase Austin around a track? Lizette will show off big-time, and it will be fun. I love go-karts."

"I've never done it."

Amanda goes off to organize, and I make the mistake of coming through the lobby, where I see Trey and Jerry arguing in the middle of the ornate carpet. Guests are walking around them, trying to reach the front desk.

"Could you two come with me for a moment?" They follow me to an out-of-the-way corner.

"What on earth is going on? You're making a spectacle of yourselves."

"I cannot be responsible for making sure all his luggage gets on a trolley," Jerry says. "I have enough baggage of my own."

"So what am I supposed to wear at tonight's charm ceremony? The airline still hasn't found my bags. I am the host. What you wear makes no difference. You're fiddling with lights."

"You're always lording it over me, the fact that you're the host. What the hell do you do other than say *Austin, when you're ready?*"

"I resent that."

"I don't give a flying f—"

My eyes widen. "Shhhh! This is a classy place."

"I don't need this agro." Jerry storms off towards the elevators.

"If it was *his* suit, he'd be upset."

"Would you like a cup of tea, Trey?"

We order tea and crumpets and sit in the lounge by the large window. It's amazing how calming tea can be. Trey is an interesting person when you get to know him.

"How long have you and Jerry been together?"

"Fifteen years."

"How have you managed to last that long?"

"When you find the right person, you don't let them go."

"You do nothing but argue."

"We disagree. There's a difference."

"Wouldn't it be better to be...calmer?"

"You're young, Miss Sparrow. One day you'll know passion."

"I'm going to be an old maid like my aunt."

Trey laughs as he pours us another cup of tea. "I see the way men look at you."

"They do?"

He holds his teacup in the air. "Are you pulling my leg? If you end up alone, it's all down to you."

"What do you mean?"

"You obviously don't see yourself as others see you."

"To be quite candid, Trey, when you've lived alone for most of your life, you tend to disappear."

"Well, my advice is to keep your eyes open."

CHAPTER TWELVE

Everyone is excited about Amanda's idea to race go-karts. We head over on a bus in the late afternoon. One of the keys to making this show interesting is to film our cast at different times of the day. It's visually more appealing with the occasional sunset in the background.

We set up, our camera guys at different angles along the course. It's been decided that whoever beats Austin to the finish line is the girl who gets tomorrow's date. We haven't told them that they'll be bungee jumping.

As predicted, Lizette is ahead around the first corner, but Austin is no pushover as he catches up to her, Jocelyn on his tail. Jennifer, Kate, Sarah, and Sandy flounder behind them. Thankfully there's only one each now, but from behind they look the same with their flowing dark hair. All of these girls are beautiful. No wonder Austin kept them around. As I watch him zooming around the track, I'm not sure if I like that.

In the end there's a huge upset. Jocelyn beats everyone to the finish line and Lizette is fuming. This was her chance to show off and it backfired. She stalks off and gets back in the bus, the other girls having a giggle at her expense.

Once the important shooting is done, the crew begs to have a turn. It's getting late and it's been a long day, but what the heck. Brian's like a little kid tearing around the track, and Trey and Jerry have me in stitches with their antics. Amanda is a madwoman, cackling into the wind when she passes the guys.

"Get out here, Sparrow! Don't be a chicken!"

It does look like fun. I attempt to put my helmet on, but I'm doing something wrong with the clasp. Austin comes over and adjusts it for me.

"You've never been in a go-kart?"

"I don't get—"

"Yes, I know."

Once I'm off, I take a few turns around the track to acclimatize myself to the feel of the cart. This is so much fun! Brian and Trey come up behind and pass me on either side.

I shake my fist in the air. "Curses!"

Jerry and I are the slow pokes, but for the first time in a long time, I'm enjoying myself. Amanda shouts, "Outta the way!"

She bumps me from behind, and my cart smashes into the tires piled up along the sides, flips over, and scrapes along the track before finally stopping. I'm upside down.

Honest to God.

Austin gets to me first.

"A I bweeding?"

"Uh, yeah, stay down."

Fade to black.

❦

IN THE HOSPITAL EMERGENCY ROOM, THEY TELL ME I HAVE A concussion, a broken right wrist, a broken pinkie finger on my left hand, whiplash, and a very swollen tongue. Apparently I bit it, and now it's hanging out of my mouth like I'm a panting dog. Amanda has been crying ever since we got here, so she's been no comfort at all.

When they release me, a nurse pushes me in a wheelchair to the hospital door, whereupon Austin and Brian help me into the rented car, Amanda still snivelling behind me. I'd like to tell her to knock it off, but I can't talk without drooling. I'm tired, achy, and thoroughly miserable. Brian carries me up to my room, and Amanda stays with me. Austin asks if there's anything I need. I close my eyes and he kisses my forehead. "Try and get some rest."

I hear the others crowded around my door. Trey, Jerry, and the girls call out that they'll see me in the morning and hope I feel better.

Amanda takes my hand. "It kills me to say this, but you need to go home, Chloe. You can't stay here alone, and we'll be gone all day. I've arranged for a driver to take you back. We'll recline your seat and you can sleep. A few days' rest and you'll be as good as new."

Two big tears fall down my cheeks.

"I'll never forgive myself for this," she says.

I'll never forgive you, either.

When I arrive back home, Gramps is furious. "We're suing! Do you hear me? Suing!"

Even Aunt Ollie's hot under the collar. "The CBC is negligent, as far as I'm concerned. You've been practically killed for this show. What are they going to do about it? You need a bodyguard. You need protection. I'm sick of seeing you look like a war victim."

My aunt and grandfather open their arms and give me a big hug.

❀

BATHING WITH A CAST AND A COLLAR ON IS NO PICNIC. AT LEAST the collar comes off, but at a price. On top of that my cast is itchy, so every hour or so I shove a sharp knife into it and scrape away skin cells. When there is evidence of blood I stop.

My tongue looks like a slab of canned corn beef. I'm alternating soaking it in a bowl of warm water and baking soda and sucking on the Popsicles Gramps picked up for me. Both help, but I still talk like someone's strangling me.

Lunch consists of yogurt. Damn Amanda. What if I'd broken my neck?

Even though I can't talk properly, Amanda calls to let me know that Jocelyn survived the bungee jump, and Austin let Jennifer go. All the departures are difficult now, for everyone.

A day later, just when I'm feeling very low, I get a call asking me to come to Mr. Gardner's office. I have a bad feeling about this and try to protect myself. *I wish to not cry in Mr. Gardner's office.*

Gramps drives me downtown. "Do you want me to come in with you?"

I shake my head.

"I'll be waiting right here, unless some traffic cop decides to be a jerk. In that case, I'll keep circling the block."

I'm about to get out of the car when he grabs my hand. "Don't take any shit off this bastard, ya hear me?"

I nod.

The elevator whisks me to Mr. Gardner's floor. His personal assistant picks up the phone and tells her boss I'm here. She hangs up. "You can go right in."

My cast keeps interfering with my ability to turn a doorknob, but I eventually get it. The door swings open and Mr. Gardner rises from his chair. So does Amanda.

This I wasn't expecting. I thought she was still in Quebec City.

"Sit down, Chloe."

I take a seat next to Amanda, who looks embarrassed and refuses to meet my eyes.

"How are you feeling, Chloe?" Mr. Gardner asks.

"...ood."

"This is very difficult to say the least," he begins. "You've had an incredible string of bad luck lately and we feel terrible about that, but in the end this is a business. I can't keep you on the show any longer, not with you incapacitated like this. You can't speak properly and we're coming up to a very busy and important time in the schedule, with the family visits and orchestrating the final episodes. Amanda has agreed to take over. I think you'll concur that she did a great job in Alberta while you were under the weather."

If he's waiting for me to nod my head, he's out of luck. Mr. Gardner and Amanda exchange glances and Amanda turns to me.

"You know how badly I feel about all this. When Mr. Gardner asked me to step in I was reluctant because this is your show, but in light of the circumstances, I want to do the very best job I can so you'll be proud of the final product."

My wish comes true. No tears, just a volcano of hate.

Mr. Gardner clears his throat. "When you recover, you'll be back at your desk doing the great job you always do. We're extremely lucky to have your talent here at the CBC."

I stand up. "I...uit."

Amanda jumps out of her chair in a panic. "Chloe, you can't quit! This is just a temporary setback!"

"Don't be hasty, Chloe," Mr. Gardner frowns. "You're being unprofessional."

Since I can't say what I want to say clearly, I won't bother. I walk out the door. Amanda comes after me, so I turn around and hold my arm out to stop her. She gets the message. I take the elevator down to my floor and go to my desk. People I work with are about to approach me, but when I glare at them, they back off. It doesn't stop them from whispering to each other.

There are very few things I need to take with me. I gather up my picture of Norton, my coffee cup, a stapler, some gel pens, and a pair of slippers I keep under my desk. One of my colleagues approaches and hands me an empty wastepaper basket to put my belongings in—a good idea, since I have two bum hands. The last thing I add is my nasty sweater that's been hanging off my chair all summer.

I walk out the door and don't look back. Gramps is where he said he'd be, and when he sees me coming with the wastepaper basket, he hops out of the car and takes it from me, opening my door so I can get in.

When he joins me in the front seat he looks at me. "Fuck them."

We drive away.

❈

AUNT OLLIE BRINGS NORTON AND THE KITTENS OVER TO SEE me sometimes—all except Bobby, who refuses to be moved from Gramps's lap. It turns out the male is the biggest baby of the three. They are very sweet, but since I'm not much fun to be with, they always howl at the front door to go back home. So now I don't have cats, a job, or a friend.

I've been in bed since the day I quit. My cell has buzzed, rung, sung, peeped, tingled, and lit up ever since I left the CBC building. It's now under my parents' mattress so I can't hear it. Aunt Ollie reports that various people have tried to reach me through them, but Gramps keeps telling them to go to hell. For the first time in my life my relatives are putting my needs ahead of their own. I'll appreciate it for however long it lasts.

Aunt Ollie whips up scrambled eggs and bowls of pudding, but mostly relies on ice cream to fill me.

She also makes me go see Dr. McDermott. This maternal spurt of hers is just another form of bossiness. Gramps drives me over and says he'll nap in the car until I'm finished.

"You've lost five pounds."

"It shtill hurtsth when I ee."

"Headaches?"

"Yeth."

"Do you feel dozy or irritable?"

"Yeth."

"That's from the concussion. The symptoms might linger. Your aunt tells me you quit your job. I don't want you getting down in the dumps about this, Chloe, because that will make things worse. Drink your protein drink and milkshakes. I want you to take a good multi-vitamin. You have to look after yourself. I want you to come see me on a regular basis."

Soon cards and letters start coming through the mail slot from Mr. Gardner, Amanda, Austin, Trey, Jerry, Brian, Jocelyn, Lizette, Kate, Sandy, and Sarah. Now that my tongue is better, I curse as I gather them up and throw them in my CBC waste-paper basket. Maybe someday I'll set them on fire.

As the days pass, *The Single Guy* cast and crew become entwined in my mind into one super entity that has given me nothing but heartache since the beginning. If I think of one person, it inevitably leads to thinking of someone else, and I refuse to dwell on any of them anymore—except to say that Amanda stole my job, which is what she wanted from the beginning, and Austin flirts with me but keeps his arms wrapped around other women.

I wish for Austin to kick off Jocelyn and Lizette.

There. Why make things easy for any of them.

Flowers start to arrive, one bunch after another. This must be the new strategy to make me remember them. Austin sends me roses, there are pink Shasta daisies from Austin's mother Harriet, a huge bouquet from Amanda, an edible arrangement from Trey and Jerry, and a cactus from Brian. His note says *To use as a weapon on CBC employees.* Good old Brian.

The very next day another bouquet arrives at the door. Steve is holding it.

"Did Amanda send you?"

"No. She doesn't know we're friends."

"Is that what we are?"

"I'd like to think so. May I come in?"

I don't care if he does or not, so I leave the door open and walk into the living room. He follows me and puts the flowers on the glass, gold-framed coffee table that was old-fashioned when my mother was alive. I recline on Dad's chair.

"You look like shit, Chloe."

"Thanks. Your opinion means a lot."

"I obviously heard what happened through family gossip. I'm sorry it turned out this way."

"I'm sure Amanda is enjoying herself, so that's all that matters."

"I spoke with Jason. She's having a hard time."

"My heart bleeds. So what are you up to these days, Ramon?"

"This and that."

I shake my head at him. "So you haven't quit your day job."

"But you did. Why?"

"That's none of your business."

"Okay. Would you like to go to our German bakery?"

At the moment I'm wearing rags. "No."

"Why don't I go and bring some goodies back here?"

It's not like I have anything else to do. When he returns we stuff our faces in the living room, because I don't want to eat at the kitchen table. Then I sit back in the recliner and promptly fall asleep. When I wake up he's gone, the remnants of our meal cleaned up.

That's the kind of visit I can handle. He leaves a note. *I won't come again unless you call me.*

Steve gets it.

❊

IT'S NOW SEPTEMBER, WHICH MEANS THE SHOW HAS WRAPPED. Not that I'm interested, but it does explain the fact that Austin is walking down the street towards me as I sit in my rocking chair on the porch. My energy level is pretty low these days, so I don't stomp off, which he seems to take as a good sign. He walks up the steps and sits on the last one.

"Hi, Chloe. It's good to see you."

"Hi."

"I've been worried about you."

"Whatever for?"

"Your cast is off. That must be a relief."

"Not really. I found it handy for whacking unwanted visitors."

"Why are you mad at me?"

Time to look offended. "I'm not mad at you."

"Yes, you are. You're this lovely girl one minute, and then a prickly pear the next. I never know where I stand with you."

He's awfully cute at the moment, with his jeans and sky-blue sweater, but I can't let that distract me. "Perhaps my multiple injuries have put me in a bad mood. Or maybe it's because you're the single guy and I hate everything related to that show."

His grey-green eyes light up—with irritation, I'm guessing.

"I haven't done a damn thing to deserve this. My only role has been to pick you up and dust you off from one disaster after another. Do you ever wonder why these things happen to you?"

Ignore him.

"Chloe, you're so busy keeping everyone at arm's length and so preoccupied with controlling the universe, the gods have to do something to get your attention."

"I resent that."

"You can resent it all you want. I'm going to give you a little medical advice. The more rigid you are, the worse the break. This is true for all species. You have to give a little. Stop lifting the world on your shoulders and then barking at the people who can help you lighten the load."

"Listen here. I've held up my world by myself for as long as I can remember and I've done a damn good job. I don't need anyone helping me, and I certainly don't need you to tell me what I should and shouldn't feel. What do *you* know? Your wonderful mother has made your life perfect. It's not so easy for some of us. You think I wouldn't love a mother like that? Why do *you* deserve her, and not me? Why do I even care what you think? You've spent the last three months breaking hearts. I won't let you break mine. I don't need you. I don't need anyone."

I march into the house and slam the door and then stomp up the stairs. My canopy bed and black walls are waiting for me. Now I slam my bedroom door and get under my blankets.

I wish Austin would leave me alone.

❁

THE NEXT DAY THE DOORBELL RINGS. I THINK IT'S THE GERMAN bakery delivering my fattening food, but when I open the door, Amanda is there, looking pale with dark circles under her eyes.

"Please let me in. Please. We need to talk."

"No, we don't."

"I know you hate me—"

"I don't hate you."

"Then why won't you pick up the phone?"

"I have nothing to say."

"Aren't you the least bit interested about what happened at the end of the show?"

"No."

She stamps her foot. "Stop it, Chloe! I've been punished enough."

Aunt Ollie sticks her head out of her front door. "What's going on?"

Amanda gathers herself. "I'm here to talk to Chloe, if you don't mind."

"I do mind, you sanctimonious bitch."

Amanda turns bright red. "You have no right to talk to me like that."

"I can say what I damn well please. Now get off this porch and leave my niece alone. You CBC people have done nothing but hurt her. Get goin' before I get my broom."

Amanda gives me a shocked look.

I shrug.

Down the stairs she goes and hurries over to her car, driving away without looking at us.

"Good riddance to bad rubbish." Aunt Ollie disappears back into her house and I disappear back into mine.

❊

I'VE DISCOVERED EATING FATTENING FOOD IS A WOMAN'S BEST friend. What started as an attempt to gain back the weight I lost has turned into a mission. I've gone from no appetite, to nothing but. All I think about is food, and none of it is healthy. Gramps and Aunt Ollie don't care what I chomp on.

I'm over at their place in late September. The air is chilly and it's getting dark earlier. The dark and I are good friends. I'm comfortable with black. Tonight we're having Chinese food we ordered in. My fortune cookie says *A diamond is a hunk of coal that stuck with it.*

Rubbish.

"Have you thought about getting another job?" Gramps puffs on his pipe.

"No."

"What are you going to live on?"

"I have money."

"I'm not used to seeing you mope around. Usually you never sit still."

"I haven't had a rest in ten years. I'm taking a little time off, okay? Good night."

Once I'm back in my house, I go to bed. The next morning I get out of bed and scream. The frayed sheets are covered in blood. For a millisecond I think someone attacked me with a knife, and then I remember my long lost friend. After changing the sheets, I celebrate by going back to bed.

I stay there for three months.

CHAPTER THIRTEEN

IT'S NOW JANUARY, AUNT OLLIE TELLS ME. I DON'T REMEMBER Christmas, but we never do much celebrating anyway. This is a new year and I'm a new person. I'm addicted to sleep, food, and reality television.

This would blow my mind if I could care, but I can't muster up the energy to care. I spend entire days watching shows I've always dismissed with contempt. I'm now emotionally invested in people trying to lose three hundred pounds in six weeks, or looking for a wedding dress, or being a New Jersey housewife. Mothers who subject their babies to beauty pageants fascinate me. Why are they all fat? Being a Gypsy seems like a lot of fun, until they get married. *The Amazing Race* is amazing; *Survivor* isn't but I still watch it. Mob wives terrify me and boy can they curse.

Then there are the talk shows that are actually paternity clinics, and others where people come to confess their sins and thoroughly enjoy it. I boo at bad people and clap when they're fixed before the end of the show. Now I get the fascination. When you have no life of your own, you live it through the television set. These people are your friends when you have no friends.

However, there is one show that premieres this month that I do not plan to watch. Every time a commercial for it comes on, I change the channel.

My hair grew while I was sleeping. I'm now a terrier with pierced ears, but bedhead is sexy, so I don't have to do a thing to it. The buttons on my pyjamas have gaps of skin between them, which is rather unsightly, but I'm the only one who sees them. At least, I am until the day Dr. McDermott shows up at my door. Wait till I get my hands on Aunt Ollie.

"You look terrible," he says.

"Thank you."

"You were supposed to come and see me." He grabs my wrist and takes my pulse in the porch before he escorts me into the living room and opens his ancient leather doctor's bag. This bag has fascinated me for years. It seems to have no bottom, and its contents are always different from visit to visit. He listens to my heart, takes my blood pressure—boring things that don't mean anything.

"Go get your scale."

"No."

He points at the door, so I go and get it. Once I'm on it, he grunts, but I don't bother looking. It doesn't mean anything.

"Did you get your period yet?"

"Yes. Now I wish it would go away."

"You've packed on twenty pounds, and this is where it ends. You need to exercise and turn this new heft into muscle, not fat."

When I don't respond, he looks at me from under his bushy eyebrows. "Did you hear me?"

"Maybe."

Now he gets his pad out. "I'm sending you for more blood work, we'll check your hormone levels, and I'll arrange for an MRI, just to make sure that noggin of yours is functioning properly. Concussions can have lasting effects."

When I don't respond, he looks at me from under his bushy eyebrows. "Did you hear me?"

"Maybe."

"I'm also sending you to a psychiatrist. You're exhibiting symptoms of depression, and I want to nip it in the bud before you spiral downward."

"That's already happened."

"You'll find another job. A girl with your talent and education would be an asset to any company."

"I'm not going back to work."

He eyes me. "Ever?"

"If I'm careful, I can live on my inheritance. And someday, God forbid, I'll sell Gramps's house and make another pile of money, so I don't need to go anywhere forever and ever."

He passes me the prescription. "Amen."

❧

OUT OF NOWHERE, AUNT OLLIE SAYS, "I'M STARTING MY OWN book club."

"You don't read books."

"I would if I had a minute to myself."

"Who will join you?"

"Are you insinuating I have no friends?"

"No...but do you?"

"That's neither here nor there. You become friends after you join."

Norton stretches on my lap as I rub her neck. "Do you have a favourite book?"

"I liked *Anne of Green Gables*."

"Anything more recent?"

"*Nancy Drew*."

"Great idea, Aunt Ollie. Have a blast."

"You could join the club."

"I could, but I probably won't."

She frowns. "You're turning into me, and you're too young to do that."

Later that night, while I watch *Ice Truckers*, my cell rings. I took it out of its hiding spot long ago and deleted the texts and voicemails before I looked at them. Now no one calls, and that's the way I like it, so I'm reluctant to pick it up.

It's Steve. "I got tired of waiting for you to call me. I miss you."

"How can you miss me? You're not my boyfriend. You can't say you miss me like we have a relationship."

"We do. We eat together."

"I'm not allowed to eat anymore."

"You sound tired."

"I'm tired of everything."

"I have the solution. Come away with me."

"Where?"

"You choose. Anywhere you'd like to go."

"Jamaica."

"I'll make the arrangements."

"Don't you dare. I'm kidding."

"Just for a week. You can lie on a beach and I'll rub suntan oil on your back."

"Suntan oil is a big no-no. Sunscreen is better."

"Your wish is my command."

"Don't. You have no idea how powerful wishes can be. So what have you been up to?"

"I have a new job. Advertising. Boring stuff."

"Still, it's a start."

"What about you, Chloe? Are you working?"

"No."

"If you ever need to get out, call me. Promise?"

"Okay."

"Take care, Chloe."

After we hang up I think about that. I have no one to take care of.

❁

IT'S WHILE I'M WATCHING TWO TEAMS OF HYSTERICAL BAKERS have a butter meltdown that I realize I want my own car. I do know how to drive, I just haven't. At this point in my life I don't care about the environment. The world is going to end because human beings are so revoltingly terrible to this planet and my not driving won't tip the scales.

I mention it to Gramps. "Can I take your car for a drive? I want to refresh my memory."

He looks concerned. "I'm not sure about that."

"I took driver's ed, unlike you, who learned in a field when you were seven."

Aunt Ollie comes into the kitchen with a load of laundry to fold. She dumps it on the table and the three of us pick at it. For some reason, I love folding laundry. The warmth of the clothes feels nice against my chest.

"Chloe wants to take my car for a drive. What do you think?"

"I think you should go with her in case something happens."

"I'm not sure that's a good idea. It'll make me nervous."

"No, Ollie's right. I'll go with you."

Aunt Ollie pretends to have a heart attack. "I'm right? Merciful God, will wonders never cease."

This old station wagon reeks of tobacco. There's a huge stain of nicotine directly over my head. Strange that I never noticed it before, but then I've never paid much attention to the inside of this car. Gramps starts grumbling when I mention the stink.

"Never bothered you before."

The gizmo to bring the seat forward doesn't work until I force matters and end up squeezed against the wheel.

"Now you broke it. You have to be gentle with it. I'll never get it back in the right place."

I turn the heater on and get a blast of cold air. "Doesn't the heater work? This is the air conditioner, which we don't need in January in Canada."

"You need it in the summer."

Now I turn on the radio. Nothing but static. "Gramps, how old is this car?"

"I can't remember."

It starts to snow halfway down the block. At a red light I try to locate the windshield wiper switch, but I turn on the lights, turn signals, and defroster instead.

"What are you doing?" Gramps yells.

Cars beep behind me when the light turns green. I can hardly see, but I put my foot on the gas, whereupon the car backfires, a plume of dark smoke pouring out the back. Undaunted, I take one more stab at a dial and the wipers start, but they only reach halfway up the window, rubber strips hanging off them precariously. They scrape the glass every time they move.

"Why haven't you fixed this?"

"I was going to."

Two cars pass by and both drivers point at my back end with exasperation. "What are they pointing at?"

"Don't know. Someone did that to me the other day."

So I pull into the nearest gas station to get out and look. Gramps joins me. "Something's missing, probably the tailpipe. Ask the young guy to come outside and help us."

The young guy confirms Gramps's diagnosis.

"Is that bad?"

"Yeah, didn't you notice the engine sounded louder?"

"No."

He points at the tires. "These are in pretty rough shape, and they're low to boot. You should put some air in them."

"How do I do that?"

He points to what I gather is an air pump. "Sorry, I have customers." He jogs back to the station, leaving us to our own devices. It can't be that hard, surely. Gramps looks like he knows what he's doing. He rummages in the glove compartment. "I don't have a tire gauge. Go in and ask for one."

The snow is falling fast and furious and I'm not dressed properly, but I retrieve a tire gauge and give it to Gramps. He checks the tires and then takes the hose and puts air in them. "I think we'll be okay now."

I give back the tire gauge and run to the car. Once inside, I look at him. "Have you ever had an emissions test done?"

Gramps strokes his chin. "Can't say I remember."

"You're supposed to every two years!"

"That's a rip-off, a way for the goddamn government to take more of our hard-earned money."

"So that's a no. At this moment, off the top of my head we need new tires, a new tailpipe, a new heater, new wipers, and a new radio. That's just what we know about. I have a feeling you're very lucky this heap didn't blow up years ago."

"Listen, missy, I'm retired. Money doesn't grow on trees. Ollie doesn't work. I have to watch my pennies."

"That is drivel. I know full well you and Dad made a fortune on stocks before the market crashed. You've told me often enough. I think it's time for you to buy a new car."

"I don't know about that. What will Ollie say?"

"*Hallelujah*, I imagine. I'm sure she doesn't like freezing to death when she goes for groceries."

"What kind of car?"

"We'll figure that out when we get there."

We noisily belch exhaust every twenty feet and I'm getting the finger from drivers on all sides, so I steer into the first dealership I see, which is Mazda. Two hours later Gramps is the new owner of a jet black Mazda 6. The salesman asks me if I'm in the market to buy a car and I think, why not.

"I'll have that one over there. I like the colour."

"I love you," the guy says. Now I have a spirited green Mazda 2. I tell Gramps that his car is three times better than mine and he seems chuffed.

It takes another hour for the salesman to explain the new features to Gramps, and to tell the truth, to me as well. These babies can do everything but babysit, but the only thing Gramps is really impressed with are the heated seats. Me too.

We drive them home in a convoy through a snow squall with our temporary license plates, Gramps leading the way. When we get home we hustle Aunt Ollie outside so she can look at our new purchases, and then we take turns driving her around the block.

She's madly in love with the heated seats as well. "I think I'll sleep in here."

We put Gramps's new car in the garage and leave mine outside, since I'll have an easier time wiping snow off my vehicle. We celebrate by drinking hot chocolate with marshmallows.

"Why didn't we think of this years ago?" Gramps puzzles.

"People get into ruts," Aunt Ollie says. "That's what I'm in. Hopefully my book club will change that."

"Are you telling me there's going to be highbrow women in this house looking down their noses at me?"

"Think of the trays of sandwiches, Gramps."

He mulls this over. "True."

I take my car out the next day to run to the grocery store for boxes of Smarties. Out of the corner of my eye I see a colourful sheet of paper on the public bulletin board. *Love Books? Me too. Join my book club.* Aunt Ollie's phone number is repeated on pieces of fringed paper at the bottom, making it easier for a prospective member to rip off.

All the numbers are still there. Poor Aunt Ollie. I grab three pieces and put them in my pocket. People will think others are interested and be more inclined to take a piece themselves. Two days later I go back to the store to get more cat food and check Aunt Ollie's poster and notice another piece of paper missing. Thank God. When I turn to leave, I notice a similar poster.

Are you the woman of my dreams? I'm a young seventy with my own house, my own teeth, and a brand new car. Call me for a good time.

Guess who.

It takes me a good minute before I recover and another minute to realize that all his phone numbers have been ripped away. When I drop the cat food off, my grandfather is on the phone while Aunt Ollie frets by the stove.

"Every time that damn phone rings, I think it might be for my book club, but now he's got every old widow in the neighbourhood on speed dial."

"He'll be out of your hair."

"He copied me, and now he's ruined everything."

When I sit at the table, Norton jumps up on my lap and Gramps gets off the phone.

"Gramps, you don't have all your own teeth."

"I have two bridges, not dentures. There's a difference. Are you going to be a sourpuss about my new hobby too? Olive here is carrying on like I've ruined her life."

"I don't care about your fancy women. Why aren't people calling about my book club?"

The phone rings.

"Let me guess, it's for you," Aunt Ollie gripes.

Gramps picks up the phone. "Hello there, you're speaking to Wilfred Butterworth, but you can call me Fred or you can call me to dinner, your choice."

Aunt Ollie rolls her eyes.

Gramps listens. "Yes, she's here. Are you sure you want to speak to her?" He hands Aunt Ollie the phone. "It's for you."

Aunt Ollie runs down the hall to pick up the phone in her room. Gramps hangs up. "Judging by her voice, she's a dried up old prune."

❧

TODAY IS MY FIRST PSYCHIATRIST'S APPOINTMENT WITH A DR. McDermott—either the weirdest coincidence ever or evidence that my pediatrician is messing with my head. This Dr. McDermott's office is in a rundown apartment building. I can't tell if it's derelict or terribly chic. A labyrinth of hallways dissect each other on the first floor, and are seemingly endless, like an indoor maze.

Eventually I come to the office and the door is open. There's a handwritten sign on the wall. *Knock loud and come in.* So I do. The place looks like someone is moving in or moving out. Moving out, more likely; who'd want to stay here?

There's no receptionist.

"Hello?"

A door opens and a young guy sticks his head out. "I'll be with you in a minute."

Is that the doctor? This is ridiculous. I'm going to take advice from someone even younger than me?

He eventually emerges, escorting a little old man with a cane. "I'll see you in two weeks, Mr. Finkel. Hopefully by then I'll have chairs in the waiting room." Then he looks at me and ushers me in his door. "Sorry to keep you waiting. Please, come in."

The office is in an uproar as well, but at least there's a chair for me and one for him. No couch, thankfully.

"I'm Dr. McDermott. It's nice to meet you. My uncle referred you. Chloe Sparrow, isn't it?" He takes out a notepad and sets it on his knee while looking at my file.

"How old are you?" I ask him.

"Old enough to be a psychiatrist. How old are you?"

"Old enough to be a patient."

"Uncle Matthew is worried about you."

He looks very familiar to me. "Did anyone ever tell you that you look like that *Mad Magazine* guy, Alfred E. Neuman?"

"Frequently. Usually while holding my head in the toilet at school."

"Kids suck."

"Yes, they do. According to my uncle you've had a pretty traumatic time of it these last few months."

"No."

"Perhaps I have the wrong file." He shuffles through some papers and quickly reads one out loud. "You quit your job."

"Yeah."

"You've had a broken nose, a concussion, a broken wrist and finger, and sprained ankle."

"So?"

"Your weight is fluctuating, your menses unpredictable."

"Good grief, he actually told you that? Is nothing sacred?"

"Not to a shrink. You lost your parents in a terrible accident when you were fifteen."

"I killed them."

He writes it down. "That I didn't know. Were you tried and convicted in a court of law?"

"Yeah."

"How much time did you serve?"

"Ten years, three months, four days, seven hours, and fifty-five minutes. Make that fifty-six."

He writes that down as well.

"I have to go."

When I stand up, he does too.

"No problem. Please come back for your appointment in two weeks, same time, or Uncle Matthew will hunt you down. You know what he's like. I'm hoping to have chairs by then."

CHAPTER FOURTEEN

I'M NOT USING MY CAR AS MUCH AS I THOUGHT I WOULD, BUT then I have nowhere to go and nothing to do. Which is fine. You can't get hurt when you're by yourself.

At least, I thought I was by myself, but then one day Gramps and Aunt Ollie don't come home for dinner. I'm used to them going out from time to time, but they always come home for supper. Not that I usually eat with them, but it's comforting to hear them banging, stomping, and hollering at each other through the wall.

As it gets later and later, I go next door and bring the cats back with me. That keeps me calm for about an hour. I watch a modelling show and eat a box of animal crackers, but now that it's past nine and there's still no sign of them, I'm getting concerned. There's no way to get in touch with them because they don't have cellphones, so I pace back and forth in front of my living room window waiting for them to show up. Tomorrow I'm going out and buying them both a phone. Why haven't I thought of this before? An elderly man shouldn't be driving around a big, bad city unable to call for help. And Aunt Ollie... well, she's a perfect victim for any one of a hundred crimes.

At ten o'clock, I call the police.

"Have they been missing for twenty-four hours?"

"No, but it's not like them. I'm telling you something's wrong."

"Okay, calm down. We don't file a report until they've been missing for a full twenty-four hours, so call us tomorrow if you still haven't heard from them. I'm sure they're fine. Usually these cases turn out to be nothing. Call their friends."

"They don't have any friends! It's just the three of us and now I'm alone." Talking to this guy is useless, so I hang up. What should I do?

Oh, for cryin' out loud.

I wish Gramps and Aunt Ollie would come home right this minute.

One more glance out the window and I see Gramps's car turning into the driveway, just as an unfamiliar car stops in front of the house and lets Aunt Ollie out. The relief is overwhelming, but it changes to anger before long. I walk out onto the cold and blustery porch.

"Where were you guys? You scared me half to death!"

"I was on a date. I took Effie to the movies and then we went out for coffee."

"And what's your excuse?" I glare at Aunt Ollie. "You could've left a note!"

"I was at my book club."

"It's supposed to be *your* book club. Why aren't you having it in *your* house?"

"I wanted to go over there. It's not far, and it's a change of scenery, if you must know."

Now that my heart has stopped racing, I gather my wits. "Next time, please leave a note telling me where you are."

"I'm freezing," Gramps says. "Is the interrogation over?"

"Sorry, yes. The cats are with me. Good night."

Around nine in the morning I go over to their place to discuss buying cellphones, but there's no one home. There are two notes on the table.

I've been invited to Gladys's house. We're going for a drive and then she's making me dinner, so I won't be home till tonight. Don't wait up.

Chloe, Agatha and I are going to the library and then on a stakeout. I have no idea when I'll be home, so don't wait up.

A stakeout! What does that mean? Somehow my reclusive aunt and grandfather have developed more interesting social lives than me.

❧

I'M IN MY PYJAMAS WITH THE LIGHTS OUT IN THE LIVING ROOM so no one can see me at the window. It's now eleven, and I should've been in bed two hours ago, but Gramps and Aunt Ollie aren't home yet. It's damned inconsiderate not to call and give me a rough idea of when to expect them.

The cats sit on the windowsills staring out into the dark unknown. Their company makes things so much better.

Aunt Ollie comes home first. She struggles out of an old Cadillac, bending down to have a quick word with the driver, and then shuts the door and waves until the car disappears. As she hauls herself up the stairs I'm trying to figure out what's different about her. That's when I realize she's smiling and doesn't have those dumb curlers in her hair.

Gramps comes home about fifteen minutes later. He whistles as he comes up the steps. There's something different about him, too. It looks like he went to a barber and had the springy grey hair removed from his facial orifices. Even his eyebrows look tamed. He's positively dapper.

Thank goodness I can drag my weary body to bed now, knowing they're safe. But three little kittens decide they don't want to go to bed and chase each other around my room and then jump from the furniture onto the bed. They get me up at four in the morning, howling because they want something to eat. Norton sleeps through it all.

Since I'm up early anyway, I listen for signs of life next door. I want to catch Gramps and Aunt Ollie before they disappear again. They need to provide me with more information than I currently have.

The toilet flushes next door. That's my cue to go over.

"Yoo-hoo...good morning."

"We're in here." Gramps is at the table while Aunt Ollie stands by the stove waiting on his four-minute boiled eggs.

"Would you like some toast?" Aunt Ollie asks me.

"Sure, that would be great." My bum hits the nearest chair.

"I'd like two slices as well," she says.

Up I get to put on the toast. "So you guys had a busy day yesterday."

They both nod, but it doesn't look like they're listening to me. There is no sense in continuing this until they're both at the table. When we're seated, I try again.

"So what's Gladys like and what happened to Effie?"

Gramps grins from ear to ear. "Different day, different woman. Gladys is a swell gal. And cook! Her dinner was the best I've had in years."

I expect Aunt Ollie to start hollering that he can make his own damn dinners, but she doesn't. She puts jam on her toast instead.

"You must be having fun with your new friend, Aunt Ollie. You say she lives nearby?"

She nods. "Agatha lives about ten minutes from here in a duplex. It's a little rundown, but she's getting older."

"Doesn't she have family who can help?"

"No. She's single like me."

"So, what did you mean about going on a stakeout? I thought it was a book club."

Aunt Ollie slathers more jam on her crust. "She's a mystery buff who loves Agatha Christie novels, and she runs her own detective agency. She calls it Nosy Parker, because her last name is Parker."

"Do you mean she actually follows people around? Isn't that dangerous? I'm not sure I like the idea of that."

"You don't have to. You're not my mother."

Now I'm concerned. "You can't chase criminals around. They carry guns!"

"Oh good gravy, she's not the FBI! She does favours for her neighbours, like check out when so-and-so left their house, or what time someone came home...that sort of thing. Agatha says she makes a great snoop because old ladies are practically invisible."

"Promise me you won't get involved in her escapades. A cheating husband could go after you with a baseball bat if he thought you were squealing to his wife."

"Leave the girl alone. This is the most fun she's had in forty years."

I find a pad of paper and a pencil. "I want their names and addresses and phone numbers, so that if anything happens I know who to call."

They reluctantly gather the information and scribble it down.

"Thank you. Now, what are you up to today?"

"Greta wants me to help her move some boxes."

"Who is Greta? Never mind...put her name and address down too. Please don't have a heart attack lifting those boxes. And you?"

Aunt Ollie eats the last of the jam out of the jar. "We're going on another stakeout."

"Oh, Jesus."

"It's like having a picnic in the car, only you keep your eyes peeled while you're eating. I'll be fine."

"I'm going to buy you cellphones so you can call me if you're running late. I'll teach you how to use them."

"I'm not going to call you like I'm a little kid," Gramps grumps.

"Fine, but I want you to have one so I can call you if I need to."

"A lot of nonsense."

"Before you go, Chloe, your grandfather and I have discussed this, and we think the cats are better off with you fulltime, our schedules are so hectic now. But we want visitation rights every other weekend."

I leave feeling like I don't recognize anyone anymore.

❦

MY *KIDS* HAVE ME UP ALL NIGHT, EVERY NIGHT. IF PEANUT ISN'T yowling about something, then Bobby's getting stuck somewhere. When Rosemary wants to use the litter box, the other two decide they do too, with disastrous results. I clean, feed, referee, and roller fur, and I step on surprise bits of throwup in the process. All the toys I bought out of guilt are now strewn from one end of my house to the other. Mess bothers me, which I never knew before, as I've never had anyone to pick up after.

I start doing internet research on the best brands of cat food to buy, and quickly discover that if you don't want your precious pets to die of cancer, you have to cook their meals with organic food. So now I'm buying free-range eggs and chicken and bags of flax seed and I crush supplements into their meals. They are eating better than I am. It's true what they say. Mothers will do anything for their children—but those same saints become martyrs very quickly, and I can hardly complain to Aunt Ollie. I begin to miss Amanda.

I'm moping around the house trying to get up the energy to go buy those cellphones when my doorbell rings. It's Trey, holding a large box of chocolates.

"Hi Trey, what a nice surprise."

"Chloe, you look like an unmade bed! What happened to the little spitfire I know and love?"

"She left long ago. Come in."

He follows me into the living room and hands me my gift before his eyes roam around the room.

"I know, it's awful. I have to redecorate."

"You have to decorate it before you can redecorate it. A flower-covered fence wallpaper border belongs in the Smithsonian."

"I've missed you." I open my box of goodies and pop one in my mouth. "Help yourself."

He sits beside me on the pitiful couch. "You've been on my mind. The premiere is coming up and the crew thought we'd get together to watch it. You have to come."

"I can't. I'd only ruin it for everyone."

"That's ridiculous. Everyone cares about you."

"Amanda doesn't."

"She tried to call you for weeks but you never answered. Then your bulldog Aunt Ollie threatened her with a broom. What's she supposed to think? People won't run after you forever."

"Trey, I don't have the energy to fix things right now."

"Are you getting help?"

"I saw a shrink for five minutes. How's Jerry?"

"He's still driving me crazy, so everything is right with the world." He takes out one of his business cards and turns it over to write on the back. "This is my address. Come around eight, a week from Monday night. It won't be the same if my favourite Girl Guide's not there." He stands up. "I better go, you look tired. Take care, Chloe." He gives me a hug before he sees himself out. I take the chocolates to bed and eat all of them.

The next day I buy the phones and crawl back to bed. The day after that I show Gramps and Aunt Ollie how to use them. It doesn't go smoothly. We holler at each other for an hour.

On the third day I'm sorting through the kittens' stuff and find their health records, which recommend they be spayed or neutered when they're seven months old, so I count the weeks on the calendar and sure enough, the end of January is it. Now I'm panicked. I can't go and see Austin. I call Gramps on his cellphone. It rings twenty times before he finally figures out how to answer it.

"Who's this?"

"It's me, the only person who knows you have a phone. Gramps, can you take the cats to the vet for me?"

"No. Lois and I have plans." He hangs up.

I try Aunt Ollie. She only needs ten rings to answer. "No dear, I'm busy. We're following a suspect through Shoppers Drug Mart and we can't lose him now." Click.

There's nothing to do but make the appointment, but I schedule it with one of Austin's partners. It would be wiser for me to go to another clinic altogether, but their files are already there and I do owe some loyalty to Austin after all. He was there at the beginning when they were cute and helpless. But right now they're in the car driving me crazy with their complaining and whining in both carriers. I look in the rear-view mirror at their devilish faces through the mesh. "Don't make me come back there!"

The babies are bawling by the time I get to the waiting room, so it's not like people don't notice me. Everyone asks me how many cats I have and one little kid keeps poking at the mesh with his disgustingly dirty finger.

"Go away," I say quietly so his mother won't hear me.

"Make me."

I vow to myself to never have human kids.

I spend the endless wait thinking Austin will come around the corner at any moment. We're finally called in and I put both carriers on the floor of the examining room. "The doctor will be with you in a moment."

"Thanks."

The kittens aren't pleased about their imprisonment. I look at my watch. I have to get home to watch Honey Boo Boo reruns.

After another long wait, Austin walks in the door.

I stare at him. "What are you doing here? I made an appointment with Dr. Buck."

"Chloe?"

"Yes! You don't remember me?"

"You look...different."

"You don't look so hot yourself." He doesn't. He's thinner and he's cut his hair. I don't like it.

"Dr. Buck called in sick today."

"Let's just get this over with, then. I've got Norton and the three kids. I want them all spayed and neutered so I don't become an even crazier cat lady down the road. You might as well give them any shots they need while you're at it."

"I'll make the arrangements. I'll take them now, shall I?"

"No! I have to say goodbye first." I put both carriers up on the examining table and unzip the mesh. All four come cautiously nosing their way out. It hits me how adorable they are and how if anything happened to one of them I'd die. Now I'm blubbering.

"You have to make sure they're going to be okay. You should operate on them. You're their father."

After many kisses and hugs I zip them back up and Austin hands them over to an assistant out back. Their pitiful mews pierce my heart.

I wish for Norton, Bobby, Rosemary, and Peanut to come through their surgeries with absolutely no problems at all.

"I'll make sure they're fine."

I didn't realize I had wished my wish out loud.

Now that the kittens are gone, it feels as if a cavernous hole has opened up between us while we stand on either side of the examining table. I wipe my tears with the back of my hand. "How have you been?"

"Okay. You?"

"Just peachy. Trey came by and mentioned the launch party. Are you going?"

"He asked me, but I don't think so. I've had quite enough of *The Single Guy.*"

"Ditto."

He doesn't smile.

"So who did you choose?"

"I can't tell you that until the last episode airs. I signed a contract."

I roll my eyes. "You can tell me."

The pupils in his hazel eyes seem to narrow to a point. If he had dog's ears, they'd be flat. "You've made it quite clear that I'm no longer a friend of yours, so my personal information is none of your business."

"When did I say that?"

"That's another thing that's always irritated me. You conveniently forget what you say to people."

"When have I done that?"

"You live in Chloe world. The rest of us don't exist."

"Now you're being ridiculous."

"Was my mother kind to you?"

"Of course she was."

"She was a little hurt that you didn't acknowledge the flowers she sent you."

Now I'm horrified. "But I didn't acknowledge anyone's."

"Exactly."

Once again I'm blubbering. "So you're saying I'm rude and selfish?"

"I'm saying you don't care about other people until they can do something for you, like drive you around in the middle of the night to deliver kittens. Or how about now? You dismiss my friendship for months and yet expect me to operate on your four cats. I'm sure once I'm done I won't see you until one of them has another problem. Please do me a big favour, Chloe, and take your pets somewhere else from now on. It's too hard to see you."

He walks out of the room.

My sobbing has now reached its peak. When I pay my bill at the desk the other clients think I've just put my pet down. They look at me with sympathy. One woman even comes over and pats my shoulder.

"I know, dear, I know. It's the worst thing in the world."

I'm driving in my car, bawling, but instead of going home, where there are zilch people or animals, I drive to my psychiatrist's office. Not that I have an appointment. His door is closed and another woman is standing there because he still doesn't have chairs. We nod, but she's trying to avoid me. I'm still crying.

When Dr. McDermott comes out with a patient, he takes one look at me and asks the other lady if she would mind waiting a few more minutes. She says of course not. The minute I'm in his office, we sit and he hands me a tissue. "What's wrong?"

"Do I seem selfish and rude?"

"That's hard to answer. I've only known you for about ten minutes total. I'll be able to give you an opinion if you stay a little longer at your sessions."

"Okay."

He scribbles on his prescription pad. "I was going to give this to you at your next appointment, so you might as well take it now." He hands me the paper. "The first one is a mild antidepressant that you take twice a day and the other is a low dose of anxiety medication that will see you through episodes like this. Don't take it unless you feel out of control."

I put the small piece of paper in my pocket.

"Are you all right to drive home?"

"Yes."

"I'll see you at your regular appointment, but call if you need me before that."

"Thank you."

He leads me out of the office, and I nod at the woman who was kind enough to let me go ahead of her. I wonder if I would've done that in her position.

When I get home from the pharmacy at suppertime it's dark. There are no lights on at Ollie's, so she must be with Agatha, and my grandfather's car is gone, which means he's flirting with someone named Mildred or Joyce. I take a tiny anti-anxiety pill and give Steve a call. By the time he arrives, I'm calm. Calm enough to agree that revisiting the kitchen table is a great idea.

Until the utensil drawer starts to shake.

"Okay, I'm done with this kitchen," he pants.

"Come up to my creepy bedroom, then."

"If it's creepy like this kitchen, I'm outta here."

"Oh, it's creepy, but in a decor kind of way."

"That I can deal with."

We have a nice evening.

CHAPTER FIFTEEN

I FINALLY MEET AGATHA.

I go over to Aunt Ollie's to ask Gramps if he can pick up the kittens, but he's off skating with Lenore.

"Chloe, this is my good friend, Agatha Parker. Agatha, this is my niece, Chloe."

"It's nice to meet you, Agatha. I've heard a lot about you." I shake her hand before I sit at the table. Aunt Ollie makes tea and puts cookie packages in front of us.

Agatha has pure white hair that sticks out from under a beret. She's round and wearing a pair of cat's-eye glasses that are so old they're back in style. Her clothes look like she might have found them in a bin. Everything about her is instantly forgettable.

"I've heard a lot about you, too," Agatha says in a way that implies she knows my every secret.

"Did you want something?" Aunt Ollie passes us our tea.

"I don't only come over when I want something."

"Could have fooled me."

"I thought I might ask Gramps if he could pick up the cats."

"You have a brand new car. Do it yourself."

"I can't. The vet and I had a falling out."

"That nice young man who delivered Peanut?"

"I can't discuss it right now, Aunt Ollie."

She sips on her tea and takes a fistful of oatmeal cookies. So does Agatha, so why not. I join in.

"You can say whatever you want in front of Agatha. You'd be surprised what she knows."

That I don't doubt.

"Ollie and I can pick them up," Agatha says. "But I need gas money."

It's five minutes away.

"Sure, thanks. I appreciate it."

"I know you do. And one day you'll be able to help me. That's the way it works."

Okay, now I think she may be a cult leader.

❊

MY DEPRESSION MEDICATION OBVIOUSLY HASN'T HAD TIME TO kick in yet, but now that I have my tiny anti-anxiety wonder drug, I think I'll go to Trey's party. He said everyone wants to see me. Maybe they don't think I'm selfish and rude.

Fingers crossed.

Nothing in my closet fits. Nothing. I visit many stores in the mall and all the mirrors say the same thing: I'm not me anymore. Still, I'm kind of digging the fact that I have cleavage. I buy a little black dress and a little black coat and little black boots. As long as I only go to parties and funerals, I have a wardrobe.

I ask Aunt Ollie and Agatha if they'll babysit the cats for me. Aunt Ollie looks at Agatha. I don't know why she needs her opinion.

"I charge twelve dollars an hour," Agatha says. Aunt Ollie nods.

I agree, since I'm nervous about leaving them alone so soon after surgery. It's a very cold night and when I walk from my parking space to Trey's condo, the snow squeaks under my boots. When I was a kid I loved that sound.

As I make my way up to the eighteenth floor, the mirror in the elevator confirms the fact that my hair is a mess. I shouldn't be here. I need to go home. The elevator doors open and across the hall I see Trey greeting Brian in his foyer. They spy me at the same time.

"She's here! How wonderful."

Trey kisses both cheeks and Brian gives me a big bear hug.

"Come in, come in."

Now there is chaos as Trey takes our coats and we remove our boots. Jerry shows up with a tray of drinks and is happy to see us. There is laughter and conversation going on in the living room. I grab Brian's arm. "Can I stay by you?"

"Sure thing."

We emerge into the living room and there is the whole crew. They roar when they see me. It's overwhelming. Everyone wants to know how I am, and I say fine and smile a lot before I hold up my hands. "Before we go any farther, I'd like to thank each and every one of you for sending me such nice cards and flowers when I was recovering. It meant a great deal to me, and I'm sorry I didn't acknowledge that right away."

There's a murmuring of dismissive noises, telling me not to worry and it was nothing; the kind things people say when they really mean *It's about time*.

And then I see Amanda. She's turned away from me—deliberately, it seems. My saliva immediately evaporates.

Trey says, "Amanda?"

She turns around and looks at me. There's an awkward pause.

"So how have you been, Chloe?"

"Great."

"You look good."

"No, I don't, but thank you for saying so."

"I'm sorry I haven't been in touch. I've been so busy."

"Oh yes, I can imagine."

I'm aware that even though Jason is talking to someone else, he's keeping his eyes on Amanda. For God's sake, I'm not going to choke her. This is unbearable.

"Look, Amanda, I apologize for not calling you back and not talking to you that day on the porch. I was hurt and didn't know how to handle it."

She grabs my arm. "Of course you were hurt. I understand completely. It was my fault you were out of commission and then they put me in charge. I don't blame you for ignoring me, but you have no idea how often I've wanted to call you about the show. I hope we can be friends again. I've missed you a lot."

The party goes full throttle, and it is gratifying to see everyone. Jerry keeps trying to give me wine, but I'm not in the mood. He offers mineral water instead. Amanda and I toast each other, and then Jason comes over and hugs me. He's such a nice guy.

The canapés are delicious. I find myself standing by the buffet table sampling everything and am almost sorry when Trey pulls me away.

"Okay, everyone, it's almost nine. Take your seats!"

We sit and stare up at Trey's enormous flat-screen television over the stylish and sleek gas fireplace.

"I forgot one thing!" Trey turns to me. "You are the only one here who doesn't know who Austin picked. Do you want to know or shall we forever hold our peace?"

"I don't want to know."

"You heard her, folks! Not a word!"

And then it starts. We are amazed at how good it looks,

everything seamlessly cut. Trey cries, "Look at the lighting! Is that not the best lighting in the world?"

Everyone claps and Jerry takes a bow. "That means a lot coming from the best host in the world!"

Which sets everyone off.

"That is the best makeup in the world!"

"Look at that camera angle! Brian rules!"

"Look at Sydney's flattened nipples!"

"And look at that fabulous man!" Amanda says when Austin comes on the screen. Everyone goes wild. And he does look fabulous. Everything about him is perfect.

"Who's Ryan Gosling again? Because he doesn't have anything on our boy!"

No one is listening to the dialogue. Everyone is too busy remembering what went on behind the cameras during each scene.

Jerry jumps up and points at the screen. "This was about eighteen hours into the first shoot. Look at the bags under Trey's eyes. That's your fault, Chloe. You nearly killed him!"

The girls look so happy and hopeful chatting together on that first night, their hearts not yet broken.

All at once my own heart is fluttering. It's scary and I want to leave, but I don't want to ruin the party. I excuse myself, "Off to the loo!" and no one pays attention. Once I get to the hallway I search for my coat, which is among a pile of others on the bed in Trey and Jerry's room. I tiptoe back to the foyer and zip my boots as Trey comes out of the kitchen with yet another bottle of wine.

He looks concerned. "What are you doing?"

"I really need to go, Trey. Please say goodbye to everyone."

"You're upset, Chloe."

"No, no. I had a wonderful time. Thank you for everything." I kiss his cheek and then literally run out the door and head to the nearest stairwell. I'm afraid someone might come out of the apartment and try to dissuade me while I wait for the elevator.

I get back on the elevator three floors down, my heart still racing. Once I hit the cold air outside, I take great gulps of air and the panic recedes a bit. By the time I squeak back to my car, I'm not shaking anymore.

When I get back home, Aunt Ollie and Agatha are in the living room watching the last hour of *The Single Guy*, with the cats spread out around them.

"We're watching your show," Aunt Ollie says. "So far it's not bad."

Agatha shakes her head. "It's a load of shit if you ask me."

I run up the stairs and lock myself in the bathroom, trying not to die because that's what it feels like. Aunt Ollie follows me upstairs and bangs on the door. "Are you okay?"

When I don't answer, she paces in front of the door. Then I hear Agatha at the top of the stairs.

"She owes me thirty-six dollars."

"She'll give it to you in the morning, isn't that right, Chloe? You'll give Agatha her money in the morning."

I take two twenty-dollar bills out of my wallet and slide them under the door. "Keep the change!"

❧

AMANDA CALLS ME FIRST THING. I DON'T WANT TO TALK, BUT I'm stuck.

"Chloe, what happened last night?"

"My stomach was upset. It must have been something I ate. I needed to get home. You know what that's like."

"I'm so relieved. I thought it had something to do with the show. Look, why don't you come over for lunch on the weekend and we can get caught up."

"Sounds good."

"Feel better."

"Thanks."

When I turn on my laptop a few days later the CBC website is filled with commentary about the show. *The Single Guy* is a hit, number one in its time slot across Canada. Every single woman across the country is in love with Austin, at least that's what the message boards say.

I should be pleased, but I don't feel anything at all.

❦

I'M BACK FOR MY APPOINTMENT WITH THE YOUNG DR. McDermott. There are now lawn chairs in the reception area. My ass is poking through one of them. Once again, he's late, and he escorts his patient to the door before waving me in.

"Lawn chairs?"

"I know, I know. I don't have the time to go out and get more."

He settles in the chair by his messy desk. "Now, where were we?"

"You still don't have a receptionist."

"Again, a time issue."

"What's your first name?"

"Dexter. I know, I know, I got that look while being shoved into my locker at school."

"Kids suck."

"You're right."

"Do you mind if I call you Dexter? Every time I say Dr. McDermott I picture your uncle."

"No problem. So, how was your week?"

"The same as any other."

"Any more panic attacks?"

"I had one, but the smaller seismic ones that rumble all day under the surface are worse."

"What caused the big one?"

"I went to a party with my cast."

"You have a cast?"

"I was the producer of *The Single Guy*."

Dexter sits back in his chair. "Wow. That got great reviews this week. My mother and sister watched it. They love the guy."

"Austin. He thinks I'm rude and selfish."

He scribbles something down on his pad. "You're no longer the producer?"

I shake my head.

"What happened?"

I stand up. "Sorry, I have to go."

He gets up too. "I wish all my patients were as speedy as you. Same time next week."

I'm almost out the office door when I turn around. "How come you don't mind if I go after five minutes?"

"I'm sure you have more important things to do."

As I pass his reception area I turn around again. "I can buy you some chairs if you want and you can pay me back."

"Fantastic! What a great idea."

"What kind do you want?"

"Isn't one chair as good as another?"

"Do you want comfortable, so that your patients lounge here all day, or hard as a rock to move them along?"

"How about something in between?"

"How much do you want to spend?"

"My budget is very limited. I have a ton of student loans."

"So does Austin."

❁

EVER SINCE AUSTIN TOLD ME I ONLY CARE ABOUT PEOPLE WHEN I want something from them, I'm acutely aware of it. Like getting Aunt Ollie and Agatha to babysit, and now borrowing Gramps's bigger car to haul chairs.

"I'll drive," Gramps says. "Effie won't mind a little detour. That way you don't have to carry them yourself."

"Thanks, Gramps."

Off we go to get Effie. "So you're back to dating Effie?"

"I have my gals on rotation. They all know about each other. They live in the same senior citizen's facility." He starts whistling.

"But doesn't it bother them to share you like that?"

"No. They know there are plenty of other widows who'll take their place. It's all because you persuaded me to buy the new car. I have a new lease on life."

"Aunt Ollie is enjoying her new friendship, even though Agatha's a crackpot."

"Now we have to work on you." He looks directly at me.

We stop by Dexter's office, and Gramps and I carry the chairs in. He's in his office with the door closed, so I arrange the chairs in a waiting-room fashion and leave. It'll be a surprise.

My lunch with Amanda is the next day, and I feel like I need a tiny pill to get through it. I don't understand why, exactly, but I take it anyway.

The Partridge boys are beyond busy today. J. J. and Callum are running after each other brandishing all manner of rubber toys like they're weapons. It's difficult to talk at the kitchen table with all the noise. Amanda might be acclimatized, but I'm in hell.

Eventually Jason comes home and lassoes them, taking them upstairs for a nap. They're both crying as they go, but scarcely two minutes later, all is quiet.

"Jason lets them lie on our bed and he has a nap with them. It's the best part of the day."

She takes my plate. "Would you like a cup of coffee? I finally got a new coffeemaker for Christmas, like the one at the office. It only takes a minute."

"Sure."

We sip our coffee and eat Arrowroots. She puts down her mug. "How are you really doing?"

"Not good."

"Oh, Chloe, don't get upset. The series is better than people expected, and that's down to you. I only came in at the end and tied things up."

"I've never failed at anything before."

"You didn't fail. It was rotten luck. If you went to Mr. Gardner, I wouldn't be surprised if he gave you your job back. You are very talented and he knows that."

"I don't want to work."

She gives my hand a little shake. "You don't mean that."

I sit upright in the chair. "Don't tell me what I don't mean. I'm sick of hearing from other people about what I should do. I feel like everyone wants me to hurry up and get back to normal, but the way I was living wasn't normal, so I have to find a new way to cope."

"I can help you! I read a great book—"

"Amanda, stop being bossy."

"I'm not bossy."

I nod my head. "Yes, you are."

"But I'm older and wiser. You could benefit from my experience."

"I need to do this myself."

She gives a great big sigh. "Fine. I'm here if you need anything."

"I did need something, my lunch. Thank you."

❁

WHEN I ARRIVE AT MY NEXT APPOINTMENT, THE CHAIRS ARE every which way, so I put them back where they're supposed to be and sit on one of them. They're perfect.

Dexter opens the door and emerges with a large woman who's obviously been crying. "See you in two months."

Once she's gone, he turns to me with a goofy grin. "I love my new chairs. How much do I owe you?"

The receipt is in my purse. I hand it to him. "We went to a used furniture place because everything was too expensive in a regular store. They were a hundred dollars for the four of them."

"Excellent job. Are you interested in finding me a desk for the receptionist?"

"You hired one?"

"Not yet. I should have a place for them to work first."

"Okay, but you'll have to pay for delivery. I don't have a big enough car."

"No problem. Thanks, Chloe. I'll see you next week."

He heads for his office.

"Aren't I supposed to have an appointment?"

He turns back and taps his forehead. "I completely forgot. Come in."

Once we're settled he starts with his usual question. "So how was your week?"

"I bought chairs."

"Anything else exciting?"

"I discovered my grandfather is dating the female residents of an entire wing in an old folk's home."

"How does that make you feel?"

"I miss him."

Scribbling.

"I went to my friend's house for lunch and told her I didn't need her advice."

"Everyone needs a friend's advice."

"I'm making this journey alone."

Scribble.

"Do you notice any improvement in your mood?"

"No."

"Don't worry; it takes time to get into your system."

"Oh yeah, my Aunt Ollie's new friend is bananas. Since my aunt is already odd, it's like the blind leading the blind."

"Like attracts like. They might be just what the other needs."

That's enough psychobabble for me. "Have to run."

"Okay. See ya."

It's only when I'm driving home that I realize I left before he gave me my money. I've got to stop being so hasty. It's not like I have anything to do.

❀

NEARING THE END OF FEBRUARY I'M SICK OF MY OWN COMPANY. This hiding away from the world is great, up to a point. Today I asked the kittens a question and expected them to answer me. They did their best, turning their heads one way and then the other, but none of them had an opinion.

Every so often, Amanda, Trey, or Brian will call me, but since I'm no fun to talk to the conversations are short and sweet. No one comes to the house and I don't go out, unless it's to buy a desk, which I did almost ten days ago. Dexter paid me for the chairs and the desk and asked if I'd pick up a filing cabinet for him. Why on earth doesn't he give me a list of the stuff he wants and be done with it? Last time I stayed at my appointment for fifteen minutes but left because I don't want him to think I need him.

There is one errand I've been putting off, and I need to get it over with. It's all I can think about.

When I arrive at Austin's mother's door I have a big arrangement of flowers that are quickly withering in the cold. When Harriet opens her door she's surprised, but I can't tell if it's in a good or bad way.

"Chloe. Come in."

"Hi, Mrs. Hawke."

She doesn't say, *Call me Harriet.*

"These are for you."

She takes them. "That's very nice. What's the occasion?"

I take a deep breath. "It was very thoughtful of you to send me flowers when I was recovering and I never sent you a thank-you note, which was terribly rude because I did appreciate it. So I'd like to apologize for that."

"Well, thank you, dear. Would you like to come in for a cup of tea?"

"Sure."

We sit at her kitchen table drinking tea and eating slices of cherry cake.

"How are you feeling now?" she asks.

"I'm okay."

She puts down her teacup. "I'm sorry, but the mother in me has to say that you look very sad. Is there anything I can do to help?"

Oh hell. Here come the waterworks.

"I'm a complete mess! Austin hates me because I was mean to him, and he's only ever been nice to me, and my grandfather and aunt are ignoring me, I have no job, I have fraying sheets, I love Amanda but I still resent the fact that she took over my job. I can't stand watching my show, but I do anyway and I cry the entire time. I'm seeing a shrink, but I only stay for a few minutes because I'm afraid of what he's going to say. I have no friends, no mom, my doctor tells me I have to eat healthy and I'm not. I have this guy who comes around, but I'm not sure why. I have a new car that I hardly use, my hair looks like a puppy chewed it, and now I can't believe I just told you all this."

She gets up from the table, gets a tissue box and plunks it in front of me. "There now, don't you feel better?"

Amazingly, I do.

"You're adrift at the moment, but that will change, I promise you."

"Austin hates me."

"Austin doesn't hate you."

"I don't even know who he picked in the end or if they're still together."

"I don't know either. He won't tell me."

"You see! He's such a good guy. He never cheats and he fixed my kittens and I don't know what to do because he doesn't want to see me anymore. He told me to go to another vet!"

"Austin doesn't divulge much of his personal life to me, but as his mother I can see that this experience has been a difficult one for him. I'd say he regrets it, but being the man he is, he saw it through until the end. Give him and yourself some time to get over this. You'll be friends again."

"Do you think so?"

"My mother instincts say yes."

"Thank you, Mrs. Hawke."

"Call me Harriet."

CHAPTER SIXTEEN

MARCH COMES IN LIKE A LAMB. THE WEATHER IS SURPRISINGLY warm and the snow we had is now melting, making huge puddles that could be two inches deep or twenty. I never know, I just take my chances and sometimes I win—but not often. The dirty slush covering the sidewalks reminds me of colourless margaritas. When I walk down the street, big drops fall on my head from power lines or rooftops. It's that time of year when I'm not sure if I should wear my boots or running shoes and I always make the wrong choice.

Canadian weather is known for lulling citizens into a false sense of security. Just when you think spring is around the corner, the biggest blizzard of the year comes screaming down from the north, burying everyone in lost optimism and snow.

So I'm walking in this mixed bag of weather conditions when it occurs to me I'm outside, walking. When was the last time that happened? I didn't even notice when I made the decision to get some fresh air instead of watching *Scared Straight*. Could I be feeling better? I'm afraid to ask myself this question in case I get slammed by some unforeseen miserable moment, the kind that creeps up on me and flattens me against a wall.

I clearly have to stop thinking about it or I'll drive myself bonkers, so when Agatha and Aunt Ollie ask me if I can drive them to a stakeout while Agatha's car is being fixed, I agree.

Agatha sits in front with me. Aunt Ollie has the cooler in the back seat with her.

"What's that for?"

"In case we get hungry."

"How long do these stakeouts last?"

"What a ridiculous question," Agatha says. "Each case is different. Now drive."

"Where am I going? I'll punch it into the GPS."

Agatha looks suspicious. "What's that?"

"It shows you your destination. Give me the address."

I can tell Agatha's very interested in what this little gadget does, but she doesn't want to admit it. We set off.

"What's the job today?"

Aunt Ollie leans forward in her seat and grabs my headrest. In the rear-view mirror I can see she's excited. "We have a woman who thinks her ex is seeing someone else."

"Isn't he allowed to if he's her ex-husband?"

"We don't judge."

That couldn't be further from the truth.

"And then we have a woman who's sure her husband is pretending he's in a wheelchair to get out of household chores."

"What a sleaze."

"We might not get them both done today, but there's always tomorrow," Agatha says.

"How long will your car be in the garage?"

"It could be a week. Why, is there a problem?"

"No, no problem." I'm still slightly leery of Agatha.

After an hour I'm wishing I'd brought a magazine. The other two are telling each other knock-knock jokes and cracking themselves up. Thankfully Aunt Ollie passes around a bag of nuts.

So fitting.

As I sit here staring at a nondescript apartment building, a thought occurs to me. "You know, there's no reason why Gramps can't do the occasional stakeout for you. He loves to drive his babes around. If you share the work, you guys could get twice as much done in a day and make even more money."

"I don't know about that," Agatha frowns. "Your grandfather is a bit of a jerk."

My mind is whirling. "For that matter, I could use my car and do a few jobs on occasion. We need to create a logo of some kind and make business cards if we're going to be serious about this career."

Aunt Ollie bites her lip. "I don't know if I want it to be a career. That sounds like work. Right now it's just fun."

"We could run seminars on how to snoop properly. We could have satellite groups all over the city. We'd have workshops on how to follow a car or how to talk yourself out of a situation if the suspect suspects you. There are endless things to learn. This could be a little goldmine..."

"There she is," Agatha interrupts, pointing her finger at the windshield. "That's the woman in our picture. There's no reason for her to be at this apartment except that the ex lives here, so the wife is right about her suspicions."

"The nasty ex-wife, you mean."

Agatha takes a few pictures of the woman going into the building and then we crack open the Thermoses and nibble on cheese and crackers and grapes. Aunt Ollie even had the good sense to bring bars of chocolate.

We wait for three hours. By now my ass and legs have gone numb, and worst of all they won't let me listen to my music CDs.

"I'm sorry, but are you seriously suggesting Conway Twitty is better than Adele?"

"You know it," Agatha shouts.

"You can forget about me helping you with this business stuff. You guys do your little thing and I'll stay out of it."

"Good! Who asked you to be involved anyway?" Agatha says.

Then we have a fight about turning the car off for the sake of the environment.

"When you get old, you get cold," Aunt Ollie pouts.

Mercifully, the woman finally emerges. After we take ten pictures of the woman walking to her car, Agatha calls the ex-wife and gives her our report before she hangs up.

"She was very thankful and says the cheque will be in the mail."

"Okay, hold it," I say. "You didn't get paid up front?"

"She asked if she could put if off for a few days until she got her pay."

"We sat here all afternoon, and I can tell you with certainty that this lunatic will never send that cheque. Is this what you've been doing all along?"

The Nosy Parkers look guilty.

"From now on, you quote them a price from the price list I'll make up for you and get the money in your hot little hand first or tell them you won't do the job. Got it?"

"I thought you didn't want to get involved?" Aunt Ollie pipes up.

"I don't, but you shouldn't be taken advantage of either. Agatha, I'm surprised at you. You made me pay for babysitting while I was hiding in the bathroom. Why so lax with everyone else?"

"I know you."

I'm not sure what she means by that.

The wheelchair caper is a rousing success. We track the guy down in a parking lot, and while Agatha and Aunt Ollie man the video camera in the car, I sashay over to him and drop a bag of groceries in the slushy muck. I stand there, helpless and forlorn. The guy gets out of his wheelchair and helps me pick up the food items. I thank him very much and tell him he's a wonderful man before running back to the car.

"Did you get it?"

"Perfect!" Agatha says. "You're a natural."

For some reason this pleases me to no end.

❊

"How was your week?"

"I went on a few stakeouts and I took a walk."

Dexter writes something on his pad and then looks up smiling. "Good job. I'm not sure what the stakeouts entail, but if they get you out of the house, wonderful. Dare I ask if you notice a change in your mood?"

"I'm brighter, I think—when I'm not feeling lousy about how I have no job and ruined my career. Being confused about Austin makes me miserable, and it's depressing to know that he's probably in love with someone I picked."

"Austin's opinion means a great deal to you. That usually means something."

"Okay, gotta run."

I stand up, but he waves me back into my chair. "I want to ask you something. Would you be my receptionist?"

"Me?"

"I realize you're a big-time television producer and this job is dead boring, but I need someone to organize my life here in the office and I think you'd be perfect for the job. I like you."

"Would you still be my shrink? Isn't that a conflict of interest?"

"I can refer you to someone else, but I'd miss you. You're one of my favourites."

"Why?"

"You don't go on and on and on."

"Okay."

❁

When I call Amanda to ask her to meet me for lunch, she's thrilled.

"Where should we go? I heard about this great little place close to work…"

"I don't want to be within fifteen miles of the CBC building."

"I can't meet you otherwise. I'm swamped. You need to get out of your comfort zone."

"Fine."

So here I sit in my casual attire while all around me business types hobnob over lunch. Amanda whirls in looking every inch the professional woman, with her black suit and bow-collared white blouse underneath her wool poncho. She's wearing high heels, something I've forgotten the feel of. She waves and comes towards me, saying hello to a few people at other tables before she kisses my cheek and sits down opposite me.

"It's so good to see you, Chloe. I'm thrilled you called me."

"It's good to see you, too."

She shrugs off her poncho, drops her elegant gold-chained bag in the chair beside her, and leans towards me. "We need wine."

"Not for me, I'm on drugs. You look wonderful."

"Believe me, this look doesn't come easy. I've had to up my game since they hired that little bastard—oh…sorry."

"My replacement?"

She nods. "He's one of those kids who think the world owes him a living. Honest to God, if my boys grow up to be like him I'll be heartbroken. I asked him to go to the editing room for me today and he said, *Why should I? You've got legs.* I nearly knocked his teeth out."

The waiter comes by with the menus and glasses of water. Amanda takes a sip. "So what have you been up to?"

"I'm going to be a secretary for a young psychiatrist just starting out."

She screams. Literally. Everyone in our section looks at her. "Sorry! Sorry about that!" Then she gets low to the table and thrusts her head at me. "You're joking. A secretary?"

"Excuse me. What is wrong with being a secretary? The origins of the word go back to 1350 Middle English. The word *secretarie* is medieval Latin. A person who keeps records and writes letters, originally for a king. Someone trusted with private or secret matters; a confidant. I'll take the word *secretary* any day over *receptionist* or *office manager*."

"You're right. What was I thinking?"

Now I take a drag of my water. "Stop it. I have to take baby steps here."

She reaches out to hold my hand. "Yes, you're right. It just upsets me that your talent is being wasted."

"I don't know what my talent is yet."

"You produced the number one hit show in Canada."

"I produced it because someone told me to."

"Okay, I won't badger you." She proceeds to size up the menu. "How about a pulled pork sandwich."

"I refuse to eat Wilbur."

"That's hogwash. Get it? *Hogwash!*" She looks behind me with surprise. "Hey, look who just walked in. Steve! Steve!"

I look over my shoulder in time to see Steve approaching us while his date stands by the door.

"Fancy seeing you guys here," he laughs. "How are you, sis? Chloe?"

"Good," I say.

"Who's that?" Amanda asks. "An art patron trying to whittle down the price of a painting?"

"No, just a friend."

"I thought you were working in advertising."

"Advertising? Chloe, I told you he worked at an art gallery."

"Oh, yes, I forgot." I don't bother looking at him.

"Well, good to see you two. I better shove off."

"Come for supper next week. Bring your friend."

He waves, goes back to the woman and escorts her out the door immediately.

"Why are they leaving? That's strange." Amanda shakes her head. "I wish he'd settle down. He's not getting any younger."

I've lost my appetite.

❊

WHEN MY DOORBELL RINGS LATER THAT AFTERNOON I KNOW it's him. I open the door.

"Yes."

"I'm sorry."

"For what?"

"Can I come in? It's a little chilly out here."

I walk down the hallway to the kitchen Steve hates and lean against the sink. At least he looks ashamed. "Why did you lie?"

"Your opinion of me means a lot."

"Why is what I think important?"

"I care about you, but you don't take me seriously."

"Are you still an escort?"

"Basically."

"You're an idiot."

"I never claimed to be otherwise."

"So what now?"

"I'm lonely. I thought maybe you were too."

"So you thought we could comfort each other in bed, because that's what you know."

"See? You just blurt out the truth all the time. I've never had anyone tell me the truth before."

"Get out."

"Chloe—"

I grab a dinner plate and smash it against the wall. "Get out! I've been lonely all my life. I'm not going to soothe that away having mindless sex with you. I already told you. You helped me and I'm grateful. I don't mind being your friend, but I can't do this. If you want to love someone, Steve, love yourself. That's who you need to pay attention to."

Gramps appears at my front door. "What's going on in here? Are you all right?"

"Everything's fine. My friend is just leaving."

Steve takes two steps closer and stands in front of me. "I'm glad I met you, Chloe Sparrow." He kisses my cheek and then turns to leave. As he passes Dad's study door, it slams shut. Steve jumps and lets out a yelp before he hurries down the hall and past Gramps.

"Nut case," Gramps mutters before he comes into the kitchen and holds his arms out. I walk into them.

"Is this a good thing or a bad thing?"

"It's a thing thing."

"That clears that up."

CHAPTER SEVENTEEN

My first day at the new job is a disaster. The patients hate me because I can't find them on the computer and their files are still in deep piles on the floor, so they have to wait while I search for the one I need. None of these miserable people say anything about it to Dexter. They think it's cute that he's disorganized and in a flap, but they give me an earful. How can he stand all the doom and gloom that floats in the air here?

The minute I start to make some progress organizing the office, the phone rings or some other misery guts walks in and I have to pretend I like them.

"Good morning."

"Is it?" Some goth girl who can barely summon the energy to chew her gum looks at me with contempt.

"Do you have an appointment?"

"Would I be here talking to you if I didn't?"

"Your name?"

"Wiccan."

"The name your parents call you?"

"Bitch, slut, whore..."

"That's how your parents talk to you? That's awful."

"You're calling my parents awful? Are you some kind of fucking social worker?"

There's another patient putting on his coat to leave. He looks very uncomfortable with this exchange.

"I apologize. May I have your birth name, please?"

"Tinkerbell Crawley."

I get a case of the giggles. Dexter's door opens. "Oh, hi, Tinker. Come on in."

We break for lunch at noon. Dexter pokes his head out. "I made some tuna sandwiches this morning. Want to share them with me?"

We settle down in his office. I supply the juice, yogurt, fruit, and éclairs.

"How are you making out?"

"It's slow going. I'll have to come in here on a weekend and organize these files so your patients stop glaring at me."

"Do they all glare at you?"

"I'm not being paranoid! Your patients have issues."

"Most people do."

I reach for another half of a sandwich. "Take Tinkerbell. Who on earth names their child Tinkerbell?"

"I knew a Marilyn Munro once, and the poor girl was no prize. Parents make lots of mistakes. My parents hounded me for years to be a lawyer like my dad, but I always wanted to be a firefighter."

"When I was five I told my mother I wanted to be a bal-lerina, and she said that it wasn't a practical occupation."

"She said that to a five-year-old?"

"When I was ten I wanted to be a vet...I'd forgotten that."

"Why didn't you?"

"I wasn't allowed a pet, so it seemed pointless."

"What did your parents want you to be?"

"A person who was educated and dedicated, who contrib-uted to the betterment of society."

"I hate to tell you, but society will always be screwed up, with or without you. It's not your personal responsibility to save the world."

I stand up. "I have to go."

"Where?"

"To my desk."

Halfway out the door, I turn back. "Speaking of desks, can your budget handle a few green plants, a nameplate, a couple of gallons of paint, and a rug?"

"Sure, but painting walls and ceilings are not in your job description."

"Do you want to be taken seriously or not? If this place looks like a dump, you'll never get anywhere in this world. And on that note, get yourself a few new shirts and ties and iron your pants."

"Aye-aye, Captain."

I'm a great one to talk. I go to Winners to buy myself professional clothes after work. The only secretaries I know are Mr. Gardner's old bitch and James Bond's Miss Moneypenny, so I come home with a bunch of skirts and cardigans. My hair is longer now and still horrific, so I pull it all back and make a very tiny bun. It looks ridiculous, but I feel like a secretary. To complete the transformation I buy sensible shoes. When I look in the mirror, Mom looks back at me.

I miss her.

Every week I promise myself I won't watch *The Single Guy* and every week I do, usually while snivelling and eating liquorice in my bed. Tonight he kicks off Lizette. I knew he would, of course, but no one else saw it coming.

She's furious and actually shoves Austin backwards before she gets in the limo. He steadies himself and looks forlorn.

Lizette points her finger at him. "Tu es complètement débile!" which roughly means *you're a complete moron.*

To which Austin replies, "Je suis désolé." *I'm sorry.*

"Casse-toi, Englishman!" I believe that's *piss off, Englishman.*
Then she slams the door in his face. He stands there and takes
it.

Amanda texts me. *Did you watch it?*

I text back. *No. What happened?*

He kicked off Lizette! None of us could believe it.

☹

I know! TTYL.

❀

BECAUSE I HAVE NOTHING ELSE TO DO WITH MY LIFE, DEXTER'S
office becomes my drug of choice. It takes me an entire
weekend to paint the walls in bright cheerful colours. Dexter
shows up to help, but he's lousy at it and gets in my way so I
send him home.

The super allows me to put up Dexter's nameplate on the
outside of his office and beside the front door going into the
building. I scatter the green plants, put an area rug between
the chairs, hang wooden blinds, and tack up modern artwork.
The place looks like it came out of a magazine. The last thing
I do is take Dexter's diplomas and have them professionally
framed to hang in his office.

All the files are filed, my desk is spotless, and there's a
coffee machine for the patients. I have a toaster oven in a small
supply room out back, where I spoon pre-mixed chocolate
chip cookie dough on the tray and make six cookies at a time,
putting each of them in its own wax paper sleeve and then in
a wicker basket on the coffee table I bought for thirty dollars.
The sight and smell when people come in is comforting. When
I can keep Dexter from eating all of them.

Since I've started working here, Dexter's clients have

doubled—no doubt through word-of-mouth about how great the office is. I'm sure they like Dexter too, but if he'd stayed in his rat's nest it wouldn't matter how great a psychiatrist he is, no one would've stayed to find out.

Dexter insists on taking me to dinner to thank me for my hard work. He wants to go somewhere fancy, but I choose a local Chinese restaurant. We both order the number three.

"When you're not toiling away in my doctor cave, what are you up to?"

"Nothing."

"You do nothing? I didn't think that was possible."

"I've kind of become an extra member of a detective agency called Nosy Parkers. I've made up a list of prices for different jobs because gas is expensive and I don't want it coming out of Aunt Ollie's or Agatha's pocket."

"Did you say a...detective agency?"

"It's my aunt and her friend doing favours for the neighbours. It keeps them from wasting away on a couch in front of the television."

"But what you do for yourself? What are your hobbies?"

"Don't have any, unless you consider wrestling with kittens a sport."

Our plates of fried rice, chow mein, chicken balls, and egg rolls show up. Dexter eats with chopsticks. I'm a fork kind of gal.

"I was talking to Uncle Matthew the other day and your name came up. He was very surprised to find out you work for me. He actually said it was beneath you."

My fork stabs the air. "What does that mean? Who decides which job is more important than any other job? The world puts too much emphasis on status. Now that I'm allowing myself sometimes to think about my old job at the CBC, I realize there were days when I hated it. The daily push to be better, trying to do more, striving for a bigger viewing audience—it's numbing after a while."

"Well, I very much appreciate what you've done for me. I owe you."

"It's nothing."

He stares me down. "But for me, it's made all the difference in the world. I didn't feel like a psychiatrist until you created the illusion that I was and I started to believe it myself. That's a wonderful gift."

Lying in bed that night, I think about what Dexter said. I look around. This is the room of an unhappy teenager. I'm now an unhappy adult, but I'm an unhappy adult with way better taste than I did when I was fifteen. I'm going to paint my room.

❁

I'M ON MY SIXTH COAT OF GREY PRIMER. MY LESSON FOR TODAY is, don't ever paint walls black. My arms are like noodles, so I go next door to sit for a minute and give my pussycats a cuddle. They are vacationing at Aunt Ollie's cat camp while the painting is being done.

Gramps, Aunt Ollie, and Agatha are around the kitchen table. I'm kissing kittens as I join them. "What's going on?"

"My car went back in for repairs," Agatha says. "Since you're busy painting, I'm trying to convince the old goat here to take us to our job today."

"And Dad is being a pain about it, as usual," Aunt Ollie frowns.

"Your car is obviously a lemon. Get a new one," he says.

"I may look like I'm made of money, but I'm not."

"No, I wouldn't say that."

"Gramps!" I turn to Aunt Ollie. "I'll take you. I need a break anyway."

"Thanks for nothing, Dad."

"Listen here, I'm off to court someone new. I have to be on my A game."

"You're an F as far as I'm concerned," Agatha says.

"Don't be so damn touchy, woman." He gets up and leaves the kitchen. "I'm surrounded by sourpusses. Speaking of pusses, where's Bobby? Come here, boy."

Bobby the dog-cat streaks after him.

An hour later we're parked on a quiet street with the sun streaming through the window. Despite the chill in the air, the sun is hot on the windshield—spring isn't far now. It's still March, but the patches of grass get larger every day.

"So what's the plan?"

"We have to take a picture of someone's backyard. Our client thinks her brother is stealing stuff out of her garage when she's not home," Aunt Ollie says.

"And this stuff would be...in a backyard?"

"It's a snow blower and a snowmobile, so yes."

"Why doesn't she just take the picture herself?"

Agatha gives me an annoyed look. "She's elderly."

Should I say it? Better not.

"We're wasting time. You stay in the car, and Ollie and I will be right back."

"Why can't I go?"

"Two old ladies aren't noticeable. Someone might give you a second look."

I suppose I'll take that as a compliment. It's only after they've disappeared up the street that I wonder what an elderly woman wants with a snow blower and a snowmobile anyway.

Five minutes go by, and then ten. Does it take ten minutes

to snap a picture? I'm not sure what to do. They told me to wait here and Agatha will give me heck if I don't follow instructions. But when fifteen minutes have gone by I have no choice. I jump out of the car and head off in their direction. It suddenly dawns on me that I don't have the address—they could be in any one of backyards on this street.

I rush down one driveway, come back to the street, and then rush down another driveway, over and over, hoping no one is watching out their window. There's no sign of them. This is ridiculous. Where are they? I'm almost at the end of the block and a bit panicked when I hear a small voice to my right. It's coming from behind the house I'm standing in front of. It doesn't look like anyone's home, but I keep my voice down just in case.

"Aunt Ollie? Agatha?"

Again I hear a faint whisper. "Over here."

As I round the corner I see the two of them pressed up against the inside fence. "What are you doing? You not supposed to be *in* the yard!"

They look scared to death.

"Don't worry, I'm coming!"

They shake their heads, but undaunted I run through the gate to rescue them—from what, I don't know—until I come face to face with an enormous bulldog growling deep in his throat, so deep I didn't hear him until now. I leap over to my partners in crime and the three of us huddle together as he snarls and drools at us.

We whisper without moving our lips. "Why are you in here?"

"It's Ollie's fault."

"It is not. You wanted a closer picture."

"I asked you if there were any dogs. You said no."

"I couldn't see him under the back deck."

"Does it really matter now? Be quiet so I can think."

"*I wish this dog would go to sleep and let us pass.*"

"That's it? That's the plan?" Agatha says.

Aunt Ollie springs to my defence. "Have you got a better one?"

The dog gets closer and more menacing with each passing minute. This wish is not working! What did I do wrong? "*I wish this dog would...*"

"Drop dead!" Agatha hisses.

I know I have to do something—and then I have it. Carefully, I take my cellphone out of my pocket and call Austin's cell. Please take the call. Please.

"Hello? Chloe?"

"Austin, I need your help."

The dog gets upset and starts to charge us and then runs around in circles, still growling.

"What's wrong?"

"We're being held hostage by a very scary bulldog. He's going to attack any minute. What should I do?"

"Where are you?"

"Agatha, what's the house number?"

"How's that going to—"

"Shut up and give it to me!"

She does, and I give it to Austin. He says, "I'll be right there."

I honestly didn't mean for him to come to the house. I thought he might talk me through a few strategies for calming the animal down, but now that I know he's coming, I want to weep with relief.

"Austin's coming."

"The nice vet you were mad at?" Aunt Ollie whispers.

"Yes!" I say that too loud and now the dog starts to snap his teeth. "Oh God."

It's the longest fifteen minutes of our lives. Finally I hear Austin's voice. He runs into the yard with heavy-duty gloves on. The dog is startled, but Austin calmly takes him by the neck and gives him an injection before he can even react. Peacefully, he falls to the ground and starts to snore.

The three of us are weak and trembling. Austin comes over and helps us out of the yard and closes the gate. "He'll be out for about twenty minutes."

I grab Austin around the middle. "Thank you. Thank you for always rescuing me."

He pulls me away and holds my arms. "How the hell did this even happen? That dog was protecting his property. He didn't do anything wrong, *you* did."

"You're right. I know you're right. I'm sorry."

"Do you know the people who live here?"

I avoid looking at him. "We were trying to take a picture of the backyard."

"We are on official Nosy Parker duty. Not that it's any of your business," Agatha huffs.

"That's the dumbest thing I've ever heard. You're trespassing? What is wrong with you? I left a waiting room full of patients to come over here, only to find out you're breaking and entering. I should call the cops."

"You're bluffing," Agatha says.

"Pipe down, Agatha! I'm sorry Austin. This will never happen again."

He points at us. "Stay off other people's property. This could have been a disaster."

Our hero storms off to his car and drives away a tad too fast.

"You heard him. Let's go."

We shuffle our way back to the car and sit for a few minutes, hardly believing we don't have a scratch on us.

"I can't remember if the snow blower and snowmobile were there. Can you?" Agatha says.

❀

THAT NIGHT I WATCH THE MAN I LOVE LET JOCELYN GO ON *THE Single Guy*. He looks miserable as he struggles to tell her.

Amanda calls me. "Were you expecting that?"

"Yes."

CHAPTER EIGHTEEN

I'M BACK IN THE OFFICE THE NEXT DAY, STILL SMARTING THAT Austin gave me hell, even though I deserved it. A woman comes in looking high.

"I have an appointment."

"Dr. McDermott shouldn't be too long. You can take a seat."

So she picks up a chair and heads for the door. I scramble from behind my desk and touch her arm.

"Sorry, that's my chair."

"Oh." She puts it back down and sits on it. I give her the last cookie to take her mind off whatever it's on.

In the afternoon I've got a guy in the waiting room cracking his knuckles repeatedly and a lady sighing every time he does.

"How long before I see the doctor?" he says.

"You'll see him when he's finished with the appointment ahead of you."

"And how long will that be?"

"It shouldn't be long now."

"You said that ten minutes ago. Look, I'm only here for a doctor's note. It'll take thirty seconds and then I can get out of here."

I punch Dexter's line and he picks up.

"Not now."

Down goes the phone. "Sorry."

"I bet you are."

"You're right. I'm not sorry. Pardon me if you have to sit on your ass for ten minutes. Waiting for a doctor is not a burden, you know. There are people out there who don't have a doctor, homeless people who have no family or friends to love or care for them. *Those* are problems, not waiting in a comfortable room with magazines and coffee and warm chocolate chip cookies that I made myself. So grow up and stop being an ungrateful oaf."

When I come to my senses, Dexter has emerged from his office. He, the patient he was with, and the other two are staring at me.

"Chloe, go into my office. Mrs. Fish, we'll call you about your next appointment; Mr. Getz, I'll sign that for you right now; and if you don't mind, Mrs. Olson, I'm going to talk to my secretary for a moment."

"Someone should," Mr. Getz sputters. "She has a nerve, insulting people."

Dexter comes into his office a few minutes later and shuts the door. He sits down and leans towards me, very calm and reassuring. "You're having a hard day."

"Ya think?"

He doesn't say anything.

"I'm sorry, that was rude."

"Maybe you should take some time off."

I cross my arms. "You're firing me?"

"I didn't say that."

"Perfect, why don't I go home to an empty house? The place where my parents barely knew me before I killed them, and where my relatives live next door but they don't need me anymore and the place where I rejected Austin before I knew what he meant to me, and now because of yesterday's debacle, I've killed any hope I had of ever being with him."

"You didn't kill your parents."

I stand up. "Yes, I did! I screamed at them that I wished they'd shut up and leave me alone. So they went outside, got electrocuted, shut up forever, and left me alone. All my wishes come true. Didn't you know that? So don't get too close to me or I might wish you away."

"Please sit."

"I don't want to sit."

"Chloe..."

I sit. "What?"

"Your wishes don't come true. Not unless you work hard and reach for them. You didn't kill your parents. You told them to shut up, like teenagers sometimes do, and they were alive when you said it. We can't worry about everything we say in case someone we love dies an hour later. You can't live like that. At some point, if this terrible accident hadn't happened, you'd have told them you were sorry, and your parents would have forgiven you, and the three of you would've had just an ordinary day. Your parents were killed by electricity, not your wish."

"So my wishes don't come true. I'm not special or powerful. I'm just nothing. That's what you're saying?" I'm angry, and shaken. My wishes *do* come true. My airplane didn't come down in the storm, the cream did appear in the fridge, I got the job as producer—and my parents shut up. Although I can't help but think about the wish I made for the vicious dog to fall asleep. Which he didn't, at least not until Austin drugged him. I wonder if that counts.

"I'm saying that you are a wonderful person who's been living under a weight of guilt about something that wasn't your fault. I hate to tell you, Chloe, but the gods didn't look down and say 'Hey, we should give magical powers to one person—how about a teenager who lives in Cabbagetown, Ontario?' I mean, come on. If you were a god, would you pick Ontario?"

"...I suppose not."

"Not that there's anything wrong with Ontario, but I figure the Fiji Islands would be better. Your homework for the next month is to tell yourself every day that you did not kill your parents. They are not dead because of you. Everything that happens is not because of you."

"So you said."

"Take a few days off to regroup, and if you need me, call me day or night. I hope you realize what a privilege that is."

"I'm honoured."

"You're going to be fine, Chloe. You'll get through this and you'll be fine. I know what I'm talking about because I'm the psychiatrist and I have a big plaque that you framed on my wall that says I'm brilliant in every way." He rips off the top page of his notebook and writes something down. "There's a group I thought you should check out, people who have lost their parents. They might give you some support."

"I don't need a bunch of whiners sucking the life out of me."

Dexter thrusts the paper at me. "Take it anyway, you stubborn mule."

As I'm on my way out the door, he says, "I think you should woo Austin."

"Woo?"

"When you decide to do something, Chloe, you do it to the best of your ability. Think of Austin as your next project."

Driving home, I think about what Dexter said. I don't like that he thinks I'm completely ordinary. Intellectually I understand what he's saying, but I *know* there have been countless wishes of mine that have come true. Maybe I'm not completely to blame for my parents' deaths, but I'm not completely innocent, either. And what's wrong with thinking all your wishes come true, anyway? People walk around all the time saying they can communicate with the dead or tell the future. Maybe they're telling the truth—their truth. I'm not convinced yet that I'm part of the rabble. Something sets me apart. Even if it's just screaming at people at work.

On my time off I finish painting my bedroom. The walls are now a soft buttercream with cloud white on the window frames and moulding. The professional junk guys come and take away the hideous canopy bed and all the other furniture in the room. A few hours after they leave, the furniture store delivers my new bed set, called Country Cottage Shabby Chic. I'm in love with the bed, the dresser, the bureau, and side tables, but I'm especially enthralled with the linen, duvet cover, and pillows, all in shades of celery green, soft pinks, and ivory. It's definitely girly, and I clap my hands in glee before I take a giant leap through the air and land on my new oasis. I'm out like a light in minutes.

I'm on the same fantastic bed a week later when I watch Austin let Kate P. go. Naturally, Amanda calls me. "Now tell me you saw that coming."

"No, I didn't."

"It's between Sandy W. and Sarah C. It still boggles my mind."

❦

THIS JOB IS NOT MY CUP OF TEA.

"How can you stand being a psychiatrist? All people do is bitch and moan. Don't you feel like slapping them silly?"

Dexter shakes his head. "Believe it or not, I actually help

people, which makes them feel good, which makes me feel fulfilled."

The phone rings and he answers it. "I'll be right there." He grabs his coat. "I have to go to the hospital. Cancel my appointments."

This is a job every secretary hates—cancelling appointments that people made months ago. Most patients understand, but there's always one who runs with it.

"Mrs. Mitchell, it can't be helped. He has an emergency and won't be here this afternoon."

"That's unacceptable. It takes forever to get another appointment."

"I'll make sure you're first on the list for cancellations."

"And what's so important that he can't see me?"

"That's none of your business."

"I was hoping Dr. McDermott would talk me out of killing myself this afternoon, but now I think I'll grab my husband's razorblade and get it over with."

"Well if you're planning to be dead, then I'll take you off the cancellation list right now."

She laughs so long and hard that I start laughing, and the two of us bust a gut over something I should never have said.

"Thank you. I needed that."

"Please don't kill yourself. And please don't tell my boss what I said. He'll be furious."

"You tell him that I'll live to see another day because I have to tell my bridge group about this. I can't wait to meet you."

That night I bring home a bucket of chicken and take it next door. Aunt Ollie, Agatha, and Gramps are sitting around the table looking down in the dumps.

"What's wrong?" I put the chicken in the middle of the

table. As I get the plates and cutlery they collectively sigh. "Someone better say something."

"I miss Nosy Parkers," Agatha says.

Aunt Ollie agrees. "I miss our picnics."

Gramps takes a drumstick. "I hate women."

"I thought you were enjoying their company."

"What company? After a while they only wanted me to drive them places so they could get their groceries done or go shopping. Effie even wanted me to help her son move! I said I don't even know him and she said I was selfish because she has arthritic ankles and what was he going to do? He can call the movers like everybody else, I said. She said he was too poor and I said *I'm* poor too, what with the gas I've spent these past months. She said she never wanted to see me again and I said good riddance. So now all the old hens in that building are mad at me. I'm never going near that place again."

"You had a good run while it lasted."

Agatha puts a wing on her plate. "They all had a lucky escape, if you ask me."

"Pipe down, you old bird."

"Dad! Stop talking to my best friend like that."

"I might be a bird, but you're a birdbrain."

That gives me an idea. "Why don't you and Aunt Ollie go birdwatching? You have to drive around, use binoculars, write down your observations. You'd meet lots of new people."

"But I wouldn't make any money," Agatha says.

"I'll pay you just to get out of my house!" Gramps yells.

They start brawling. I grab two pieces of chicken and go home, where I debone the chicken for the cats and make myself some rice and beans. After that's all done I take a bag of chocolate chip cookie dough and make a huge batch for Austin.

❀

MY DAY IS INTERMINABLE. I'M JUST WAITING FOR IT TO END SO I can take my yummy cookies over to the clinic. My thought is to leave them at the front desk, but the minute I put the basket down the office staff circle like sharks. Austin won't get any this way, so I grab it back.

"May I speak to Dr. Hawke, please?"

"Do you have an appointment?"

"No. I won't take up much of his time. I want to give him these."

"Sorry, he's operating at the moment. You can leave them here and we'll make sure he gets them."

"That's okay, I'll wait."

"It might be more than an hour."

They're annoyed with me. They can smell the cookies but can't have the cookies.

"That's fine."

I wait an hour and a half. I'm starving and there are three fewer cookies for Austin. He finally emerges, taking his operating-room cap off his head. He looks like a real surgeon. He *is* a real surgeon. It's very impressive.

"You wanted to see me?"

I hold out the basket. "I wanted to give you these cookies to thank you for saving my miserable life."

He doesn't take it. "That's very nice, but I'd rather not."

"They're just cookies. You can hate me and still eat them. They're not mutually exclusive."

"If I take them, will you go?"

"Do I have to?"

"Yes."

"Okay."

He takes the basket. "Thank you."

"You're welcome."

We stand there and look at each other. I forget I'm supposed to go and only remember when he says, "Scram."

"See ya."

He's scowling as I leave. This wooing thing doesn't seem to be working. The next morning I mention it to Dexter.

"Wooing someone can take months, even years. He's not going to fall at your feet over one basket of cookies."

"This is hard."

"Anything in life worth having is hard."

The next thing I do is send him a Candygram. Obviously I don't know how it goes over. He never calls to tell me.

For my next trick I write a poem.

Roses are red

Violets are blue

I'm a stupid idiot

And you're not.

I send flowers, I send a gift certificate for the liquor store, I send tickets to a Toronto Maple Leafs hockey game. I'm at my desk at work when Austin texts me. *Please stop sending me gifts. I appreciate it but it's not going to change my mind. I have no intention of being hurt again.*

I text back. *I have no intention of hurting you. I've completed a rehab stint for spoiled brats and passed with flying colours.*

The night of *The Single Guy* finale, Amanda wants me to go over to her place to watch it, but I decline. I can't be with anyone when this happens, so I sit here alone on my wonderful bed.

It's horrifyingly stressful. Trey opens up the limousine to Sandy W. and walks her to the edge of the garden path, where

I used to drink my coffee in the early days of the show. Austin looks sick. When he tells her that he thinks a lot of her but has to listen to his heart, she tries not to weep. She spends a lot of time wiping her eyes. He hugs her goodbye and sends her on her way. She's sad in the car and wonders what she'll do now.

So he's picking Sarah C. I know he likes her, she's a sweet girl and very funny. They always got along. She looks beautiful in her grey flowing dress. My eyes fill with tears as he holds her hands and tells her he's not in love with her.

OMG.

Amanda's on the phone. "Can you believe it? It killed me not to tell you."

"Everyone will hate him now."

"Wait until the wrap-up show! Fireworks! We'll be number one in our time slot for sure."

"I'll talk to you later, Amanda."

I cover my face with my hands. He could have proposed to Sarah for the cameras and then quietly broken up with her a few months later like the rest of them, but he didn't. And he's going to pay for that now.

❦

TREY AND JERRY ASK ME TO MEET THEM FOR LUNCH AT A LOCAL café. They want to know what I think of the outcome.

"Every media outfit is lambasting him for his decision. I don't think it's fair for people to judge someone they don't even know."

Trey makes a face. "That's what television is. They'll say mean things and tear him down and then the tide will turn and they'll say he's a man with principles who didn't take the easy way out, blah blah blah. Just you watch."

"Are you glad he didn't pick anyone?" Jerry smirks.

"What are you suggesting?"

"For God's sake, Chloe," Trey sighs. "Remember in Quebec City when I told you to keep your eyes open? I knew then that he was in love with you, but I didn't dare say anything because you were already at the end of your rope."

"Did everyone know?"

"No. Amanda doesn't know yet, because she's been in another world what with her demanding schedule, and Austin was careful around everyone. I only noticed it because I'm a guy. I already know your answer, but are you in love with him?"

I nod and tell them what I've been doing to woo Austin. Jerry tries to hide his dismay.

"Stop it for a few days. Maybe even a week."

Trey sips at his butternut squash soup. "You let him know you're interested, now wait a bit. You don't want to be a stalker."

"Okay."

"I've been meaning to ask you, do you miss work?" Trey says.

"No, but I miss the people."

Jerry points his fork at me. "Brian was saying the other day that his shoots aren't nearly as interesting now that you're not there."

"Good old Brian."

"Did you hear he hooked up with Sydney?"

"No way! I always liked Sydney."

"Can I leave you with another thought?" Trey says. "For the love of God, run, don't walk, to the nearest high-end hair salon. You're not going to woo anyone looking like that."

❀

UNBELIEVABLY, I LISTEN TO HIM. NOW MY HAIR IS IMPOSSIBLY cute. I spend an hour in the bathroom at home talking to imaginary people and flipping it this way and that. Hair is definitely a barometer of the soul. Even Gramps and Aunt Ollie like my new shaggy bob. Naturally, Agatha has her opinion: "Anything would be better than the way you had it."

The reunion show airs tonight. I expected Amanda to call me afterwards; instead, she shows up at my door beforehand.

"Oh my God, I love your hair! I had to watch it with you. Do you mind?"

If only she knew how much I mind. "Come in."

We settle on the living room couch. She's brought snacks and a couple of cold Cokes. Trey introduces the hostile jury of dismissed females sitting on what look like bleachers, just waiting for Austin to come out from behind the curtain. Then there's the studio audience of freaked out *The Single Guy* fans who can't believe they watched the entire series only to be disappointed.

He emerges to a smattering of applause but mostly catcalls, and shakes Trey's hand before unbuttoning his jacket and sitting on the couch.

For two hours the women rake him over the coals. All their disappointment comes bubbling to the surface. Austin is the target for their unrequited dreams. He manages to stay calm through it all.

Not Amanda. She's completely riled up and throws taco chips at the television. "I just want to smash their faces in! Sanctimonious she-devils!"

Trey asks Austin if he's sorry he came on the show.

"No, I'm not sorry. I met some wonderful people—the ladies, obviously, but also the crew, who were a great bunch and were with us for our adventures last summer. We travelled the country together and weathered some unexpected obstacles, but all in all I'd say it was a very worthwhile experience. Obviously it didn't turn out the way I expected, and I feel badly about that. These beautiful women offered their hearts, and because they did, I needed to be truthful with them. They deserve respect, honesty, and loyalty and I didn't want to make a promise I couldn't keep."

Now everyone's melting. Trey was right.

I turn off the television. Amanda is eating a pepperoni stick. "Is he not the sweetest guy? No wonder everyone's in love with him!"

"Including me."

She stops chewing.

"I love him."

"When did that happen? I know we always said we loved him, but not *loved*, loved him. How come I was oblivious to this? Why didn't you tell me?"

Then she does her restaurant scream.

"He loves you! That's why he didn't pick anyone! That's why he got rid of Jocelyn and Lizette even though they were his favourites. So it wouldn't be as traumatic for him at the end! Sandy and Sarah were just innocent victims—sorry, wrong word—innocent bystanders. Oh my God! Wait till I go home and tell Jason! This is fantastic. I'm so pleased for you, Chloe!"

"He doesn't love me anymore. I ruined it with my pathetic ranting about how I didn't need him or any man."

"We all say stupid things we don't mean. Fight for him, Chloe!"

"That's why I got the haircut."

"Good start. Now get a mani–pedi as well."

CHAPTER NINETEEN

IT'S AROUND NINE IN THE EVENING AND RAINING. I KNOW Austin's home; I can see his Mini Coop in the parking lot of this totally dreary apartment block. His address is still in my phone, which is how I tracked him down. That sounds like I'm hunting him. Which is not entirely inaccurate.

Because my plethora of gifts didn't produce any results, I've arrived empty-handed. Tonight it's just me and my nasty sweater dodging raindrops as I run into the foyer of his building. The humidity is already affecting my new coif, but I can't worry about that now.

Press his number. Ring. Ring.

The box says, "Yes?"

"It's me. Chloe. Chloe Sparrow."

He makes me wait for thirty seconds before he buzzes me in. This doesn't bode well. He's on the third floor, so I walk to my execution rather than take the elevator.

He's not waiting with the door open, so I knock. When he finally opens the door—it takes forever—he doesn't say anything.

"Hi, Austin, may I come in?"

"Why are you here?"

"To tell you I watched the reunion show and I was so proud of you."

He leaves the doorway, so I make the assumption I'm allowed in and follow him into a very sparse apartment. Only the necessities are here. He sits at his computer desk and whirls around in the swivel chair, burning off excess hatred, I guess. I perch on the very edge of the couch, since he didn't actually invite me to sit down.

"I love your hair."

That's a good sign. "How have you been?"

"I was slapped by a woman at the grocery store yesterday. I've received hate mail and, oddly enough, about a thousand marriage proposals, so I guess you could say I'm all over the map."

"I've been having a hard time..."

"Of course you have."

"Look, I'm trying to woo you and so far I'm failing. I love you, Austin. I know I haven't given you any reason to believe that, but I do, most sincerely. It's taken me a long time to figure out how messed up I've been, and Dexter—"

"Who's Dexter?"

"My shrink-slash-boss."

"You work for a psychiatrist?"

"We're a two-man operation. He's only just graduated—but never mind him. You're the best guy I've ever met. I've never had a real boyfriend..."

"You told me you did have a boyfriend. The reserved fellow who works in an art gallery."

"I'm a liar on top of everything else. You're right, I've only been concerned with myself, but I'm getting better. Please don't hate me. I went to your mom's and apologized about the flowers. She was as lovely as always."

"Chloe, you may think you love me, and that's very flattering, but my heart can't take any more hurt, so even if I believed you I wouldn't do anything about it. I need to protect myself right now. You need to leave me alone."

"So no more wooing?"

"None."

I stand up. "I've never loved a man before, and even if we're never together again, I want you to know that I intend to be just like Aunt Ollie and love you until I'm old and grey. Be happy, Austin."

When I leave, he doesn't come after me. In my head I always picture him saying, "Wait!" but there's no sound as I close his door. My sweater gets wet going back to the car. Amanda's right: it does stink when it's wet. I drive for hours without a destination, blowing my nose a couple of hundred times.

❀

A WEEK LATER DISASTER HITS. NORTON GOES MISSING.

I look for her and call until I'm hoarse. Gramps, Aunt Ollie, and Agatha help me and we search every corner in every closet and under beds and in the basement. She's gone. I swear I haven't left a door open, so I can't figure out how or why she isn't with me anymore.

"If I didn't leave a door open, then it must have been one of you two!"

Gramps and Aunt Ollie both swear on a stack of Bibles that they have never left the door open. So I canvass every home-owner in a ten-block radius. I plaster posters everywhere, and I call the SPCA and other rescue organizations to see if they have her. I take out print ads and radio ads and offer a reward of five thousand dollars. I ask all the vet's offices in the area to be on the lookout, even Austin's. Surely he'd let me know, even if he does hate my guts.

And then one morning I notice a straight rip along the edge of the kitchen window screen. It's big enough for a cat to get through. Thinking back, I cracked that window open one night when I burnt something on the stove and forgot to close it till the morning. So here's the proof. She really did leave me.

Every night I gather the kids on my bed and cry my heart out. They're used to it now, so it doesn't bother them. How could Norton have left us like this? Someone must have stolen her, she must be trying to get back to us. The thought of it gives me nightmares.

Every day when I go to work, the first thing Dexter does is look up from his desk. When I shake my head, he grimaces. Amanda came over one night to spend time with me, but I wasn't great company so I told her to go.

I've lost ten pounds, but I don't care. Nothing matters. I'm so distraught I barely speak to Dexter's patients. At night I stand by the living room window with the lights out and watch the budding tree branches sway in the wind, hoping to see her saunter down the sidewalk. Now that it's April it's not as cold at night, but she's out there and could be hurt or starving. The dark winter of my discontent threatens to overtake me once more, which is terrifying. Memories of the night Norton came into my life haunt me.

I get on my knees and pray. *I wish Norton would come home to me.* "Please, someone up there, if you're listening, that's all I want."

The very next evening, the doorbell rings, and when I open the door Austin is standing there with Norton in his arms. I burst into tears and reach for my cat. Norton licks my face and lets me hold her for a minute, but then she wants to go and see her kids. I hug Austin. My cheek presses into his coat and he puts his arms around me. I want to stay there forever.

Eventually, I have to let him go to wipe my tears. Austin follows me into the kitchen and sits on a chair.

"I can't believe you brought her back to me. It's so good to see you, Austin. You look better."

"You look like hell."

"I've been so upset about Norton, I can't think straight. How did you find her? How did this happen?"

"An eight-year-old girl came in with her parents and they had Norton in their arms. They said that Norton showed up on their doorstep one night and walked in like she owned the joint. They brought her to me to get her checked out. When I told them I knew who owned the cat, the little girl was very disappointed."

"She can get another cat."

"She's an only child, and she's bonded with Norton. If you could see the two of them together..."

"No thanks. Norton is back with me, where she belongs." I pick her up and give her a cuddle.

"It's up to you, of course."

"What am I supposed to do? Give her my pet?"

"Do what you think is right."

I keep Norton in my arms. "Thanks a lot for the judgement. Why did you even bring her back? You could have kept your mouth shut and not told me."

"I couldn't do that to you."

"Please go, Austin. I don't have the strength for this at the moment."

He gets up out of the chair. "Eat something, will you? Promise me you'll look after yourself."

"Thank you for bringing her home." I turn away and keep my face buried in Norton's fur until I hear the front door close. A few minutes later I rush next door to tell them the good news. They're very relieved to see her and happy she's home.

Norton puts up with me fawning over her for a couple of hours and then she goes to the front door and meows.

"Norton, you just got home. You can't leave."

She stays by the door all night. Nothing I do entices her away. She looks sad and desperate to go.

"Please don't leave me, Norton. My heart will truly break."

As dawn approaches after the second night of Norton holding vigil by the front door, I realize that Norton is here physically, but her time with me is over and she won't be coming back.

"Is this what you do, Norton? Find people who need you?"

Before I go to work I take Norton in the cat carrier and drive to Austin's clinic. I ask the girl to let Austin know I'm here and then sit in the back, away from everyone. Norton is purring. She knows.

When Austin comes around the corner, he gives me a big smile and then sits beside me.

"What changed your mind?"

"Norton told me to."

"You won't regret this."

"You'll have to take her. I can't do it. Call the family and get them to come. I don't want to meet them, but I'd like to see them."

"I will do that. Can I get you anything while you wait?"

I shake my head.

Austin picks up the cat carrier and takes it with him. It's everything I can do not to weep buckets. I'm trying to be brave and focus on the fact that I am lucky enough to have Norton's babies waiting for me at home.

It dawns on me that the child will be in school so I settle in for a long wait, but twenty minutes later, a couple come in with a little girl wearing a kerchief on her head. She's bald underneath. Oh my God, she has cancer. She needs Norton right now. She looks so happy and excited. The receptionist escorts them to the offices in the back. They're in there for fifteen minutes or so, and then the family comes back out, Norton snuggled in the girl's arms.

"Isn't Princess beautiful, Mommy?"

Oh, she is that.

After they leave I can't get out of the chair. My legs won't move. I'll have to stay here for the rest of my life. Fortunately, Austin comes around the corner and realizes what's going on. He calmly takes my arm and escorts me to one of the offices and closes the door.

"Why didn't you tell me she had cancer? I feel like a selfish jerk."

"That is exactly what I didn't want."

Now I can cry in peace. Austin holds me while I do.

"Let it out," he whispers.

Bad move, Austin. I'll be here for hours; I have a lot to let out. But Austin doesn't seem to be in any hurry, so I take him at his word and bawl about everything: Norton; my parents; my loneliness; my job; my idiotic behaviour where Austin's concerned; my obsessive need to control the universe; my lousy diet; my broken, broken nose; my thick ankle...the list is endless.

When I can't cry anymore, he sits me in the chair and bends down to look at me eye to eye.

"You passed my test."

"Why didn't you tell me I was having a test? I would've studied."

"You let go of something you loved. You thought about someone other than yourself."

"Not really. Norton howled at the door. If she hadn't I'd probably still have her."

He takes my hands in his own. "Just once, will you give yourself some credit?"

"*I wish you'd kiss me.*"

And he does. Oh, how he does. It's getting much too steamy in this little office and we realize it at the same time.

"I'll come to your place tonight," he says.

"I can't wait."

"You're not going to change your mind?"

"No."

When I finally tear myself away from those marvellous lips, I hop in the car and head straight to a lingerie store, because that's what women in love do, on television anyway. The girl picks something out for me because I'm flummoxed with the choices available.

I have candles on the coffee table in the living room (since I can't use the kitchen table for obvious reasons), a frozen pizza in the oven, red wine in glasses, and music playing. My sexy lingerie is on under my jeans and silk blouse and my fabulous bedroom is on high alert, with luxurious, un-frayed sheets at the ready.

At ten o'clock, the pizza is burnt, the candles are out, the wine is gone, and the music CD was biffed across the room an hour ago. I refuse to call or text him like a pathetic needy female.

At eleven I get a text.

I'm sorry.

❊

"YOU'VE GIVEN ME THE WRONG FILE AGAIN." DEXTER HANDS me a manila folder and I pass him another one. "That's not it either."

"Find it yourself, then."

"My office."

I follow him into the office and I know the drill. He sits down, I sit down. He leans forward with a concerned look on his face, and I fold my arms and sulk for a minute.

"Austin stood me up."

"Did he explain why?"

"He sent me a text saying he was sorry. Sorry for not coming? Sorry for not liking me anymore? Sorry he missed out on pizza? What?"

"You need to be patient with him."

"Figures you'd take his side."

"There are no sides. You both had a traumatic year. Let your life happen gradually; you'll always be disappointed if you're too rigid with a self-imposed timeline. You are much too serious for your own good. Be flexible. Be mushy. Be a limp noodle."

"You are never going to become a famous psychiatrist if that's the sort of advice you dole out."

"I don't want to be famous. Send in my next patient."

Amanda and I meet for lunch at a diner close to her office because the CBC building doesn't cause me heartburn anymore. It's just a building, with good people in it, like Amanda. When I tell her what happened, she nods and grunts as she devours a smoked meat on rye. "Do you want my pickle?"

"No, I want your advice. Dexter tells me to relax and everything will work out."

"He's a guy. They have no idea of the complexity that rules the female psyche."

"So what should I do?"

"First, you call up Austin and tell him not to worry about the other night. You totally understand and you weren't ready anyway on account of Norton, etc. That puts him at ease. Enough so that he figures it might be okay if you meet for coffee. He asks you but you can't make it. You suggest an alternate time—that way he knows that you're interested but not chasing him. You go on the coffee date, you give him a peck on the cheek goodbye and say you should get together sometime, but you're vague about it. So now he's uneasy that he might be blowing it, so he'll do something more romantic and you make sure you're ready for whatever it is and then you pin him to the mat...literally. After that he's yours. It's easy."

"It doesn't sound easy. Is that how you snagged Jason?"

"No, I got knocked up."

I'm riding the bus home when two elderly women get on, so I stand up and give one of them my seat. I tap the shoulder of the young guy next to me who's plugged into his phone. He takes out one earplug.

"Do you see this lovely lady here? She could be your grandmother. It would be kind if you gave her your seat."

The kid looks around and sees that other passengers are watching this exchange, so he gets up and stands beside me. The lady smiles at both of us and sits down. That's the moment I remember I drove downtown. Good grief.

I get off at the next stop and go across the street to catch a bus back when I see the earphone kid running after me. Oh shit, this is how I die. At least my bedroom is nice. I turn to face him and he's coming right at me...with my purse.

"You left this on the seat," he pants.

"Oh, thank you. Here, let me give you a reward."

"No thanks, ma'am. My grandmother wouldn't approve."
He gives me a wave and leaves.

Did he just call me ma'am?

That night I call Austin. I know what I'm going to say— but he doesn't pick up the phone. Hmm. I text him. *Don't worry about the other night. I understand.*

I try for three nights. Nothing. Finally, I phone his mother.

"Oh dear, I wondered if you'd call."

"What's going on? Is he okay?"

"He went to Uganda to see mountain gorillas."

CHAPTER TWENTY

IT'S ALMOST MAY AND MY TRAUMA ASIDE, THE WEATHER IS GLO-rious. Tulips and daffodils are poking their heads out of the soil. Brilliant, light-green leaves unfurl on the trees. Spring is about renewal, and in spite of all my disasters, I'm feeling slightly more alive. Dexter attributes it to his meds, and I'm sure that's part of it, but at some level deep inside I'm waking up out of a long slumber.

I spend all my free time getting rid of things I don't need anymore. Peanut and Rosie have a marvellous time in the boxes and bags strewn all over the floor. Big lump Bobby lives with Gramps and doesn't want any part of this place. Cleaning up the past is liberating. I empty my parents' closets and throw most of their clothes away, but a few of the suits and coats are still in good shape so I bag those for Goodwill.

One Saturday morning I come across a small, wrapped package at the very back of Mom's top drawer. It's a gift addressed to me. The small card says *For Chloe, on her six-teenth birthday. Mom and Dad.* It's a gold necklace with a simple gold cross attached to it. It's delicate and beautiful. I put it on and it looks like it's always belonged there. Having it with me gives me the strength to get rid of a lot of their belongings. I don't have to be Miss Havisham anymore.

This spurs me on to bigger and better things. I call the 1-800-GOT-JUNK number and arrange for a massive purging. Gramps and Aunt Ollie are on the porch wringing their hands.

"What if you throw something away that was my mother's?" Aunt Ollie says.

"You hated the old bat," Gramps says.

"You hated my grandmother?!"

"Believe it or not, your mother and I liked this old fool much more than we liked her."

The things you learn.

"You're going to throw out all the furniture?" Gramps says. "Is that wise?"

"I'm keeping the good stuff, like Dad's roll-top desk, Mom's secretary desk, the old rocking chair, the antique bureau, and some lamp stands. The wingback chair is nice, too, once I cover it, and the settee. Everything else is revolting eighties junk."

A hefty fellow comes out the door with the kitchen table over his head.

"You're not throwing that away, are you?" Aunt Ollie tsks.

"Watch me." I wave at the table. "Bye-bye."

Another truck pulls up to the sidewalk.

"That's your truck."

"What do you mean?"

"These nice men are going to take every scrap of rotting newsprint, magazines, and brochures in your house. I'm not letting them take anything else until we have a chance to go through it, but I have no intention of fixing up my house when you live in a firetrap next door. If you don't comply, I'll get the municipality involved. Do you understand?"

"Why would you get the municipality involved? What business is it of theirs?"

"You are becoming borderline hoarders."

Gramps waves me away. "You watch too much television."

"And you two are plain lazy. This has been going on long enough. It's time to smarten up."

"Let me go get Bobby. The stupid bastards might take him!"

It takes hours, but eventually both trucks lumber away. In my house there's an echo, with Peanut and Rosie running from room to room with glee. The occupants next door are in shock. The place looks five times bigger.

"I'm not sure I like this." Gramps holds Bobby while they check out each room.

"I'm hiring a cleaning company to come in here and scour the place. It will look much better then."

Aunt Ollie comes out of her bedroom holding an iron. "I've been looking for this for years."

❧

NOW THAT I'VE CLEANED ALL MY WOODEN FLOORS THOROUGHLY, my new steam mop keeps them shining. Rosemary and Peanut are delighted with the slippery surface. All I need now is some furniture. My new kitchen table is coming today, which will be a godsend since I'm getting better at cooking meals for myself and freezing them. Nothing fancy, but at least they're vegetarian and wholesome.

The doorbell rings. "There's the table, girls!" Peanut and Rosie run down the hall ahead of me and then dart up the stairs. When I open the door, I am certainly not expecting to see Austin.

He's put on some weight, he's tanned and looks relaxed, his hair is longer with blonde streaks—from the African sun, I imagine.

"Hey, Chloe."

"Hi, stranger. How was Uganda?"

"The most amazing experience of my life."

Oh good, and I was over seventeen thousand kilometres away when it happened.

"May I come in? I brought you some presents."

"By all means. You'll have to sit on the floor."

The girls come streaking down the stairs and zoom around the living room before heading out again.

"They look wonderful."

"Mm."

We sit and he opens his backpack. "I have two gorgeous baskets. I thought you'd like them, and some woven red fabric from a small village, and a soapstone bracelet."

"Well, thank you so much." He hands them over and smiles. I want to smash his teeth in.

"You're welcome. A lot has happened while I was away. Someone stole your furniture."

"I'm getting rid of all the garbage in my life. I'm sure you know how that feels."

That hesitant look I know so well comes over his face. Stay calm.

"And the mountain gorillas, were they glorious?"

"I cried when I saw them. They were magnificent, a dream come true."

"That's wonderful, Austin. I'm really happy for you."

"Thanks."

We sit and look at each other. I don't feel the need to say anything else.

"I've thought a lot about you while I was away."

"That's nice."

"I'm sorry I didn't tell you before I left. It was a crazy, last-minute decision, and I was on the plane before I realized what I was doing."

I nod and smile.

"I felt like I was choking."

"Right."

"The show did my head in."

"I can imagine."

"I just needed to breathe."

"Don't we all."

He gives me that piercing Hawke-eye thing he does so well. "Will you knock it off? I'm trying to be serious."

I leap to my feet. "Thank you very much for the gifts, Austin. They're lovely and I am grateful. But you need to leave now." I walk to the front door.

He comes behind me. "I understand why you're upset. I should have handled it differently. But I think both of us needed some time to ourselves."

"You are so right, Austin. That's definitely what I need, more alone time. Say hi to your mom."

He shoots me a dirty look and I smile.

"Bye-bye!"

When I close the door I race to the kitchen and take a spatula and hit the wall about a dozen times. Aunt Ollie's muffled voice shouts, "Give it a rest!" So I run upstairs and beat the shit out of my duvet. Then I call Amanda.

"That miserable rat had the nerve to say that we needed time apart. He had the most amazing experience of his life while I was on my knees scrubbing floors like Cinderella."

"So you didn't let him say anything else?"

"Like what?"

"How he wants to proceed?"

"He can't proceed! I never want to see him again!"

"You'll change your mind."

"Amanda, I mean this in the nicest way, but fuck right off. Love you." Click.

Austin's baskets end up being new beds for the girls, the fabric is draped over my rocking chair, and the bracelet I'll wear because it's nice. Why should I suffer?

❀

A FEW WEEKS ROLL BY AND I AM SUFFERING. ALL I CAN THINK about is Austin, which ticks me off because I don't want to be thinking about him. It gets so bad I take Peanut to his office for an appointment. There's not a thing wrong with her. When I get there Austin is out on an emergency call, so I slink home. He's doing good works. I'm flipping out at Dexter's patients.

"For the third time, Mrs. O'Neill, Dr. McDermott cannot make a house call."

"I want him to."

I've been on here for five minutes trying to get through to her. "I'll tell him you called and he'll call you back."

"No."

"What do you mean, no?"

"It's not good enough. He needs to come here."

"Sorry." I hang up the phone.

She calls back. I assume it's her, but I'm not picking up to find out. It rings ten times and finally Dexter comes out of his office. "Everything all right?"

"I can't do this anymore."

"My office."

We sit in his office. "You can't do what anymore?"

"Work for you. You'll have to find someone else. I'm sorry, Dexter; I'm not suited for this job."

He nods his head. "I know. I've often wondered why you stayed so long."

"Because you were so nice to me. You'd forget I had an appointment or be cool with the fact that I'd run out ten minutes into a session. You cared and didn't rush me. I noticed even if I pretended not to."

He smiles. "What will you do?"

"I don't have a clue."

It's the middle of June when I finally finish working for Dexter. It took him that long to find someone. I'm not surprised; look how long it took him to get chairs. The woman is an efficient, middle-aged sort who knows way more than I ever did. Dexter hugs me goodbye and says he'll see me for my appointment in three months. I weep all the way home in the car. I wanted to move on, it was my decision, but what little psychotherapy I've had tells me that I will always have a hard time with change. I'm like the three-year-old in the sandbox who grabs all the toys and won't share with anyone. It's scary to acknowledge I can be a shit like everyone else and scarier still to know I'm capable of doing ridiculous things like call up Steve and ask him to take me to Jamaica.

❀

"You want to go to Jamaica in June? You'll melt."

"Okay, smartass, then where?"

"Las Vegas?"

"How about New York? It's closer."

"When do we leave?"

"This isn't what you think. I'm not interested in sleeping with you. I just need to get out of here and you're the only one I know who is irresponsible enough to drop everything and go."

"Spoken like the Chloe I know and love."

"No loving. Just eating."

"Just eating."

I pack my bags and tell Gramps and Aunt Ollie I'm going to a spa and I'll be back in a couple of weeks. They're not fussed. They're tired of seeing my gloomy face. Steve meets me at the Air Canada gate and tries to kiss me but I refuse, so he hugs me instead. We drink champagne on the flight, go to our boutique hotel room on 45th St., and don't leave the room for five days.

❦

IF I SPENT ANY TIME THINKING ABOUT THIS SITUATION I'D BE mortified, but fortunately my brain is on hiatus. I'm drugging myself silly with fattening food, bottles of wine, sex, and cartoons. We're even raiding the mini-bar, which I'll regret later, but what the heck.

Steve is so laid-back he's a bed. He suggests we go to a spa for a couple's massage.

"Ugh, creepy."

"Have you ever had a massage?"

"No."

"Then be quiet. You can hate it after you've had one."

So we end up in this very warm room on massage tables parked right next to each other. There are jungle noises coming out of a stereo somewhere in here. I'm already freaked out by the fact that I'm naked under this robe.

"I have to lie down with nothing on?"

"No, they'll cover your pretty little ass with a sheet."

I'm lying here trying to relax but not having much luck. My face is looking at the floor through the headrest attached to the table. I suppose I knew someone would have to put their hands on me, but I glossed over that part.

"Just breathe," Steve mumbles. He sounds like he's almost asleep and it hasn't even begun.

The door opens and I see four feet, two for me and two for Steve. My God, one of these Swedish ladies has huge feet. Mine puts a tissue with lavender scent by my head with her hairy knuckles. Hairy knuckles? My head pops up. There's a man standing over me.

"Umm, Steve...Steve..."

"Mmmm?" He's already enjoying the pretty girl rubbing his back.

"Look at me!"

He opens one eye. I mouth, "Mine's a guy!"

"For the love of God, Chloe, live a little."

Easy for him to say, he's got people running their fingers over him twenty-four seven. I put my face back in the hole and gag. "I'm sorry, I can't stand this smell."

"Perhaps you'd prefer peppermint?" the jolly green giant says.

"What exactly is this for?"

"So your nose doesn't get stuffed up," Steve says. "Let the man do his job."

Peppermint isn't much better, but I put up with it. This guy's hands are the size of a phone book. He could clearly break me in half if he wanted to, so that's all I think about. When he puts his hands up near my neck, I freeze. "Don't."

"Madam?"

"Don't touch my neck."

Steve sighs heavily, a cue for me to stop being a party pooper. I shout at the floor I'm staring at. "If I don't want him to touch my neck, that's for me to decide, Steve, not you."

"Are you on your honeymoon?" the pretty girl asks.

"No, thank God," we say in unison.

The giant changes strategies and proceeds to put hot rocks on my back.

"Is this really necessary?"

"It will soothe you."

"No, it won't."

There's a bit of a commotion and Steve's feet appear under the table. "I'd rather be stuck in rush-hour traffic than go through this. We're leaving."

I bolt upright and the rocks fall off my back and onto Steve's toes.

"Sorry," I say over Steve's screams.

Steve hobbles back to our room, refusing my offer to assist him. He lowers himself onto the bed and covers his eyes with his arm.

I sit on the edge of the mattress. "I didn't do it on purpose."

He lowers his arm and shakes his head. "You are incapable of letting yourself go."

"I'm here with you, aren't I?"

Steve reaches out and takes my hand. "You're only here because you have nowhere else to go. I know that. I can see now that you and I are only destined to be friends, because if we were a couple I'd have to kill you."

"I'd kill you first."

"I have a great idea. Why don't we go see New York?"

We roam the city for a week and see the sights. We browse museums, art galleries, and luxury stores. We have dinner every night after the Broadway shows. We really do have a very nice time, but now we go to sleep on either side of the king-sized bed.

"Good night, Steve," I wave at him.

"Goodbye, Chloe," he waves back.

CHAPTER TWENTY-ONE

ONE OF MY FAVOURITE PURCHASES WHILE I WAS AWAY IS A GOR-geous handbag that's as soft as butter and lined with silk. My old purses have to go, so I root around inside them, making sure I don't miss a credit card or an extra key before I throw them out. I come across the phone number Dexter gave me for his pity-party bereavement group. I toss it onto my bedside table and use it as a coaster for a week, but because I'm trying to ignore it, it becomes a beacon that shines in the dark. I've proven that I don't need people, so why would this crowd have any answers for me?

On the other hand...it's not like I'm doing anything else.

The number is now covered with circles from pop cans. I can barely make it out—the ink is bleeding into the damp patches—but I press on. It's ringing.

"Together We're Better. Mary speaking. Can I help you?"

"Probably not, Mary, but when is your next meeting?"

"It's tonight. We meet every second and fourth Tuesday of the month."

"And this is for people who've lost parents?"

"Yes."

"Is there an expiry date? It's not like I lost them last week."

"The fact that you're calling is the answer to that question."

Mary is a know-it-all. She gives me the address and says she looks forward to meeting me. I don't go until two weeks later.

The group meets in a church basement. It's spooky going down the stairs. The lights are off in the main part, but there's a door open on the right and I can hear people murmuring inside. There's a semi-circle of people sitting on chairs facing the woman I assume is Mary.

"Welcome." She smiles. "Join us."

Okay, I've run into another cult. I don't want to join them, but everyone swivels their heads to look at me. I'm trapped, so I quickly sit in the first empty chair. Thankfully, Mary continues as if I'm not there, which means I don't have to introduce myself or participate in any way.

Sad to say, I don't even listen to Mary. I'm too busy observing this diverse group. None of them would have anything to do with the others in real life, and yet here they sit together, the young with the old, the well-dressed matrons beside the party girls, the businessmen beside the street kids and college students. I'm lost in the crowd.

Most everyone speaks at one point or the other and there are some tears, but I notice this bunch doesn't flinch. Crying isn't a sin here. The stories are all different, but the result is the same: Losing your parent is like walking around with no skin. The world can hurt you now that your protection is gone. Who do you belong to? Who is there to say, "I remember the day you were born." The two people who created you have disappeared and left you alone in the universe. Shouldn't you be with them?

When I sense things coming to a close, I skedaddle so that Mary can't corner me.

❖

THAT FRIDAY IS THE START OF THE LONG WEEKEND HOLIDAY IN August. Amanda calls and asks me if I want to come over and play in their paddling pool. My life must be at a new low; I'm excited about the prospect. After loading up with candy for everyone, I arrive to find Daddy Partridge chasing the baby Partridges around the yard with a water hose. He sprays me as I come through the gate.

"Oops, sorry."

"If you're sorry, take that grin off your face."

Amanda waves me over to the chaise lounges. "Never mind them, what's in the bags?"

We settle ourselves in our chairs and eat junk food while the father of the year keeps the kids busy.

"Your husband—"

"Is amazing. I know. My mother says I don't deserve him." She holds her lollipop in the air. "Speaking of great guys, have you seen Austin?"

"No."

She pantomimes choking me. "Friggin' frig frig!"

Ignore her. "How's work?"

"They've renewed *The Single Guy* for next season."

"I hope Mr. Gardner offered it to you."

Amanda looks over at her kids. "Yeah, but I don't think I'm going to take it."

Now it's my turn to choke her. "Why? Not because of me, I hope, because I'd be thrilled for you."

She reaches over and pats my forearm. "No, not because of you. The schedule is a little too gruelling. Being away from home for months isn't fair to Jason. I'd rather work on local programs, so I can be in my own bed at night. Besides, I really missed my kids. Work isn't everything in life."

The boys run over to their mom squealing and put their cold, wet hands on her legs. She screeches and jumps up to chase them back to their kiddie pool. Jason seizes the moment and plops down in her chair.

"Any candy left?"

I pass him the overflowing bag.

"Don't you just love eating junk that you'll never let your kids have?" he grins.

"My parents wouldn't let me eat candy."

"Life without peanut butter cups and M&M's isn't worth living."

We sit for a while not saying much and watch Amanda in the pool as she helps the boys fill a bucket with water.

"I love her," I say.

"Me too. That's why I need some advice."

I turn my head to face him. "What's wrong?"

"Her brother Steve was over the other night when Amanda was with her mom. We had a few brews and he spilled his guts basically."

Instantly, I stop breathing.

"He confessed he's been a male escort for a year now."

My eyes are bugging out, which he takes as a sign that I'm as shocked as he is.

"He lost his job and went for the easy money. I couldn't believe it."

"Wow."

"He says he's finished with it. That he can't do it anymore. I don't know whether to believe him because he's a pretty good liar, but he did sell his car for some cash, so that says something. My dilemma is whether to tell Amanda or not. What do you think?"

"He told you because he's ashamed to tell his sister. He doesn't want her to think badly of him."

"I know, right?"

"He's doing something about his mistake and starting over. I'd keep it a secret. I won't say a word."

Jason nods. "That's what I thought. Thanks."

The kids call their father over and he leaves me.

Dear old Steve. I'm proud of him.

❀

AS THE WEEKS GO BY, I SPEND A LOT OF TIME OUTSIDE WITH Gramps digging up a section of the back lawn to prepare a garden for next year. It will save a lot of money on vegetables. Gramps was brought up on a farm and knows a ton about growing food. The added bonus is I won't have to mow as much grass.

"We'll put the tomato plants and pumpkins in that sunny section, over where Bobby is."

Bobby meows and rolls over on the hot ground, pointing it out to me. This cat is spooky.

I don't have a lot of strength, but between the two of us, we manage to work the soil sufficiently, adding bone meal, compost and sheep manure. The hardest part is getting Gramps to stay put while I spray sunblock on him.

"A lot of baloney!" He waves me away. "Something the government thought up, no doubt."

"You'll get skin cancer, now stay still."

He's pretty agile when he wants to be. I chase him around the yard. "Get back here!"

Aunt Ollie steps outside the back door. "What's wrong?"

"She's attacking me!"

"I am not. He's going to get skin cancer if he doesn't put on sunscreen."

"Child, the old coot is probably filled with cancer. He's been smoking since he was eight."

"Eight? Are you kidding me?"

Gramps wipes his forehead with an old handkerchief he

produces from his pocket. "Those were the good old days, when just enjoying yourself wasn't against the law."

Aunt Ollie comes and sits on the top step, her bone-white legs exposed to the sun. "Give me some of that spray."

I do, but she goes inside a minute later. "It's too hot."

It is too hot. *I wish it would rain.*

A clap of thunder sends Gramps, Bobby, and I scurrying into the house. We just escape a downpour.

There's something about rain and thunder that makes me lonely, so I end up going to the group meeting at the church hall. I attend sporadically, so Mary doesn't think I need her. This time I select a seat somewhere in the middle. I'm not here to talk, just to listen, until Mary decides to stick her nose in.

"Can you relate to any of this, young lady over here?" She points right at me.

"Yes. I'm an orphan."

"Please. You're too old to be an orphan."

I recognize the snarl. I turn my head and sure enough, it's Dexter's patient, Tinkerbell. She looks as pleasant as ever, with her black raccoon eye makeup, cheek spikes, and see-through earlobes.

Two can play this game. "The dictionary's definition of orphan is a child whose parents are dead."

"Exactly. A child. How old are you?"

She's good, but Mary's better: a counsellor who immediately jumps in to keep the argument from escalating. "A very interesting observation. How old do you have to be to feel like an orphan?"

A voice at the back says, "I'm forty and I'm heartbroken. My mother was everything to me."

The group murmurs and nods its approval. It seems my point has been made. Tinker folds her arms across her chest and glowers before jumping up and walking out of the room.

Now I feel bad. She's just a kid.

At the next meeting we only have half the crowd. Mary says it could be because of Labour Day.

"*Death Takes a Holiday*," Tinkerbell says under her breath.

She's clever. "That was the title of a movie—"

"I know. A 1934 romantic drama starring Frederic March and Evelyn Venable."

"Do you like watching movies, Tinker?" Mary asks.

"When I'm not getting drunk or blasted out of my mind on prescription drugs."

One of the other girls rolls her eyes and Tinker sees it.

"What's up with you, bitch?"

Mary puts her hands up. "Okay, these meetings can get highly emotional, but we don't insult each other."

"We're all angry," the girl continues, "but getting stoned isn't the answer."

Tinker glares at her. "How did your parents die?"

"My dad had prostate cancer."

"Well, honey, I killed mine. What advice do you have for me now?" Tinker gets up and storms out the door. Mary scans the alarmed faces in our group and tries to settle everyone down.

"She looks like the type who'd murder someone," the girl says.

"That's a terrible thing to say. She didn't murder anyone. Don't you recognize guilt when you see it?" I brush past the others and leave the room. I can hear everyone buzzing behind me. When I get outside, it's still raining and I don't see Tinker at first, but as I hurry to the car I catch sight of the glow of her cigarette. She's slumped on the bench inside a glass-enclosed bus stop. As I approach her, she looks up.

"You people are relentless." Taking a big drag, she blows smoke in my direction.

"Do you mind if I sit down?"

"It's a public space. You can piss here if you want to."

So I sit and get straight to the point. "I killed my parents too."

Tinker gives me a sideways glance. "Yeah, right."

"I did. I told them to shut up and they were electrocuted an hour later on our front lawn."

"Well, I screamed that I wanted mine dead, dead, dead, and they had a car accident that night. I swear to God they did it on purpose just to stick the knife in one more time."

"I'd be furious, too, if my parents called me a slut and a bitch and a whore."

Tinker sits up and stares at me. "Who are you?"

"I was Dr. McDermott's secretary, remember? Do you want to grab a coffee or something?"

The bus comes around the corner. Tinker grinds the cigarette out with her heel. "I'm not a charity case, lady." She climbs the bus steps and I watch as she walks down the aisle to sit at the very back.

❦

GRAMPS AND AUNT OLLIE AND AGATHA ARE AT COSTCO the next Saturday, and little Bobby cat is outside on his leash chasing bugs. "You're the only one who likes to go outside."

Bobby nods. I swear on a stack of Bibles, he does. And then I look at him closely and see his nose is three times the size it should be. It doesn't matter what my relationship is or isn't with Austin. He's the only doctor I trust with our family's feline health.

I'm at the vet's office in fifteen minutes.

"No, I don't have an appointment, but this is an emergency. I must see Austin. Bobby might have trouble breathing. Look at this nose."

Bobby looks like Jimmy Durante but otherwise as healthy as a horse, so she tells me to take a seat. I make my way over to the back corner and sit beside an elderly woman with the most gorgeous dog I've ever seen. I'm actually distracted from my own medical crisis.

"Oh my, what a sweetheart."

"He's my Dudley," she sniffs.

Dudley is a fat basset hound with velvet ears that hang to the floor, his woe-is-me expression magnified ten times by his big beautiful brown eyes. I reach over and touch Dudley's soft head. He gets to his feet and puts his head in my lap so I can continue to stroke him. "You must love him very much."

"I do." Her voice cracks and she begins to weep.

"Oh, I'm sorry. I didn't mean to upset you." Reaching into my new handbag I find a packet of tissues. "Here, please take this."

She wipes her tears and gathers herself.

"Poor Dudley must be sick, is he?"

"No, he's fine. But I have to go into a home that doesn't allow dogs and I have no one to care for him. I've agonized over my decision to put him down because he'll just die without me."

All thoughts about logistics leave my mind. "I'll take him! I'll take him and bring him to visit you."

She looks shocked. "But...but I don't know you."

"I'm a very nice person. I own two cats, but I have a huge house and a big backyard and Dudley could be happy there. I can get references. The vet, Dr. Hawke knows me, and he can vouch for me. I really mean it, Mrs...."

"Miss Elwood."

"Oh, Miss Elwood, please reconsider! Dudley is adorable. I love him already."

"Well, I don't know...I'm so confused."

"Take a deep breath and think about it."

Austin comes out from an examining room and looks at the chart. "Dudley Elwood." Then he looks up and does a double take when he sees me, so I wave and smile. As Miss Elwood rises from her chair, I put my hand on her arm. "I really, really mean it. I wouldn't have offered if I didn't mean it."

She's distracted as she leads Dudley over to Austin, and they disappear behind the closed door. Bobby meows from the carrier. I forgot all about him. "Oh, good, you're still breathing."

They are in that room for what seems like forever. Oh, please don't let her go ahead with it! Surely Austin wouldn't let that happen. *I wish for Miss Elwood to give me Dudley.*

Finally Austin pokes his head out and beckons me with his finger. Oh yes! I leap out of the chair and leave Bobby behind.

"Your cat," someone says, pointing.

"Oh, goodness, thank you." Back I go for Bobby. "Don't tell Gramps I did that, okay?"

Twenty minutes later, I own a dog. Miss Elwood gives me her new address and we make plans to meet twice a week to take Dudley for a walk around her neighbourhood. We agree to the exchange in ten days time. That will give her a chance to get his things in order. She says I need to know the routine and what he eats and his grooming regimen, etc.

"Please, we'll get it all sorted. I'll see you soon."

"Come on, Dudley," she smiles. "Let's celebrate and buy steak for supper." She kisses me on the cheek. "God bless you, child."

Finally I'm alone with Austin. He smiles at me. "Are you sure you know what you're doing?"

"I never know what I'm doing, but it can't be that hard. I couldn't let that beautiful animal meet his end that way...at least not until he's lived his full life."

"Nice move. How are you?"

"Good. You look great."

"So do you."

Bobby says, "Meow."

"I forgot the cat!" I take Bobby out of the carrier and hold him up. "Look at his nose."

Austin takes him and gives him a gentle examination. "Looks like he lost a fight with a bumblebee."

"He'll be all right, then?"

"He'll be fine. He's learned his lesson and will probably leave bees alone the next time he sees one."

We stand there and look at each other. It's tricky.

"So, what have you been up to?" I ask him.

"This. You?"

"Nothing much."

"You're still not back at the CBC?"

"No, just as well. My mind is decaying." I rub Bobby's fur while I talk. "Austin, I'm sorry I threw you out of the house after you gave me your gifts. Miss Manners, I'm not."

"I deserved it for standing you up. Forget about it."

"Okay." Is it me, or is it getting hot in here? I want to kiss that mouth, but look what happened the last time. "I better go." Back into the carrier goes Bobby. "I'll see you around."

"Want to go for coffee?"

This is the best phrase in the world, second only to *I love you*, and *We won the lottery!*

❀

Aunt Ollie and Agatha think I'm deranged to take on a dog.

I have to listen to them because they're in the car with me, seeing as how Agatha's ancient auto is back in the shop. We're scouting out a playground to see if a boy named Preston is hurting the other kids.

Agatha looks through her binoculars. "A big old hairy thing on its last legs."

"Who? Preston?"

"No! The dog."

"He's only three years old."

"But what if Rosie and Peanut don't like him?" Aunt Ollie worries. "They come first."

"They'll get used to him. We got used to Agatha, didn't we?"

Agatha punches my arm. "Take that, you brat."

"I sense action," Aunt Ollie shouts. "Get the video camera ready."

This is my job. So I zoom in on the dratted Preston and a group of kids. I see him pull a girl's hair, but she turns around and wallops him. He does it twice more and gets an elbow and spit in the eye. "This girl is going to make mincemeat of this kid."

My attention turns to the cop car stopped down the street and a woman pointing at our car.

"Fuck!"

"Chloe! Watch your language!" Aunt Ollie shouts.

I throw the video camera at Agatha. "We've got to get out of here. A neighbour must think we're creepers. Someone called the cops."

"What's a creeper?" Agatha wants to know.

"She thinks we're pervs, and no, I'm not explaining right now!"

I pull a U-turn and zoom up the street and turn at the first right, hoping to lose sight of the police car, but no, the car's right on my tail. I'm not going to make matters worse by getting in a police chase. I pull over at the first available space and the officer parks behind me.

"Don't say anything! Let me do the talking."

Why do police officers all look gigantic when they get out of their cars and approach yours? My blood pressure spikes and I'm perspiring, which is always so attractive.

The male officer leans into the car. "Ladies."

"Good afternoon, officer—"

"This is ridiculous!" Agatha shouts. "We're not hardened criminals. We were only filming children."

We are released from the police station several hours later. Our arresting officer reads the riot act to Agatha and Aunt Ollie and tells them in no uncertain terms that it's time to hang up their binoculars. I thank them very much and promise to keep my eye on them.

The officer gives me a hard look. "Need I remind you that *you* were driving the car and manning the video camera? The warning extends to you as well."

"Of course. Don't worry. You'll never see us again."

The three of us hurry out to the car, and before I start the engine I turn in my seat. "Okay, you heard the man. No more of this. You'll have to think of something else to keep you occupied."

Agatha grunts. "What kind of dirty mind would think we were taking pictures of children for sexual purposes?"

"This is a very new world, Agatha, and unfortunately it's all about perception. The truth is sometimes lost when people automatically assume the worst of mankind."

"Take me home. I'm tired," Aunt Ollie sighs.

"So do you promise me that Nosy Parkers is out of business?"

They nod sadly.

"Don't worry. You'll find another hobby."

I wish for Aunt Ollie and Agatha to find a new way to occupy themselves.

CHAPTER TWENTY-TWO

OUR COFFEE DATE IS A GREAT SUCCESS. WE SIT UNDER THE umbrellas of a sidewalk café and people-watch. The sights you see, when you just stay still.

"What are you going to do now, Chloe?" Austin puts the cup up to his lips. Oh, to be that cup.

"I'm picking up Dudley tomorrow. I can't wait."

"I mean for the next hundred years."

I've been practising my coquettish manner in the bathroom mirror, so it comes quite naturally when I toss my hair and twitter demurely.

He leans closer. "Did you swallow a fly?"

"You total jerk. You always ruin the mood. I put on this polka-dot dress and these itchy espadrilles just for you. I could be on the cover of a magazine."

He gives me that cheeky smile and wrinkles his nose. I *love* when he does that. "You only need to be you. You're not a model, you're not on *The Single Guy*, and you're not one of these exotic creatures walking down the sidewalk with designer price tags hanging all over their bodies."

Bat your eyelashes. "What am I, then?"

"Have you got something in your eye...I'm kidding!" He puts up his hands and laughs before he leans back in his chair. "What are you? Let me see. You were my boss, and then you were my friend, and then I was hoping you'd be my girlfriend, but it turned out you were a thorn in my side. Thankfully, you're now my friend again. I hope."

I put my sunglasses on the top of my head so I can squint at him. "I ask you what I am and that's your answer? Haven't you read any romance novels?"

He nods his head slowly. "Oh, it's like that, is it? Well, here's my answer." He takes my face in his hands and kisses me softly in front of the whole patio. Oh wow. I'm in a movie. This feels amazing...

"Chloe?"

I was unaware he'd stopped kissing me. "Yes."

"Pay attention."

"Sorry."

"Ask your question again."

"What question?"

He drops his head in frustration.

"Oh! Sorry, sorry. What am I, then?"

He smiles when he looks up. "You're my everything."

❀

DUDLEY HAS BEEN WITH ME NOW FOR A COUPLE OF WEEKS. HE'S become part of the garden gang. He and Bobby are fast friends, though Rosie and Peanut aren't as thrilled. When they're not hissing at him, they're hiding from him—but the good thing about Dudley is he can't be insulted. He's happy about everything.

I was so worried when I actually put him in the car and drove away. From the way Miss Elwood talked, I expected Dudley to roll down the window and shout that he was being kidnapped—but no. He grinned at me the whole time. At least, I think he was grinning. It's hard to tell with his folds of saggy jowls. The minute I introduced him to the family, Gramps became his pal, and even Aunt Ollie and Agatha were smitten. It's like I've always had him. He is definitely the canine version of Norton.

Austin and I take him for walks and we visit his real mother, but Dudley loves going for car rides the best. His ears flap in the breeze out the passenger-side window, like two velvet banners announcing his arrival. When I stop at red lights, the drivers next to us all point and wave at him. He makes people feel good.

Wait a minute. He makes people feel good.

It's mid-September when I attend Mary's class and bring Dudley with me. Everyone's face lights up, but I don't care about everyone. I care about Tinker. She's at the back, looking gloomy as usual, but I'm on to her. She can be saucy all she wants and give everyone the silent treatment, but she's still showing up every week.

I purposely sit next to her and nod hello, but then I concentrate on Mary at the front of the class. Dudley works his magic with his sweet temperament. Before long, Tinker is scratching behind his ear, and just like he did to me, he sits up and puts his head on Tinker's lap for a cuddle. I don't dare look at them.

At the end of the meeting, I notice Tinker delay her exit. She's usually the first out, so I strike.

"Would you mind doing me a favour?" I ask her. "I think Dudley needs to pee. Can you take him outside while I talk to Mary for a second?"

"You trust me to take your dog?"

"Shouldn't I?"

Dudley looks at her with his soulful eyes and gives an impatient wiggle. He knows the word *outside*.

So off Dudley goes with the devil herself holding his leash. If Miss Elwood saw this she'd have a heart attack. Mary is cleaning up the coffee cups and putting napkins away. I go up to her.

"I was wondering, do you often get cases where young people think they're responsible for their parent's death?"

"It happens, but often we never know it because it's so difficult to talk about."

"That's true. Okay, thank you."

She holds out her hand. "Why do you ask?"

"Just a gut feeling."

When I go outside, Tinker and Dudley are halfway down the block. Dudley is sniffing at everything while Tinker patiently waits for him. I watch them for a while before Tinker turns around and sees me. She starts to come back.

"Well, well, well," I smile. "Looks like Dudley has a new friend."

Tinker reaches down to pat his head. "He's a great dog."

"Isn't he? I just love him. Do you have a dog?"

"No."

"My parents never let me have a pet."

"Mine neither. Although I did have a hamster once. My dad killed it. He said he thought it was a rat."

Keep calm and carry on.

"Hey, it's only eight-thirty. Why don't we get a coffee at the drive-through and Dudley and I can drive you home? Beats taking the bus."

"Okay."

"My name is Chloe Sparrow, by the way."

"Don't expect me to shake your hand."

When the lady hands us our coffee, she spies Dudley in the back seat and insists on giving him a Timbit. Now I can see why Dudley is such a butterball. Everyone and his dog insists on giving him something to eat.

Tinker doesn't say much on the drive home, but I happily chat about nothing at all. Just the fact that she allowed me to get this close to her is a major victory. We pull up to a nonde-script, two-storey house.

"Thanks for the ride." She opens her door.

"Tinker, what's your schedule like?"

"My schedule? I think I'm having lunch with Justin Bieber on Thursday. Why?"

"My vet told me that Dudley needs to lose a few pounds and that I should be walking him more often, but I'm really busy. Would you be interested in walking Dudley three or four times a week after school? I'd pay you, of course."

She takes her time thinking about it. "What do you want from me?"

"Nothing. If you're not interested, that's okay. I'm going to put an ad on the bulletin board at Superstore tomorrow. I'm sure there are lots of students looking to make money."

"No kid does anything if they can help it. If they want money they sell a few pills."

"That's awful."

"What would you know about it, with your fancy clothes, and car, and designer dog. You don't have a clue."

"You're probably right. I'm sorry I bothered you. Good night."

She gets out of the car and slams the door in my face.

❀

I'M ON MY LAPTOP READING ABOUT GRIEF AND THE POWER OF animals to ease distress. Every day there are articles about dogs being used as companions for servicepeople suffering from Post Traumatic Stress Disorder, or PTSD. This is where my years of research prove valuable. I'm relentless when I want to know something, and I'm not satisfied until I know everything.

I mention it to Dexter at my appointment in late September.

"Can I just say that you seem lighter than air?" he grins. "What a huge difference. What's your secret?"

"Let's see." I count on my fingers. "I credit my meds, walking dogs, kissing Austin and my cats, digging in dirt, thinking about Tinker, research, and my plans for the future. The list is long."

"She mentioned you at her last appointment."

"I haven't seen her lately. She seems to have stopped going to the bereavement group."

"Don't give up on her, Chloe. You are exactly what she needs."

Three days later there's a knock at the door. Most people use the doorbell. When I open it, there's Tinker.

"Hello! How did you find me?"

"Dr. McDermott. He said you wouldn't mind."

"Not at all. Come on in. Dudley! Tinker's here."

Dudley is asleep on his favourite chair, the one I'm supposed to get reupholstered. He opens one droopy eye and closes it again. "Just give him a minute. He's like an old man when you wake him."

Tinker looks around. "You don't have any furniture. I thought you were rich."

"No, I'm not rich. I'm comfortable. Come into the kitchen and have a drink while you're waiting."

She follows me into the kitchen and sits at the table while I open the fridge. "I have sparkling water, mango-pineapple juice, or almond milk perhaps. There's also coconut water."

"No rot-your-gut Coke or Pepsi?"

"I do, but it's warm."

"I'll have the juice."

While I pour her a glass, Rosie and Peanut roar into the kitchen. They skid to a stop when they see Tinker.

"Cute cats."

"They're my babies. Their brother lives next door with my Gramps and Aunt Ollie."

The cats decide that Tinker is an interesting new landmark in their landscape and won't leave her alone. I bring over the juice and join her at the table.

"Don't let them crawl all over you. You'll be covered in fur in no time."

"I don't mind."

As the cats continue to sniff and try to climb up her legs, the armour that surrounds Tinker softens a little. Of course, you'd still be scared to death to meet her in an alley, but this is the beauty of the animal mind. It's your energy that matters, not what you look like.

"So you live here alone," she says.

"Yes."

"Don't you have a man?"

"I do, as a matter of fact, but he has his own place."

"That's dumb."

"Maybe, but I'm used to living by myself. Ever since my parents died when I was a teenager I've had to manage on my own, but I was lucky enough to have my grandfather and aunt live next door, so they helped me. Well, they tried to help me. Still, I love them and I'm grateful for their support. Someone is better than no one."

Tinker takes a sip of her drink. "That's not always true."

She's only ten years younger than I am, but I want to take her in my arms and rock her like a baby.

"Do you work? I mean, now that you're not Dr. McDermott's secretary?" she asks.

"I did, before I was a secretary. I produced the television show *The Single Guy*."

"Fuck off! You did not!"

"I did, I swear."

"You're too young to do something that cool."

"It was very hard work, believe me."

She looks at me with new respect. "So you know Austin Hawke?"

"He's my boyfriend."

"No way!"

"Would you like to meet him sometime?"

I see a flicker of a smile. "Are you serious?"

"Sure. You'll probably meet him if you take the dog-walking job. Is that why you're here?"

She nods and looks pleased.

Dudley lumbers into the kitchen with a yawn. "Ready to go for a walk?"

He knows the word *walk*, too, so the wiggling begins. I give Tinker his leash. "There's a little park around the corner. He loves sniffing around there. Here's a bag to clean up after him."

"Eww. I'm not doin' that shit."

"Okay, but if you get arrested, I'm not making bail."

She's trying not to smile. She takes the bag and walks out the door with Dudley. It's just the beginning, but it's a start.

❦

THE WEATHER IS SPECTACULAR THIS FALL, AND THE SOFT, buttery tones of the dying leaves and melting sun put me in a mellow frame of mind. Perhaps I'm noticing the weather more because Gramps and I have spent so much time in the backyard. When I look back on my life, I realize I've barely spent any time outside. That's such a shame. It's amazing the energy that seeps into your bones when you go about your day under a bright blue sky. I think the fresh air is helping Tinker as well, and all the walking has given Dudley a sleeker silhouette. Miss Elwood is delighted that he looks so well. I tell her that he has Tinker to thank for that. She says she wants to meet Tinker. I'm still trying to figure out how that's going to go.

Today I'm meeting Amanda for lunch. We haven't seen each other in a while and I miss her in my life. As soon as I sit down at the table, she's gobsmacked.

"You look like a different person! You've got colour in those chubby cheeks, and is that a muscle I see on your arm?"

"I haven't noticed a muscle, but I do feel stronger. It's all the work Gramps and I did for our vegetable patch. I think I'll study gardening and do something with my front yard."

Amanda picks up her water glass. "Oh God, the Gardens of Versailles will pale in comparison when you're done."

"That's what Austin said."

"How is he? What's the status?"

The waiter interrupts. We order and I continue.

"There is no status. We're taking it slow."

She almost spits out her roll. "Taking it slow? You've been crazy about each other since the day you met. What the hell are you waiting for?"

As usual, I feel like a kid when Amanda starts lecturing me. "We've had a bumpy road. Neither one of us wants to make a mistake."

"Don't be an idiot. There's such a thing as being too careful. Look what happened to your poor Aunt Ollie. You snooze, you lose."

"I'm sure we'll muddle through without your help."

"Damn, girl. Make that man yours before someone comes along and jumps the queue."

I ask about Jason and the kids just to shut her up. That takes up the rest of lunch. Then off we go to buy her an outfit for some mucky-muck cocktail party Mr. Gardner is hosting. While she's in the dressing room, I'm outside holding some of her choices. She emerges in a gold lame top and pencil skirt.

"What do you think?"

"You look like someone's Rolex watch."

Back she goes and tries on a green flowered number.

"Lily pad."

"Fine, but floral is the latest trend. Pass me the red one."

While she's trying it on I ask her about work. "Do you think they miss me?"

"We're just numbers on a pay stub, Chloe. Everyone is replaceable."

"You could have said no."

"No."

"Good. Now I can move on."

She appears from behind the curtain.

"That dress won't be on for long."

She looks pleased.

❀

CATCHING UP WITH OLD FRIENDS IS FUN, BUT I INVITE TREY and Jerry over with a purpose in mind. After we polish off the cheesecake, we take our coffee in the living room.

"I am in love with this dog!" Trey says. "We have got to buy a bassett hound, Jerry."

"No, Austin says you should adopt a rescue animal from a shelter."

"Fine, we'll get one of those too, but I still need this dog."

"You can't have him. Now what do you think about this room? I'm asking you because your place is so fabulous, you must have some tips for me."

"Burn it to the ground?" Jerry says.

"Besides that."

"I have no clue. We pay someone to do ours," Trey says.

"But..."

"You think all gay men are fabulous decorators? I'm highly insulted. It's such a stereotype and you should know better."

"Sorry."

"But if you want advice about musical theatre...."

Jerry gets up and moves about the room, Rosie and Peanut at his feet. "The first thing you have to do is get some light in here. That fireplace is beautiful, but you can't see it in the dark, so if you added a big sparkling mirror above the mantel with two crystal light sconces on either side that would help enormously. Then you're going to need a stunning crystal chandelier with a ceiling medallion, some pot lights, and two lamp stands and some table lamps—"

"I'd have an operating room! Would I need that much?"

Jerry gives me his impatient eye roll. "Who's the lighting expert here? Everything will be on a dimmer switch to suit your mood."

"What's your decorator's name? Although, I don't want anything too modern, like Lucite chairs or sofas with no arms."

"We have Lucite chairs and sofas with no arms."

"Yes, in your modern condo. This is a turn-of-the-century house. I want to keep the integrity of the space."

"Integrity? This place has been hanging its head in shame for decades. It's used to being neglected and ugly. *Anything* would be an improvement!"

"Dudley, go bite that bad man."

Dudley snores on.

"If you want inspiration," Jerry says, "walk up and down your street. Every single one of these houses is perfection. You and the house next door are the poor relations."

"Thank you for your insults. They've motivated me to never invite you over again."

Before I go to bed I wonder around my empty rooms. Am I really going to do this? Make changes my parents might not approve of? Then I remind myself that they're ghosts and other than cracked china and swinging doors, what are they going to do about it?

When Tinker shows up later that day, I decide to tag along for Dudley's walk and really take a good look at my street. The houses are immaculate, with gorgeous landscaping. Then I look at Gramps's and mine with a new perspective. We're eyesores! It's a wonder the entire street hasn't served us with a petition from a betterment committee. Our two houses look sad, like no one cares.

I care. Suddenly I care very much.

On the walk home, Tinker opens up. "Have you ever stopped thinking you were responsible for...you know?"

"Yes and no. There's a part of me that carries that burden, but now that I'm older I see that I didn't make them go up that ladder. My father should've known better."

Tinker looks away. "It's different with a car accident."

"Were you driving the car?"

"No, but they left the house because of me."

"People leave their houses ever day and get in a car of their own free will. We are always at risk. It's the luck of the draw whether we make it home safely or not."

Tinker doesn't look at me as she bends down to pat Dudley's soft head. "I told my mom that Dad was abusing me and she didn't believe me. They said I was a liar and needed to get away from me. Do you think that's awful too?"

"Yes, Tinker. I do think that's awful. They didn't deserve to die, but as your parents it was their duty to protect you. Nothing in this situation now or when you were growing up is your fault. They were the adults. You're the child."

"I hate them."

"That's okay."

"But I miss them."

I'm aware that tears are falling down her face, but she hides them from me.

"Of course you do. They were your parents, and you'll never get the chance to fix things now. That's what's making you sad. You can hate them for what they did and still wish they were here. I was often very angry at my parents. They wouldn't let me have a pet, or have friends over, and they didn't pay much attention to me. I always felt like I was in the way. But I still love them. They're still with me."

Should I tell her about my parental spirits? Nah. Better not.

"It's going to hurt for a long time, Tinker. But I know you're going to be okay, because you have a mind like a steel trap."

She wipes her eyes and stands up. "What do you mean?"

"You're clever. I recognize it. I'm clever too...in some areas. In other areas I'm hopeless, but I think you have the strength to rise above your lot in life and make something of yourself."

"I do?"

"And I need a personal assistant, because I'm going to start a new venture. I don't have it completely formed at the moment, but for the first time in my life, I know what I want. And it involves you."

Despite herself, her face brightens. "You mean on television?"

"Maybe. We'll see."

When we arrive at the house, Austin is sitting on the top step. "Hey there, you must be Tinker." He stands up and holds out his hand. "Great to meet you."

I know Tinker is quietly losing her mind, but she hides it well. At least she shakes his hand, unlike mine at the bus stop.

"And how's our Dudley?" Dudley starts squirming. He loves Austin slightly more than the rest of us.

"I came with pizza."

"Perfect. We're starving."

We sit around the kitchen table and hear about Austin's day. Then I tell Austin about Trey and Jerry's visit and how I'm going to completely renovate the inside and outside of this house.

He shakes his head and looks at Tinker. "She's small but she's mighty."

Tinker takes a gulp of her pop and then says out of the blue, "How come you don't have a key?"

"Because he doesn't live here."

"He's your boyfriend. You must trust him."

"Of course I trust him. I'm just...private."

"I don't think she does trust me, Tinker. She pretends to be a free spirit, but she's actually old-fashioned. She still worries about what her grandfather thinks and she's almost thirty."

"Not so fast! I'm twenty-six!"

"Still an adult, wouldn't you say?"

Tinker agrees. "You need to grow up. You are very immature."

"Thanks a bunch."

Austin and I drive Tinker home and on the way back I tell him about my progress with her.

"Impressive. She seems like a tough nut to crack."

"She's not that tough, God love her. Imagine what she's been through. It makes me want to cry."

When we get home, all three critters meet us at the door. We've only been gone fifteen minutes.

"How about some dessert?" Austin says. "Any of that cheesecake left?"

"No, but I'll make it up to you."

He turns around.

"Tinker's right. I need to grow up and give you a key to this place. But there's something I want to give you first."

I dash up the stairs and he dashes up behind me. Dudley, Rosie and Peanut are excited, until we dash their hopes and shut the bedroom door.

CHAPTER TWENTY-THREE

It takes me a while to summon up the courage to tell Gramps and Aunt Ollie that I've invited Austin to live with me. It's November, and Austin is getting impatient.

"I'm the one who sneaks out the back door in the morning. Not exactly a pleasant way to start the day."

So I go to the store and buy a lot of ice cream and brownies and dole them out to the three amigos, who are perched around their messy kitchen table. They look a little bored and unhappy, which doesn't make my mission any easier. I'm about to open my mouth when Agatha speaks up.

"When are you going to tell that Bluebell to stop dressing like a freak? She looks ridiculous."

"She's expressing herself."

"She looks like the bride of Beetlejuice," Aunt Ollie says with her mouth full.

"You've actually heard of Beetlejuice? You surprise me sometimes, Aunt Ollie."

"Agatha and I watch cable television now that we have nothing else to do."

"You could volunteer at a soup kitchen, or offer to work with Meals on Wheels, or read to invalids, or help collect for any of a thousand charities around this city."

"And what would *I* get out of it?"

"The satisfaction of knowing you helped someone."

"I never had anyone help me."

"Okay, forget it. Watch television."

"We will."

Aunt Ollie has Winston Churchill's glower down pat.

"How about you, Gramps? Any projects in the works?"

He puffs on his pipe. "No."

I wait for him to say something else, because he always does, but today he doesn't. Maybe this is a good day after all. I clear my throat.

"I've asked Austin to come and live with me, and before you say anything, I want to point out what a good idea this is. Gramps, Austin loves to work outside and he can help us with the garden next summer. If you need any heavy lifting, Aunt Ollie, you can count on Austin. We'd always have a vet on site if anything happened to the cats or Dudley. His mother is a great cook and always sends over delicious baking. He can shovel the driveway, paint on tall ladders, carry groceries, protect us if a burglar broke in...it just makes good sense, to me, at least, so I hope you'll support me."

Complete silence.

"Well?"

Agatha scrapes her bowl. "Do you even love this guy? Sounds like you expect him to be a slave."

"Of course. I'm just saying—"

"Then why not marry him?" Aunt Ollie asks.

"I'm not ready yet. There are things I have to do first."

Gramps gets up and sits on his rocker. Bobby immediately pounces and drapes himself over Gramps's shoulders. "Like get a job?"

"Eventually. This is the first time I've ever taken any time off, and it's helped me to see things clearly. For a start, I want to spruce up our property."

"It's almost winter. How much sprucing can you do?"

Agatha points her finger at me. "I say we tell Austin to head for the hills before she works him to death."

Not for the first time, I wonder if I'll ever have a normal conversation with these people. It's draining to deal with them.

"So? Do I have your blessing?"

"I don't care," says Gramps.

"I don't care either," says Aunt Ollie.

"It's none of my business, and I couldn't care less," says Agatha.

I'm a little let down.

❊

LIVING WITH A MAN IS COMPLETELY DIFFERENT FROM JUST sleeping with him. I find Austin's stuff everywhere. He doesn't hang towels correctly, and he never drinks all the milk in his cereal bowl. There are toast crumbs in the butter, lids left off jam jars, and he leaves all the kitchen cupboard doors open. My ghostly mother closes them on occasion.

He puts stuff away and I can't find anything; he opens the window too wide at night; he likes to dance around the house with music blaring; he even puts all the crap from his pockets on my beautiful dresser.

The more he settles in, the more trapped I feel. His big feet stomp up the stairs, he talks too loud on his cell, and he feeds Dudley at the table. I finally blow up when he leaves the inner plastic liner behind the shower curtain out of the tub. There's water on the bathroom floor everywhere. He apologizes, but then uses my best towel to clean it up. Not only that, he used my favourite soap and now it's got man hairs stuck all over it.

"You are driving me crazy!"

He comes up behind me with a damp towel around his waist and rubs his cheek on mine. "Soft, isn't it? I bought a five-blade razor just for you."

"Why? So I can slit my throat?" I push his hands away.

"What's wrong?"

"Everything! This doesn't feel like my house anymore. It's like an alien landed and is now systematically destroying my environment."

Fortunately, Austin is used to my hissy fits. "Can I point out some benefits?"

"If you must."

"You'd ace any Cosmopolitan sex quiz about keeping your man satisfied, thanks to all the practice you've had lately."

"Here we go."

"I rub your stinky feet."

"They are not stinky."

"Says you." He advances towards me while I back out of the bathroom. "I make sure you have a good breakfast in the morning. You have to give me that."

"Fine. What else?"

"I volunteered to paint for you."

"Okay."

"I saved you from that weirdo in the grocery store parking lot."

"He was weird."

I'm backed into the bedroom and he continues to move forward. "And don't forget the scary movie I wouldn't let you watch."

"You watched it."

"I also tickle you when you come home from next door with steam coming out of your ears."

"True."

"And I do kiss you all night, don't forget."

I fall back on the bed. "Okay, you can stay."

He covers me with his body and puts his soft cheek against mine. "I knew you'd see it my way."

❀

I MAKE AN APPOINTMENT TO SEE DEXTER, BECAUSE I NEED HIS opinion about an idea I have.

"I'm no psychiatrist, but I do have first-hand experience. My proposal is to gather a group of teenaged children who've lost parents and bring them together with animals, as a form of therapy. Austin has already made inquiries at local SPCAs and animal shelters and they are always looking for volunteers to help out with exercise and grooming and just keeping the animals company while they try to find homes. I've seen what a difference it's made with Tinker."

"She's come a long way."

"Once I get this program up and running, the real fun starts. I want to make a documentary about it, to add to the voices out there trying to make people see what a beneficial experience it is for someone's who suffering to feel the love of an animal, and how we can help them at the same time. We are all living beings, beings that can help each other heal."

"Sounds ambitious."

"But best of all, Tinker will be the face of this project, the one who can reassure new participants. They'll open up to her more easily than an adult. She can talk to them, and slowly they will talk to each other as time goes on. I'm going to make it such a great program that when Amanda presents it to Mr. Gardner as a freelance project, the CBC will have no choice but to air it. It's costing them nothing. This is my money I'm dusting off."

Dexter grins at me. "You know what I think of when I look at you? Spit and vinegar."

"And best of all, I'm honouring my parents. They always wanted me to make a difference, and I believe I *am* making a difference in Tinker's life. I want to help all the other Tinkers out there who think they're alone. So will you help me?"

"I would be delighted."

Fortunately, Mary feels the same way. She said she would make enquiries from other social agencies to suggest clients who might be interested in such a program.

But the best moment is when I tell Tinker my plan. We are walking Dudley, the snow falling gently around us. It's not accumulating, it's still too warm for that, but it gives me that first thrill of the changing season. For the first time in a long time I'm looking forward to Christmas.

Her eyes sparkle. "Me? You want me to be on camera?"

"You're perfect. You've walked the walk, you're their age, and you live in their world. You understand what it's like to navigate the stress that young people feel today. You couldn't be more perfect."

She touches her hair. "I'm not pretty enough."

"That's ridiculous, but I do know some pretty fabulous makeup people and hairdressers who will do anything you want. I don't have a problem with your look now, but you might decide to soften it up a bit. Television can be very unforgiving. We will really need to see your eyes. You can't communicate when you're wearing a mask."

I let all that sink in.

"And you don't have to ask anyone's permission for me to do this?"

"I'm the boss. What I say goes."

"Awesome. I want to be a boss some day."

"I have every faith you will."

❀

T₀ THINK ABOUT AN IDEA IS ONE THING. T₀ BRING IT TO LIFE IS another. My scheme is embraced by the people who matter to me, but bureaucrats and their red tape can stop a project in its tracks. The more I run into brick walls, the more I realize that this project isn't suited for mainstream television. I rethink my strategies and go the social media route, where ideas can become viral in a matter of hours thanks to YouTube and Facebook. I want an underground vibe to appeal to the kids who would never visit a social worker or psychiatrist. The kids who not only fall through the cracks, but break their dead mothers' backs.

Brian has offered his camera skills, and I'm using every contact I made at the CBC to align myself with sites to give me maximum exposure on the net. Tinker comes up with a great name for our project—Creature Comfort.

The difference between us and a structured bereaved group meeting is that there is no expectation for the kids to explain their feelings. My mission is just to make them feel better and get out of their own heads. Tinker can become their friend—and Lord knows she needs as many friends as she can get. The animals will work their magic all by themselves.

One night at dinner I bring my laptop to the table. I have a plan for a national program and a strategy to set up satellite groups across the country. It will be fantastic, just as soon as I connect all the dots and bring the various factions together. I've got the orchestra ready, I just need to start conducting.

Austin reaches across the table and pushes my computer screen from behind with his finger. I'm still typing as it slowly lowers.

"Just a sec!" I finish my sentence. "What?"

"Dudley, Peanut, and Rosie cornered me when I came home

tonight and asked me to speak to you. They're concerned that you don't love them anymore."

"That's silly."

"Their father thinks the same thing."

"Even sillier."

"Chloe, I'm thrilled that you're fired up about this project and I want it to succeed, but you need to learn how to balance your life and work. I can see the stressed-out Chloe I knew on the set of *The Single Guy*. This is the third night in a row you've eaten nothing on your plate. You don't live alone anymore, remember?"

"But I have to—"

"You have to have your first meeting before you create a network across Canada. Just sayin'."

"Okay. What do you suggest we do?"

"Wrestle? Strip poker?"

"That's it! We'll strip wallpaper! Genius idea!"

The look on his face is priceless. That will teach him.

❁

Creature Comforts grinds to a halt at Christmas, as do most things, because no one has time to think about anything other than gifts, turkey, and parties. Take Amanda.

"Jason and I are throwing a Christmas party on Boxing Day, if you and Austin would like to come."

"That sounds nice. I suppose I should be doing things like that now."

"No offence, Chloe, but your domicile is as bare as Mrs. Hubbard's cupboard. How do you stand it?"

"We live in the bedroom."

"Braggart."

Gramps comes over about a week before Christmas and says he wants a real tree. We've never had a real tree. My mom and dad had a tabletop plastic one, and Gramps and Aunt Ollie have never bothered.

"Why the change?"

"For one thing we have the room, and for another, I don't have that many Christmases left."

"Don't say that!"

"This is one of those jobs you said Austin could do for us," he puffs away. "We'll go to a tree farm and chop one down."

Austin looks at me. "What jobs?"

"Nothing. Don't listen to him."

Gramps's car is the only one big enough to hold the five of us (why Agatha needs to come, I have no idea). He drives, with Austin in the front seat and the three females in the back. It's a good thing I'm small, because I'm suffocating back here as it is. Aunt Ollie's rolls are like bread dough and Agatha's old coat smells like mothballs.

"Are you sure we can tie the tree to the roof of the car?" Aunt Ollie bellows. She seems to think that no one can hear her from the back seat.

"I brought rope," Austin assures her.

"Gramps, I don't think we can chop down our own tree. You can only pick it out and they do it for you. They wrap it up, too."

Gramps looks at me in the rear-view mirror. "You never told me that! I don't want some jackass cutting it for me."

"Sorry. That's the way it works on tree farms."

"Nuts to that," he says. "We'll get one ourselves."

"Where?"

"The side of the road."

Oh, brother.

It's now getting dark, and we have a small tree that looked

perfect when viewed face-on but is a disaster in the back. We'll put it in a corner and no one will be the wiser. We want to head home, but Agatha is stuck in a ditch. We told her to go around it, but no. She marched into the trench and went up to her knees in oozing sludge and snow. It looks like she will be a permanent fixture unless we come up with a solution. Aunt Ollie holds the tree and yells instructions that none of us listen to.

"You'll be all right, dear heart! Should I call 911?"

"Stop fussing, Aunt Ollie. They're doing their best."

Gramps and Austin are on either side of Agatha with their arms around her armpits.

"When I say *three*, give her all ya got!" Gramps yells. "One, two three."

They pull with all their might and we hear a mighty sucking noise. Agatha pops out of her winter boots, which remain buried, never to be seen again.

Gramps has a fit as she crawls into the backseat with muddy pants, but what can the poor woman do?

"Turn up the heated seats!" Aunt Ollie orders. "She's perished."

I'll say this for Aunt Ollie: She dotes on her only friend.

We are a very sorry lot by the time we make it home. Austin and I are sent back to the store when Gramps realizes he has no Christmas ornaments. There are very few nice ones on the shelves at this time of year, but golden glitter balls are better than nothing.

"We can make strings of popcorn and cranberries," I tell Austin as we get out of his car. "I saw that in a magazine once, and it looked so homey."

He walks around the Mini and takes me in his arms. "You are so cute."

I'm not so cute when I find out Harriet wants Austin to come home for Christmas Eve and Christmas morning. I'm invited for Christmas dinner later in the day. For some reason I thought we'd be spending Christmas together with the critters, but I was clearly mistaken.

Austin tries to explain. "Ever since my dad died, Mom gets very emotional on holidays and she likes having us around. It's only for one night. I'm sure your relatives want you with them."

If only that were true. If I didn't show up they wouldn't even notice right away. I offer to make them dinner on Christmas Eve so I can see them.

Austin leaves for home, hugging me goodbye like he'll never see me again. I hold up Peanut and Rosie and make a pathetic face. Dudley was born to look sad, so we make a perfect vignette of guilt. He rolls down the car window as he drives off. "Will you knock it off? I'm dying here!"

I buy big red bows to put on the kids, and one for Bobby as well. My mission is to get them all in the same picture with Gramps, Aunt Ollie, and Agatha. They squeeze together on the hideous living room couch, the elders holding one cat each with Dudley at their feet.

"Say cheese!"

"Cheese!"

When the flash goes off, Peanut freaks out and flies out of Agatha's arms. Rosie does everything Peanut does, so off she goes. Bobby and Dudley stay put, so I take a few more of them.

"Agatha, would you mind taking a picture of me with Gramps and Aunt Ollie?"

She agrees, but has no idea how the camera works. I end up having to get up and down a half a dozen times before she's confident enough to shoot and click. Against all odds, the picture is rather nice. I'll print a copy for them.

They sit around my kitchen table, which looks very festive with a red tablecloth and white and green candles with holly. Gramps rubs his hands together.

"Turkey. My favourite."

I bend down and take the casserole dish out of the oven. "I made cheese-stuffed ravioli."

"For Christmas!"

"I don't kill turkeys."

"You don't mind melting cheese and boiling pasta alive!"

"I also have tea biscuits and a salad and a big chocolate cake for dessert."

Aunt Ollie digs in. "Stop your bellyaching. If you want turkey, go get one and cook it yourself."

"It's not the same," he mumbles.

After dinner we go back to their place and sit around our tree. We decide to be like the French and open our gifts tonight. I bought Gramps a new sweater and slippers, Aunt Ollie a silk nightgown and perfume, Agatha bath gel, soap, and body lotion. Hopefully she'll take the hint.

My gifts are a frying pan, a hat, and nail polish.

After listening to some Christmas music on the radio, Agatha says good night and I'm ready to go too. I kiss my kin and go back to my place. Dudley needs to go out, so I take him for a walk in the crisp, cold air. I've always loved Christmas Eve. It's much better than Christmas Day. There's still hope and expectation in the air. As I pass my neighbours, I see their windows glowing with the light from within, their Christmas trees twinkling, the front doors decorated with holly, cedar, and red berries.

Last Christmas I slept through the entire holiday, trying to make myself disappear. Now I have furry babies at home and my Dudley right here, who I want to hug to bits. I think of Austin, making his mom happy tonight. He and his sister will go to church with her, even though it makes him break out in hives when she insists on talking to everyone, showing them off as if they were toddlers. It's the one thing he and Julia agree on.

I'm about to turn around when I see a familiar figure walking alone up the sidewalk. It's Tinker.

"Fancy seeing you here!"

Dudley strains at his leash, so I let it go. He runs to her and she greets him with open arms. After a thorough patting, she straightens up and holds out a card. "This is for you."

I can't believe I forgot to get her something. Shit.

"Thank you."

"I don't want you to open it here."

"Okay. Do you want to come back to my place?"

"No. I have to get back."

"Let me drive you."

"No. I want to be by myself. I'm okay alone."

"I have to go to Austin's for dinner tomorrow and we have a party on Boxing Day, but why don't you come the day after? We can talk shop and I'll give you your present."

"You didn't have to get me anything."

I didn't…shit, shit, shit.

She stands there and looks at me for a moment. I'm not sure if she wants to hug me.

"See ya." She turns around and walks away, so I hurry back to the house because I'm dying to see what's in the card. I go to the kitchen table with the dirty dishes still piled on it and open the envelope. It's a store-bought card. The cover is a water-colour painting of a sparrow singing in a tree. Inside it says, "Thank you. Tinker."

That's enough. I put it on the fireplace mantel.

The kids and I go to bed, and when I pull back the covers, I see a wrapped gift tucked up by my pillows.

"I wonder who this is from." I smile.

Peanut and Rosie play with the ribbon and Dudley rips at the giftwrap with his paws. I open the box and there's a bracelet with *The Single Guy* charms, plus a heart with our names engraved around a message. *It was you all along.*

Aww. I inspect each of the charms one by one, and I notice there are two other extra charms, a cat and a dog. "What a sweetie pie. Right, guys?"

They agree, and after several kisses each, it's lights out.

I'm awakened in the middle of the night by Aunt Ollie looming over my bed and scaring the life out of me. "What's wrong?"

"Daddy's dead."

It takes me a moment to realize I'm not dreaming, and even then I'm not clear on what's happening.

"What?"

"Dad doesn't look like he's breathing. Bobby woke me up."

"Call 911."

"I did!"

I run out the door and don't even remember getting to Gramps's bedroom. Bobby's on his chest, licking his face. Gramps does look dead, but I refuse to believe it, so I push Bobby off and listen for a breath, then blow in his mouth and start chest compressions.

"Breathe, Gramps! Don't leave me!"

Aunt Ollie is behind me in the doorway. "They're on their way. What should I do?"

I keep pumping his chest. "Go to the front door and let them in."

This is a battle I'm going to win. *"I wish you'd wake up, Gramps."*

Nothing.

"Come on, you stubborn old coot! Bobby needs you!"

There's a little gasp of air, or at least I think there is. Maybe it's my wishful thinking. Just as I pushed Bobby away, the paramedics shove me aside. I grab Bobby and we huddle in the corner. I can't watch anymore, so I close my eyes. The conversation between the medics is calm and reassuring. If they're not panicked, then I don't need to panic. Unfortunately Aunt Ollie gets in everyone's way.

"What should I do?"

"Put the kettle on," I tell her.

"What for?"

"He might want a cup of tea."

"Right." Out she goes.

"He's coming around," they say.

I open my eyes and walk to his bedside. "Gramps? Can you see us?"

"Bobby," he whispers.

"That's right, Bobby saved you."

The rest of the night and Christmas morning are a bit of a blur. Aunt Ollie and I sit in Gramps's hospital room and wait for some test results. Gramps looks smaller and a bit frightened, so I hold his hand to reassure him he's not alone.

The doctor comes in and stands beside the bed. "Mr. Butterworth? You are a lucky man. You had a heart attack, but fortunately help was quick in arriving. You're going to need surgery to open up your blocked arteries. Do you smoke?"

"A little," he whispers.

"That's over. And you'll be changing your diet. You're not

over the hill yet, Mr. Butterworth. With these changes you will add years to your life."

"Who says I want to?"

After the doctor goes, Gramps makes a face. "How old was he? Fifteen?"

My cellphone goes off. Austin! I totally forgot about him. "Hello?"

"Merry Christmas! Did you like your gift?"

"What?"

"Your bracelet."

"Oh, of course. I love it, thank you."

"Is everything all right?"

"Gramps had a heart attack last night."

"Oh no. Where are you? I'll be right there."

I turn my back on Gramps and Aunt Ollie. "If you don't mind, I'd rather you stayed with your mother."

"But Chloe...you need me."

"Not right now. I'll call you." And I hang up on him. Even as I cut him off, I wonder why. When I return to Gramps's side, he rolls his head to look at me. "Ollie told me what you did last night."

I burst into tears. "I didn't make you a turkey dinner! When I leave here, I'm going right to a farm and cutting the head off the first turkey I see."

"Make sure you cook it."

❋

BETWEEN CHRISTMAS AND NEW YEAR'S I'M SO PREOCCUPIED with my relatives that I don't pay enough attention to anyone else. I'm aware of Austin in the background, looking after the critters, and Tinker comes over to walk Dudley and Amanda shows up with a casserole, but it's like they're in black and white and only Gramps, Aunt Ollie, and I are in colour.

Agatha hung around for a while, but Aunt Ollie snapped one day that it was her fault her father almost died.

"You had to get stuck in that mud, didn't you? He overexerted himself rescuing you. You never listen to anyone!"

We haven't seen Agatha since.

Gramps has his surgery and everything goes very well, despite his smoking addiction. While he's in the hospital Aunt Ollie and I overhaul his bedroom. We take everything out, wash the nicotine off the walls, and apply a fresh coat of paint. Then I buy him a new bedroom set and have everything ready when he comes home.

"Now, why would you go and do that?" he grumbles, but he looks chuffed. Bobby is on the bed waiting for him.

"There's my little buddy. Did you miss me?"

Bobby nods. I swear he does.

I make menus for Aunt Ollie to follow from recipes the dietician gave me. "You should eat this as well. I don't want you to get sick."

"No one would miss me," she frowns.

"I'd miss you."

Aunt Ollie sits glumly at the kitchen table. "Agatha wouldn't."

"Call her. Tell her you're sorry."

"But I meant it. Dad's always getting hot and bothered when she's around. He hates her."

"I'm not so sure about that. I think Gramps is like that kid in the park, always picking on the girl he likes."

Now she gets red in the face. "She's fifteen years younger than he is!"

"I'm not suggesting he's interested in her romantically, but he does like a good argument, and she provides that non-stop."

I have to admit that things are kind of dull without Agatha around.

It's New Year's Eve and Austin wants us to go out and party with the CBC gang at a nightclub, but I just can't do it, so now he's fed up. We bump into each other in the bathroom. I brush my teeth while he opens the medicine cabinet to get his after-shave.

"The only time you come alive is when you're caught up with death, dying, grief, bereavement groups, sorrow, and loss. What about just being happy? Why not come dancing with me? You've done everything you can do for your grandfather. He's recovering and he's comfortable. Why not enjoy some time with the other man who loves you?"

"You don't understand. I could lose him."

"You could lose me, Chloe."

He gets dressed up and leaves the house. I go over to say good night to Gramps. I'm happy to say Aunt Ollie is on the phone with Agatha and there's a lot of sniffing going on. I sit on the side of the bed.

"Why are you here on New Year's Eve?"

"I didn't feel like going out."

"Where's Austin?"

"He left."

"That's not good."

This ruffles my feathers. "Look, when my family needs me—"

"I don't need you. It is not your job to babysit me. I sure as hell don't want to be responsible for you letting that young man die on the vine. Now go, I'm tired."

So I go home and sit on my bed. Only it's not just my bed anymore. I pick up Austin's pillow and breathe in his scent. What am I doing? I can't save the world. I don't know anything, really. I'm afraid to admit to people that I'm scared most of the time.

I wish I were brave.

It's almost ten-thirty. If I hurry, I can be dressed and at the club by midnight. I shower, powder, perfume, spray, and slink into a black dress. The kids are asleep when I leave. I'm in a race against time now and the streets are a bit slippery. The whole way there I yell at myself for being a stupid bitch. Why can't I just grow up and behave? I either smother people or completely ignore them. The problem is I'm still fixated on myself. The world according to Chloe Sparrow. Who do I think I am? I'm nothing special. Lots of people lose family members in pretty horrible ways. I didn't stab my parents or choke them, or push them off a cliff. I was in my room sulking when they met their maker.

It's now 11:50 and I can't find a parking space, so I pull into someone's driveway. Who cares if I get a tongue-lashing or a ticket? In my hurry I forgot to put boots on, so I slip and slide in my high heels as I jump a curb and a pile of snow. There's a lineup and the doors are roped off. I implore the bouncer to let me in, while the people in line heckle me.

"Sorry, darlin'. You'll have to wait like everyone else."

"I wish you'd open that door. It's a matter of life and death!"

The doors open and a group of drunken people come spilling out. In the mayhem I slip inside. According to my watch, I have four minutes to find Austin in this madness. The music is blaring and everyone is on the dance floor, most of them with a drink in their hands.

"Austin! Austin!"

I elbow my way through the crowd. A few men grab me and

want to dance. I elbow them and keep going. Wait! I think I see Jason.

"Jason!"

Now I see Amanda. "Amanda!"

She turns around and looks very happy to see me. We head towards each other in slow motion. The DJ tells everyone we only have a minute to go. I don't have much time. When she gets to me, I shout in her ear. "Where's Austin?"

She points over the crowd. "Some cougar is all over him."

"Well, he is a vet."

"Go knock her teeth out!" Amanda yells.

I'm wading through people and my shoe comes off, but I finally see him. This insane old woman is trying to grab Austin's ass and manoeuvre herself so she can kiss him when the clock strikes midnight.

"Ten, nine, eight, seven..."

"Austin! Austin!"

He looks around but doesn't see me.

"Six, five..."

"I'm here!"

He finally spots me and pushes his way towards me with a big grin on his face.

"Four, three..."

He lifts me up and I'm in his arms.

"Two, one...."

"Happy New Year!" we shout together before we kiss each other for what seems like forever.

"I'm so happy you came," he says in my ear. "I love you, Chloe."

I put my hands on his face. "Austin?"

"Yes?"

"Will you marry me?"

CHAPTER TWENTY-FOUR

So now, on top of everything else, I have to plan a wedding. My lists are beginning to get out of hand, so I make Austin stay in bed the next weekend to discuss it.

"I don't care what you do. It's all good."

"You're supposed to be more interested than that."

"Just include my mother in some of the planning and you'll have my everlasting gratitude. Julia says she's never having a wedding and Mom is down in the dumps about it. Let her plan your bridal shower, or whatever."

"Do I need a bridal shower?"

He gets out of bed and puts on his running clothes. "We could use a few things. There's an echo in this place."

"I hate to disappoint you, but people are not going to buy us a dining room table or a loveseat as a shower gift."

"When are we having this wedding?"

"Soon? Or should we wait?"

He reaches down and kisses my head. "Soon, please. I've waited long enough. Come on, Dudley, let's get some exercise."

Dudley comes out from under the bed and hurries after him. The girls are left with me. "I suppose I should call Harriet."

She answers on the first ring. I ask her if she'd like to host the bridal shower and she's beside herself with excitement. There, that's done.

Next I get a text message from Amanda. *You don't have to do a thing. I'm hosting your bridal shower.*

I'm finishing breakfast when Aunt Ollie shows up and

sits at my table. "Agatha and I are thinking of having a bridal shower for you."

My surprise is such that I spit my tea into the sink. "Seriously?"

"Isn't that what a female relative of the bride is supposed to do? I know your mom isn't here, and I'm second-best..."

I run over and give her a big hug while she's still seated. "You're not second-best, Aunt Ollie. That's so sweet of you. I'd be happy to have you host my shower!"

"That's settled, then. Now, you're going to have to tell me what to do because I have no idea."

Sigh.

This requires diplomacy, so I show up at Harriet's door.

"Hello Chloe! What a nice surprise. I'm already full of ideas for your shower."

"That's what I've come to talk about."

"Wonderful! I'll make us some coffee."

So I drink the coffee and try to butt in every few minutes, but she's off to the races with her themes and colours and appetizers. She eventually realizes I'm not saying much.

"Are you all right, dear?"

"I don't know how to tell you this, but my Aunt Ollie came over this morning and said she wanted to host my bridal shower. I never thought she'd offer in a million years, so the fact that she has leaves me in an awkward situation. I don't want to disappoint anyone, and you've been so kind..."

"I see." Her face falls a little.

"But she doesn't know how to do it, so if you could help her with it, I'd be so grateful."

"Of course."

"And I'll need you in the coming days for a million other things..."

She smiles at me. "You've let me down gently, Chloe. I'm fine. I'm here for you, so don't fret."

Now I give my second big hug of the day. Harriet smells like lilacs and baby powder. My heart stops racing almost instantly.

On my way home I stop off at Amanda's. She's cleaning out her fridge while Jason has the boys on a grocery run. I try and let her down gently, but she's not that gracious about it.

"What? You're letting Aunt Ollie organize this? Are you nuts? She'll serve Melba toast and fruit cocktail if we're lucky." She throws her sponge in the sink. "I had all the wine picked out and everything."

"Harriet is going to help her."

"Does that poor woman know what she's in for? How do you get Aunt Ollie to do anything? Not to mention that meatball, Agatha."

I shouldn't laugh, but I do. "It's going to be a disaster of epic proportions."

"And this is just the shower. Can you imagine the wedding?"

❁

CREATURE COMFORT'S FIRST MEETING IS ON SUNDAY AT OUR local animal shelter. They are prepared for ten kids to come and spend time with the dogs and cats. I almost cry when Tinker shows up. She's still got spikes and earrings, but her raccoon eyes have gone, thanks to the tutelage of one of the CBC's makeup gals. Her hair is in a high ponytail. I've never seen it off her face.

"You look amazing!" I hug her, but she stiffens up so I back off.

"I'm nervous."

"That's completely normal. If you weren't nervous I wouldn't want you. It means you care."

Austin drives us over to the shelter. Dexter and Mary plan on being here, chaperoning this first venture. Brian, my cameraman, and Sydney wave as the shelter people welcome us. Mary thought of bringing hot chocolate and cookies, thank goodness. It's pretty cold today.

I introduce Tinker to Brian, who tells her what he wants her to do. She's going to interview the shelter people and do a once-around of the animals involved. Off they go to do their part before the kids arrive.

Austin has a clinic, so he's going to come back later. He wishes us luck, while Dexter, Mary, and I confer on what sort of progress we've made. I'm anxious to get going.

Only seven teenagers of various ages show up, but those seven have a great time. They walk and brush the animals, clean out their kennels, and horse around with them, although I do have a couple of boys who spend most of their time trying to get near Sydney and her big boobs. Tinker does an awesome job talking to the kids. With a microphone in her hand, all her insecurities fall by the wayside. I'm thrilled for her, and she looks flushed and happy.

After three hours we're all pooped, but by the look of it, we have relaxed kids, happy shelter people, and a whole bunch of sleepy dogs and cats. The kids get picked up one by one, and all of them have rosy cheeks. To me, that's success.

While we wait for Austin, Brian has a suggestion. "I'm certainly available, but it seems to me that Tinker is a natural. Why don't you get her a good video camera and she can shoot and interview at the same time? It's a lot more intimate and more conducive to the style of your reporting. She can upload her film right onto the blog."

"You're right. Would you like that, Tinker?"

"Oh, yes."

Brian and Sydney get ready to leave. I stand by their truck. "So, did you hear our news?"

"What news?"

"Austin and I are getting married."

Sydney shrieks right in Brian's ear. "Oh my God! You little vixen! You won *The Single Guy*!"

"Christ almighty, woman, my ears are ringing," Brian shouts.

She waves him away. "I'm really happy for you, Chloe. You make a very cute couple. I hope we're invited to the wedding."

"Of course. We'll be in touch."

Everyone's gone but Tinker and me. We sit on the bench outside the shelter door.

"Do you think we made a difference today?" I ask her.

"Definitely. The manager said that little beagle hadn't wagged his tail in weeks till just now."

❦

AFTER A COUPLE OF MONTHS, TINKER AND I HAVE THIS DOWN pat. Thanks to our posts, we have more and more kids showing up, and sometimes we divide the kids between shelters if we have too many. Other agencies get in touch and want the kids to visit their facilities, so it's a matter of coordinating who's going where. It's extremely satisfying, and I have enough video footage to start to bring the documentary to fruition, but there are still experts to be consulted and research to be done. The work hangs over me like a weight-bearing branch.

But one amazing thing happened that we never expected. Some of the shelters called to say their adoptions have gone up. Kids are falling in love with particular animals and want them full-time. Even Tinker's foster mother says she can adopt the little beagle she was worried about.

It's the evening of April Fool's Day when Austin and I finish wallpapering the living room. I have to say, it looks stunning— a Victorian pattern with a modern twist. It almost shimmers. Austin says it looks beige. It's not beige, it's golden. Our new sectional is a soft orange, with brown and yellow patterned pillows. I've already ordered the armchair and my mother's secretary desk looks great between the windows. Amanda was over one day and suggested I put interior louvered shutters on the bottoms of my windows and flank them with silk curtains hung from the ceiling. Does she know how much silk curtains cost when you have twelve-foot-high ceilings?

That's something else that keeps me up nights. I need a job to pay for this wedding. My funds are not endless, or so my bank manager pointed out when I dipped into my savings accounts recently.

We snuggle together on our new sofa.

"I've been thinking," Austin says. "I'd like to start my own practice."

I slap him on the chest. "That's amazing! I could help you. I can run your office. Maybe we should move to the country and help farm animals. It could be like a ranch for my kids who are struggling. We could have horses! Lots of horses, or maybe even make it a vacation destination by putting up cabins that people can rent for the summer. People who need to get out of the city..."

"Take a breath and stop talking." He looks annoyed, so I do what he says.

"I'll start again. I'd like my own practice somewhere in this general area. I prefer dealing with small animals. I have built up a large clientele who say they will follow me to my new space. That way I'm not starting from scratch. I'm going to need these people in the first years. There's a small store I've looked at, and I think I can afford it, if Mac comes in with me."

"The new vet, right?"

"He's just out of school and raring to go. He's a hard worker and we get along really well."

I keep quiet in case he needs to tell me something else. Seconds tick by.

"Well?" he says.

"It's perfect. You should definitely do it. I'm behind you one hundred percent."

He takes my hand and kisses it. "Thank you."

"Although—"

"No."

"You don't even know what I was going to say."

He kisses my hand again. "I do not want my practice bigger, more sophisticated, or edgy. I'm a mom-and-pop operation. I cater to average folks who just want to look after their dogs, and cats, and hamsters."

"Sounds good."

Austin keeps rubbing my fingers. "If I do this, I can't afford an engagement ring."

"I don't want one. I have my bracelet. That means more to me than anything."

We christen the sectional.

❀

DESPITE MY LISTS, I HAVE YET TO DECIDE ON ANYTHING FOR THE wedding. Every time I call about a venue, they're booked a year and a half ahead, or they want an obscene amount of money.

Amanda is breathing down my neck to make some decisions so she can go out and buy a dress. She's always at work when she calls.

"You have your red dress, remember?"

"Am I your matron-of-honour?"

"No."

"You big shithead."

"I'm not having all that."

"This is once in a lifetime, Chloe. Don't cheat yourself out of this experience. You will rationalize this to death and squeeze the joy out of it. I know you."

"I don't want to waste money on one day. It's ludicrous."

"You said you were rolling in money."

"Kind of like you told me you run five kilometres a day."

"I'm hanging up."

Finally comes the evening of my bridal shower. I'm a nervous wreck. Austin and Dudley are lying on the bed with a bowl of chips, watching me get ready.

"How come this shower has been arranged and we're still no closer to the wedding?"

"Feel free to take over."

"Wear that." He points at my navy skirt and polka-dot blouse.

"What are you doing tonight while I'm held hostage next door?"

"Jason invited me, Brian, Trey, and Jerry over for a couple of beers."

"Take me with you."

I bid farewell and go next door. "Hello?"

Everything is quiet. Maybe I have the wrong day. I step into the doorway of the living room and my motley crew shouts, "Surprise!" even though it isn't a surprise.

This moment will remain in my memory forever. On one hand we have the normal-people section, with Harriet, Julia, Amanda, Sydney, and two of Austin's cousins I met at their

Uncle Sam's funeral, and on the other side we have Bobby draped over Gramps, Aunt Ollie with a new perm that looks like a human brain on her head, Agatha in a lace tablecloth, and Tinker with a new tattoo of a skull that has flowers growing out of the eye sockets.

One side of the room is filled with yellow balloons and a huge crêpe-paper banner; the other features a chair draped in a cashmere throw, surrounded by real flowers, ribbons, tulle, crystal candlesticks, and a display of beautifully wrapped gifts.

Aunt Ollie gets to me first. "I'll take your coat." She grabs me by the arm and we head to her bedroom.

"That infuriating woman Harriet has taken over this entire party. She even brought canapés, after I told her I had Breton crackers and old cheese. Agatha worked hard on those. We bought six bottles of ginger ale and fruit punch, but that snotty friend of yours insisted on bringing bottles of wine and wineglasses. What's wrong with our glasses?"

"They're trying to be helpful. Let's just enjoy this. We're in your home, so you trumped them all."

"I'll be damned if I bring out their cake. Mine is just as nice."

Aunt Ollie heads back to the kitchen and I scoot into the bathroom, but Harriet nabs me before I shut the door.

"I'm sorry, dear, but I had to bring some food with me. I asked your aunt if I could contribute anything and she said no, that she had three packages of Breton crackers and a pound of old cheese. I nearly died. Your aunt is a very stubborn woman."

I put my hand on Harriet's shoulder. "I am well aware of my aunt's way of doing things, and she's not always easy, but she means well. Please don't take it the wrong way if I end up eating only the crackers and cheese, for the sake of family harmony. Serve your delicious food to the guests, and thank you for everything."

"All right."

I've almost got the door closed when someone's fingers reach around. It's Amanda.

"For fuck's sake! Fruit juice and Breton crackers!"

"I know, I know. Do me a favour and get everyone drunk."

I'm finally seated in my chair and everyone remembers what they're here for.

My grandfather's jokes. There's nothing he likes better than to have a captive female audience. "A priest, a rabbi, and an atheist walk into a bar…"

Everyone looks uncomfortable. Aunt Ollie is no help but unbelievably, it's Agatha to the rescue.

"I forgot to tell you Fred, I think I hit your car bumper earlier. Come outside and look."

"What?!" Gramps immediately gets off his rocker and shuffles out of the room, with Bobby behind him. "You pinheaded woman! How did you manage that? You're more trouble than a skunk at a church picnic! Where's my coat?"

We commence and I have a grand time opening up my gifts. I've never had a party thrown for me before. The feeling is like bubbles in my chest. I can't stop smiling.

Harriet and Julia made us a beautiful quilt. I'm overwhelmed. Wait until I tell Austin the work his sister put into it. Amanda bought us a gorgeous platter to use on special occasions, and Trey and Jerry sent a crystal decanter. Sydney crocheted us a table runner and the cousins gave us a really nice blender.

I open Aunt Ollie and Agatha's present. They went the tea-towel-and-dishcloth route, which of all the gifts are the things I really need.

Gramps got us a toolkit. Another winner.

I open Tinker's last. It's a new leash for Dudley. "His old one is fraying."

"Perfect. Thank you."

Gramps comes inside and mumbles down the hallway. Agatha gives me a thumbs-up.

I eat the Breton crackers and old cheese and drink the fruit punch. Both Harriet and Aunt Ollie show up in the doorway carrying their cakes. Harriet's is a masterpiece and Aunt Ollie's is a Betty Crocker, but both are delicious and after all the wine we pour down our throats, no one cares.

Everyone piles into taxis to go home after I thank them profusely. Then I help Aunt Ollie and Agatha clean up, because they didn't want Harriet in their kitchen.

"What a fun night. Thank you for the wonderful shower. I'll never forget it."

Aunt Ollie picks up a dishtowel and dries a plate. "Your mother would be very proud of you."

These words ring in my ears as I unlock my front door. What would she be like now? Would we be friends? At this moment I miss her.

Dudley gets a bedtime walk with his new leash and when we come back in, I turn on the kitchen lights to give him a Milk-Bone. My mother's favourite teacup is on the counter. She must have enjoyed the shower too.

I'm getting into my pyjamas when Austin comes in. He looks four-beers happy. Brian drove him home.

"So did we get lots of loot?"

"I'll bring the gifts over in the morning. Everything's perfect."

"We had a good time too. I met Jason's brother-in-law Steve for the first time. What a great guy."

My buzz disappears.

"He says he's met you a few times."

"Yeah, over at Amanda's."

"I think he likes you."

"Don't be crazy."

"No, he said you were very special and that I'm a lucky guy. I totally concur."

He jumps on the bed, kisses my cheek, and is out like a light in seconds.

CHAPTER TWENTY-FIVE

By June I have a full-blown panic attack in the local pharmacy while picking up pills for Gramps. The pharmacist makes me sit in a chair off to the side until I stop hyperventilating.

"Have you had a lot of stress recently?" she asks kindly.

"I have a wedding to plan, renovations to do in my house and garden, a charity to run, and a documentary to write. I'm helping my fiancé open his new office while I look for a job. And I now have two more dogs to add to the one I already had and all of them love sleeping on our new sectional and chasing the cats. My crazy aunt and her loopy friend have decided they want to sail around the world. So now my grandfather has heartburn, and he's probably going to have another heart attack. Other than that, I'm fine."

She blinks. "I find Valium helps. Or vodka."

When I lurch into the house carrying two big bags of dog food, the dogs herald my arrival to the neighbours. Dudley never opened his mouth until Gauge and Hector came to live with us. Gauge is a young black lab who's as stunned as a bag of hammers. Hector is some sort of rat variety, all mouth and no legs. Both were in danger of being put down and I couldn't have that on my conscience, so I dragged them home. Austin just shook his head.

Because we run into so many needy pets in our therapy sessions, Tinker has started a Walk the Plank wall on our blog. She puts up pictures of the animals walking the plank, with mean pirates brandishing swords. *If you don't want this horrible fate to happen to Rex, Ernie, and Milo this week, call and save their lives!* She draws clothes on them and puts little captions over their heads. *Don't hurt me! I'm too young to die!*

It's been amazingly effective. The trouble is, now I can't stop worrying about all the stray animals in the city. Austin is worried about me.

"Go see Dexter," he says.

So I do. I spill my guts for an hour and even he looks tired by the time I'm finished.

"Here's what I want you to do."

I rummage in my purse. "I need a piece of paper to write it down. Do you have a pen?"

"Forget the pen and paper and look at me."

So I look at him.

"If your wedding plans are causing you misery, couldn't you get married in a registry office and go for lunch afterwards?"

"I suppose so."

"With the money you save on the wedding, you could hire a landscaping firm for your outdoor projects and get a decorator to help you do a room at a time. It doesn't all have to be done this year."

"True."

"Your charitable work is practically running itself. Pay Tinker to see to the schedule and make phone calls. She told me she has her driver's license now. You could lend her your car on occasion."

"Right."

"Austin is a big boy and he can open his office by himself. You can pitch in from time to time, but leave the planning to him."

"Okay."

"You can't have enough pets, as far as I'm concerned. Throw some old blankets on your sectional for now and just enjoy the little buggers."

"Whatever you say."

"Your aunt, her friend, and your grandfather are adults, and what they do with their lives is none of your business."

"They make it my business."

"It takes practice to keep your nose out of other people's affairs. Now as for the documentary, you're not in a time crunch. This sort of project needs attention, and you can't give it your all if you're looking for a job. Finding employment is your number-one goal."

"I'll feel guilty if I lessen my commitment to Creature Comfort."

Dexter leans forward in his chair. "Now, this is your prescription. I don't want you in the bereavement business right now. Your mission is to be happy, and enjoy your engagement and have fun with Austin. You need to find balance. The constant talking about death, dealing with death, grief management, and loss seminars have depleted your spirit over the years. It's time for other things. This is very important Chloe. I don't want you to dismiss this."

I sigh. "I thought I was going to change the world."

"You have, Chloe. You've completely changed your world and the people in it. Think about it."

Everything he says makes sense when I'm in Dexter's office, but the minute I leave, my hair stands on end. Where do I start? I text Amanda and arrange to meet her in a coffee shop on her lunch hour. When she walks in, I'm floored.

"What happened to your tan?"

"My new guru says I'm poisoning my body by dousing it in chemicals every morning."

"Guru?"

"That's what I call my new yoga instructor." She holds up her hand for the waiter. "You should come with me. I feel so much better."

Yoga sounds relaxing. This is the type of thing Dexter would approve of. I buy a mat and yoga pants and stand by Amanda in class, but I can't hear the guru because she's so soft-spoken, so I mimic Amanda's moves.

"You are about as elastic as a brick," she whispers.

"You're such a comfort, Amanda."

"SHHH!" The lady to the left is annoyed with me.

"Sorry."

I make a face at Amanda and she makes one back, which naturally sets me off. The two of us try not to make a sound and alert the others, but our shoulders are shaking. With a supreme effort we pull ourselves together and I faintly hear the guru say "downward dog." Don't know what that is, so I once again look at Amanda and she's bent over with her hands on the ground and her butt in the air.

The minute I assume the position, someone passes wind—and with growing mortification, I realize it's me. Amanda is now on her mat holding her stomach and crying with laughter. I leap up, grab my mat, and run to the dressing room. She appears ten seconds later, and the two of us can't speak we're laughing so hard.

"I can never show my face again!" I cry.

"It's not your face you need to worry about."

"If you ever tell anyone about this, I'll have to kill you."

"So much for getting rid of your stress."

❀

THINGS START TO LOOK UP. AUNT OLLIE AND AGATHA ARE NOT sailing around the world. They went out for a cruise on a sailboat rented from the nearest marina and were seasick within ten minutes. Austin suggests they fly over to Torquay, in Devon, the birthplace of Agatha Christie, and go on her authentic vintage bus tour. Now they're all excited.

"Can Aunt Ollie afford to go?" I ask Gramps.

"I'm paying for it. Anything to get them out of the house. Bobby and I need a break."

"But what about Agatha? How's she able to manage it?"

"I told you. I'm taking care of it."

I kiss the top of Gramps head as he rocks in his chair. "You're a nice man."

"I'm a sucker."

Gramps has improved in spite of himself. The smoke-free atmosphere is heavenly and he goes for a walk every day. He takes Bobby on a leash. All the neighbours get a great kick out of it. The kids always crowd around. Bobby puts on a show, ham that he is. He rolls around on the sidewalk and shows his belly to everyone.

Austin is completely distracted with his new venture, but he whistles when he's home or playing with the dogs outside. He calls me one day to ask if we have room for a cockatoo that needs a good home. So now Jethro, who's ten, spends his life dancing to Queen on the stereo or driving the cats bonkers. They don't know what to make of him, but they know not to go near him. One nip was all it took to get that message across.

It's now summer and the trees and flowers are blooming. I'm outside, supervising the painters who are sprucing up the woodwork, trim, and porches. There's a landscaper taking measurements of the yards at the front and back. There's so much going on that I have to stop and take it all in. Two years ago I was a lonely workaholic with no friends. As it turns out, *The Single Guy* was the greatest thing that ever happened to me. Where would I be if I hadn't made that wish in the CBC bathroom? I'm almost afraid to think about it.

Tinker arrives to take all three dogs out for a walk. She is almost unrecognizable. Her face is soft, her manner confident. She met her boyfriend Joe at one of the shelters, and the two of them are a great team for Creature Comforts. Joe now works with the older teens and Tinker enjoys being with the ten- to thirteen-year-old groups. Of all the improvements I've made in the last little while, I think helping Tinker is my proudest achievement. She doesn't know it, but I'm going to offer to send her to Ryerson after she finishes high school. Or wherever she wants to go. I've put money aside for that. She is my little sister, after all.

In the middle of this mayhem my cell goes off. It's Herb Gardner, of all people. He asks me to come see him at his office tomorrow. I immediately text Amanda. *What is going on?*

I don't have a clue!

I don't believe her. When Austin comes home after work, I tell him about it. We sit on the back porch drinking our green tea, dogs at our feet and Jethro, mimic that he is, barking.

"If he offers you a job, you don't have to take it, you know. It's whatever makes *you* happy, not him. We'll support you either way, right guys?" Austin looks at the critters and I swear they look back and smile. I'm not kidding.

I wear my pinstripe suit to the meeting with Mr. Gardner. My tummy is nervous—with excitement, I realize. Amanda rides up with me on the elevator. She holds my shoulders and shakes me a bit. "You can do this! Come down to my office when it's over."

She waves goodbye as the elevator doors close. Mr. Gardner's grumpy secretary is still grumpy. After a few minutes she says I can go in.

I come out an hour later.

Amanda is at the elevator doors when they open on her floor. She drags me into her office. "So? Spill the beans!"

I have to sit first. She gives me a bottle of water and then perches on the edge of her desk, impaling herself with her letter opener.

"He wants me to run the documentary division. You knew that, didn't you?"

Now she leaps in the air. "I did! I almost told you a dozen times! I have no nails left."

"I told him no."

She freezes in mid-air. "You what? Are you joking? With this opportunity, you can okay any documentary you want."

"I told him no to running it, and yes to working in the department part-time."

Now she puts her hand over her mouth. "He said yes to that?"

"Hard to believe, but he did."

"Why part-time?"

"I have a project I'm working on."

Amanda shakes her head. "You sly fox. Why didn't you tell me?"

"I don't have to tell you everything, Amanda."

"That's where you're wrong."

❈

Now that the mirror is over the mantel and the sconces and crystal chandelier are in place, as well as the shutters and silk curtains, the living room looks mighty fine. It worried me that the shiny new lights might upset my ghostly parents, but they seem to be mellowing. They've been remarkable quiet lately, or perhaps the house is too noisy for me to notice.

Austin and I are standing in the middle of our new room with our arms around each other, surveying the space, but quickly head in two directions when Gauge and Hector chase Peanut and Rosie into the room and up those silk curtains. We're yelling and Jethro is in the kitchen screeching, "Bad dogs! Bad dogs!"

Once that drama is over, we decide it's time to have a party for our friends and family. A housewarming, if you will. We don't have a dining room table yet, but we can put out goodies on the kitchen table. We settle for July 1, Canada Day.

Now that I'm proud of my house—the rooms that are done, anyway—I do my best to make everything look great, so that means the living room, the kitchen, and the bathroom are always pristine. We have flags draped everywhere, which is totally tacky but it's not Canada Day without flags. Our new outdoor furniture has arrived, so if the weather cooperates, Austin will barbeque hamburgers and hot dogs. Veggie burgers for me. We even have fireworks to end the evening. The two of us are so excited.

We invite everyone who has been part of our journey so far. Gramps, Aunt Ollie, and Agatha, of course, Harriet and Julia and all the CBC team—Amanda and Jason, Trey and Jerry, Brian and Sydney. Tinker is coming, and we even invited the two Dr. McDermotts.

Everyone shows up in the early afternoon and the place is hopping. Trey corners Amanda and I overhear him say, "Have you seen the claw marks on these silk curtains already?"

Amanda peers closer. "I'm going to kill you, Chloe!"

"Killing the cats would be more productive," Trey says.

I throw a cracker at him.

Harriet is cornered by Aunt Ollie and Agatha after she makes the mistake of asking about their upcoming trip. Gramps sidles up to Sydney and has a hard time keeping his eyes on her face. Brian is the bartender and then takes over the barbeque, telling Austin he's doing a lousy job. And Julia shows Tinker how to play her guitar.

At the height of the hilarity the doorbell rings. "Okay!" Austin shouts. "Everyone in the living room for the big surprise."

The gang hustles into the best room in the house, all of them puzzled. Austin walks in with a very dignified gentleman. Harriet gives a little shout and the tears start.

"Everyone, this is Reverend Knox. He's here to perform our wedding ceremony."

Now everyone shouts, and Amanda grabs me. "I thought your dress was a little too nice for this party! I can't believe you didn't tell me!"

It takes a good ten minutes for things to calm down. The animals are excited, especially Jethro, who doesn't want to be left out, so Austin puts his perch in the living room.

We're almost ready to get underway when Austin says, "I forgot. Someone else wanted to be here." He goes out of the room and brings back a big box.

"This is for you, my love."

I open the box and there's Norton. She jumps into my arms

and rubs my face, purring. The dogs start to run in circles, but Norton ignores them. "How did this happen? The little girl?"

"She and her parents have moved overseas for the next six months to try some experimental treatment and they couldn't take Norton. I proposed a time-share option and they were thrilled."

"Oh, Austin. You are the world's nicest guy."

"Norton introduced us, so she needed to be here."

Eventually we recover our senses, and Austin and I stand facing each other and hold hands while Reverend Knox performs the ceremony. We didn't write our own vows. We knew neither of us would be able to speak, so it's a very traditional service. We exchange thin gold bands and it's over.

I'm Mrs. Sparrow-Hawke. Hawke-Sparrow? I think I'll keep the Sparrow and he can have the Hawke.

Everyone is very happy for us, beaming faces all around. Trey holds up a glass.

"To the best Girl Guide I ever knew! Thank you for saving us from a dreary reception and rubber chicken!"

Everyone cheers.

But I have one more surprise. I ask everyone to be quiet and take Austin's hands again.

"I have a wedding gift for you. The newest member of the family." I reach over and put his hands on my tummy. His mouth drops open. "Are you serious? How did that happen?"

"The usual way, I imagine...wine, a nice dinner."

He softly rubs our little bump. "I can't believe it."

"Neither can I!" His mother bursts into happy tears.

"She's a little girl, and her name is Phoebe."

"How do you know?"

"I made a wish."

NICOLA DAVISON

Lesley Crewe is the author of twelve novels, including the *Globe & Mail* bestselling and 2022 Canada Reads longlisted *The Spoon Stealer*, *Beholden*, *Mary, Mary, Amazing Grace, Kin*, and *Relative Happiness*, which was adapted into a feature film. She has also published two collections of essays, the Leacock–longlisted *Are You Kidding Me?!* and *I Kid You Not!* Lesley lives in Homeville, Nova Scotia. Visit her at lesleycrewe.com.